STILL WATERS

BY
DEBRA WEBB

All rights reserved including the right of reproduction in whole or in part in any form. This edition is published by arrangement with Harlequin Books S.A.

This is a work of fiction. Names, characters, places, locations and incidents are purely fictional and bear no relationship to any real life individuals, living or dead, or to any actual places, business establishments, locations, events or incidents. Any resemblance is entirely coincidental.

This book is sold subject to the condition that it shall not, by way of trade or otherwise, be lent, resold, hired out or otherwise circulated without the prior consent of the publisher in any form of binding or cover other than that in which it is published and without a similar condition including this condition being imposed on the subsequent purchaser.

® and ™ are trademarks owned and used by the trademark owner and/or its licensee. Trademarks marked with ® are registered with the United Kingdom Patent Office and/or the Office for Harmonisation in the Internal Market and in other countries.

First Published in Great Britain 2016
By Mills & Boon, an imprint of HarperCollins*Publishers*
1 London Bridge Street, London, SE1 9GF

© 2016 Debra Webb

ISBN: 978-0-263-91918-9

46-1016

Our policy is to use papers that are natural, renewable and recyclable products and made from wood grown in sustainable forests. The logging and manufacturing processes conform to the legal environmental regulations of the country of origin.

Printed and bound in Spain
by CPI, Barcelona

Debra Webb is the award-winning *USA TODAY* bestselling author of more than one hundred novels, including reader-favorite series Faces of Evil, the Colby Agency and Shades of Death. With more than four million books sold in numerous languages and countries, Debra's love of storytelling goes back to childhood on a farm in Alabama. Visit Debra at www.debrawebb.com.

ROTHERHAM LIBRARY SERVICE	
B53104581	
Bertrams	13/09/2016
AF	£5.99
BSU	ROM

I feel so blessed to be surrounded by wonderful, supportive friends. Among those many amazing friends are the members of my incredible Street Team. Thank you for all you do and for simply being you.

Chapter One

Jess Harris Burnett had just poured her third cup of decaf when the jingle of the bell over the door sounded. As she walked toward the lobby, she heard receptionist Rebecca Scott welcoming the visitor to B&C Investigations. The office had been open almost a whole month now. Jess and her lifelong friend Buddy Corlew had made a good decision going into business together. With a nineteen-month-old daughter and a son due in a mcre six weeks—Jess rubbed her enormous belly—stepping away from her position as deputy chief of Birmingham's major crimes team had been the right move.

The memory of being held prisoner by Ted Holmes attempted to bully into her thoughts, and Jess pushed it away. Holmes, like the many serial killers before him she had helped track down, was history now. Still, Jess was well aware that there would always be a new face of evil just around the next corner. She intended to leave tracking down the killers to the Birmingham PD. Her goal now was to concentrate on the victims. With B&C Investigations, she was accomplishing that goal.

"I'll let Mrs. Burnett know you're here, Ms. Coleman," Rebecca said as Jess came into the lobby.

"Gina, what brings you here this morning?" Jess flashed a smile for the receptionist. "Thank you, Rebecca. We'll be in my office."

Gina Coleman, Birmingham's beloved and award-winning television journalist, gave Jess a hug. "You look great!"

"You're the one who looks great," Jess countered. "Married life agrees with you."

Gina smiled and gave Jess another quick hug. On the way to her office, Jess grabbed her coffee and offered her friend a cup.

"No, thanks. I've had way too much already this morning."

When they were settled in Jess's office, Gina surveyed the small space. "You've done a wonderful job of making this place comfortable."

Jess was proud of how their offices had turned out. The downtown location was good for business even if the building was a very old one. In Jess's opinion, the exposed brick walls gave the place character. It was a good fit. Anyone who knew them would say that she and Buddy had more than a little character.

"Thanks." Jess sipped her decaf and smiled. "You really do seem happy." Gina looked amazing, as always. Her long brunette hair and runway-model looks had ensured her a position in the world of television news, but it was her incredible ability to find the story that had made her a highly sought-after journalist. Her personal bravery, too, inspired Jess. Gina had taken some fire when she'd announced she was gay and married the woman she loved. Standing firm, Gina had weathered the storm.

"I am very happy." Gina stared at her hands a moment. When she met Jess's gaze once more, her face was cluttered with worry. "Barb and I need your help."

"What can I do? Name it." Jess set her coffee aside.

"A couple of hours ago Barb's younger sister, Amber, was called into the BPD about a murder."

A frown lined Jess's brow, reminding her that by the time this baby was in high school she would look like his grandmother rather than his mother. She spotted a new wrinkle every time she looked in the mirror. *Don't even go there.*

"I hadn't heard. There was a homicide last night?" This time a few months ago and Jess would have known the persons of interest and the prime suspects in every homicide long before an arrest was made in the city of Birmingham. Not anymore. Dan made it a point not to discuss work when he came home. Though she could still nudge him for details when the need arose, it was one of the perks of being married to the chief of police. A sense of well-being warmed her when she thought of her husband. He was a genuinely good man.

"Dan explained as much as he was at liberty to share. He assured me it was routine questioning, but I'm worried. I told him I was coming to you." Gina sighed. "I don't think he was very happy about my decision. He obviously prefers to keep murder and mayhem away from the mother of his children."

Two years ago Jess would have been jealous at hearing Gina had spoken to Dan. The two had once been an on-again, off-again item. Now she counted Gina as a good friend. "Don't worry about Dan." Jess shook her head. "I've warned him time and again that just because I'm no longer a cop doesn't mean I won't be investigating murders."

"If he had his way, you'd retire," Gina teased. "We both know how he feels about keeping you safe."

Jess had been cursed with more than her fair share of obsessed killers during her career first as an FBI profiler and then as a deputy chief in the Birmingham PD. Dan's concern was understandable if unwarranted. Just because she was a mother now didn't mean she couldn't take care of herself. Admittedly, she had grown considerably more cautious.

"Tell me about the case." Considering it was a murder case, she could get the details from Lieutenant Chet Harper or Sergeant Lori Wells. Chet had recently been named acting chief of the small major crimes team— SPU, Special Problems Unit—Jess had started. Lori was reassigned to Crimes Against Persons. One or the other would be investigating the homicide case. Jess hoped the case was with Harper. She counted Lori as her best friend, but the new chief of the Crimes Against Persons Division, Captain Vanessa Aldridge, was brash and obstinate, and carried the biggest chip on her shoulder Jess had ever encountered.

Though they'd only met once or twice, Jess was familiar with Barbara's younger sister. Amber Roberts was a reporter at the same station, Channel Six, as Gina. She was young, beautiful and talented. Her and Barbara's parents were from old money, but Gina would be the first to attest to the fact that a sparkling pedigree didn't exempt one from murder. Gina's own sister had paid the price for her part in a long-ago tragedy.

"Kyle Adler's body was found in his home yesterday. He'd been stabbed repeatedly. Amber hardly knew the man. The very notion is ludicrous." Gina held up a hand. "I know you're probably thinking that I felt the same way about Julie, but this is different. Amber had nothing to do with this man's murder."

As much as Jess sympathized with Gina, Amber would not have been questioned if the police hadn't found some sort of connection between her and the victim. "The police have something," she reminded her friend. "You know this. What about the murder weapon—was it found?"

"They haven't found the murder weapon." Gina shook her head. "The whole thing is insane. Amber swears the only time she ever saw this guy was when he made a delivery to her or someone at the station. Apparently he made a living delivering for various shops around town. But the cops claim they found evidence indicating she'd been in his house. Unless someone is framing her, it simply isn't possible."

Jess chewed her bottom lip a moment. "It's conceivable someone may have wanted Adler dead and set it up to look as though another person, like Amber, committed the act."

"If that's true—" Gina leaned forward "—not only do we need help finding the actual murderer that the police may not even try to find, we also need to protect Amber. She could be in danger from the real killer."

Jess sent a text to Harper. "Let's see who's working the case first. Then we'll know whether or not we have to worry about finding the truth. As for the other, I agree. If Amber is being framed, it's quite possible she could be in danger. Personal security would be a wise step until we know what we're dealing with."

"Buddy said you do protective services as well as private investigations."

"We do," Jess agreed. "Right now the only investigator we have available is Sean Douglas."

Gina's gaze narrowed. "I'm sensing some hesitation. Do you have reservations as to whether he can handle the job?"

Jess considered how to answer the question. "He spent the past five years as a bodyguard to various celebrities in Hollywood." She shrugged. "Based on our research into his background, he was very, very good at his job. For two years prior to that he was a cop with the LAPD. He's had all the right training, and his references are impeccable."

Gina said, "There's a *but* coming."

"His last assignment was Lacy James."

Gina sat back in her chair. "Damn."

Lacy James had been a rising pop star. The rumors about drug abuse had followed her from singing in the church choir in her hometown of Memphis all the way to her Grammy nomination in LA last year.

"Her agent hired Douglas to keep an eye on her," Jess explained. "According to Douglas, she had been straight for a while and her agent wanted to ensure she stayed that way. Six months into the assignment, she died of an overdose."

Gina pressed her hands to her face, then took a breath. "Do you think what happened was in some way his fault?"

Jess shook her head. "Responsibility for what happened to Lacy James lies with her agent and her other handlers. They cared more about her career than they did her health and welfare. My only hesitation is that

Douglas is a little too cocky for his own good. I think he uses attitude to cover the pain and guilt he feels about James's death." Jess paused to weigh her words. "I'm concerned his need to prove himself again might be an issue, but as for his ability to protect a client, he's more than capable."

Gina's expression brightened. "Trust me—whatever this guy's attitude, Amber can handle it. You don't rise as rapidly in my business as she has without a tough skin and a little attitude. I'm desperate, Jess. I promised Barb I would take care of this."

Jess felt confident Gina was right about Amber. Putting herself in front of the camera every day was hard work, and it wasn't for the faint of heart. "Why don't I learn all I can from the BPD and then I'll brief Douglas. I'll arrange a meeting with Amber, and we'll go from there."

"I will be forever in your debt."

"We'll take care of Amber," Jess assured her friend.

Gina stood. Jess did the same, albeit a little less gracefully.

"I'm aware that we don't always know a person as well as we believe—even the people closest to us," Gina confessed. "But I would wager all I own that Amber had nothing to do with this man's death."

Jess nodded resolutely. "Then all we need to do is ensure she stays safe until the BPD can find the killer."

Chapter Two

Forest Brook Drive, Homewood, 12:32 p.m.

Amber Roberts entered the necessary code to stop the infernal beeping of her security system, tossed her keys on the table by the door and then kicked off her heels. This had been the longest morning of her life. She closed her eyes and reminded herself to breathe as the man assigned to keep an eye on her rushed past her to have a look before she went any farther into the house.

Forcing her mind and body to focus on her normal routine, she locked the front door and set the alarm. Without waiting to hear the all-clear signal, she grabbed her shoes and headed for her bedroom. This was her home. The alarm had still been set, for God's sake. If anyone was in her house, he or she had been there since Amber left that morning. Otherwise the alarm would have gone off, right? She closed her eyes for a moment. At this point she wasn't sure of anything.

Her stomach knotted at the memory of the police showing up just as her early morning news broadcast ended. Everyone had watched as the detective explained she was needed downtown and then escorted her from the station. She didn't have to look to know her face would be plastered all over the evening papers as well as the internet and television broadcasts.

The damage control had to start now. She'd already tweeted and posted on Instagram and Facebook. The station had backed her up, as well. If the reaction didn't make her sound petty and paranoid, she would swear Gerard Stevens from the station's primary competitor had set her up.

Amber walked into her closet and shoved her shoes into their slots. Her head spun as she dragged off the dress that would forever remind her of the interview room where she'd endured a relentless interrogation by one of the BPD's finest. She tossed the dress into the dry-cleaning hamper and reached for a pair of sweatpants and a tee. Worst of all, a man was dead. Though she only knew him in passing, she felt bad about his murder. He was someone's son. Probably someone's brother and significant other. She pulled on the sweatpants. Most people had a life—unlike her. Gina and Barb warned her repeatedly that she was going to be sorry for allowing her life to fly by while she was totally absorbed by work.

Who had time for a social life? Gina should know better than anyone. Amber was fairly confident her mentor was saying what Barb expected her to say. It didn't matter either way. Amber was twenty-eight; her top priority was her career. She still had decades for falling in love and building a family.

Even if her narrow focus on her career did get lonely sometimes.

She yanked on the tee and kicked the thought aside. The police believed she was somehow involved in a man's murder. Her love life, or lack thereof, was the least of her worries.

How the hell the police could think she was involved was the million-dollar question. Why in the world would she hurt this man, much less kill him? She scarcely knew him. He had made a few deliveries to her house. He was always pleasant, but they never exchanged more than a dozen words. None of what she'd been told by the police so far made the slightest bit of sense.

"The house is clear."

Amber jumped, slamming her elbow into the wall. Frowning at the broad-shouldered man filling the doorway to her closet, she rubbed her funny bone.

"Thank you," she said even though she didn't quite feel thankful. She did not want a babysitter. She hadn't killed anyone, and there was no reason for a soul to want to harm her. Reporting the news for the past six-plus years had given her certain insights into situations like this one, and hiring a bodyguard this early in the investigation was overreacting. There could only be two potential explanations for her current dilemma: mistaken identity or a frame job. Both happened. As hard as she tried, she could come up with no other explanation.

Her bodyguard's gaze roamed from her face all the way to her toes and back with a couple of unnecessary pauses in between. Now that annoyed her. He was here to keep her safe—supposedly. He had no business looking at her as if she was the next conquest on his radar. Though she suspected Mr. Sexy-as-Hell usually didn't have to work very hard to get what he wanted. The man was gorgeous. Tall, with those broad shoulders that narrowed into a lean waist. Thick blond hair just the right length for threading your fingers through and deep blue eyes. His muscular build attested to his dedicated workout ethics. With every extra thump of her pulse she understood that beneath his smooth, tanned skin was an ego large enough for the Vulcan iron man that watched over the city of Birmingham from high atop Red Mountain.

Sean Douglas was hot, and he damn well knew it.

As if he agreed wholeheartedly with her assessment, he gifted her with a nod and disappeared.

Amber sighed. She should pull herself together. Her attorney was on the way over with whatever details the police had shared with him. They'd done nothing but ask questions this morning. Each time her attorney had asked about the evidence, the detective had evaded the question. Still, she hadn't needed a lawyer to tell her that she wouldn't have been called in and so thoroughly questioned had there been no evidence. Friends, colleagues and people acquainted with the victim were questioned in their homes or workplaces. Only the ones about to be named a person of interest—or, worse, a suspect—were hauled to the station and interviewed. The police had wanted her off balance—which was not a good thing.

How the hell was this possible?

She needed a couple of cocktails and a good night's sleep. Maybe she'd wake up in the morning and discover this had all been just one big old bad nightmare.

Finding Sean Douglas kicked back on the sofa in her living room reminded her that the situation was all too real.

"I put on a pot of coffee." He leaned forward and braced his forearms on his knees. "I figured some caffeine would be useful the next few hours."

She would have preferred a caramel latte, but she'd been too emotional to think of dropping by her favorite coffee shop after leaving the police department. Her parents were beside themselves. They were in a remote part of Africa on a medical aid mission and couldn't get back for days. She and Barbara had insisted they stay and do the important work they'd gone there to do. This entire business was nothing more than a mistake. Surely it would be cleared up in a day or two.

Belatedly she remembered to say, "Thank you." Her attorney, Frank Teller, was a coffee drinker. Vaguely she wondered how Douglas had known this or if he was a coffee guy, too.

"I can call in some lunch for delivery. I'm guessing you didn't take time for breakfast this morning."

She appreciated the offer but said, "I had a protein smoothie. I'm fine."

He dismissed her response with a wave of his hand. "How about a pizza or a burger? Your choice."

She couldn't possibly eat. "I'm not hungry. Feel free to raid my kitchen or order something for yourself."

His mouth eased into a lopsided grin. "Already done that. You're fresh out of real food."

A frown furrowed her brow. He'd prowled through her kitchen? What kind of bodyguard checked the fridge?

"Why don't you tell me about yourself," he suggested with a pat of the sofa cushion next to him.

Amber felt sure that inviting pat worked well for him under normal circumstances, but those blue eyes and that hopeful smile did little more than annoy her at the moment. "Weren't you briefed on my case?"

The need for personal security was entirely new to her, but instinct told her a man assigned to protect her would certainly have been briefed about the situation. Small talk was the furthest thing from her mind.

He needed to find a way to entertain himself if he was bored. She had no desire to chat.

"I was." He clasped his hands between his spread thighs.

"What else do you need to know?" She gave herself a mental pat on the back for not sounding as snippy as she felt.

"Until this situation is resolved," he began, tracking her movements with those blue eyes as she settled in a chair a few feet away, "we'll be spending a lot of time together. It's helpful to know a little more than the facts of the case. What time do you like to get up in the mornings? What's your usual bedtime? Do you watch television or read or just relax in the evenings? Should I expect company? Is there a boyfriend to accommodate?" He shrugged. "Things like that are good to know."

For the love of Mike. Amber shook off the frustration. His request had merit. *No need to be unreasonable.* "I'm up at six unless I'm called to a scene earlier or I host the morning news the way I did this morning. I go to bed right after the ten o'clock news assuming I haven't been called out to a scene. I usually leave the television turned on all night." She glanced at the dark screen hanging on the wall above her fireplace. She imagined that every channel was running stories about her and the murder. "I might be taking a break from that habit for a few days."

"Understandable." He cocked an eyebrow. "What about a boyfriend?"

"There is no boyfriend." Somehow saying it out loud sounded far worse than simply knowing it. She hadn't been in a serious relationship in more than a year. Maybe there wouldn't be another one. Who had time? More important, who cared? She had everything she needed. *If that's so, why the sudden need to justify your status?*

He made a knowing sound as something like surprise flashed across his face. "A girlfriend then?"

"No girlfriend."

He made one of those male grunts that could convey surprise as easily as indifference. Either way, the sound got on her already-frazzled nerves.

"Your degree is in mass communications," he said, changing the subject. "When did you decide you preferred working in front of the camera versus behind it?"

"I didn't decide. The journalist I assisted during my first assignment was in a car accident. Everyone was on the scene except her and the cameraman told me to get in front of the camera and do the job. The audience responded well to me, so that's where the powers that be decided I should be—on-screen."

"But you had aspirations?"

Amber nodded. "I had my heart set on hosting one of the big entertainment news shows." She laughed, remembering the horror on her parents' faces when she'd told them. "It wasn't exactly the career my family had hoped for."

He smiled. It was nice. Really nice. *Too nice, damn it.* "Your parents and your sister are all doctors."

"Yes. I'm the black sheep." The realization that her words had never been truer stole the air from her lungs. Now she was a potential suspect in a homicide.

The doorbell saved her from going down that pity path. She stood to go to the door, but Douglas moved ahead of her and checked the security viewfinder.

"It's Mr. Teller."

Douglas opened the door, and Teller came inside.

He'd already been introduced to the man who would be keeping watch over her. There was just something wrong with calling him a bodyguard. Particularly since she continued to have a bit of trouble keeping her attention off *his* body. The foolish reaction had to be about sex. She hadn't been intimate with anyone since she and Josh had ended their relationship.

Her gaze drifted to the man assigned to protect her. *Don't even go there.*

"We should speak privately," Frank Teller announced before saying hello. He looked from Amber to Douglas and back.

"I'd like him to stay," Amber countered. Douglas and his boss would need to be kept up to speed anyway.

When Teller relented, Douglas insisted on serving the coffee. Amber was happy to let him do the honors. Her knees were feeling a little weak as she sank back into a chair. Maybe it was the grim expression Teller wore.

He placed his briefcase on the coffee table and opened it. "The news is not good."

Amber's stomach did the sinking now. "What sort of evidence could they possibly have? I don't even know this man! He…he made deliveries to my house and the station a couple of times." Maybe more than a couple of times. Still, the whole thing was incredible.

"Amber." Teller closed his briefcase and placed the folder he'd removed atop it. "I've known your family for most of my life. Your father is my father's personal physician. Your mother was my pediatrician. I, of all people, know this is wrong. You couldn't possibly have harmed this man. Yet the evidence is enough to make even me have second thoughts."

The trembling she had experienced that morning after

the initial shock that no one was playing a joke on her started anew. The police had mentioned evidence without providing the details. "What evidence? I don't know how they could find evidence that leads back to me in a home where I've never been...on a body I've never touched."

"They found a teacup with your prints on it."

"What?" The situation had just gone from unbelievable to incomprehensible. "If there is anything in that poor man's house that either belonged to me or bore my prints, someone—besides me—put it there."

Before Teller could respond, Douglas returned with the coffee. He'd gone to the trouble to find her grandmother's serving tray and to dig out the china cups and saucers rather than the stoneware mugs. He'd even prepared the creamer and sugar servers. Her disbelief was temporarily sidelined by the idea that he would think to go to so much trouble.

Douglas placed the tray on the coffee table, and she noted there were only two cups. "If you need me for anything—" he hitched his thumb toward the rear of the house "—I'll be outside checking the perimeter."

"Thank you." Amber suddenly didn't want anyone else to hear these incredible lies—at least not until she had heard them.

When Douglas was gone, Teller said, "Amber, I realize this is shocking."

He'd certainly nailed her feelings with that statement. "I don't understand how any of this happened." She shook her head, overwhelmed and confused and, honestly, terrified. "You see it on television or in the movies, but this is real life. *My* life."

"Do you drink a tea called Paradise Peach?"

Something cold and dark welled inside her. She moistened her lips and cleared her throat. "Yes. It's my favorite. There's a specialty shop downtown that stocks it."

"A can of Paradise Peach tea was found in the victim's home. Your prints were on the can."

Worry furrowed her brow and bumped her pulse rate to a faster rhythm. "Maybe he shopped there, too. He may have picked up a can after I did." Hope knotted in her chest, but it was short-lived. How did a person prove a theory as full of circumstantial holes as the one she'd just suggested?

"Certainly," he agreed. "Bear in mind that the burden of proof is not ours. It will be up to the BPD to make their case. For that they need evidence, which brings us to the cup that also bore your prints."

The rationale she had attempted to use earlier vanished. Dear Lord she felt as if she had just awakened in the middle of a horror film and she was the next victim. All she had to do now was scream.

"Take a look at these crime scene photos." He opened the folder and removed two eight-by-ten photographs. He scooted his briefcase and the serving platter to the far side of the table and placed the photographs in front of her. "These are copies, so they're not the best quality."

The first one showed the victim lying on the floor next to the dining table in what she presumed was his kitchen. Blood had soaked his shirt. He appeared to have multiple stab wounds to the chest. *Poor man.* She swallowed back the lump of emotion that rose in her throat and moved on to the second one. The second was a wider-angle view showing more of the room. Definitely the kitchen. Her attention zeroed in on the table. The table was set for two. Teacups sat in matching saucers, each flanked by a spoon and linen napkin. She squinted at the pattern on the cups. A floral pattern for sure, but difficult to distinguish.

"He was having tea with someone." She lifted her gaze to Teller's. "Whoever that person was, he or she is likely the one who killed him. Based on the prints found at the scene, the police believe that person was you."

Hands shaking, she pressed her fingers to her mouth to hold back the cry of outrage. "The medical examiner is certain about the time of death?"

Teller nodded. "Last Friday night, around eight. It'll be a while before we have the autopsy results, which will tell us what he had for dinner and various other details that may or may not help our case."

Amber made a face.

"Knowing what and where he ate might help us," Teller explained. "The police might be able to track down the restaurant—if he ate out—and someone there might remember if he was alone."

Sounded like a long shot to her. The detectives had pressed her over and over about her whereabouts on Friday night. It was the one time she'd come home early and hit the sack. She hadn't spent any time doing research at the station, she hadn't spoken to anyone and she'd had no company. None of her neighbors could confirm she was home. She hadn't done any work on her home computer, which might have confirmed her whereabouts. Bottom line, she had no alibi.

Disgusted, she shook her head. "Single people all over the world should be terrified of spending a quiet evening at home alone." If she were married or involved in a relationship, she might have spent time or at least spoken to her plus one that evening.

"There's more."

His somber tone caused her heart to skip a beat.

"A pair of panties were found in his bed. There was trace evidence. A pubic hair and a much longer hair…" He touched his head. "They want you to agree to a DNA test."

The heart that had stumbled a moment ago slammed against her ribs now. "Do you think I should?" Considering her fingerprints were there, she couldn't help but feel somewhat tentative as to how to proceed. "I know I haven't been in his house or his bed, so I have nothing to hide, but my fingerprints were there." She pressed a hand to her throat. "If someone is setting me up…"

He reached into his folder and removed another photograph. "Do you recognize these?"

The red panties in the photograph stole her ability to draw in air. She shot to her feet and rushed to her bedroom. Opening drawer after drawer, she rifled through her things and then slammed each door closed in turn. Her pulse pounding, she moved to the laundry hamper.

The panties weren't there.

Teller stood at her bedroom door, worry lining his face. "Lots of women have red panties. My wife has red panties. How can you be sure you recognize these?"

Her lungs finally filled with air. "The little bows." She paused to release the big breath she'd managed to draw in. "There should be a little satin red bow on each side. One is missing. It annoys me every time I see it. I've meant to throw them away…"

Of course any woman with red panties that sported little red bows could be missing a bow. In her gut, Amber knew better than to believe it was a mere coincidence. Her red one-bowed panties were missing. There was a teacup in the man's house, for God's sake, with her prints on it. She didn't need a DNA test to prove a damned thing. The hair and any other trace evidence would be hers, as well. Whoever wanted her to appear guilty had done a bang-up job.

Douglas appeared behind Teller. "Is everything okay?"

No. Everything was not okay. In fact, nothing was okay.

"I'll do the DNA test," Amber said to the man representing her.

Teller gave her a resigned nod. "I'll set it up."

Dear God. She was in serious trouble here.

Chapter Three

The mouthpiece hung around awhile longer, asking more questions and making Amber even more upset. Sean had heard of the guy. All the rich folks in Jefferson County used him. Teller didn't need billboards or commercials with catchy jingles. The family name got him all the business he would ever need. It didn't hurt that he had a reputation for being the best damn attorney in town.

Sean turned his attention back to assessing Amber's place. If the items found in the victim's residence were Amber's and she hadn't put them there, someone had been in her home. The reality likely hadn't sunk in for her just yet. It would hit her soon enough. It was time to start considering who would want to see Amber go down for murder. There had to be an old schoolmate or ex-bestie, maybe even a competitor at a rival television station with a grudge against her. Revenge, jealousy, there were all kinds of potential motives.

No matter that he'd only been employed at B&C Investigations for a month, he'd learned a lot from the boss already. Jess had a motto: find the motive, find the killer. When looking for the source of trouble, there was no better advice. The boss didn't exactly have a lot of confidence in Sean just yet. She'd been reluctant to assign him this case—which was exactly why he had to do the best job possible. Of course, he always wanted to do a good job, but he couldn't allow even a single misstep this time. He had a feeling the first mistake and he would be out at B&C Investigations.

For damned sure he would never again allow the kind of mistake he'd made on his last security assignment. His bad judgment had cost a life.

His fingers stilled on the back door's lock mechanism. How could he blame Jess Burnett for not fully trusting him? No matter that he had years of outstanding work history under his belt, his last assignment for his former employer had gone to hell. The only reason he'd gotten the job with B&C Investigations was because Buddy Corlew and Sean's older brother, Chase, were friends. They'd played high school football together—against each other, actually. Chase had warned Sean that a year of moping around was enough. Sean had to get on with his life. During his time in Hollywood he'd built up considerable savings. Private security in the entertainment world paid extremely well. Finding a new job hadn't been necessary the first year after he returned home, but his brother was right. Sean had to get on with at least part of his life. His personal life might never recover from his mistake with Lacy, but there was no excuse for allowing his professional life to stay in the toilet.

"Is there something wrong with my door?"

Amber's question snapped him from his worrisome thoughts. He closed the door and shook his head. "I've checked front and back doors, and so far no sign of forced entry. The windows are next."

A frown dragged down the corners of her lips. She had nice lips. Full and pink. Her red hair and green eyes were a vivid contrast to her pale skin. The sprinkling of freckles across her nose she worked so hard to cover with makeup made him want to smile. She was a gorgeous lady, no doubt, but not the kind of overdone Hollywood beauty he'd disliked in California. Amber's was natural and completely unpretentious. He'd been watching her and fantasizing for months.

Fantasies and casual encounters were all he had anymore. He wasn't sure he would ever trust himself in a real relationship again, and he would never permit work to become personal. Of course, his brother warned him that a guy still six months from thirty shouldn't be throwing in the towel.

Realization dawned in the lady's pretty green eyes. "You think someone broke into my home and took my... the evidence the police found." The frown reappeared. "But how did they get my prints on the teacup?"

When he looked confused, she quickly explained about the evidence the BPD had discovered in the murder victim's home.

Sean inspected the second of three kitchen windows. "Trust me," he said in answer to her question, "there are ways to get into any place—home or business—if a person wants in badly enough."

Amber followed him into the living room. She watched silently as he confirmed the windows were locked and that all the locking mechanisms were in working order.

"You mean like overriding security codes?"

"That's one way, yes." He shrugged. "Folks who make it their business to break and enter can unlock about any kind of lock with or without a key."

Rather than continue with her hovering too close and

watching his every move, he decided to run a few questions by her. Why not start with the most obvious ones she'd already answered for his boss and more than likely for the police? "Do you have any enemies, Amber?"

Her arms crossed protectively over her chest, and she dropped into the nearest chair. "Your boss and the police asked me that question along with a barrage of others. The answer is no. I've never had any sort of trouble with anyone. I've never had a stalker. Never received strange emails or Facebook messages. The fan mail from viewers is never threatening or overly negative. Someone might disagree with the way I reported an issue or event, but so far no one has taken it any further."

"Lucky you. Most celebrities get their fair share of threatening or nasty mail." Sean meant the comment as a compliment, but judging by her sigh she didn't feel so lucky. He hitched his head toward the hall that led to the bedrooms. "How about persistent fans or admirers? Any of those?"

Amber pushed to her feet and trailed after him. "The usual. I typically receive flowers at the station a couple of times a week, depending on the stories I've covered. The high-profile stories generate the most reaction from viewers. Letters, food baskets, the occasional gift." She rubbed at the back of her neck and then stretched it from side to side. "Nothing negative."

The single window in the hall bath was secure. Sean moved to the first of the three bedrooms. "Any that are unsigned or from repeat senders?"

"A few."

Both windows in bedroom one were secure. "Define 'a few.'"

Following him to the next bedroom, she shrugged

and said, "Four or five fans who consistently send little gifts. The occasional unsigned letter, maybe once or twice a month."

"Have you ever met any of the four or five gift senders?" He progressed from the first window to the second before moving on to the final bedroom—her private space.

"The station has a big community day twice a year." She crossed her arms over her chest, drawing his errant attention momentarily to her breasts. "You know, to thank the viewers. We do photos and giveaways. Have games and hot dogs. There's always a clown and a couple of cartoon characters for the kids. Sometimes the people who write to me or send me gifts or flowers come by and say hi. No drama or discomfort. Just a friendly hello and a request for an autograph."

The instant he entered her bedroom he felt completely out of place. The room smelled like her. Whatever perfume she wore was restrained but unmistakable. Light and citrusy. The delicate fragrance was barely there but so uniquely her, as if the subtle sweetness came from all that soft, satiny skin. He gave his head a mental shake. Evidently the skintight tee she wore had his imagination running a little wild.

The bed was big, too large for a woman to lie in alone. The bedding was pure white, lush and natural— like Amber. It didn't take much to summon the image of that long, curly red hair flowing over those white linens. His body tightened with need at the thought of climbing onto that bed and kissing his way up her naked body.

Do the job, man. "Do you keep the unsigned letters?" He walked to the nearest window and confirmed it was locked. "Some of those may be from the same person."

She massaged her temples as if a headache had begun there. Who wouldn't have a headache? She was a person of interest in a murder case. That was enough to give anyone a headache.

"I never looked to see if there were similarities in the handwriting. I don't keep them all. Only the ones that touch me in some way. In fact, Gina and I did a special about how feedback from viewers added a richness to our work." She smiled; his pulse reacted. "We each shared things about ourselves that viewers could hopefully relate to. It was one of the most watched local programs last year."

Her bedroom windows were secure. He stepped into the en suite bath. The only window was one of the half-moon types above the shower and it didn't open. Like the rest of her home, the bathroom was organized and well-appointed. The house was a traditional one-story brick in an upscale, older neighborhood. According to the background report Jess had given him, Amber had lived here since graduating college. She'd inherited the house from her grandmother.

He returned to the bedroom, where she waited in the middle of the room looking very much like a lost little girl. "You keep the fan mail here or at work?"

"Here." She opened the double doors leading to what he presumed would be the closet.

He hesitated in the doorway. The closet was almost as large as the bedroom with a sliding library-style ladder that provided access to the upper shelves that banded all the way around the space above the hanging clothes.

"The house used to have four bedrooms," she explained as she adjusted the ladder. "I used the fourth bedroom to expand the bathroom and for this closet."

"Looks like you made a smart move." He surveyed the rods and rods of clothes and the rows of shoes and whistled. "This could be a supermodel's closet."

"Ha-ha. Viewers notice if you wear the same outfit." She climbed up the ladder and reached for a box covered in a floral pattern resting on the first shelf.

"Let me take that." He stepped over to the ladder and reached up to take the box.

"I suppose you'd know a supermodel's closet when you saw one. My sister told me you were a bodyguard to the stars."

He accepted the box and waited for her to climb down the few rungs. "I may have seen one or two."

She pushed the ladder back into its storage position. "Don't be modest, Mr. Douglas. Barbara says you had quite the reputation in Hollywood as a top security specialist as well as a ladies' man."

Apparently she hadn't heard the whole story. "Where do you want these?" He was damned ready to get out of her bedroom. Being surrounded by her scent and her private things in what now felt like a small space was too much.

"Kitchen table."

Rather than be a gentleman and wait for her to go first, he got the hell out of her closet and her bedroom. A few deep breaths and he still hadn't cleared her scent from his lungs. He shook off the uneasiness and placed the box on the round table that stood in the breakfast alcove of the kitchen.

The red and pink rose-patterned box wasn't a typical file storage size. Handholds were formed on each end. Judging by the weight, it was made of heavy-gauge cardboard. He'd noted several of varying sizes on the uppermost shelf of her closet. Some he recognized as photograph boxes. All were neatly arranged by size and color. His mother had similar tastes and organizing habits. From what he'd seen so far, his mother would like Amber.

He booted the concept out of his head. Maybe he needed more coffee. He was sure as hell having a hard time keeping his head on straight.

Amber joined him at the table. She pressed a hand to her flat belly and made a face.

"Look." He took her by the shoulders and turned her to face him. "I know you TV personalities don't like to eat for fear of gaining half an ounce, but you're going through some serious trauma right now. You need to eat."

Her green eyes were wide with surprise or indignation because he'd touched her or that he'd dared to give her an order or both. He released her and dropped his hands back to his sides.

"No need for strong-arm tactics, Mr. Douglas. I was just thinking that I needed to eat." She turned gracefully and marched to the refrigerator.

Strong-arm tactics? Well, at least she was smart enough to listen to good advice.

She pulled open the freezer drawer and selected a frozen dinner—the organic, calorie-conscious kind. While she removed the outer packaging, she flashed him a fake smile and said, "Take your pick. I highly recommend the pecan chicken and rice."

While she nuked her meal, he rummaged through the selection. He chose the pizza. The photo on the box looked normal enough, though he doubted one would ever be enough. The way his stomach was protesting, he could eat his weight in steak and potatoes about now.

"Water or coffee?" She grabbed a bottle of water from the fridge for herself.

"Water would be great."

Ten minutes later they were seated at the table with their little prepackaged meals—*little* being the operative word. The first bite of the pizza did two things. Burned the hell out of his mouth and confirmed that although it looked nothing like the one on the box, it tasted exactly like the box.

"Gina says you grew up in Birmingham." She twirled her fork in the noodles of her meal. She'd picked out the little chicken and broccoli chunks.

He imagined the noodles tasted somewhat similar to his pizza. "I did. When I graduated high school I went for a criminal justice degree. After that I headed out to Cali with my best friend. We both went to work for the LAPD. My friend's parents had divorced when he was a kid. His father promised him a job with the department if he wanted to move out to California after school."

"So you both became cops?"

He tore off another chunk of the tasteless pizza and nodded. "Two years later the top personal security team in the LA area offered me a position with a salary I couldn't refuse."

"You must have done something to grab their attention?" She smiled, and his pulse executed another of those crazy dips.

"I might have saved a couple of lives in a nightclub shoot-out while off duty and without a firearm." He shoved the last of the pizza into his mouth to prevent having to say more. The doped-up ex-husband who'd come after his wife in a crowded club with a cocked and loaded nine millimeter had every intention of killing anyone in the room with her. There hadn't been time to think, only to act. Sean had thrown himself at the guy. Two shots had hissed by his head, close enough to have him wishing he'd gone to church a little more often. Clips from the club's security cameras had played on all the local networks and even a couple of national ones for days. The notoriety had bothered him. He'd done the right thing. Maybe that might have made him a hero to some.

"Had you always envisioned yourself as a bodyguard to the stars?" Amber set her fork aside and sipped her water.

"Never crossed my mind until they knocked on my door."

"What was it like? Are the big stars as difficult to work with as the gossip rags suggest?"

He really didn't want to talk about his past. Things always ventured into the territory he still couldn't revisit. The only reason he hadn't changed the subject already was because she looked relaxed for the first time since they'd met.

"Stars are like anyone else. You've got the nice ones, and you've got the jerks. They put on their pants the same way you and I do."

"According to Gina, you're the best."

He pushed back from the table and stood. "Your friend might have exaggerated just a little." He carried his plate to the sink and rinsed it before depositing it into the dishwasher. Amber did the same with her bowl and fork.

"We need a notepad or something to list the names of

the people who've written to you repeatedly." He moved back to the table. The sooner they focused on the reason he was here, the quicker she would forget about all the questions she appeared to have for him. Not that he had expected anything less from the lady. Amber might not be a big-screen celebrity, but she was damned sure a big star in Birmingham. "Anyone who seems overly interested in your career or you as a person is what we're looking for."

She opened a drawer and came up with a notepad and pen.

"We should talk about your neighbors," he went on. "Friends. Ex-boyfriends. Former girlfriends. Anyone who knows your routine. Anyone who knows you well enough to have a handle on your likes and dislikes. Paradise Peach tea, for instance. Who would know about your taste in tea?"

When she'd settled back at the table, she placed the pen next to the pad and looked him straight in the eye. "My sister and my parents. My colleagues at work. None of them would do this any more than I would. Most of my neighbors are the same ones who lived here when my grandmother was still alive. They're older, and I've known them forever. I have no former girlfriends. I only have current ones."

"No fallings-out. No estrangements of any kind?"

"There are people with whom I've lost touch, but nothing like you're suggesting."

"What about ex-boyfriends? Even the one-night stands—especially the one-night stands."

"I don't do one-night stands, Mr. Douglas. This is not Hollywood."

"But it is the twenty-first century. Even people in Alabama do one-night stands, Ms. Roberts."

"Not this person." Her eyebrows shot up her forehead. "And before you jump to that conclusion, I'm not a prude, either."

"Ex-boyfriends?"

"We talked about this already."

He exhaled a big breath and reached for patience. "I need more details."

"There have been three."

Did she just say three? "Three?" he echoed.

She gave him a sharp look that answered the question. "One in high school. We started dating when we were freshmen. We broke up when we went our separate ways to college. He's married with three children and lives in Wyoming. My second boyfriend was in college. He decided he wanted to travel the world before settling down. To my knowledge he's still doing so. Last year I broke up with the man to whom I'd been engaged for two years."

"Please tell me you dated a few guys in between."

"A few. Yes. I was very busy with my education and then with building my career, Mr. Douglas."

"Sean," he countered. "The Mr. Douglas thing makes me feel old."

"I certainly wouldn't want to make you feel old, *Sean*," she acquiesced.

Like every other ridiculous reaction he'd experienced since coming into her home, the sound of his first name on those pink lips disrupted the rhythm of his pulse again. "The ex-fiancé has no reason to want to cause you trouble?"

She sent him a look. "Killing a man and leaving my

panties in his bed is a little more than causing me trouble—wouldn't you say?"

He nodded. She had him there. "I'll take that as a no."

"We broke up because he confessed that he'd never stopped loving his college sweetheart. They're married with a baby on the way. They live in Mobile. I'm certain I'm the last person on his mind these days."

The guy must have been a total idiot.

Sean cleared his throat and his head. "That leaves us with strangers." More often than not, crimes of this nature were committed by an intimate, but not always. Occasionally strangers formed fantasy relationships or attachments with high-profile personalities. Once in a while those bonds led to murder.

"Okay." She stood, took the lid from the box and set it aside. "I have quite a few letters and cards here." She reached inside and lifted a mound of envelopes. She placed them on the table. She reached into the box once more and stalled. "What in the world?" Her eyes widened with horror. "Oh, my God."

Sean moved to her side. In the box, amid the stacks of envelopes addressed to Amber Roberts, was a knife. Nothing elaborate or exotic, just a stock kitchen butcher knife, with an eight-or ten-inch blade covered in dried blood.

It was time to call his boss.

Chapter Four

Captain Vanessa Aldridge stared directly at Amber. "You want me to believe that you just happened to have a knife from the victim's kitchen in your home. A knife, I might add, that is covered in his blood."

The head of the Crimes Against Persons Division had asked Amber this same question several different ways over the past three hours. The lab had confirmed the blood on the knife was in fact Kyle Adler's. The knife apparently was part of a set from his home. Dear God, how had this happened? Why would anyone do this to her? Her home had been searched by the forensic team for any other potential evidence. It was all completely insane.

"Your prints are on the knife handle, Ms. Roberts."

Amber blinked. Her mind wouldn't stay focused on the moment.

"Of course her prints are on the handle," Teller countered. "She touched it while she was searching through a box of saved fan mail."

"Do you have some way of proving her prints weren't already there?" Aldridge argued.

"Do you have some way of proving they were?" Teller fired back. "I have no burden to prove anything, as you well know. You're the one who needs to prove your accusations. And unless you can do that, Captain Aldridge, I would suggest you stop harassing my client."

Amber felt sick. "I have never seen that knife before. I have no idea how it got in my house."

Teller put his hand on her arm to silence her. He didn't want her to make any spontaneous remarks. Only the prepared ones they had discussed before this meeting. This was wrong. All of it. And it was escalating. She was terrified at the idea of what might happen next. It felt surreal, like someone else's life was spiraling out of control.

"You have a security system. Who else knows the access code?" Aldridge demanded for the third time.

"My client is uncertain of the answer," Teller replied without hesitation.

"You don't recall who you gave something as important as your security code? An old boyfriend? An associate from work? You can't expect me to believe you have no idea who else might have access to your own home."

The captain stared directly at her, ensuring Amber understood the questions and comments were meant for her regardless of the attorney seated beside her. Amber merely stared back. She'd already answered those questions. Teller had reminded her repeatedly not to allow Aldridge to drag her into a discussion. The captain's job, according to Teller, was to trip Amber up and make her say something she didn't mean. The truth was, Amber couldn't have answered at the moment even if Teller had wanted her to. Some level of shock had descended, and she couldn't think quickly enough to piece together a proper response.

"Ms. Roberts, I'm aware your attorney is supposed to work in your best interest, but frankly I'm concerned as to why he feels compelled to answer for you—if you have nothing to hide."

Teller launched a protest.

Amber held up her hands. "Are we done here?" They had been at this for three hours. Her answers weren't going to change whether she gave the prepared ones or the ones straight from her heart—assuming she could get the right words out. "Or do you plan to arrest me?"

Aldridge laid one hand atop the other on the table and smiled. "We're done for now, but rest assured, Ms. Roberts, we will be speaking again. Soon, so don't leave town."

Amber wanted out of this room. She tried to slow her racing heart, tried to still her churning stomach. *Who would do this?* The question echoed in her brain. She could think of no one who wanted to hurt her this way.

Captain Aldridge walked to the door, glancing over her shoulder one last time before exiting. The silence that ensued left Amber feeling hollow and alone.

"Let's get you home."

Amber followed Teller's prompts and exited the interview room. Douglas—Sean waited in the corridor.

"We're going out the back," he said to Teller.

Teller nodded. "I'll go out the front and hopefully keep the media entertained long enough to allow the two of you to escape.

Escape. Amber had been one of those reporters more times than she could count. Desperate to get the story. Determined to discover what the person in the spotlight was hiding. Certain the police were holding back crucial information.

"No." Amber shook her head. "I'm not running from the press."

Teller urged her to listen to reason as they boarded the elevator. She ignored him. As the doors opened into the lobby, he launched a final plea. "I can't do my job if you don't cooperate. Every step you take makes an impression. If this case goes to trial, the jury will be made up of people who watch the news and read the paper."

Amber had had enough. She turned to him. "I'm certain you'll be able to do your job under whatever circumstances arise, Frank."

Teller held up his hands and backed off. "I've said my piece."

As she approached the main entrance, Sean pulled her close. "I'm not going to try to talk you out of something you're obviously intent on doing, but we will do it my way." Her gaze locked with his as he went on. "You will stay right beside me. You will not reach out to anyone who reaches toward you. You will stay focused on moving forward while giving whatever responses you intend to give quickly and concisely."

His eyes and the stony set of his jaw warned there would be no changing his mind. Unable to do otherwise, Amber nodded her agreement.

"Good. Let's do this." He pushed through the door, moving her along with confident strides.

Lights flashed and questions were hurled at her. As Sean had predicted, hands extended toward her. Amber felt as if she were being pulled in every direction. The few faces she recognized blurred with the many she did not.

"Amber, did you murder Kyle Adler?"

"Amber, have you been arrested?"

"Amber, were you and Kyle involved?"

She wanted to answer. Her feet stumbled, and her tongue felt tied. Her heart pushed into her throat.

"Give us your side, Amber!" a vaguely familiar voice shouted.

Behind her, Teller assured the crowd that Amber had not been arrested and was not involved with Kyle Adler. He firmly stated that she certainly had not murdered him.

Sean pushed his way through the microphones and the cameras stretching toward them. Amber moved along in his wake, able to remain upright and progress forward only because he held tightly to her arm.

They reached his car, and suddenly she was in the passenger seat. He slid behind the wheel, and they started to roll slowly through the seemingly endless crowd. The situation was completely alien to her. She felt lost and uncertain. This was what she did every day. How could she feel so completely out of place on this side of the story? Where was her professional training? Where was her courage? She should have answered those questions. She should have looked directly into the camera and told the world that she was innocent no matter what Sean or Teller told her to do.

How many times had she watched someone do exactly what she just did and doubted the veracity of his or her claims of innocence?

People watching the news would think precisely that about her. They would believe she'd killed a man. They would believe she knew all the tricks to avoid being found guilty because she was a reporter. They would believe she was lying because her job was to spin stories into the kind of news viewers couldn't resist.

"I'm telling the truth." She turned to Sean as he accelerated, leaving the horde of reporters behind. "I *am* telling the truth."

He glanced at her. "I believe you."

Did anyone else?

"We're going to the office," he explained as he made the next turn. "My boss wants to speak with you."

Amber managed a nod. His boss was former deputy chief Jess Burnett. Gina trusted her. Amber had been working her way up the ranks when Jess first returned to Birmingham. She remembered the buzz about the FBI's top profiler helping with the Murray case. No one would ever forget how serial killer Eric Spears had followed Jess here. Amber had read the stories about her and how she could find the face of evil when no one else could.

Please let her be able to find this one.

Fourth Avenue North

"Amber, I know this is unsettling."

Amber produced a smile for Jess Burnett. "I never thought I'd say this, but yes, this is terrifying." Had she been such a coward all this time?

"Being the target of breaking news is far different from finding the breaking news. Trust me on that one," Jess assured her.

Certainly the former profiler would know. Amber remembered well when Jess had been the target of those who thought she'd brought evil to town with her—that she was on some level partially responsible for the heinous murders committed by Eric Spears and his followers.

"I appreciate that you understand," Amber confessed. "What I really want to hear is that you can help prove I'm telling the truth. I don't think Captain Aldridge believes me."

"We'll do all we can—you have our word on that," Buddy Corlew assured her.

Buddy sat next to Jess. Amber knew a little about him, as well. He'd grown up in a rough neighborhood and he'd beaten the odds. He'd served in the military and the Birmingham Police Department. Even when his career as a detective had tanked, he'd built a thriving private investigation agency. The man was a fighter as well as the new husband of the recently named Jefferson County medical examiner.

If the people in this room couldn't help her prove her innocence, Amber felt reasonably confident she was screwed.

Next to her Sean shifted in his chair as if he'd read her mind and recognized that she had left him out of her deduction. Bearing in mind that they'd found a bloody knife in her house—which confirmed beyond all doubt that someone had been in her home without her knowledge—she was pretty damned sure she needed him, too. And her attorney, Frank Teller, was the best. Amber would need them all to get through this nightmare.

"We didn't invite Teller to this meeting," Corlew said, "since what we're about to tell you is off the record and he doesn't need to know about it. For now."

Was she thinking out loud or were they all mind readers? Amber took a breath and forced the crazy thought aside. She needed to calm down and focus. "I understand."

"Buddy and I have contacts inside the department, and they've shared details with us that Captain Aldridge might not be ready to disclose at this time," Jess explained. "However, none of what we're about to tell you is breaking the law. We're only bending it a bit."

"I'm grateful for any insights into what the captain is thinking." The woman gave every indication of being on a witch hunt. Amber had pondered the possibility that this was the captain's opportunity to get back at the press. Since taking over as head of Crimes Against Persons, she had been cast in a bad light more often than not.

"I've had the opportunity to review the findings by the evidence technicians," Jess began, "as well as the lead detective's assessment." She turned to a new page in her notepad. "The victim's home is meticulously organized and painstakingly clean. No journal or personal notes were discovered, but I've asked the detective to have another look for any items that may be connected to other ongoing or unsolved cases."

Tension coiled inside Amber. "You believe he may have been involved in some sort of illegal activity?"

Jess hesitated but only for a moment. "The china teacups found on his table were the only pieces in that pattern found in his home." She removed a photo from a folder and passed it to Amber. "I've blown up the photo provided by the lead detective on the case. Look closely at the pattern. Is it possible those teacups and saucers came from your home?"

Amber studied the image, and her breath caught. She hadn't been able to see the pattern very well in the photos Teller had shown her. "This is my grandmother's china." Her heart pounded. "He or someone he knew was in my house." *Maybe more than once*, she realized as she thought of the knife.

Jess nodded. "Now we're getting somewhere."

Amber looked from Jess to the photo and back. "What does this mean?"

"It means," Sean interjected, drawing her attention to him, "that *you* have been a victim without even knowing it."

He was right. She'd been so focused on finding something that would prove she was telling the truth that she hadn't considered herself a victim.

"Kyle Adler may have been obsessed with you," Jess explained. "He may have come into your home on numerous occasions. He has no criminal record, but we're operating under the assumption that he simply hadn't been caught. His need to have something of yours may have caused him to cross the line, ultimately perhaps drawing him into association with the person who murdered him."

Amber looked from Jess to Sean and back. "So it's possible his killer may have saved my life. Is that what you're suggesting?"

"In some perverted way perhaps," Jess agreed. "Envy may have driven him or her. The unknown subject—unsub—may have been Adler's lover who learned of his obsession with you and killed him in a fit of rage. When your name and face hit the news as a person of interest in the case, this person may have put the knife in your house to further implicate you as the murderer. Or if he or she was working with Adler all along, the knife may have been in your home since the day it was used as a murder weapon."

"How could he or she have known I would look in that particular box?"

"The choice was too specific to believe it's a mere co-incidence," Jess agreed. "At this point my opinion would be that the unsub took his time and selected a place that wouldn't be too obvious to the police but wouldn't go unnoticed by you. Does anyone else know about the box of fan mail you keep in your closet?"

Amber started to say no, but the memory of the special she and Gina had done stopped her. "Gina and I did a special." She looked at Sean. "I told you about it earlier." To Jess she said, "We both shared a little about how our professional and personal lives intersect. I talked about the letters and…" Amber sighed. "And how I kept them in a lovely box on a shelf in my closet."

Jess nodded. "He was watching. He's using all he knows about you to frame you for murder."

"He's certainly done a top-notch job so far." Every piece of evidence in the case pointed to her as the murderer. How could her entire life be turned upside down in less than twenty-four hours?

"With your permission," Jess said, "the detective in charge of the case wants to have a couple of evidence techs go through your house a second time to see if they can pick up any overlooked prints left by the victim or any other potential unsub." Jess removed her reading glasses and placed them on her desk. "It's a long shot, but we shouldn't ignore the possibility that one or both may have been in your home many times."

Amber held up her hands. "I have no problem with them turning my house upside down if it helps find the real killer."

"There's always the possibility," Corlew warned, "they'll find more planted evidence that could hurt your case. You might want to run this by Teller before you commit."

Amber pressed her hand to her lips. She hadn't thought of that scenario. She shook her head. "I have nothing to hide. If something else has been hidden in my home, I want to know."

Jess nodded. "All right. I'll let Sergeant Wells know. She'll call Sean in the morning with a time."

"Meanwhile," Sean spoke up again, "I have a locksmith at your house changing the locks as we speak. As soon as we get back there, you should change your access code and your password for your security system."

Amber's head was spinning again. "I've never given anyone—not even my own parents—the access code or password to my security system. At least not that I can remember."

"There are other ways," Corlew assured her. "Perps can order electronic equipment on the internet that overrides or breaks access codes."

"Which is another reason," Jess cut in, "we believe the person who murdered Adler and planted the evidence in your home has done this before. He's too smooth to be a first timer."

Amber thought of the man Kyle Adler. She couldn't recall ever seeing him except for the occasional delivery. On those occasions he'd always seemed so kind and shy. His was not a face she would have associated with evil.

Sean spoke up again. "Does your station keep the original footage from your assignments or just the part that doesn't end up on the cutting room floor—so to speak."

"The station stores the footage that airs, but not the raw footage before it's edited." Hope welled in her chest. "My cameraman may keep all the raw footage. I can check with him."

"If Adler was watching you," Sean offered, "we might find him in the crowd wherever you were reporting breaking news. It's worth a shot."

Jess agreed.

Amber couldn't believe she hadn't thought of checking the footage. She had to clear her head and focus. Her future depended on how this turned out. She could spend the rest of her life in prison or end up on death row. Worse, a murderer could get away with his heinous act.

"Go home, Amber," Jess said. "Try to get some rest, but don't clean your house tonight," she added with a smile.

"Don't worry." Amber stood. "I won't touch anything I don't have to touch."

"Good idea," Jess granted.

As they left the building, Sean exited ahead of her. He scanned the street and checked his car before motioning for her to cross the sidewalk and climb in. He closed her door and went around to the other side. Dusk had the street lamps flickering on against the coming darkness. She closed her eyes and leaned fully into the seat. This day couldn't be over soon enough for her.

When the car moved down the street, she opened her eyes and turned to the driver. "Do you really believe we'll be able to find all the pieces of this puzzle?"

He glanced at her. "Don't worry—we'll find him."

Amber stared out at the darkness. "I hope so."

She didn't want the next story about a person who spent years in prison before being exonerated to be about her.

Chapter Five

Hugo L. Black United States Courthouse
1729 Fifth Avenue North
Tuesday, October 18, 10:30 a.m.

Sean did not like this one bit. He'd had no sleep since Amber had paced the floors most of the night. She'd insisted that was what she did when she battled insomnia. She'd also insisted he should take one of the bedrooms and just ignore her.

Impossible.

The loose fit of the pink flannel pajamas showed nothing of her curves or all that pale, creamy skin. There wasn't one thing sexy about the overly modest sleeping apparel, and still he couldn't keep his mind off her. At one point he'd even covered his head with the pillow. The move hadn't helped an iota.

He'd opted to sleep on the sofa since the layout of the family room and kitchen gave him a view of both the front and rear doors. The house was an older one, but it had been renovated at some point, opening up the main living space. The locks had been changed and her security system had a new access code and password.

First thing this morning she had informed him that

she had to get back to work. She wouldn't discuss taking a vacation. She had ongoing assignments, she'd insisted. Apparently last night's insomnia had evolved into today's determination to pretend nothing had happened.

Three cups of coffee and one caramel latte later and Amber was rushing around the station prepping for the McAllister assignment. On the way to the federal courthouse, she'd explained that Forrest McAllister had been the go-to guy for investments by the who's who of Birmingham for many years. Eight months ago he'd been charged with insider trading. Now that same who's who were doing all within their power to distance themselves from the man. His trial started today.

Sean had heard something about the big story, but he hadn't followed it. Apparently, he was going to now.

Watching Amber wasn't a hardship. The blue skirt and sweater she wore today fit her petite body perfectly. Her hair hung in soft waves, and those cute little freckles were faintly visible across the bridge of her nose.

Get your head back on the job, man. The cameraman had promised to dig through the work they'd done together. He couldn't promise he had anything Amber was looking for. Her first cameraman had retired more than a year ago. She hadn't been able to reach him yet. Sean intended to remind her to follow up with both men later today.

Vehicles sporting the logos of television stations and newspapers from all over the southeast ringed the block. Security had the courthouse locked down. The street, however, was brimming with people—mostly newshounds. Between the horde of reporters, the occasional helicopter overhead and the blaring horns of frustrated drivers attempting to navigate Fifth Avenue, the situation was a security specialist's worst nightmare.

There was no way to cover every direction from which trouble could come. He was left with no recourse but to stay as close as possible to his client. Sweat lined his brow. He felt as if he were guiding a rocker client through the crowd for a sold-out concert. It never ceased to amaze him how many megastars felt the need to brush shoulders with thousands of fans despite the risk that one of them might be a wacko. Sean had navigated the crowds, ever watchful and barely breathing. Like now. His senses were on full-alert. Adrenaline had his heart in the fight-or-flight zone. Every muscle was tense, ready to react to the first sign of trouble.

The hearing had started at nine. Since the date and time of the hearing had been a closely guarded secret, the reporters following the case had missed McAllister's arrival. Word had traveled like wildfire as soon as the man was spotted entering the courthouse. Now they all waited for his exit and any sound bite his team of attorneys would permit to slip. Amber had managed a spot right up front, near the steps into the building. In the event of trouble, maneuvering through the crowd behind them would not be an easy task. Just his luck.

Suddenly, the towering entrance doors opened and a group of men exited. Sean recognized the main player from the shots he'd seen on the news and in the papers. The suits all around him were a combination of security and lawyers. The difference was easy to spot; the lawyers carried the briefcases while the others wore communication devices in their ears and constantly scanned the area around their client.

As if floodgates had been opened, the rush of reporters swelled into a tide of bodies, microphones and cameras. Sean wrapped his fingers around Amber's left forearm to keep her close. Intent on getting some word on how the hearing turned out, she ignored his move. Questions were hurled at the group exiting the building. Amber's was the loudest voice. For such a petite woman, she had a set of pipes and she knew how to use them.

The cameraman slipped in front of Sean, blocking his view forward. Sean held tighter to Amber and elbowed his way between her and the big guy.

Once the group reached the sidewalk, the crush of bodies was too close for comfort. Sean didn't like this. He angled his body to stay close to Amber. She stretched toward her target.

The huddle of security guards and lawyers abruptly stopped. McAllister stepped forward. A hush fell over the crowd of reporters. "Today was the first step in proving my innocence," he announced. "See you next week."

As soon as he was swallowed by his guards, the attorneys shouted, "That's all for today!"

Amber twisted to face her cameraman. "Did you get that?"

"Got it," the man fondly known as Bear assured her.

"Let's find a quiet place and do a lead-in," Amber directed.

Before Sean could suggest they get the hell off the street, she was climbing the steps to the building's entrance. She took a position and smoothed a hand over her hair.

"Hair and makeup are good," the cameraman assured her. "We are live in the studio in ten, nine..."

As he counted down, Sean scanned the crowd that had followed McAllister to the waiting limos. Behind him, Amber delivered a thirty-or forty-second overview of the case and introduced this morning's hearing results. When she signed off the air, Sean was able to breathe again.

The position they were in was far too open, not to mention they were backed against a wall—literally. No overt threats to Amber's life had been posed, but his orders were to assume the worst. If the attempts to frame her for murder failed, the perp might very well choose a different strategy.

"Can we get out of here now?" Sean asked as the cameraman packed up his equipment.

"We can." Amber moved toward him. "There's a clerk inside I want to follow up with first."

As long as they were off the street, Sean would be happy.

"See you at the station," Bear tossed over his shoulder as he hustled away.

Sean reached to open the door for her as a dozen or so of the reporters who'd only moments ago been hanging on McAllister's every move were suddenly closing in on them. He stepped in front of Amber.

"Amber, is it true the murder weapon was found in your home?" the nearest reporter shouted.

Sean turned his head and whispered to her, "Go inside. Now."

"Did they find your prints on the weapon?" another voice shouted.

"If you didn't know the victim as you claim, can you explain how this happened?"

"Were you and Kyle Adler having an affair?"

More questions speared through the crisp morning air. Rather than go inside, Amber stood stone still, staring at the people who were her colleagues—colleagues determined to get the story even if it meant turning on one of their own.

"What about those red panties they found in his bed?" a man accused as he moved to the front of the horde. "Are you going to deny they're yours?"

Sean didn't wait for Amber to react. He opened the door and dragged her inside. Two security guards immediately stopped them.

"We have a meeting," Sean announced, hoping Amber would snap out of her coma and get them past these guys.

"Paula Vicks," she said, her voice shaky. "She's expecting us."

After passing through security, Amber seemed to regain her composure. They moved to the elevators and she selected a floor. Sean kept his mouth shut as the car shuttled them upward. The elevators, like every other part of the building, would be monitored by security.

The elevator bumped to a stop, and the doors opened. She took a right down the corridor, and he eased up close beside her. "You okay?"

"Why wouldn't I be?"

He wasn't going to touch that one. "Good."

She seemed to square her shoulders as she reached for the door. He followed her inside. A woman about Amber's age, tall and thin with blond hair and brown eyes, was waiting. She shepherded them into a small office and closed the door.

"I can't talk to you about the McAllister case, Amber. I can't talk to you about anything."

Amber appeared surprised. "What's going on, Paula?"

"Rumor is you're about to be charged with murder.

I've taken too many risks giving you tidbits already. Anything or anyone related to you is about to come under intense scrutiny. I can't be a part of that. I'm sorry."

Amber nodded. "I understand. If you can just tell me the date of the next hearing on the McAllister case, we'll leave it at that."

"A week from today. Same time."

"Thanks." Amber exited Paula's office without another word.

Sean kept his mouth shut until they were back in the first-floor lobby. The tension radiating from Amber said loads. This ugly business had just trickled into her career. For a woman whose career came first, this new reality was devastating. Outside the reporters had thankfully vanished. They reached his car without incident.

Once they were inside, he asked, "Where to now?"

"My office. I need to dig up everything I can find on Kyle Adler."

"Then we need to go to Corlew's office instead."

Amber hesitated at the door he'd opened. "I thought your firm had already given me everything they had on Adler."

Sean shrugged. "You have everything obtained through the usual channels. It's time we checked out a few others."

When she didn't argue, Sean closed her door and rounded the hood. He'd call Corlew en route. If Corlew's contacts couldn't find it, it didn't exist.

The Garage Café, Tenth Terrace South, 11:15 a.m.

SEAN WAS NO stranger to the Garage, but Buddy Corlew considered the place his conference room. He held more meetings here than he did at the office. This particular meeting couldn't be held at the office anyway. Jess knew Buddy skirted the law from time to time, he'd done it for years as a PI before he and Jess formed their partnership. Jess, being the boss, had one rule: never break the law. So Buddy conducted whatever business Jess might not approve of here.

Buddy acknowledged their entrance with a nod. Sean ushered Amber to his table. She had asked a lot of questions on the way, and he'd assured her that Buddy could answer just about anything she wanted to know. Sean worried that no one was asking the right questions. To some degree the dilemma was understandable. At this point, the motive for Adler's murder was unclear. The motive for framing Amber was even foggier.

Buddy stood as Amber took the chair Sean pulled out. "I saw you on the news a little while ago." Buddy gestured to the screens hanging around the bar. "You think McAllister is innocent?"

Amber smiled, looking relaxed for the first time this morning. "I do not, but that conclusion is based primarily on the fact that I just don't like him." She leaned forward. "If you tell anyone I said that, I'll make my next exposé about you, Mr. Corlew."

Buddy held up his hands. "No worries here. I've never met a woman who could tolerate a man who gave her secrets away."

"What about Kyle Adler's secrets?" she asked.

Sean wasn't surprised. The lady had built a career on getting straight to the point. He'd seen her falter a bit the past twenty-four hours, but she didn't give up.

"Mr. Adler was a strange one." Buddy rested his forearms on the table, leaning in a little closer. "He didn't go to college and still he was twenty-seven before he held a steady job and moved out of his parents' basement. He rented a small home over on Eagle Ridge Drive about two years ago. He made a living delivering *things*."

"Things besides flowers and dry cleaning?" Amber asked.

She stood by her certainty that the few times Adler had shown up at her door to make a delivery he hadn't come inside. Sean had pressed her to consider whether or not she'd ever turned her back for even a few moments. Had she gone to get a tip from her purse in the other room? Even a couple of minutes could have given him the opportunity he needed to make a move.

"Groceries, prescriptions, flowers, dry cleaning, you name it," Buddy said in answer to her question. "Your books overdue at the library? Just give him a call, and he would pick them up and drop them off for you. But he made his real money driving folks home from the clubs and bars around town."

A waitress appeared and took their orders. Buddy insisted they have lunch on him. Amber hadn't eaten that morning. After seeing what she kept in her fridge and cabinets, Sean expected her to order a salad. A woman as tiny as she was couldn't possibly eat more than a spoonful at a time anyway. She surprised him by ordering a burger, fries and a regular cola. Maybe she felt the need for carbs. He damned sure did. He'd been starving all morning.

"Did Adler ever drive you home?" Sean asked once the waitress was on her way.

Amber shook her head. "Absolutely not. I haven't spent much time on the club scene in years. Occasionally I meet friends or colleagues at a bar, but I always leave under my own steam."

Buddy pulled a folded piece of paper from his shirt pocket. "I compiled a list of the businesses he operated from the most frequently." He passed the list to Amber. "It's possible your encounters with him may have been more frequent than you realize. We shouldn't rule out anything. Start with that list and compile your own. Any deliveries, pickups, drives to the airport or to pick up your car after it was serviced, whatever you can think of that required assistance from another person."

She studied the list. "I recognize a number of these business. The dry cleaner." She pointed to another name. "The alteration shop. Still, I'm certain I've never seen him beyond a couple of flower deliveries and I think something from the dry cleaner's that once."

"We can't ignore the possibility that he disguised himself when he was delivering to you," Buddy countered. "You may not have recognized him."

"Oh." Amber frowned as she surveyed the list again. "I hadn't thought of that."

Buddy was right. If Adler was obsessed with Amber so much that he went to such extremes to be close to her, the possibilities for encounters were endless. "It's a little like looking for a needle in a haystack," Sean commented.

"It's a lot like looking for a needle in a haystack," Buddy agreed. "You just have to remember that the haystack can come apart the same way it went together, one row at a time."

"Has the BPD turned over any of the inventory lists of things found in his home or vehicle?" Sean looked from the list of businesses to Buddy. "It would seem to me they'd find the tools of his trade. Anything he used to get into houses like Amber's. Disguises, if he used them."

"Jess received a list from Lori Wells, the lead detective on the case," Buddy said to Amber, "but there wasn't the first tool or electronic gadget one would need for breaking into a house found."

Uncertainty nudged Sean. "Then he has to have a secondary go-to place. A storage unit or somewhere he keeps his gear."

"Or a somebody," Buddy countered. "The more Jess and I learn about this guy, the less we feel he was capable of anything worse than stalking."

"If we can't find the motive or the killer, the only way his murder makes sense—" Amber met Sean's gaze before shifting her attention to Buddy and going on "—is if we were friends or lovers and I killed him."

Her words hung in the air as the waitress delivered their drinks. When she'd gone, Amber continued, "The problem is, I hardly knew him. He's a face I barely recall. A smile of appreciation for a good tip after making a delivery."

"Did Detective Wells mention whether or not Adler had a cell phone and if they'd subpoenaed the records?" Sean suspected the BPD was already working on any cell phones and social media Adler used.

"They have," Buddy confirmed. "But it'll take a few days with all the hoops they have to jump through." He grinned. "I, on the other hand, have my own source. We'll have his phone records by morning."

"I'm impressed, Mr. Corlew," Amber said. "I guess Gina was right when she said B&C was the best."

Buddy gave her a pointed look. "First, no one calls me mister anything. It's Buddy. And second, just make sure you remember that my methods for being the best are trade secrets."

Amber smiled, the confident, relaxed expression she wore whenever she was on camera. Sean was glad to see it.

"You have my word, Buddy. I'm putting all my trust in you." She glanced at Sean when she spoke. "The two of you," she amended.

Sean would not let her down. He wondered, though, if she knew the last woman he had been assigned to protect and who had trusted him had ended up dead.

Chapter Six

Thrasher Floral, Pearson Avenue, 3:10 p.m.

Amber wasn't entirely convinced about this route, but she had nothing to lose beyond a little time by taking it.

"Stick to your story," Sean reminded her. "Don't allow your emotions to get involved."

Amber's jaw dropped. He did not just say that to her. "Excuse me?"

How many years had she been reporting breaking stories? She'd waited for hours in the rain and freezing cold. She had followed leads into the darkest back streets and alleys of the Magic City. She had endured the latest trends in health, fitness and fashion. She never lost her cool or came unglued. Never.

At least not until today…

"You're a pro at digging into a story and finding the details," he offered. "This isn't just another story—this is *your* story. It might not be as easy to do."

"I've got this." Not about to debate the subject, she grabbed her bag and reached for the door. She'd barely opened it and gotten out when he moved up beside her.

"It wasn't my intention to offend you," he said as they crossed the sidewalk.

"You didn't," she lied.

He opened the door and a bell jingled. Inside the smell of flowers overwhelmed all else. As much as she loved receiving flowers, visiting a floral shop was one of her least favorite things to do. It always reminded her of funeral homes and the day she'd had to go with her mother to select flowers for her grandmother. Amber shuddered. She hated this smell.

Sean leaned closer. "You okay?"

She flashed him a frustrated smile. "I'm fine."

Who knew how annoying having a bodyguard could be? No wonder celebrities were always coming unhinged in public. What kind of life was this? Someone watching every move a person made? Ordering that person around for her own good?

Then again, she decided as she reached the counter, there was little chance of feeling afraid…or lonely. Sean Douglas paused next to her and sent her a sideways smile. Her heart bumped into a faster rhythm. Why in the world did her bodyguard have to be so damned handsome?

"Good afternoon," the clerk announced. "How may I help you?" She looked from Amber to Sean and back. "Do you have a special occasion coming up?"

Summoning her game smile, Amber glanced at her name tag. "Kayla, I'm Amber Roberts, and this is Sean Douglas. We're here to speak to Mr. Thrasher."

Kayla made an aha face. "Sure. He's in the back working on arrangements. I'll let him know you're here."

Amber thanked her as she disappeared through the staff-only door behind the counter. She'd researched the shop on the way here. Peter Thrasher was the owner. His mother had opened the shop forty years ago, nearly a decade before he was born. An old lifestyle interview from the *Birmingham News* during Thrasher's senior year in high school quoted him as saying flowers were his life. His mother had passed away the year before last. According to the obituary, she was preceded in death by her husband and Peter was her only child. If he had ever been married, Amber had found no announcement. Kyle Adler delivered flowers for only one floral shop, and this was the one.

The door opened once more and Peter Thrasher appeared. The six-foot-two man matched the few images she'd found in her Google search. His white button-down shirt sported the shop logo over the breast pocket. His brown hair was neatly trimmed and his brown eyes appeared overly large behind the black-rimmed glasses.

"Ms. Roberts." He gave her an acknowledging nod. "Welcome to my shop. How can I help you? I've just received a beautiful shipment of fall flowers. Gerber daisies, chrysanthemums and classic roses. I'm certain I have just what you're looking for."

"Sounds lovely." She reached into her purse and removed the photo of Kyle Adler she'd printed from her Google search last night. "I was hoping you could help me with a story I'm doing on Kyle Adler." She showed him the photo. "He was murdered a few days ago."

Thrasher looked from the photo to her. "I heard about his death." He gave a shrug, the gesture uncertain. "I also saw on the news that the police were talking to you about it."

"Did you know him?" Amber forged ahead despite the turmoil of abrupt emotions his words had stirred inside her. Maybe Sean had been right to warn her. This was not the same as chasing a story about someone else.

Thrasher nodded. "Not really. Not until he started his delivery service anyway. He was a friendly guy. Easygoing, quiet. It's a real shame, what happened to him."

"It really is," Amber agreed. "I want to do all I can to ensure justice for Mr. Adler."

Thrasher glanced at Sean. "Were you and Kyle... involved? I mean, after what I saw on the news last night..." His words trailed off as his gaze settled on Amber once more.

"I didn't know him. He delivered flowers from your shop to my home a couple of times. They were lovely, by the way." She searched Thrasher's face. "Did he ever mention me?"

Thrasher's expression turned defensive. "I see. You think he was some sort of stalker or obsessed fan."

"I don't think that at all," Amber denied. "I believe whoever killed Kyle is using me to get away with murder. I'm hoping that his friends and colleagues can help me find out who killed him."

"Isn't that what the police are supposed to do?" Thrasher stared at her expectantly.

Amber couldn't get a read on the man. Was he being indifferent or accusatory? His tone gave nothing away.

"Sometimes," Sean said, his tone undeniably pointed, "the police are too busy with other leads to see the real ones they need to follow. If you counted yourself a friend of Adler's, we're hoping you can help us find the truth."

"Anything you recall," Amber cut in, "might prove helpful. Did Kyle have any close friends that we might speak to?"

Thrasher stared at her for so long without saying a word, Amber was sure he wasn't going to answer. "Kyle was a loner. He didn't have any friends that I know of."

"How well did you know him?" Sean pressed.

Thrasher visibly withdrew. His shoulders went back and he eased a few inches from the counter. "I really didn't know him. He made deliveries for me. He was quiet and reliable. That's all I know. I have work to do, so if you'll excuse me."

He had already turned and reached for the door when Amber said, "You seemed disturbed by the idea that I might consider Kyle a stalker or an obsessed fan." Thrasher hesitated but didn't turn around. "If you didn't know him very well, why would that bother you?"

Thrasher turned back to face her. Whatever he felt or thought, he had wiped his face clean of any reaction. "I don't like the idea of anyone being made to look bad when he's not here to defend himself," he said, his tone barely above freezing. "Have a nice day."

Amber mulled over his words as she and Sean exited the shop.

"Strange guy," Sean muttered as he opened her car door.

She turned back to the shop before getting into the car. "A little."

When she was settled into the passenger seat and Sean had climbed behind the wheel, he said, "He lied about his relationship with Adler."

Amber had sensed that, as well. Thrasher's defensive reaction had been his only slip. "The question is, does he simply not want to get involved or is he protecting his friend by not revealing some not-so-flattering secret?"

"You may have missed your true calling." Sean grinned. "Maybe you're the one who should be a PI."

4:15 p.m.

"THAT'S IT." AMBER POINTED to the alterations shop. "Martha Sews."

Sean maneuvered into a parking spot. The alterations shop had a great location in one of the city's oldest neighborhoods that had gone commercial. Martha's shop was near Mountain Brook among a row of small houses converted to businesses whose front yards served as parking lots. Unlike the other shop owners, Martha had maintained the lovely flowering shrubs that lined the foundation of the house. With rocking chairs on the front porch, the place still looked like a home. Amber doubted the owner, who continued to live in the house as well as to operate her business, knew Kyle Adler any better than she did, but no stone could go unturned.

Amber sighed. She still found it incredible that the facts she needed to find were to clear her name. How had this happened? Her gaze settled on the driver as he shut off the engine. How had he handled the situation when his life was turned upside down? At some point she wanted to ask him about Lacy James. There had been endless speculation about the relationship between the star and her bodyguard in the media after her death. Sean had never acknowledged or denied they were lovers. Ultimately her death had been ruled an accidental overdose. But not before Sean had been crucified by the media. Unfortunately, being targeted by the media was only the tip of the iceberg where Amber's troubles were concerned.

"We going in or what?"

Amber blinked and turned away from the scrutiny of his blue eyes. "Yes." She grabbed her bag and reached for the door. As usual he was out of the car and waiting for her as she emerged.

He closed her door. She said, "Thank you."

As they moved toward the shop, rather than dwell on how Thrasher's slightly odd behavior had rattled her, she tried to remember all she could about Sean. She'd heard about his disappearance from Hollywood. At the time, no one seemed to know where he'd gone. She had vaguely wondered if he'd returned home, but then another local story had come along and she'd forgotten all about the disgraced bodyguard and the deceased pop star. Funny how fate had a way of bringing things and people back around. Maybe she'd have the opportunity to get the real story from him. His side should be told.

He reached for the door to Martha Sews but hesitated before he opened it. "I don't give interviews, Amber."

Clearly she was wearing her every thought on her face for all to see. It was the only explanation for how everyone seemed to read her mind lately. "I don't know what you mean."

"Part of my job is to recognize what a person is thinking before they act."

She would have disagreed with his conclusion, but he opened the door for her to go inside. It wasn't as if she could refute his statement. She had been wondering about an interview. She was curious about the man charged with her safety. His credentials should be of concern. Except he worked for Jess Burnett, and that said it all.

Annoyed now, as much with herself as with him, she

struggled to pull off a smile for the lady who emerged from the back of the shop to greet them. "Martha, how are you?"

"I'm just fine, Amber. How are you this lovely afternoon?" The older lady frowned. "Were you scheduled to pick up your dress today and I forgot?"

Amber had almost forgotten the dress herself. "No. I think that's Friday." How had she let the dress slip her mind? She had a huge fund-raising event on Friday night. Assuming she wasn't in jail.

Martha nodded as she glanced at Sean. "It's always nice to see one of my favorite customers. What can I do for you and your friend today?"

"Actually…" Amber stalled. She surveyed the retail side of the shop. Martha sold all sorts of vintage items as well as one-of-a-kind scarves and handmade jewelry. If Amber recalled correctly, most of the items were on consignment. The extra income tided her over when the alternations were slow. Amber doubted that happened very often anymore. "My friend—" she wrapped her arm around Sean's "—needs a vintage bow tie for a fund-raiser we're attending."

"I see." Martha beamed. "Does your friend have a name?"

Amber put her hand to her chest, feigning embarrassment but also because her heart was suddenly and foolishly pounding after touching him. "Of course. Martha Guynes, meet Sean Douglas."

Sean extended his hand. "Nice to meet you, Ms. Guynes."

Martha blushed. "Call me Martha. Everyone does."

"Martha," he said with such charm that even Amber melted a little more.

"Let me show you what I have, Sean." Martha directed them to the far left side of the small shop, where ties and handkerchiefs stocked a vintage display case. She moved behind the case and slid open a door. "Do you see one you like?"

While Sean perused the bow ties, Amber said, "I was telling him you'd been in business more than a quarter of a century. Everyone who's anyone brings their alternation needs to you."

Martha gave a nod. "It seems like only yesterday that I was praying for some sort of answer from the good Lord. My husband had come home from a mission in the Middle East with undiagnosed PTSD. He drank all the time and was either deeply depressed and couldn't get out of bed or was on a rampage breaking things around the house." She sighed. "It was a hard time for me and our son."

Amber reached across the counter and touched her hand. "So many husbands and fathers returned with wounds no one but the immediate family could see."

Martha drew in a deep breath. "I was worried sick about just surviving. Since his troubles were undiagnosed, there was no money coming in. I had to find a way to make ends meet. I remembered back to the days before his illness when I would have coffee and play cards with the ladies from church. It never failed that when the holidays came around and folks needed costumes or clothes altered, Ruby Jean would say, 'Don't fret, girls. Martha sews.' I suddenly realized my old friend was right, and I opened this shop in my own living room. Here we are better than twenty-five years later."

"What an inspiring story," Amber said.

Martha shrugged. "We do what we have to do."

"I'll take that one," Douglas said, selecting a classic black bow tie that required hand tying.

"One of my favorites," Martha said. "It takes a man who knows what he's doing to get the bow just right."

"My father refused to wear a tie that came with a clip," Sean said. "I learned the art of hand tying at an early age."

"A sign of character and breeding," Martha said with a smile.

While Sean paid for his tie, Amber considered all the framed photos hanging around the room. Customers, including Amber, modeling Martha's work. Everyone she knew used Martha for her alterations. The lady was a household name.

"I was sorry to hear you're having some trouble," Martha said to Amber as she passed Sean a paper bag emblazoned with her sewing machine logo. "I swear, some reporters will make up anything for headlines. Anybody with one eye and half sense would know you wouldn't hurt a fly." She shook her head. "A disgrace, that's what it is."

Amber drummed up what she hoped was a passable smile. "Thank you. I'm sure the police will get to the bottom of what really happened."

Martha came around the counter and patted Amber on the arm. "You'll be in my prayers, hon."

"I appreciate that." Amber showed Martha the photo of Adler. "I know he made deliveries for you. Did you know him well?"

Martha considered the question before answering. "He was reliable. Pleasant. He went out of his way to be helpful." She shrugged. "I can't imagine who would want to hurt him. He was such a shy fellow."

"Did he have a girlfriend?" He may have been a very nice man, but her panties and her grandmother's teacups had wound up in his house somehow. Amber kept that part to herself.

Martha crossed her arms over her chest then and pressed a finger to her cheek as if contemplating the question. "I thought he was a bit of a loner. If he had any friends or a girlfriend, I never saw or heard about them. Why do you ask?"

The few details the police had shared with Amber had not been released to the press, which meant she couldn't share those with Martha. "Curious, I suppose. I'm hoping to find someone who knew him well."

"Are you doing a story on his murder?"

Amber shook her head. "I'm looking for the truth. And maybe a few answers about why I'm a person of interest in the case. Maybe he was an obsessed fan. I don't know. I feel like there's something the police haven't seen."

"You know," Martha said, "now that you mention it, I do remember him stopping once to watch you." She gestured to the small television that sat on one end of her counter. "He picked up the deliveries for the day, and he noticed you on the screen. He didn't move until the channel had returned to the regular program."

"Do you recall when this happened?"

Martha shook her head. "I'm sorry. I don't remember. A few weeks or so ago."

"You're certain he never mentioned any friends or places he frequented?"

"I think he played video games," Martha offered. "He brought my son a new game now and then." Her smile returned. "I think they spoke the same language when it came to video games."

"How is Delbert?" Amber felt terrible she'd forgotten to ask Martha about her son. Delbert was wheelchair bound and very reclusive. His father had died in a car crash and then poor Delbert had been paralyzed in a football injury. Keeping a roof over their heads and food on the table were only parts of the burden Martha carried. Caring for a physically challenged child was incredibly difficult to do alone. Few could handle the stress, much less the workload of operating a thriving alterations shop.

"He's doing well—thank you for asking. These days he helps me remember where I leave things and what I'm supposed to be doing. I'd be awfully lonesome without him."

"Does Delbert know his friend is dead?"

"We talked about it. He'll be a little more withdrawn than usual for a while." She sighed. "I'll just have to find another way to keep him entertained. Would you like to say hello? He'd be thrilled to see you. That boy thinks you're the prettiest thing."

Amber smiled. "I'd love to say hello."

Martha ushered them through her kitchen, where the scent of something wonderful emanated from the Crock-Pot. The house had originally been a three bedroom, but Martha had turned the larger of the three into a family room since the living room and dining room were lost to the business.

Delbert sat in his wheelchair in front of the television, his focus on winning the game playing out on the screen. The cozy room had Martha's touches all over it. Crocheted throws and framed needlepoint art. Amber often wondered if sewing was Martha's way of escaping reality. Everyone needed an outlet.

"Delbert, look who stopped by to see you," Martha cooed.

Her son looked up, his attention shifting to Amber. He smiled.

Amber moved closer to him and crouched down to his eye level. "One of these days I need to learn to play that game." She couldn't remember the name of it, but it was all the rage with gamers.

Delbert glanced from her to Sean. His smile faded, and he shut off the game and stared at the floor.

After several moments of silence, Martha offered, "We'll let you get back to your game."

"I'll see you next time, Delbert," Amber promised. Back in the shop, she said, "I hope Sean's presence didn't upset him."

"He'll be fine." To Sean, Martha said. "He's just not very good with strangers."

Delbert's story was such a sad one. Not long after the paralyzing injury he'd tried to take his own life with a drug overdose. He'd survived but the close encounter with death had left him with some amount of brain damage.

"I understand. I was in his territory. By the way," Sean went on, "do you know the name of the video game store where Mr. Adler shopped?"

"That place over on Riverview Parkway, I believe."

"Game Master?" Sean asked.

Amber was glad he knew about game shops. She knew nothing about video games and had no desire to learn. Several of her friends knew the lingo and all the newest games. They warned Amber that when she had kids she would have to learn. Since she had no prospects—even if she were interested—in a relationship, she doubted there would be children. Her gaze lingered on Sean. Did he want kids?

Where in the world had that thought come from? Had to be the stress. Her mind was playing games with her.

"That's the one," Martha confirmed. "I remember the bags." She frowned. "Do you think I should call that detective who questioned me and tell her about Kyle bringing those games to Delbert?"

"It could be significant," Amber advised. At this point anything could be significant. "We should be going. We've taken up too much of your time. I hope you'll call me if you think of anything else that might help us learn more about Mr. Adler's life."

"Of course." Martha shook her head. "It's such a senseless tragedy."

Amber prayed one tragedy didn't become two. One way or another they had to find Kyle Adler's killer.

When they were back in Sean's car and he'd driven out of the parking lot, he turned to Amber. "What's the story on her son?"

Amber gave him the details Martha had given her after they became friends. "He's completely reliant on his mother."

"I guess that takes him out of the suspect pool."

No kidding. "I can't see Delbert as a suspect even if his physical and mental challenges didn't exist." These were people Amber had known for years.

"You see—" Sean glanced at her "—that's where you'd fall down in your investigation."

She shook her head. "What're you talking about? What motive could that boy possibly have?"

"First, he's not a boy. He's a man. And just because he's in a wheelchair and dependent on his mother doesn't mean he doesn't think like a man."

"Okay. How is that motive?"

"It isn't, but *you* are."

Now she was totally confused.

"He lit up like a Christmas tree when he saw you," Sean explained. "His own mother said he adores you."

Amber frowned, understanding dawning. "Then he withdrew when he saw you."

"He also shut off his game. He didn't want to share anything with me. He closed me out."

"Are you really suggesting Delbert is a suspect?" *Please.* There was no way. Even if he did think like a man where she was concerned.

Sean flashed her a lopsided grin. "I'm just pointing out how easy it is to miss clues when you're emotionally involved. Like Mrs. Guynes's comment about Adler being shy. Still waters run deep."

"Point taken." Amber tamped down her frustration. She'd thought the same thing about Adler. Just another reminder that the face of evil rarely looked the way one expected. "What we do know is that according to the police report there was no evidence of forced entry, which suggests Adler knew his killer."

"I found no signs of forced entry at your place." Sean glanced at her again. "Someone still got in and left that bloody knife in your fan mail box for you."

"Good point." Amber stared out the window. "If the police don't find the killer, how will I prove I didn't do this?"

Sean braked for a light and settled his blue gaze on

her once more. "More important, how will you ever be safe if we don't find the person who did this?"

Amber's hand went to her lips. He was right. As much as she wanted to pretend this tragedy wasn't about her, somehow it was. She was part of the motive that had caused Kyle Adler's death.

"Let's go back to who might want to hurt you," Sean suggested. "And how that person could connect to Kyle Adler."

Amber wished she knew.

THE VIDEO GAME store proved a waste of time. No one who worked there recognized Adler. Defeat had set in nice and deep by the time they pulled into her driveway. Amber stared at the house where she'd felt safe as far back as she could remember. The kitchen had always smelled of fresh-baked cookies. Her grandmother had made her feel as if this house were her home away from home.

How could she ever feel that way again knowing a killer had been in her house...had touched her things?

Would there be Channel Six viewers out there—or maybe even friends—who would forever believe she'd had something to do with this man's murder?

She felt as if some part of her identity had been stolen, leaving a hole she might not be able to repair as easily as Martha mended a failing hem or split seam. No matter that she was twenty-eight years old, she suddenly wished her parents were in town. She'd insisted they not rush back. If they learned about the knife, they would be very upset. She'd have to make sure Barb didn't tell them.

"Is it your birthday or something?"

Her gaze followed Sean's, landing on the vase of

flowers waiting on her porch. "No." She started around the hood of the car, but he moved in front of her.

She waited at the bottom of the steps while he inspected the large bouquet of red roses. Who would send her roses? If they weren't from her parents, she had no idea. Though she couldn't fathom her parents finding now a good time to send her flowers. The station? A fan? She went to a great deal of trouble to ensure most of her personal information, including her address, was kept private.

Sean removed the small envelope from the bouquet and opened it. He read the card and then showed it to her. "Looks like you have another admirer."

I'm watching you.

The stamp on the back of the envelope was the Thrasher flower shop. Amber checked the time on her cell. "We might be able to get back there before the shop closes."

"Let's bag the card before we do anything else."

Amber hurried into the house and returned with a sandwich bag. "We have to hurry."

"Dodging traffic is one of my finer talents," he assured her as he carefully bagged the card and tucked it away.

When they were settled in the car and he'd started the engine, he glanced at her before taking off. "You might not want to watch."

Deciding to take him at his word, Amber closed her eyes. Unfortunately, the terrifying images her mind conjured about the man who'd been murdered and the one who'd been in her house—perhaps more than once—proved utterly disturbing.

Sean was right. A connection of some sort existed between her and Kyle and maybe between her and his killer. How on earth did she find it? She'd done enough investigative reporting to know if a person didn't want to be found, they wouldn't be. A serial killer might use the same MO repeatedly and get away with it because he was too careful, too meticulous to leave even trace evidence.

Sean was right about that, too. In a case like this, the only way to find the killer was to find the motive for the murder.

Chapter Seven

The visit to the floral shop had been pointless. Sean had pushed Thrasher as far as he could without a badge and a warrant. The flowers had been ordered online, paid for with a gift card. The payment method was a dead end. It would take a warrant and considerable effort to trace the IP address of the computer used for the purchase. None of that was necessary in Sean's opinion. Whoever killed Adler had ordered the flowers the day before he was murdered with instructions they were to be delivered on this date.

The cops would see that element as proof Adler had ordered the flowers. In Sean's opinion the date the flowers were ordered didn't change the fact that Adler likely had a partner in whatever weirdness he was into. And that partner was in all probability his killer. Sean's conclusion confirmed the concept that Amber Roberts was in no way connected to the murder of Kyle Adler. She was a victim. All he had to do now was turn the card with the ominous message over to the BPD. Detective Lori Wells would follow up.

The boss called as they left the floral shop. Evidently

the BPD had uncovered new evidence and wanted to meet with Amber. The drive to the office was tense. He could feel Amber growing more anxious. As soon as they arrived, he passed the card he'd bagged to Jess, told her about the flower delivery and brought her up to speed on the rest.

Ten minutes later they were still waiting in the conference room. Amber sat next to Sean. She kept fidgeting with her bag or the hem of her skirt. She was nervous, but Sean wasn't worried about her going down for Adler's murder. It didn't take a detective's shield to see she was being framed. Whatever the motive, the killer wanted Amber to suffer this roller-coaster ride or worse. It was the *worse* part that worried Sean.

Unless the detectives had found more evidence that would connect to the perp, he'd get away with murder. Why risk being caught by sending flowers to Amber? If eliminating Adler had been the goal, why continue taking risks?

"Sergeant Wells and Lieutenant Harper should be here anytime now," Jess announced, breaking the thick silence.

"You have no idea what this new evidence is?" Frank Teller asked.

Sean glanced to the other side of Amber, where Teller sat, his fingers drumming on the table.

"We'll all know soon enough what they've found," Jess assured him.

Sean liked his boss even if he wasn't so sure whether she liked him or not. He'd never met anyone quite like her. She was smart and brave. As far as he could tell, she wasn't afraid of a damned thing. She and Corlew were a strange combination. Both determined to get the job done but with different perspectives and from different avenues. Corlew didn't blink at crossing the line if that was what it took. *Oil and water*, Sean decided. Yet somehow they meshed. There was a long history between the two. One of these days Sean was going to ask Corlew about it. Maybe over a beer.

A bell jingled and the sound of Corlew's deep voice filled the lobby, followed by Lori Wells's laughter and Chet Harper's quiet response to whatever Corlew had said. The two detectives were part of the family, Jess told Sean frequently. Along with Clint Hayes, Chad Cook and Corlew's wife, Sylvia. More of those close ties, bound by history. Sean wondered if he would ever again have those beyond his immediate family. The fact that his gaze moved to Amber at the thought made him want to kick his own backside.

The truth was, he'd thought he was ready for a lifetime commitment back in LA. He'd had the woman, the friends and the job. Life had been damned good. His life-shattering mistake had sent his friends running. The great job went next. The ties fell apart.

Maybe it was better not to get tangled up in close ties. No worries about being let down if you kept your expectations low. His gaze drifted to Amber. He didn't need complications like her, either. Getting involved with a client was always a bad idea. He'd learned that lesson the hard way.

Corlew and the detectives entered the room and settled around the table. Sean nodded to Lori and Harper. Since they all knew each other there was no need for introductions.

"What is it that couldn't wait until morning, Detectives?" Teller steered the conversation to business with his usual dry style.

Lori placed a folder on the table. She removed two photographs and passed them around. "Meet Rhiana Pettie and Kimberly McCorkle."

Both women looked to be twenty-five to thirty; Pettie was a blonde, and McCorkle was a brunette. Sean passed the photos on to Jess.

"Both are deceased," Harper said. "Strangled. Ligature marks indicate they were held captive for several days before being strangled. No indication of sexual assault."

"These two victims are related to our case how?" Jess asked as she handed the photos to Teller.

"We believe both women were victims of Adler and whoever killed him," Lori said.

Next to him, Amber drew in a harsh breath. Sean resisted the urge to reach for her hand and give it a squeeze.

Lori withdrew more photos and passed them on. "We located a storage unit near Riverview Parkway rented under Adler's name. Inside were three small plastic boxes. The kind you'd purchase to store a pair of shoes." She used her hands to indicate the size. "In each box was a pair of panties. A single pubic hair as well as one from the scalp was folded into each. Analysis confirmed the respective hairs belonged to the two victims." She indicated the photos that had made their way back around to Harper. "Along with Pettie's panties was a wineglass. The lab confirmed her prints were on the glass. In the box with McCorkle's was a coffee mug bearing her prints."

"Like my teacup and..."

Amber didn't have to say "red panties." Sean had struggled to keep images of her wearing nothing but those panties out of his head more than once.

Lori nodded in answer to Amber's unfinished question.

"Where were the bodies found and how were they dumped?" Jess asked.

"Pettie was taken Valentine's Day. She left work and never made it home. Her body was found a week later in the woods off Highway 280. McCorkle disappeared on June 20. Same scenario. She left work and wasn't heard from again until her body was discovered in a drainage ditch in Bessemer ten days later. Both were dressed in skimpy lingerie. McCorkle was still bound by the thin nylon rope used to secure her. Lengths of the rope were secured to each wrist like a bracelet. The one from Pettie's right wrist was missing."

Harper pulled yet another photo from the folder. This one showed a piece of blue nylon rope. "Considering this new evidence, we did another sweep of Adler's house. We found the rope tucked inside a family photo album."

"Did you find anything else like this?" Jess asked as she spread the photos of the items found on the table.

"We took his house apart," Lori answered. "We didn't find any other evidence anywhere on the property."

Jess removed her eyeglasses. "Ladies and gentlemen, we're looking at the work of a fledgling serial killer or killers. The MO is the same, though things were a bit sloppier with Pettie. The killer or killers had cleaned up their act a bit by the time they murdered McCorkle." She turned to Amber. "If I'm right, you were supposed to be the next victim."

Amber eyes widened. The pulse at the base of her throat fluttered. "Oh, my God."

"The third box found in his storage unit was empty," Lori explained. "The items belonging to you would have likely ended up there if Adler hadn't been murdered."

"We're assuming he was working with a partner," Harper said. "And that partner killed him and planted the evidence to point to Ms. Roberts. We just don't know why yet. We also can't say whether Adler was involved in the murders."

"Does that mean my client is no longer a person of interest in the case?" Teller demanded.

"We have every reason to believe," Lori explained, "Ms. Roberts had nothing to do with Adler's murder. But until we know more she's still a part of this case."

"But she has been cleared of suspicion—is that correct?" Teller pressed.

"She has been cleared of suspicion," Harper confirmed. "At this point, we believe she may be in danger from whoever Adler was working with."

"Crimes Against Persons is officially handing off the case to the Special Problems Unit," Lori explained. "Captain Aldridge is not happy about it since the search she ordered turned up significant evidence, but the chief called it a couple of hours ago. Chet will be in charge of the case now."

"Excuse me." Amber stood and hurried from the room.

Sean followed. She went into the restroom, and he waited in the hall. As grateful as he was certain she felt to be cleared of suspicion, the other news had been startling.

Learning you were the next victim on a serial killer's hit list wasn't exactly like being named prom queen.

At least now he knew what the *worse* part was.

AMBER LET THE faucet run until the water was as cold as it was going to get, and then she bent forward and splashed it on her face. She gripped the sink to keep herself steady.

The dead man, Kyle Adler, had come into her home and taken her things. He could have touched any or all of her possessions.

Fear twisted inside her, churning in her stomach.

He'd taken her panties into his bed and fantasized about...*her*.

He'd wanted to kill her.

He'd probably killed or been a party to the murders of those other two women.

Amber drew in a shuddering breath as she stared at her reflection. She had been next.

Another deep breath and then another. *Calm down.* She needed to get back in there and hear the rest.

Reaching for a paper towel, she braced her hip against the sink. She patted her face and dried her hands. She could do this. Adler was dead. He couldn't hurt her or anyone else now.

Except he had a partner...who'd in all probability been in her house, too.

Amber tossed the damp paper towel and opened the door.

Sean was waiting for her. "You okay?"

She pushed a smile in place. "I'm many things, but okay is not one of them at the moment."

He gestured for her to go ahead of him.

Amber squared her shoulders and returned to the conference room. She could do this. She was strong, and she had a bodyguard.

Jess offered a kind smile as Amber took her seat once more. "We were just discussing that you and the other two—" she gestured to the folder on the table in front of Lori Wells "—have nothing beyond being female in common."

Amber listened, struggling to keep her face clear of the fear pounding in her veins, as the detectives, Jess and Corlew, discussed the facts. Pettie was much taller than Amber and a little heavier. She had been on staff at one of the city's prestigious law firms. McCorkle was average height with a tiny waist and extra wide hips. She was an architectural engineer at one of the city's top firms. They shared no physical traits, as Jess said, except being female.

"The common characteristic that drew Adler may have simply been physical beauty," Jess suggested. "Or personality. Possibly body language. Whatever the commonality, he was drawn to each victim."

Amber wanted to know more about the partner. "How does a team of serial killers work?"

"One is usually dominant," Jess said. "Adler may have been the scout. He observed the target. Perhaps even lured her into a trap. The partner may have been the one to decide when and how she died. He may have been the one to make the kill, or they may have taken that step together."

"He left no evidence?" Amber was aware there were criminals capable of operating without leaving behind even trace evidence, but she didn't want this killer to be one of them.

"None we've found," Harper confirmed. "We'll continue interviewing friends, relatives, associates—anyone who knew Adler."

Amber appreciated their efforts. She moistened her lips and asked the question ramming into her brain. "What do I do until you find him?"

"You take extra precautions," Lori said. "You watch every step you make."

"Sean will be assigned as your personal security for as long as necessary," Jess added.

The churning started in Amber's stomach again. She swallowed back the bitter taste of bile. "How long will it take to find him?" She knew they couldn't answer that question. She, of all people, understood how these things went. She closed her eyes and shook her head. "I'm sorry. That was a ridiculous question." They might never find him. She might never know the name of the man watching her…waiting for the perfect moment to act.

"We'll do all we can as quickly as we can," Harper assured her.

"We've already taken initial precautions," Sean spoke up. "New locks. New security codes."

Amber's attention drifted. How could this man—this killer—have been watching her and she hadn't realized he was so close?

Chairs scraped across the floor and fabric rustled. Amber blinked. The meeting was over. She hadn't even realized the conversation had ended. She stood. The detectives were assuring Teller they would keep in touch with any new developments. Jess was speaking quietly with Sean.

Amber pushed in her chair and picked up her purse. Corlew joined the huddle with Jess and Sean.

"Amber, don't worry." Teller moved up beside her. "Between Jess and the BPD, we'll get through this."

She tried to summon a smile, but her lips wouldn't quite make the transition. "Thank you."

Teller gave her a reassuring pat on the arm, and then he followed the path the detectives had taken. Amber took a breath and lifted her chin. She should call her sister and her parents and let them know this latest news before they heard it some other way. This was good news on one level, she argued with herself.

Sean and the others broke their huddle, all eyes turning toward her.

After more assurances from both Jess and Corlew, it was time to go home.

Sean surveyed the sidewalk and checked the car before allowing her inside. Numb, she settled in the seat. He shut the door, and she flinched. *Deep breath. They will find this guy.*

She should call the station manager and discuss the situation. Was her cameraman in danger working with her? She glanced at the man driving. He was in danger, as well. Her sister. Gina. Maybe it would be best if she took some time off work. Gina was a reasonable person. Hopefully she could convince Barb to stay away from Amber until this killer was found.

Amber stared out at the familiar landscape. The plan seemed like a good one. Reasonable.

So she was going to put her life on hold because some evil, twisted bastard had targeted her?

No way.

"I need to go to the station."

Sean glanced at her. "Did you get called in for an assignment?"

"No. The computers at the office are better for what I need to do."

He made the necessary turn for the new destination. "Would you like to let me in on what we're doing?"

She considered his profile for a moment. Strong jaw and forehead with a nice nose balanced perfectly between gorgeous blue eyes. She wondered how often he'd been asked why he wasn't on the big screen. He had the looks, the charm. He could have gone for an acting or a modeling gig. Amber dismissed the silly notion. Her mind was working overtime to distract her from the worry.

Rather than answer his question, she asked one of her own. "What did Jess and Corlew say to you after the meeting?"

He glanced at her. "Not to let you out of my sight."

"Really? I thought that was already the plan. Isn't that why you're sleeping on my sofa?"

"Guess so." His lips quirked with a need to grin.

He likely wouldn't find the situation so amusing if the shoe were on the other foot. Still, she couldn't deny that seeing his lopsided smiles and grins were almost worth the worry and frustration. Maybe that was an exaggeration. Just another indication that her mind was on overload.

"So, what's on tonight's agenda?" He shot her a look. "I'm not going to let you out of my sight, but you're still the boss."

Amber relaxed the tiniest bit and told him what he wanted to know. "We're going to find out all we can about those two women Adler and his partner killed.

Those women and I shared some common trait or connection that drew Adler and his partner. We have to figure out what it was."

"We should get food," he suggested. "I work better on a full tank."

She hadn't even thought of food. She wasn't sure her stomach could handle food. Two women were dead, but Amber had survived whatever the bastards had planned for her. The least she could do was help find the other person responsible for their deaths.

Going into hiding wouldn't be fair. Rhiana Pettie and Kimberly McCorkle and their families deserved justice.

Amber had an obligation to help them find it.

Chapter Eight

Thornberry Drive, 9:05 p.m.

"You're sure you want to show up at someone's door at this hour and announce you might know who killed their daughter?"

The idea sounded much better when she said it. "I have to do something."

Was she being selfish? The McCorkles had waited four months to hear who had taken the life of their daughter; the Petties even longer. Still, Sean had a point. She couldn't just show up at their door and announce that she knew the murderer. Not to mention the detectives on the case would not be happy with her, and the last thing she needed to do was to annoy or enrage the BPD. Odds were, the lead detective in the case, Chet Harper, had already spoken to the families.

Still, Amber had to do this.

"I'll be subtler than that," she assured him.

Sean grunted in that way only males could, the sound a warning that he had his doubts. *Fine.* She didn't need his approval.

She hadn't been able to reach anyone at the Pettie home. Mrs. McCorkle had insisted she was happy to meet tonight. If Amber had a daughter who had been murdered, she wouldn't care what time of the day or night news came; she would want to hear it as soon as possible.

Sean parked at the street in front of the ranch-style home. "Just remember, Harper's going above and beyond to solve this case. Don't do anything to make them regret the extra effort to keep you in the loop."

"Is that what your boss warned you about after the briefing?"

He shifted his attention straight ahead, and Amber knew she'd hit the nail on the head.

"Something like that," he admitted.

"I would never do anything to jeopardize my relationship with the BPD or with Jess Burnett." As a journalist, she understood the value of the relationships she'd built. As her mentor, Gina had kept that golden rule in front of Amber. She was no rank amateur.

Sean flashed her one of those killer smiles as he opened his door. "Well, all righty then."

As usual he was at her door before she was out of the car. He surveyed the street and the homes on either side of the McCorkle home before ushering her up the sidewalk to the porch. Amber rang the bell and found herself holding her breath.

The door opened, and an older woman, fifty or so perhaps, with dark hair looked from Amber to Sean and back.

"Mrs. McCorkle?" Amber asked.

"You're Amber Roberts," the woman said. "I recognize you from TV."

"This is my friend Sean Douglas." Amber indicated the man beside her.

Mrs. McCorkle gave a nod. "Come in."

When the door opened wider, Amber stepped inside. Sean stayed close behind her. Maybe a little too close. The heat from his body made her tremble. *You really have lost it, Amber.*

"You're certain we're not disturbing you, Mrs. Mc-Corkle?" The guilt was making an appearance. Damn Sean for making her second-guess this move. If she weren't so vulnerable right now, he would never have been able to accomplish that feat. Investigative report-ers ferreted out information on cases all the time. It was part of the job. More often than not the police weren't particularly pleased, but it generally worked out to ev-eryone's benefit.

The lady shook her head adamantly. "I want to do all I can to help find the monster who took my baby."

Amber understood. She glanced around the neat liv-ing room. Framed photos of Kimberly were everywhere. "Is Mr. McCorkle home?"

The older woman looked away. "He's gone to bed." She wrung her hands. "It's hard on him. Truth is, he drinks enough beer every night after work to render him unconscious by the time he goes to bed."

"We all have our own way of dealing with loss," Sean spoke up. "As long as it doesn't hurt anyone else."

Amber wondered what he had done to deal with the loss of his lover when Lacy James died. Had he struggled to sleep at night? Tried to drown his sorrows? Why was it she suddenly wanted to know all there was to know about him? Yes, he was the man tasked with her safety, but she suspected there was more to it than that.

Mrs. McCorkle nodded her agreement with Sean's un-derstanding words. "I tell myself that every night." She sighed. "Sometimes I feel like we're muddling through some alternate reality. How can this be our lives?" She waved off the words. "Please, make yourselves at home. Would you like coffee or hot tea?"

"No, thank you," Amber said as she perched on the edge of the sofa. "Was Kimberly a hot tea drinker?"

The lady shook her head. "That would be me. Kim loved her coffee in the morning, iced tea for lunch and dinner was a cold beer. She allowed herself one or two each night, the same as her father. He always warned that overindulgence was a bad thing. But that was before…"

"I love the flavored teas," Amber said, keeping her tone light. "Paradise Peach."

"I guess I'm a purist. Earl Grey for me."

"Green tea chai for me," Sean tossed in. "Only I cheat—I buy the instant stuff."

The man drank hot tea? When he shot her another of those amused looks, Amber closed her gaping mouth. She would need to be careful around him. He kept her off balance, and he knew it.

Time to get to the point of this meeting. "Mrs. Mc-Corkle, I believe the man or men who hurt your daughter may have been targeting me, as well."

The woman's eyes widened. "Has someone else gone missing?" Her hand went to her chest. "Mercy, I've prayed nonstop that he would be caught. I don't understand why the police can't find whoever did this. They were here this evening asking more questions, but they weren't giving me any answers."

"I'm certain they're doing all they can," Amber assured her. "I'm wondering if your daughter and I had any hobbies, shopping habits or interests in common.

May we talk for a few minutes about the things she liked to do?"

Mrs. McCorkle's eyes brightened, but the perpetual sadness created by the loss of her daughter lined her face. "She always loved building things as a child. It was no surprise when she decided to become an architect. She took great pride in her work."

"What about her hobbies?" Amber reached into her purse for a notepad.

"She loved playing basketball," Mrs. McCorkle said, her eyes growing distant. "She played in high school, you know. No matter that she was a foot or more shorter than the rest of the team—she was a force to be reckoned with when she got her hands on the ball."

"Was she dating anyone in particular?" Amber asked.

Mrs. McCorkle shook her head. "She had a lot of friends and dates, but she didn't date anyone regularly. Kimberly said she was in no hurry to get serious. She was busy building her career."

Amber's instincts started to hum. "I can relate."

"Kimberly had big plans. She wanted to have her own firm one day. She was going to take care of me and her dad. She promised we'd never have to worry about anything." Mrs. McCorkle's lips trembled. "She sure saw to that. She carried a million-dollar life insurance policy. We had no idea until we saw the paperwork among her personal papers."

"Do you mind sharing the name of her insurance company?" Amber, too, carried a significant policy. The day before she'd started her job her father had insisted on a "business" talk. He'd urged her to be smart with her money from the beginning. Setting up a savings plan was at the top of his list. Insurance and investments were next. Six years later Amber was grateful for that talk.

Mrs. McCorkle told her the name of the company, but it wasn't the one Amber used. After half an hour, Amber learned that she and Kimberly had very little in common beyond their single-mindedness regarding their careers. As significant as that similarity was, their careers were so different Amber wasn't sure how that had drawn a killer's attention. The firm where Kimberly was employed was nowhere near Channel Six. Maybe they shared the same maintenance crew, or maybe Adler had made deliveries to both offices or to their homes. The architectural firm hadn't been on the list, but maybe that was only because he'd delivered there fewer times.

By ten thirty Amber realized the woman would have gladly stayed up all night talking about her daughter. She passed Mrs. McCorkle a business card. "This is my cell number. Call me anytime, day or night, if you think of anything you believe would be helpful."

Mrs. McCorkle saw them to the door. "I hope they catch him soon."

Amber squeezed her arm. "I'm certain they will."

When goodbyes were exchanged and the door closed behind them, Amber felt exhausted. The meeting had been far more emotional than she'd expected. She had conducted plenty of interviews with families who had lost loved ones, but somehow this time had been more difficult. Certainly it was more personal. Those people could have been her parents…

Sean abruptly moved in front of her. She bumped into his back. His hand went under his jacket where she'd seen the weapon stationed at his hip. She peeked around one broad shoulder and spotted the trouble. A man stepped out of the shadows.

Gerard Stevens.

Irritation seared through Amber. "What do you want?" She stepped around Sean, but he stopped her with one strong hand before she could move toward Stevens.

"So the rumors that Adler is connected to the McCorkle and Pettie murders are true," Stevens stated with a satisfied smile.

"You know this guy?" Sean asked, his fingers still biting into her arm.

"She knows me," Stevens mouthed off. "She knows me *very* well."

"Adler was stalking me," Amber said, anger building faster than she would have liked. "I'm considering an exposé on women who're murdered by obsessed men. You better watch out or you'll end up in the story."

"I'll nudge my contacts at the BPD and confirm for myself."

Sean was urging her toward the car.

"You do that," Amber tossed at the jerk before Sean ushered her into the car. Stevens had made far too many enemies at the BPD to have any reliable contacts left. He was bluffing. How the hell had she ever been attracted to the arrogant bastard?

Sean echoed the question as he drove away from the McCorkle neighborhood. "You dated that guy?"

"Once or twice." More like six times. She closed her eyes and shuddered at the memory of the time they'd spent together. The moment Gina had found out, she'd told Amber that Stevens liked to bed all the new female competition, and then he bragged to his male peers.

Gerard Stevens had been her one big career mistake. Cutting herself a little slack, she had been young and eager to make all the right contacts in the business. At the time Stevens had seemed like a great contact. *Live and learn.*

"I guess pretty boys like him attract lots of women."

Amber considered the remark as they drove through the night. For such a handsome guy, Sean almost sounded envious. She wouldn't tell him, but he was far better-looking and more charismatic than Stevens would ever be.

"Trust me—his ego is sickening. What you see is definitely not what you get. As a date he's a massive letdown."

"Ouch," he teased. "Remind me never to let you down."

During the fifteen or so minutes it took to drive to her house, Amber weighed the few facts she knew. If Pettie had been a career-oriented woman, that could very well be the attraction the three of them shared. Still, the killer had to have come into contact with each of them somewhere. What places or people did they have in common? Mrs. McCorkle hadn't been able to provide much in the way of places her daughter frequented. She had promised to talk to some of Kimberly's friends and get back with Amber.

Now if she could just get an appointment with the Petties tomorrow.

Sean checked the street before allowing Amber out of the car. He ordered her to wait in the living room while he checked the rest of the house no matter that the security system had been armed. Honestly, she didn't see how celebrities lived like this. She would lose her mind.

"Clear," he announced as he returned to the living room.

"Great." She needed to think. A cup of tea and some quiet time would hopefully go a long way in making her feel a little more in control of her life. "I'm having tea. You want anything?"

"I'm good." He peeled off his jacket and tossed it over the arm of the sofa.

Yes, she mused, he was very good.

"I have wine," she offered as she lit the flame under the teakettle.

"No drinking while on duty." He reached up and plowed his fingers through his hair. "I'll just take a quick shower while you have your tea."

She shifted her attention to preparing her tea and tried her very best to block the images of him naked beneath the hot spray of water. She was tired and confused and plenty worried. There was no other explanation for her sudden inability to think straight.

While the water boiled she went to her closet and put her shoes away. She stripped off her clothes and pulled on a pair of pajama pants and a tee. It felt good to simply relax. She washed her face and dabbed on her nightly moisturizer. Her mother had taught Amber from an early age how important the nightly rituals were. Her father had been the one to insist she set and maintain a workout routine. Her parents were health nuts, and she was glad. So many of her friends struggled with finding the time to take care of themselves in their busy lives. The routines her parents had instilled had become part of her day, so she didn't have to make time.

The whistle of the kettle drew her back to the kitchen. She gave herself a pat on the back for only hesitating a mere second or two in front of the hall bath door. The sound of spraying water had ceased. She could imagine Sean in there toweling off that muscular body. She sighed. Maybe she just needed the relief of thinking about anything else besides her current fears. Or maybe it had been too long since she'd bothered with a personal life. So many of her colleagues had the same problem. There just wasn't enough time to establish an upwardly mobile career and to have a life, as well. A few, like her, had abandoned the idea of marriage and children for the foreseeable future. Most, however, went the other way. She had no idea how people like Jess Burnett and Lori Wells juggled such demanding careers while raising children. Maybe it was time she asked.

While her tea steeped, she prowled through the cupboards until she found a package of her favorite cheese straws. With her teacup and snack ready, she settled on the sofa with her notes. Sean wandered into the room, but she kept her attention on the notes. From the corner of her eye, she noticed he'd donned the same trousers and his shirt was only partly buttoned. She refused to look directly at him. She certainly didn't need to see any part of that body uncovered.

She sipped her tea and nibbled on the cheese straws. A short list of potential places where she and McCorkle may have run into each other was easy enough to make. A few boutique shops that catered to the professional woman. The dry cleaner. The municipal building. As an architect, McCorkle would likely be in and out checking property lines and zoning ordinances. Amber followed court cases. She spent a good deal of time at or around the city offices. Town hall meetings.

The same possibilities were true of Pettie, as well.

Since she had worked for a law firm, they may have been involved with the same case at some point. Amber didn't recognize either woman beyond the reports she'd seen about their abductions and the subsequent discovery of their bodies. But then, she was usually so focused on her assignment she often had tunnel vision.

If she could get her hands on Adler's credit card records, nailing down shops and restaurants he frequented would help tremendously. Corlew was working on the phone records. Maybe he could get the man's credit card records, too.

Amber blinked. Her cup found its way to the saucer hard enough that it was a miracle it didn't crack the fine china. Her mouth felt numb. She set her notes aside and tried to stand. Her legs were rubbery. Saliva leaked from her mouth. She wiped it away. *What the hell?*

"You okay?"

Sean stood beside her. She hadn't even realized he'd moved.

"I don't know. I feel…" She tapped her lips and tried to swallow all the excess saliva. She swayed, her shoulder bumping into his.

"We're going to the ER."

She stared at him. His words were not really making sense to her. "What?"

"Are you drinking the tea from the can on the counter?"

She nodded, or she thought she did.

He sat her down in the nearest chair and disappeared. Her stomach roiled violently. "You'd better get a bag or a bucket." God, her mouth felt so damned weird. Numb and yet burning.

Sean's arms were suddenly around her, supporting her. "Let's go."

Before she could respond or catch her breath, she was in his car. How had they gotten there so fast?

He handed her a plastic trash bag, and then the car started to move.

Amber closed her eyes and fought the urge to vomit.

"Don't hold back." His words floated through the darkness. "Try to get it up."

As if his suggestion somehow triggered a response in her belly, she hurled.

"Good girl," he praised.

Funny. It didn't feel good at all.

Chapter Nine

University of Alabama–Birmingham Hospital
Wednesday, October 19, 3:15 a.m.

Sean's teeth felt ready to crack he'd clenched so long and hard. He'd only relaxed when Amber had stopped vomiting and started to get comfortable. Her mouth wasn't numb or burning anymore, and she could stand, walk and communicate normally.

"We believe whatever toxin you ingested has broken down in the digestive tract," Dr. Chaconas explained. We've taken the necessary detox precautions and given you lots of fluids. Your vitals are good. I think we're out of the woods."

"So I can go home now?" Amber asked, her voice still a little weak.

Chaconas glanced at her chart. "I don't see any reason to keep you." He made a few notes on the chart. "Come back here immediately if you experience any more symptoms, and stay hydrated. Check in with your personal physician as soon as possible."

"Thank you." Amber accepted the discharge papers.

As soon as the doctor was out the door, Harper came back in. "Looks like you're going home."

"Thank God," Amber said.

"I know you've been through a lot," Harper began, "but we're gonna need to go through your house again— top to bottom this time." He glanced at Sean. "I believe it's best if you stay somewhere else until we determine if there're any other toxins in your home. We wouldn't need more than a day or two and we should know within the next forty-eight hours what was in your tea. Is that doable?"

"My parents are out of town. I could…" Amber began. She frowned as if attempting to decide what to say next.

"She'll be staying with me."

Sean was as startled by the announcement as Amber appeared to be. Harper looked from one to the other and gave a nod. "I think that's a good idea," he agreed.

Amber drew in a big breath. "Whatever it takes."

"Good. We'll be in touch with updates."

When Harper was gone Sean offered Amber a hand as she hopped off the exam table. She swayed a bit; he steadied her.

"I, ah…" She moistened her lips. "I should probably call my sister."

Sean guided her into the corridor and toward the doors that would take them back to the lobby. "I believe I mentioned that when we first arrived."

"You're going to say I told you so? After what I just went through?"

He opened the passenger-side door. When she was settled in the seat, he passed her his cell. "You make the call—I'll get you someplace safe."

Sean rounded the hood and slid behind the wheel. He told himself he was doing the right thing. She couldn't go back home. She was his responsibility. It was his job to keep her safe. B&C Investigations didn't have a safe house as of yet. There was no need to wake up Jess or Buddy at this hour. He'd made the right decision.

Amber spoke quietly to her sister. Her sister wasn't so calm. Sean could hear the concern in her voice as she demanded answers. Amber responded steadily. He had to hand it to the lady, she was a trouper. She'd puked her guts out and was weak as a kitten, but she'd hung in there. While she had been undergoing the barrage of tests, he'd called Harper and notified him of the turn of events.

He was confident in his decision to take her home with him. Then why the hell was his gut in knots? Maybe because the last client he'd taken home with him had ended up dead.

His palms started to sweat. His heart raced. Now that they were driving away from the safety of the hospital, Amber was calmer than he was and she was the one who'd been poisoned.

Sean tightened his grip on the steering wheel. *You've got this, man. Shake it off.*

"Well." Amber passed his cell back to him. "That went over like a lead balloon."

"Yeah, big sisters like to be called during the crisis, not after." Another one of those life lessons he'd learned the hard way.

Sean braked for the traffic signal. The street lamp chased away the darkness between them. Despite the unpleasantness of the past few hours, a faint smile tilted her lips. "I see. You have an older sister?"

"Five years older and fifty times smarter." He laughed. "In her opinion, of course."

"Which is the only opinion that counts."

A smile tugged at his lips, and he relaxed a fraction. "Definitely."

The city was quiet at this hour. Back in high school he'd liked this time of the morning better than any other time of the day. The night was over, but it wasn't quite daylight...a fresh start. Anything was possible.

He had clung to that motto all the way up to the morning—about this time—when he'd made the biggest mistake of his life.

Sean checked his mirrors once more to ensure he wasn't being tailed, then he hit the remote to raise the overhead door of his garage. Once they were inside, he shut off the engine and closed the door. He hopped out and unlocked the door that led into the kitchen.

Amber closed her door and leaned against the car. "I hope you have something I can borrow to sleep in." She pulled at her tee. "This is a little gross."

"I'm pretty sure I can come up with something."

Sean flipped on the lights as he entered the house ahead of her. He didn't have a security system like the one she had, but he had something even better.

Rebel sat in the middle of the kitchen, staring expectantly at his master. The tan-and-white boxer turned his attention to Amber. Amber stalled.

Sean patted his leg. "Come on over here, boy. He's the friendliest dog you'll ever meet."

"He's big."

"He's a teddy bear. Take a break, buddy." Sean pointed to the back door. Rebel bounded to it and scooted out the doggy door. "Follow me," he said to Amber, "and I'll get you settled."

"Why didn't he bark when he heard us coming?"

"He knows the sound of my car." He paused at the

door to the spare bedroom. "Trust me—if anyone besides me had come into this house, Rebel would have taken him down."

"Who takes care of him when you're not here?" She surveyed the room as she asked the question.

His home was a classic bungalow, not nearly as large as hers, but with a decent-size yard for Rebel. It was on a quiet street in a nice neighborhood. "My sister. She helps with rescued dogs. That's how I got Rebel. No one else wanted him since he's kind of big and he's a little past his prime."

"So you took him." Amber smiled, the genuine article despite how lousy she no doubt still felt. "I would never have guessed you have such a soft side."

"Do me a favor, don't tell anyone. It would wreck my image."

She held up a hand. "Your secret is safe with me. Besides, I'm expecting you to keep any and all descriptions of my projectile vomiting to yourself."

"No one will ever know," he promised.

"I could use a shower, the sooner the better, and something to sleep in." She tugged at her tee again and made a face.

"And bottled water," he reminded her.

She pressed a hand to her stomach. "Right."

Sean rounded up a couple of bottles of water, a toothbrush and a Crimson Tide T-shirt. Amber was already in the hall bath, frowning at her reflection.

"I look like hell."

He placed the water and toothbrush on the counter and passed her the tee. "You look damned good considering. If you need anything else, just let me know. I'm at the end of the hall."

She touched his arm, stopping him. Even through the fabric of his shirt the contact sparked the desire already simmering in his veins.

"Thanks, Sean. I'm really glad you were there to take care of me."

He nodded and headed for his room. He needed a shower, too. A long, cold one.

8:15 a.m.

AMBER STARED AT the broth Sean had prepared for her. "I'm sorry. I just don't think I can do this." She had no appetite. She felt like hell. Her stomach still felt queasy and crampy.

"Just following the instructions on the discharge papers." Sean sipped his coffee.

Amber groaned. He was right. She needed to follow the doctor's orders. Slowly, she lifted the spoon to her lips and tasted. Her stomach clenched, but she kept going. One spoonful after the other, until she emptied the bowl. She washed it down with plenty of water. When she was finished, she pushed the bowl away and summoned a smile. "I feel better already."

Sean gave that one-sided grin that somehow made him even more handsome. "Liar."

She laughed. "Yeah. I feel…" She groaned. "Quite blah and very grateful for your quick thinking."

He gave a nod. "It's nice to be the hero from time to time."

Amber studied him a long moment. He really was a nice guy and completely committed to the job. She didn't see him as the type to fail a client. There had to be more to the story. "You know pretty much everything about me. I'd like to know more about you."

His relaxed expression hardened the slightest bit. "You know all the important stuff."

"Wives? Kids? Significant others?"

"Nope, nope and nope."

"You've never been married or engaged?"

He shook his head.

"Long-term relationships?" She reminded herself to sip her water.

"A couple. Nothing particularly memorable." He stared into his coffee.

"What really happened in LA?" She snapped her lips together. She actually hadn't been planning to blurt out the question.

He studied her for a long moment before he answered. "I made a mistake."

"Yeah, that's what you said before, but I think there's a lot more to it than just a mistake." She smoothed a hand over her ponytail. She'd been too exhausted to dry her hair after her shower. Her only option when she'd gotten up was to restrain the wild mass of curls. "I just feel like I deserve full disclosure from the man who's seen me at my absolute worst."

His lips quirked with the need to smile in spite of that stony profile. "I guess you have a point there."

Anticipation zinged through her. "So, let's hear it."

"Lacy James was smart and talented. And beautiful," he said, awe in his voice. "No matter that I worked extra hard to stay focused on the job, I was mesmerized by her. She had this ethereal beauty and incredible depth of soul that no one ever saw onstage."

"She was incredibly talented and beautiful," Amber

agreed, feeling strangely jealous of the way he described her. For the first time in ages she longed to know a man saw her that way.

"I'd been in LA for six long years. I was lonely. I'd dated plenty between assignments but nothing serious. I was almost twenty-nine and maybe I was feeling the need for something real."

Amber's stomach took a little dive, and she was reasonably sure it wasn't about the poison. She'd been feeling exactly that way—as if something was missing in her life. No matter that her career had taken off; something was still lacking. She needed more than work. More than coming home to an empty house and an equally empty bed. But how did she trust anyone with her heart? The world was so full of people who cared only for themselves. In her profession she saw so much *fake*—it felt impossible to sort the real from the make-believe. Oddly, this moment—this man—felt real.

"The next thing I knew we were…together." He fell silent for a moment. "She had a short break before the next leg of her tour started, and we never left the house. It felt exactly like what was missing in my life. It felt real and good, and I wanted it to last forever."

Amber watched the pain clutter his handsome face. The memories still hurt even though a year had passed. Was he still in love with her memory?

"When I was briefed on the assignment, her agent warned me not to trust her. She was never allowed to overindulge in alcohol, and if I spotted drugs, I was to get her out ASAP." His gaze met Amber's, and the agony there tugged at her heart. "Lacy was an addict. Had been since she was thirteen. When we met she'd been straight for two years."

"No one is responsible for what an addict chooses to do," Amber reminded him softly.

He nodded. "I know. But that doesn't change the responsibility I feel. I was with her 24/7 for weeks. I took my eyes off her for one minute at a party while she went to the bathroom and she scored. That night after I went to sleep, she overdosed on cocaine. She was sitting right there in the room watching me. I didn't even know she'd gotten out of bed." He stood and gathered her bowl and spoon. "That's what happens when you get too comfortable. Your sense of caution becomes dulled. You miss things. Lacy's dead because I didn't see how getting personally involved with me made her feel out of control. Made her wish for things she couldn't have if she wanted to keep her career on track."

"Are we all doomed to that choice?" Amber bit her lips together. She hadn't meant to say those words out loud. What was it about this man that made her feel the need to be so forthcoming? "I mean, can't a woman or a man have an astonishingly successful career and a personal life? Why do we have to choose only one?"

"There's a career," Sean said, his tone somber, "and there's a *career*. When you choose the latter, there's nothing else. It's all-encompassing. After the funeral, the one trusted friend she had told me I reminded Lacy how much she regretted the choices she'd made. She'd given up everything—her first love, the child they'd had together—to follow her dream. Falling in love again sent her hurtling back into the pain and loss."

Amber stood and pushed in her chair. "It isn't fair that she had to give up one or the other. Why couldn't she have had both?" Her heart was pounding. What she was really asking was why couldn't she have both?

What made women like her—like her sister and Gina and even Jess Burnett—believe they had to give up a real life for their careers? Though the dilemma rarely affected men the same way, Sean seemed to be stuck in that same place.

"It took me nearly a year of soul-searching and no small amount of counseling to come to terms with the answer to that question, Amber. Are you sure you want to hear it?"

She blinked, taken aback. "Why wouldn't I?"

"Lacy couldn't have both because she was an addict. Staying completely focused on her career helped her keep it together—helped her stay clean. I disrupted the rhythm she'd come to depend on. I should have recognized the issue, but I was too infatuated, too caught up in my own needs. I failed to do my job, and for that I'm in part responsible for her death."

"Are you suggesting I'm addicted to my work? That I don't care about anything else?"

Sean exhaled a big breath. "I'm suggesting if you can't see yourself living a personal life in addition to your career, then you won't be able to have both. You'll have to choose one or the other, and there will always be regrets with whichever choice you make. Isn't that the true definition of addiction? Being willing to sacrifice everything else for the one thing you want most?"

The doorbell rang, and Amber jerked at the sound. "Barbara said she'd bring me some of her clothes."

"I'll get the door."

Amber took a deep breath and let it out slowly. Why in the world had they been discussing her love life and career decisions? It was her own fault. She'd started it. The conversation was meant to learn more about him and what happened in LA. It was never intended to dissect her life.

Could he possibly be right about her? Was she incapable of balance? She couldn't deny being singularly focused. She'd recognized her type A personality at the ripe old age of twelve. She'd decided then that she wanted to be the next Barbara Walters.

Barb's voice in the other room drew her from her thoughts. This wasn't the time to worry about her love life. Two women were dead—possibly murdered by the same man who had poisoned her. Finding Adler's partner and presumably his murderer had to be top priority right now. Just because Sean Douglas made her heart pound and her pulse skip was no excuse to revert to being controlled by adolescent hormones.

Amber squared her shoulders and joined her sister and Sean in the living room. Barb took one look at her and rushed to where she stood. She grabbed Amber in a bear hug. "Don't you ever do that again!"

Amber tried to breathe. Sean stood on the other side of the room, his arms loaded with clothes, shoes and a small bag hanging from his long fingers.

"Really, I'm okay," Amber assured her.

Barb drew back and surveyed her from head to toe and back. "You look like hell. You definitely need all that makeup Gina shoved into the bag the cutie-pie over there is holding."

Sean looked at the floor in an attempt to hide his grin.

"Thanks." Amber knew she was okay when her big sister told her she needed makeup. Barbara Roberts hated makeup. How she ever fell in love with a television journalist like Gina was a mystery to Amber. "The cutie-pie," she said, using Barb's term, "is Sean Douglas."

"A pleasure." Barb gave him an approving nod and grabbed the bag he held. "Come on, little sister." She reached for one of the outfits he held, as well. "We have work to do. You'll have to excuse us, Mr. Douglas."

"Take your time," he suggested. "I'll follow up with Lieutenant Harper."

Amber flashed him a smile as her sister ushered her from the room. What was it about a near-death experience that made a woman suddenly bemoan all she'd given up for a career?

How did she capture that elusive thing called balance?

As soon as the person trying to kill her was caught, she intended to find her balance.

She glanced over her shoulder one last time. Maybe she would start with Sean.

Chapter Ten

Frontier Drive, Vestavia Hills, 11:00 a.m.

Rhiana Pettie's mother had agreed to a meeting.

Amber looked considerably better even if she still felt weak and weary. Barb had helped her pull herself together. Her head was still just a little foggy, but an extrasweet café mocha had helped immensely.

Sean parked at the curb and checked his cell. "Harper sent me a text. So far your place is coming up clean for toxins, but he'd feel better if you gave them another day just to be sure."

"I can live with that." She searched his eyes. "Can you?" After all, he was the one sharing his place.

"My job is to keep you safe, Amber. I can do that just about anywhere."

"I guess it's settled then. I'll be at your place again tonight."

His blue eyes darkened. "Technically it'll be your first night at my place. It was already morning when I took you there today."

"I used your shower and spent time sleeping in your guest bed."

He nodded. "You did."

"I rest my case." Amber reached for the door. As usual, he somehow managed to appear at her side of the car before she emerged.

Forty-eight hours ago she'd found his persistent presence frustrating, annoying even. Now she was very grateful he was here. The reality that someone had come into her house and touched her things was bad enough. To recognize that he'd meant her physical harm made it all the worse. It was one thing to have an obsessive fan, even a stalker; it was entirely another to be targeted for death.

Amber turned her attention to the brick home nestled on the corner of Frontier and Kingswood. According to her research, the Petties had lived here for thirty-five years. Rachel and Tom, Rhiana's parents, had three grown children, but she had been their only daughter. People always pointed out statistics like those. If they'd had another daughter, would Rhiana's death have been easier? Of course not.

The door opened, and Mrs. Pettie stared at them as if she'd forgotten they were coming.

"Mrs. Pettie, I'm Amber Roberts. We spoke about an hour ago. You said my associate Sean Douglas and I could come by to speak with you about Rhiana."

She nodded and opened the door wider. "You look different than you do on television."

Amber relaxed a little as she crossed the threshold. "Most people say I look much taller on TV."

Pettie managed a faint smile. "I think they're right. You do look taller on-screen."

Rhiana's mother went through the usual steps, offering refreshments, which they both declined, and steering them toward the sofa. Pettie was tall like Rhiana. Her blond hair was more gray now than blond, but the resemblance to her daughter was unmistakable. Amber had inherited her red hair and green eyes from her mother. Barb, on the other hand, had inherited their father's rich brown hair and dark eyes. People who didn't know them rarely believed they were sisters.

"The police told me they may have found the man who took her from us."

Amber nodded. "Yes. I hope the BPD can confirm those suspicions soon. I'm certain they'll contact you again as soon as they do."

Pettie's brow furrowed into a frown. "Are you reporting on the investigation?"

Amber glanced at Sean. This was where things got a little muddled and a whole lot sticky.

"Mrs. Pettie," Sean answered for her, "the police have reason to believe Amber was the next victim on the killer's list. As you can imagine, she's anxious to help solve the case."

"Is that why they thought you killed him?"

Amber hoped that debacle wasn't going to follow her forever. "I was and still am a person of interest in the case, but the police have cleared me of any suspicion related to his murder." It felt really good to be able to say those words.

"Can you tell us about the last few days before your daughter went missing?" Sean asked. "Had she met anyone new? Was she working on a new case at the firm?"

Amber flinched. He'd gone straight to the point rather than easing into the hard questions.

"The police already asked questions about those days," Pettie said, her gaze drifting to the floor. "After she first went missing and then again yesterday."

"Sometimes it helps to have new eyes and ears on a case. That's why we're here," he explained gently.

Pettie cleared her throat. "Rhiana was a hard worker," she said softly. "She put in a lot of long hours. I cleaned her apartment for her every couple of weeks." She smiled. "I didn't mind. Anytime she was home in the evenings she had dinner with her father and me. I think that's what I miss most…doing things for her. I loved hearing about her day. She would share the details she could, and it was always so exciting."

The loss she felt thickened in the room. It was moments like this when Amber wondered how on earth anyone could bear to have a child. How did a parent survive losing a child? *Keep your attention on the goal—finding this bastard.*

Amber braced for a no. "Can we see her apartment?"

Pettie hesitated, but then she stood. "I've left it just as it was. 'Course, the police went through her room twice, but otherwise it's exactly the way she left it."

"We'll be very careful," Sean promised.

"Follow me," Pettie offered.

There was something immensely comforting about Sean's hand at the small of her back as Amber followed Pettie up the exterior stairs that led to the apartment over the garage. She unlocked the door and stood back for them to enter first.

Rhiana had a large space that included a small bathroom and kitchenette. It was roomier than Amber's first apartment out of college. She'd refused the offer to move back in with her parents. The tiny apartment had been her only option.

The pajamas Rhiana had slept in the night before she disappeared were on the unmade bed. The bowl and coffee mug she'd used that morning were in the sink. A large bouquet of dead flowers sat on the coffee table in front of the small sofa. Amber leaned down for a closer inspection. Roses…red ones, she suspected, though they had turned black, many of the petals falling to the table.

"She was excited about the flowers," Pettie said. "She thought the junior partner she'd been smitten with for a year had finally noticed her." Her face fell. "When he was questioned, he told the police he didn't send them."

"Were they delivered here or at her office?" Sean asked.

"Her office. She brought them home with her the same day she received them. She was so excited," Pettie repeated.

Amber's heart ached for her. "Was there a card?" She searched the area around the bouquet.

The older lady wrung her hands in front of her. "There was, but as far as I know the police never found it."

Rhiana had gone missing Valentine's Day, eight months ago. The chances of finding the card now were slim to none. Amber straightened. "Did someone from the firm send home the personal items from Rhiana's office?"

Amber felt certain they would have cleared out the office reasonably soon after the body was found. The law firm where Rhiana had worked was a busy one; up-and-coming attorneys and paralegals were essential to the fast-paced operation of the firm. Office space was no doubt a premium.

"One of her colleagues packed everything in boxes, and Rhiana's father brought them home." She sighed. "At the time I wasn't up to facing people. I think he put the boxes in the garage. That's usually where he puts everything." She glanced around the room. "I meant to bring them up here, but I… I never got around to it. We can go down and look for them if you'd like."

Amber and Sean followed Pettie down to the garage. Sean pulled the two boxes from the top shelf where Mr. Pettie had stored them.

"May we have a look inside?" Sean asked.

Pettie nodded. "Are you looking for the card that came with the flowers? I think the police went through her office and didn't find it."

"We know new details now," Amber offered. "Perhaps something else we find will mean more than it would have all those months ago."

Sean opened first one box, and then the other. Rather than being sealed with tape, each had been closed by folding the flaps one over the other. Careful with the items that had likely decorated Rhiana's office, Amber emptied the first box. Sean glanced at her, and she shook her head. Nothing potentially useful to the case.

Amber's hopes plummeted as the second box provided nothing relevant to the case, either. The last item in the box was a stack of business cards bound together with a rubber band. She might as well verify that the card wasn't among them. As she reached the final three, her fingers stilled. Holding one of the cards by the edges, she turned it for Sean to see. *Thrasher Floral*.

It wasn't the warning Amber had received, but it showed a connection to the same floral shop. The police couldn't have recognized the connection when Rhiana went missing.

"Mrs. Pettie, do you have a plastic bag we could put this in?" Sean asked before Amber had the presence of mind to do so.

The lady nodded and hurried into the house.

"We need to see Kimberly McCorkle's home." Anticipation seared through Amber's veins. They were on to something here. "If we can find even the smallest connection to the floral shop, we'll have something to take to Lieutenant Harper."

"We should call him first," Sean countered. "This is evidence."

Sean was a former cop. Amber understood his desire to be a team player—particularly since the cops involved were his friends. Unfortunately there wasn't time. A murderer—possibly a serial killer—was out there, and it was more than probable that he still intended to make Amber his next victim. Not to mention there were two families who desperately needed answers sooner rather than later.

Amber made up her mind. "We can call him after we see Kimberly's house."

Sean would have argued, but Mrs. Pettie returned with a sandwich baggie.

The memory of their rush to the emergency room when Amber had been poisoned surged to the front of her mind. She had to see this through. Now.

Beckham Drive, 12:45 p.m.

SEAN WAS SURPRISED when McCorkle agreed to meet them at her daughter's home without asking the first question. He parked in front of the small house near the popular Five Points district. The cottage had been a present to Kimberly from her parents when she graduated from college. Like Rhiana Pettie's apartment, the house had been closed and left just as it was the day their daughter walked out the last time—except for the official BPD investigation.

He didn't like doing this. Despite his misgivings, he climbed out and went around to the passenger side as Amber emerged. "You know Lieutenant Harper will be ticked off," he reminded her for the third time. He had no desire to step on the toes of the BPD's finest. Jess would not be happy, either. But Amber was the client. Wasn't it his job to keep the client safe *and* happy? *Damn.*

"We will call him as soon as we're done here," Amber repeated the same response she'd given him last time he'd raised the issue.

He exhaled a big breath and followed her up the walk to the front door. McCorkle was waiting just inside. She opened the door wider as they approached.

"I was surprised when you called me again so soon." The older lady looked hopefully at Amber. "Does this mean new evidence has been found?"

Amber smiled. Sean should have looked away, but he didn't. Her smile was part of what had landed her in the television business, in his opinion. When she smiled, everything else faded into insignificance. She was genuinely beautiful.

No going there, pal. He'd spent plenty of time admiring her physical attributes before they even met. If he was completely honest with himself, he'd gone way past the admiration stage. He had to put the brakes on for now. Maybe when this assignment was finished…

Had he just made a plan to pursue something beyond work?

"We're hoping to find a connection no one knew about before," Amber explained as she glanced around the cramped living room.

Her words dragged Sean back to the here and now.

Like Rhiana Pettie's house, there was no security system, Sean noted. A small sofa and cocktail table were overpowered by a massive drawing desk and light. One wall was covered with bookshelves, but rather than filled with books, the shelves were stacked with rolls of architectural drawings. The shelves were labeled alphabetically.

No flowers in the living room.

"May we see the rest of the house?" Amber asked, her anticipation showing.

"Oh, sure." McCorkle gestured to the far side of the room. "The hall leads to the two bedrooms and a bathroom. The kitchen is that way." She indicated the doorway to the right. "The police moved things around a bit, but otherwise it's all just like she left it that last morning before she went to work."

A narrow pair of swinging doors separated the living room from the tiny kitchen. In the sink sat the vase of flowers. Adrenaline fired across Sean's nerve endings. It was way past time to call the cops.

Amber leaned close and visually examined what was obviously an arrangement of dead roses. She turned to McCorkle. "Do you know when she received the flowers?"

The older woman nodded. "The day before…"

"Did she mention who they were from or if there was a card?"

McCorkle shook her head. "She didn't. She only said that she was mad that he wouldn't let go."

Another blast of adrenaline nailed Sean. "Who did she mean? An old boyfriend?"

"Yes. They had broken up the month before, but he

kept calling. The police interviewed him and eventually ruled him out. They said he had an airtight alibi."

"What was the ex-boyfriend's name?" Amber asked.

"Quentin Yates. He works for another architectural firm in town."

"Do you mind if we look around for a card?" Sean didn't wait for Amber to ask. As mad as Harper would be, this could be a major break in the case.

"I'll help you," McCorkle offered.

Since the flowers were in the kitchen, that was the logical place to start. The evidence techs had taken the garbage to the lab. Sean figured if they'd found a card with a sinister note, they would have marked it as evidence. Since that wasn't in any of the reports, he was going with the theory it hadn't been found.

When they had checked every nook and cranny in the small kitchen, they moved to the living room. Amber chatted casually with McCorkle. Sean decided she could have been a cop herself. She had a way of prompting answers without directly asking the questions. McCorkle didn't hesitate even once. Sean doubted she realized she was being interrogated. By the time they moved on to the bedrooms, Amber knew all about Kimberly's social life and the long, hard path to her career.

"I'll take the bathroom," Sean offered. He had no desire to spend the next twenty minutes or so trapped in one of those little bedrooms with Amber. In the past twenty-four hours she had gotten deep under his skin. He wished he could regret it, but the necessary emotion just wouldn't come. He knew it was wrong, but he couldn't help savoring it.

As good as it felt, it could not go any further while

he was responsible for her safety. He could fantasize all he wanted.

Kimberly McCorkle's bathroom was crammed with the usual female necessities. Lots of hair and skin products. Loads of fragrances. Various types of razors. Toothpaste. Bodywash in a variety of scents. Amber's bathroom looked a lot like this. The first night he'd stayed at her house he'd had a hell of a time evicting her scent from his system. The subtle citrus fragrance was fresh and clean and made him long to taste every inch of her.

"Idiot," he muttered. He moved on to the medicine cabinet. No drugs other than aspirin and a half-empty prescription of antibiotics.

"Sean!"

He closed the mirrored medicine cabinet door and hurried to the bedroom at the end of the hall.

Amber pointed to the jewelry box on the dresser. "It was under the velvet lining."

He moved to her side and took a look. Amber had removed several necklaces and a watch, as well as the lining in the bottom of the jewelry box. How had the evidence techs missed this? "Was it obviously loose?"

"No. One of the necklaces hung in the fabric and pulled it away from the bottom."

At the bottom of the box were a couple of folded notes and the card from the floral shop lying right on top. It wasn't a business card; it was the one sporting the note that accompanied the bouquet. *I'm watching you.*

"We need a plastic bag," he muttered.

"I'll get one," McCorkle said, sounding breathless.

Amber reached into the jewelry box and gingerly

removed the card by its edges. "Should we look at the notes, too?"

"For sure." Sean removed the stack of notes carefully; there were four in all. Each was from the ex, Yates, who hadn't wanted to end the relationship.

"She thought the flowers were from him," Amber said. "She was keeping all this in case she needed it in the future."

But her future never came. The words echoed through Sean's head. Amber wouldn't have a future either if this bastard had anything to do with it.

McCorkle returned with a plastic sandwich bag and Sean bagged the evidence. Amber made her aware of the notes, which weren't particularly threatening, simply obsessive. Sean's mind wouldn't quit replaying those haunting words.

Did Amber have any idea how lucky she was to be alive? His throat tightened.

By the time they were at the front door, McCorkle's composure had frayed.

"We'll get this evidence to the police," Sean assured her. "They'll get this guy."

When they were in the car and headed downtown, Amber turned to him. "Before we go to the police, I want to go back to the floral shop."

Sean moved his head firmly side to side. "No way."

"It can't be a coincidence that all three flower arrangements came from the same florist and that at least two had the same warning."

Sean wouldn't deny the point. "It's still circumstantial and—" he shot her a pointed look "—we're playing fast and loose with evidence that may prove necessary to solving a double homicide."

She twisted in the seat and pled her case from a different perspective. "We have no idea what this guy does to stay ahead of the police. We do know he got past my security code. He could be listening to a police radio. I don't want him tipped off."

Sean shook his head. He had to be nuts, and yet she had a point. "What do you expect to say to Thrasher?"

She sighed. "I don't know. All I know for sure is that I don't want him to get away."

Sean braked for a light, and she touched his arm. He turned to her, and the stark fear on her face startled him. "How will I ever feel safe again if he gets away?"

Before he could stop the words, he made a promise he hoped like hell he could keep. "I won't let that happen."

Chapter Eleven

Thrasher Floral, Pearson Avenue, 3:00 p.m.

"Can we go in now?" Amber asked again.

Sean didn't like the idea of going in before they called Harper, but he'd put off the inevitable for a full fifteen minutes. If he didn't agree to going in soon, Amber would likely ignore him and go in anyway. Keeping her reasonably cooperative was essential.

"As soon as that customer comes out," he promised, "we're going in."

Amber acquiesced to his latest delay tactic with nothing more than a roll of her eyes.

The shop was in a small building on Pearson Avenue. Thrasher was thirty-one, the same age as Kyle Adler. Birmingham and its surrounding suburbs made for a fairly large population, so the two might not have grown up in the same neighborhood or have gone to school together, but they knew each other. Adler made deliveries for the floral shop—two of those deliveries had carried cards with warnings. Sean was damned certain a third one had, as well; he just couldn't prove it.

Since Adler was dead, who had delivered Amber's flowers? Thrasher? He'd denied making the delivery and claimed the employee who filled the order was out sick when Harper questioned him. If Harper had located the employee and questioned her, Sean hadn't heard about it. There was a lot happening in a short period of time. So much so that keeping everyone in the loop was difficult. Not that he and Amber had been keeping anyone informed. That had to change soon. They were way over the line already. Jess wouldn't be happy. The boss considered B&C's relationship with the BPD sacred. Maybe he'd still have a job when this case was finished.

At this point, he didn't have much to lose by putting off calling Harper for a few more minutes. If they were going to do this, they might as well do it right. It was time to ask Thrasher different questions.

The entrance opened, and the brunette they'd been watching at the counter exited with a small arrangement.

"That's our cue." He climbed from behind the wheel and moved around to meet Amber on the sidewalk. "Careful what you say," he warned. "We need him cooperative, not defensive."

She made a face. "Trust me—I've done this once or twice, Mr. Douglas."

"So I'm Mr. Douglas now?"

She eyed him skeptically. "For the moment."

Shaking his head, he opened the door. The bell jingled as they entered. The lady behind the counter looked up. "Good afternoon. Welcome to Thrasher's. How can I help you?"

"Is Mr. Thrasher in?" Amber asked, taking the lead.

Sean suppressed a grin. She might be petite, but there was nothing small about her personality. She was pretty damned fearless. Like most people who met her in person for the first time, he'd thought she would be taller, too. He decided then and there the reason was her personality. Amber Roberts was larger than life.

The clerk shook her head. "He called me this morning and said he was sick. I rushed over and opened the shop."

"Thank you—" Sean noted the name on her badge "—Louanne. We'll try to catch him again later."

Amber glared at him as he guided her out the same door they had just entered.

"What're you doing? I want to have a look around in that shop."

He ushered her to the car and opened her door. "Get in and I'll explain."

With a reluctant huff, she dropped into the seat. Sean hurried around to the driver's side and joined her.

"Let's go to his house." She dug through her purse. "I can locate his address in about thirty seconds."

"We have to call Harper. Now. No more putting it off." He pulled his cell from his pocket, ignoring her irritated glare. "We want whatever evidence we find to be admissible in court, Amber. We can't just go rummaging through the man's shop looking for clues."

"You didn't mention having issues with the idea when we were going through Rhiana's and Kimberly's homes."

"We had permission," he reminded her. "Their mothers were right there with us. We've gone as far as we can with this. It's time to let the cops do their job."

She stared at the street for a long moment. "Fine. Make the call."

Sean entered Harper's number and brought him up to speed. With the order to back off ringing in his ears, he ended the call and gave Amber the bad news.

"Detective Harper says it will take some time to get a warrant. He *suggested* we go home and wait for his call. The techs are finished at your place. He thinks it's safe if you want to go home."

"I knew this would happen." She folded her arms across her chest. "We should have nosed around when we had the chance."

He didn't bother pointing out once more that rendering evidence unusable was not their goal. "We skipped lunch. After what you went through last night, we need to rectify that oversight."

"I'm not hungry. I…"

When she remained silent, he glanced her way. She stared forward, her lips slightly parted. He licked his own and shifted his attention back to the street. The woman had amazing lips. He'd spent a lot of time watching those lips, and even when she'd been sick as a dog in the wee hours of the morning they were still tempting.

"We've been so focused on finding the evidence," she said, more to herself than to him. "We've ignored what it means." She turned to him. Her eyes round with something like disbelief. "They were watching us, and I don't mean from afar. I'm talking about up close."

Sean braked for a four-way stop. "Adler and Thrasher?"

She nodded, her gaze seeking his. "The flowers were delivered the day before each victim went missing. Mine had been ordered several days before they were delivered. They were watching." She pressed a hand to her lips. "One or the other or maybe both came into my house—into their houses—and took souvenirs, but that's not all they did while they were there."

A horn blared behind them, forcing Sean to take his eyes off her and to move forward. He got where she was headed. "You're thinking they planted cameras so they could watch."

"Oh, my God." Both hands went to her face then. "There's no other explanation."

Harper hadn't mentioned finding any surveillance devices. Sean reached over and took her hand in his. "You're okay. Adler is dead, and we're on to Thrasher. Whatever one or both did, it won't happen again."

She scrubbed at her eyes. "We have to search my house. Now. I need to know if they were watching me... I need to be sure."

"Since no other toxins have been found, I think it's safe to have a look. But I'm not letting you stay there again until this is over." Sean gave her hand a squeeze before letting go.

She held his gaze a beat longer. "Okay."

His entire being aching to lean across the seat and kiss her. He shifted his attention straight ahead. What he really wanted to do was pull over and make her feel this raging desire building inside him. She needed kissing. She needed to feel safe and cared for. For the first time in a very long time, he hoped he got the opportunity to make her feel that way.

Forest Brook Drive, Homewood

AMBER STARED AT her home for a long moment after the car stopped moving. Sean was getting out and would be at her door any second, but she suddenly couldn't move. Growing up, she had spent endless hours in this house. Louisa Roberts had been the perfect grandmother. She always baked cookies for Amber's arrival. If it was summer, there would be fresh-squeezed lemonade. If it was winter, there would be homemade hot chocolate. They read together and played games. Grandma Louisa owned every good board game made between 1950 and 1980, she'd boasted.

In this house Amber had felt completely safe and loved her entire life.

Until now.

Her door opened, and Sean waited for her to climb out. She stared up at him, conscious of her need to throw herself into his arms. She suddenly felt so isolated and completely alone. He was the one person that made her feel remotely safe right now. She wanted to know the shelter of his arms…she wanted to know him.

Shaking off the overwhelming reactions, she emerged from the car and steadied herself. When this was over, she intended to take a serious vacation. She hadn't taken a real vacation since the summer she graduated college. The job at the station was already hers, so she'd taken two weeks on the West Coast to relax and shop for a fashionable wardrobe. She'd returned well rested and seriously broke. Her grandmother had laughed and given her a high five. That winter Louisa Roberts had passed away.

Amber pushed aside the tender memories and waited while Sean unlocked her front door. The silence inside made her belly clench. Normally her security system would be screaming for attention, but she had left it disarmed for the police. Actually, they hadn't armed it when they'd raced out of here headed for the ER. How had this place that had once felt so safe suddenly become so filled with potential danger?

Her heart was pounding by the time she crossed the threshold. As terrifying as the reality that someone had broken in and touched her things was, it was still good to be home on a level no one could touch.

The evidence technicians hadn't left the mess she had expected. Everything looked just as she'd left it when they'd hurried off to the ER last night. The teacup she'd used as well as the can of tea were missing. Both were evidence now. In a day or two the lab would be able to tell her what sort of poison had been added to her tea. She'd done some Google searches before she'd fallen asleep this morning, but the symptoms for most toxins were so similar it was impossible to narrow down the possibilities. She was, however, relatively certain the culprit was some sort of plant.

"Where should we begin?" she asked, shifting to what they'd come here to do.

"The cameras might be really small. Basically they could be planted anywhere, but—" he met her gaze "—we should check the bedroom and bathroom first."

The idea made Amber sick to her stomach. "How do you want to do this?"

"Do you have a stepladder?"

She nodded. "In the garage."

Rather than go to her bedroom, Amber waited in the living room for Sean to return. She hoped the feeling of uncertainty in her own home would pass quickly. When this was over and she was on that nice, long vacation, she intended to have the house cleaned and painted. All the food products were going in the trash. Every dish and spoon and utensil would be sanitized in the dishwasher. Every single item she owned was going to be washed or dry-cleaned.

It was the only way she would ever feel comfortable in her home again.

While Sean checked the overhead light fixtures and tops of the windows, Amber started the challenging task of going through the bookshelves and clutter on the chest of drawers and dresser.

"Here we go."

She turned from the bookshelf to see him take a small object from the narrow shelf made by the plantation shutters on the window. Her heart lurched.

"We need a box," he said. "A shoe box, hatbox, whatever you have handy."

Amber rushed into her closet and grabbed the first shoe box she could get her hands on. She dumped the contents and hurried back to where he waited. He placed the small gadget in the box. She positioned the lid over it. If the thing was still live, she didn't want whoever might be watching to see anything else.

Before moving on to the next room, they covered every square foot of her bedroom and discovered one more camera, this one on top of a family portrait that her grandmother had commissioned when Amber's father was five. Even if the evidence techs had moved the painting, they wouldn't have noticed it unless they were looking specifically for something so tiny.

A third camera was found in the bathroom on the cabinet above the toilet, angled to ensure she was captured taking a bath or shower. The fear she had felt earlier was gone. Fury had taken its place. This was her home! The living room and the kitchen were bugged with one camera each. She stood in the middle of her kitchen now and allowed the rage to course through her. It was either that or throw up, and she'd done enough of that last night.

"We should take all this to Harper," Sean suggested.

Amber didn't argue.

When they left she armed the security system for all the good it would do.

Sean called Lieutenant Harper, who suggested they meet at Thrasher's home since he was en route there with a warrant.

"Did they find him?" Amber wanted to know. Sean hadn't mentioned the floral shop owner.

He shook his head. "One of the neighbors said he left this morning at the same time he always does to open the shop and he hasn't returned."

"He's gone." Amber didn't need confirmation. The man knew the police were getting close to figuring out his connection to Adler and the murdered women and he'd run. *Damn it!*

"I'm sure the BPD issued a BOLO. Thrasher won't get far."

Amber hoped he was right.

Killough Circle, 6:15 p.m.

A BPD CRUISER sat on the street in front of the house belonging to Peter Thrasher. The sedan Lieutenant Chet Harper and Detective Chad Cook had arrived in was parked in the driveway alongside the evidence techs' van. Yellow tape marked the area as a crime scene. The two uniforms guarding the perimeter had informed Amber and Sean they had to wait on the street until further notice. Two other cruisers had blocked both ends of the block. No reporters were getting in.

Amber had been pacing the sidewalk for a good forty-five minutes. She was dying to know what was going on inside the house. Had they found evidence tying

Thrasher to Adler? She rubbed at her forehead. Had they found photos or videos of her or the other women?

She hugged her arms around herself and paced in the other direction. Had the two sold the intimate look at her life to some adult site? Her stomach churned. If they had uploaded the videos they made to the internet…

"You're going to wear out that sidewalk," Sean commented.

Amber stalled and glared at him. Leaning against his car, his arms folded across his chest, ankles crossed, he appeared completely unperturbed. How could he look so calm? Two women had been murdered. She would have been number three if someone hadn't killed Adler. She might still end up murdered if Thrasher wasn't found. Reality washed over her like a dash of icy water. She would be looking over her shoulder for the rest of her life if he got away.

She couldn't fall apart now. *Deep breath.* "We've been waiting almost an hour." She looked back at the house. "Do you think they've found evidence to connect him to the cameras we found in my house?" She had stood outside the yellow tape at plenty of scenes where a crime had been committed. In her experience the longer the investigators were inside, the more likely the findings were significant.

"Chances are if they'd found nothing, we'd know it by now."

Of course they had found evidence. She really was out of sorts here. How long had she been reporting the news? Going on seven years. Granted, she rarely landed the major crime stories like serial killer Eric Spears— that was Gina Coleman's domain. Frankly, it didn't matter how many times she had worked a crime scene like this; this was different. This was personal. She was on the other side of the event this time. The reporters following this case were talking about her, which was in part why her boss had insisted she take a few vacation days. She'd been thinking about calling to do exactly that. He'd beat her to it.

Sean abruptly straightened away from his car. Amber's gaze followed his to the detective exiting the front door of Thrasher's home. Her pulse fluttered.

Detective Cook was only a couple of years younger than Amber. She'd seen him at Gina and Barb's engagement party. Cook had just popped the question to Dr. Sylvia Baron's daughter. Amber remembered feeling vaguely jealous of the couple. They had looked so in love.

Her gaze drifted to Sean. She blinked and looked away. God help her.

Cook gave Sean one of those male nods of acknowledgment, then he turned to Amber. "Ma'am, Lieutenant Harper will be out shortly. He'll brief you on what we found."

"Thank you." It was about time.

"We've got Ricky Vernon headed over here to take a look at the computers," Cook said to Sean. "Harper doesn't want to risk triggering any safety features that might shut down or wipe the systems."

"Are you saying there's more than one computer?" Amber's stomach sank.

Cook shifted his attention back to her. She held her breath as he seemed to decide how much he could tell her. "Yes, ma'am, four desktop computers and one laptop. It looks like he was watching a fourth woman. The lieutenant has sent a couple of uniforms over to check on her."

"Is she okay?"

Cook hesitated again. "We're not seeing her on any of the cameras. We've made a couple of calls already, and she wasn't at work today."

"Thrasher may have taken her." A chill bored into Amber's bones. And he was out there somewhere. She turned all the way around, scanning the neighborhood. He could be anywhere.

Chapter Twelve

Magic City Beer & Burger, 8:00 p.m.

Amber needed to relax. She sat on her side of the booth, her back ramrod straight. Sean had hoped that coming to an out-of-the-way place—one he doubted she'd ever set foot inside—would help make that happen. No such luck. She jumped every time the bell over the door jingled with a new customer.

"You should stop worrying about who walks in and just eat." He nodded to the house special on her plate. "You know the sauce is a closely guarded secret."

"I'm sure it's great." She forced a smile into place. "I'm really not hungry."

"The fries are the best in town." For emphasis he stuffed one into his mouth. Bad move. Rather than follow his example, she watched him chew. Out in LA he'd dated plenty of celebrity types. Every single one had been unique, but the one thing they all had in common was the inability to hide certain basic feelings. The flare of desire he spotted in Amber's green eyes startled him almost as much as he felt certain it did her. They'd had a couple of moments the past few days, but this was the first time she'd shown true hunger, and he was relatively certain it wasn't about the food.

"Eat," he encouraged. "You'll thank me later. Besides, you don't want to offend the chef."

She glanced over at the counter as the owner and cook shouted, "Order up," and placed a meatloaf special on the counter of the pass through window. With a sigh, she picked up her burger and took a bird-size bite. The surprise that captured her expression made him smile.

"I told you." He tore off another bite of his own sandwich.

For a few minutes they ate in silence. Amber stopped sizing up every customer who entered, and she ate not only the burger but every single fry. Apparently the lady hadn't realized how much she liked burgers. She'd polished off a good-size one at the Garage Café, too. All this time he'd been watching her on the news he'd had her figured for a vegan.

She patted her lips with her napkin. "Wow. I can't believe I ate so much."

"Good." He tossed his own crumpled napkin into his now-empty serving dish. "Would you like dessert? They make the best deep-fried Oreo cookie on the planet."

Amber held up her hands. "No, thanks. I couldn't eat another bite."

"Coffee then," he suggested.

She nodded. "Coffee would be great."

Sean waved over the waitress and ordered coffee. When she was on her way, he watched as Amber drifted back into her own troubling thoughts. "They'll find him."

She blinked as if resurfacing from a faraway place. "I hope so."

"Harper and Cook are the best."

She nodded. "They were part of the team Jess had when she was still with the department."

Sean's boss was pretty much a celebrity herself. "Lori Wells and Clint Hayes were on the team, too." Clint was the senior investigator at B&C now. One of the things Sean liked most about the older man was his straightforwardness. He didn't tolerate the games some people liked to play. Amber appeared to share that feeling. So far Sean had found her to be honest and direct. He liked that about her.

"Gina is always telling stories about Jess's FBI days and how her profiles were responsible for bringing down the worst of the worst."

"Eric Spears." Sean was still living in Hollywood when the infamous serial killer followed Jess to Birmingham, but he'd heard plenty about it from his family.

"Eric Spears was at the top of the evil scale," Amber said. "Gina did an exposé on the way Jess profiled using a scale she called the faces of evil." She laughed. "I'm sure you've heard a great deal about how amazing your boss is."

"She is amazing and tough." Sean had experienced the latter firsthand.

Amber pushed her empty plate aside and braced her crossed arms on the table. She leaned forward and looked directly into his eyes. "How many other women have been hurt or murdered by Thrasher and Adler? What if Pettie and McCorkle weren't their first victims?"

"Jess doesn't think there were other victims, but we may never know for sure," Sean allowed. The waitress arrived with two steaming cups of coffee. Sean gifted her with a smile and thanked her. He sipped his coffee, hoping Amber would do the same rather than dwell on the what-ifs.

When she followed his lead and tasted the coffee, she made an approving sound. "This place is full of surprises."

The place looked a little rough on the surface, especially with the old truck front end hanging on the wall behind the bar. Rustic but homey in Sean's opinion. The staff was extra friendly, and the craft beers were second to none. "My folks used to bring us here here as kids. It was a ritual after church on Sundays."

Amber smiled, that genuine one that made his heart beat a little faster. "You went to church?"

"Didn't you?" he teased. "You grew up in Birmingham—you must have."

"I did. I still do occasionally. Work sometimes gets in the way." She sipped her coffee and turned thoughtful for a moment. "Even when we traveled, we found a house of worship. Whether it was a Jewish temple or a Buddhist one. My parents embrace all people and their cultures."

"More people should raise their children that way." Sean damned sure intended to—if he ever had any. Now there was a thought that came out of left field. Just because he would turn thirty this year didn't mean time was running out. As far as he knew guys didn't have so-called biological clocks. He drowned the crazy idea with more coffee.

"Why does Jess believe there aren't other murder victims?" Amber's smile had disappeared. The worry was back in her eyes.

"She read the case files on Pettie and McCorkle. She concluded that the first murder, Pettie, was likely a surprise to both men. The work was sloppier. They were more careful and organized with the second victim, Mc-Corkle. Even the way the cameras were placed in the homes, Pettie's versus yours, was progressively more precise."

"So they may have started out as Peeping Toms hiding in the girls' bathroom at school or watching their sisters or mothers?"

"Exactly. The BPD confirmed the two attended the same schools. Jess believes they probably teamed up as school chums and things grew from there."

Amber shivered visibly. Sean reached across the table and placed his hand on hers. "Even if Thrasher is stupid enough to try, he'll have to go through me to get to you."

A faint smile trembled across her lips. "I'm really grateful you're here."

The warmth that had spread up his arm and across his chest from nothing more than touching her hand had him wondering how grateful she would be if she knew how much he wanted to touch all of her.

She straightened away from the table, breaking the contact. "I think maybe I'll have one of those deep-fried Oreos after all."

Rather than summon the waitress, Sean went to the counter and placed the order. He needed the distance. Allowing personal involvement with a client was a mistake he did not intend to repeat. Too bad the only part of him sticking by that motto was his brain—everything else was pulsing with need. He returned to the booth only a few minutes later with their desserts, and they both dug in.

Whether the sugar rush had her thinking again or just gave her the courage to do so, she waded into sensitive territory. "Do you think they shared the videos on the internet? Will the FBI have to be involved?"

"The guy from the BPD's lab is the top in his field. He'll be able to determine how far the sharing went, if at all," Sean explained. "If Adler and Thrasher were sharing their peep shows with friends via the Net, the FBI will more than likely be involved."

She shuddered. "I feel so exposed."

He understood. It was one thing for her to report the news on camera, but another one entirely for her private moments bathing and dressing to be videoed without her knowledge or consent. He knew a little something about feeling exposed.

"We'll know more about what we're looking at tomorrow," he promised.

"I hope they find the other woman alive." She nibbled at another bite of her dessert. "The timing would be right, you know, for another kidnapping. Pettie was in February, McCorkle in June. October makes four months. Isn't that the way serial killers work?"

"Most have a pattern." He nodded. "If Thrasher stuck to the pattern he and Adler followed and abducted a fourth victim, he did so in the past twenty-four hours. Since the other vics were held for several days before they were murdered, it makes sense that she would still be alive. Assuming, of course, the death of his partner hasn't sent him off in a different direction."

Amber sat her coffee down and stared into the cup for a moment as if searching for the right words. "Why do you suppose I was skipped? It was obvious they'd been watching me longer."

"If Thrasher murdered Adler, we have to assume the two had a falling-out. I imagine the event put Thrasher into a tailspin. Before he could regain his bearings the body was discovered and you were brought in for questioning. I've been with you since. My guess is he moved on to the next name on the list."

Amber leaned her head in her hand and rubbed her temple with her fingers. "I guess I'm the lucky one."

Sean had learned enough from Jess to know luck had nothing to do with it. Something went down between Thrasher and Adler that disrupted the timeline of the two killers. In Sean's opinion it was somehow related to Amber.

He wished the feeling that it was far from over would stop gnawing at him.

Oxmoor Glen Drive, 9:15 p.m.

SEAN TOSSED THE tennis ball across the room, and the big dog bounced after it. When he tried to take the ball back a tug-of-war ensued. Amber moistened her lips and bit back a grin. She found it far too endearing that her bodyguard played with his dog as if it were a child. He obviously loved the animal. She'd never had time for pets. Come to think of it, she rarely found time for anything other than work. Why was it the idea suddenly felt so wrong?

When Rebel had tired of playing, he curled up on the fluffy round bed in the corner. Sean gestured to the sofa. "Feel free to turn on the television. I should make sure the guest room is presentable."

"I slept in it for a couple of hours this morning," she reminded him. "I didn't have any complaints. Besides, why would I turn on the television and listen to all the speculation and theories connecting me to Adler's murder?"

"Good point." He backed into the hallway and then disappeared.

Amber released a long, weary breath and surveyed Sean's place. She hadn't really taken in many of the details in the wee hours of this morning. The kitchen, dining and living space were one fairly large room. The place was nice with most modern amenities. A gas fireplace in the living room, stainless steel appliances in the kitchen and nice high ceilings. The decor was American bachelor simple: big, comfy sofa, huge television hanging over the fireplace and a coffee table littered with sports magazines and remotes.

On the bar that separated the kitchen from the rest of the space where he'd tossed his keys, there was a framed photograph of a young Sean, his siblings and their parents. His hair was considerably longer. She estimated the shot had been taken before he left for the West Coast. A built-in bookcase next to the fireplace held several books by one of her favorite mystery authors. She reached for last year's release and smiled. So they had something besides the lack of a personal life in common after all.

"Have you picked up his latest?"

Amber closed the book and tucked it back onto the shelf. "I haven't, but I plan to. You?"

"It's on my bedside table. You're welcome to it."

Was he inviting her to his bed or to borrow his book? Her nerves jangled foolishly. She was nervous. The realization startled her. Hoping to keep that embarrassing revelation to herself, she pointed at him and gave a knowing nod. "You saw the stack on my bedside table, didn't you?"

He shrugged. "I might have noticed." He glanced at the clock in the cable box. "Would you like a beer?" Another of those completely male shrugs lifted his shoulders. "Sorry. I've been meaning to pick up a good bottle of wine for company. I'm pretty sure I have popcorn and a stash of peanuts."

Was it her imagination or was he feeling as nervous as she was? "Nothing for me, thank you."

For several seconds they stood there staring at each other.

She should say something. "I think I might shower and go to bed early." She propped her lips into a broad smile. "Do a little reading maybe—if you don't mind me borrowing that book."

"Sure thing." He hitched a thumb over his shoulder. "I'll get it for you."

Scrubbing her unexpectedly sweaty palms against her hips, she followed him down the short hall. Butterflies had taken flight in her belly. She stopped at the door rather than follow him into his bedroom. Like the main living space, the decorating was minimal. A big bed, bedside table and a chest of drawers. She was surprised not to see another massive television. What she did see was a stack of books that rivaled her own.

He grabbed a pair of boxers and a lone shoe from the floor. "You need anything else to sleep in?"

She thought of the faded crimson tee that sported the Roll Tide logo she'd slept in that morning. "The T-shirt works."

"There're clean towels in the bathroom closet." He winced. "Did your sister bring bodywash? You might not like my soap. I know you used it this morning, but that was kind of an emergency."

"It's fine." It smelled like him, but she'd been too sick to care.

He tossed the shoe and boxers into his closet and then grabbed the hardcover from the bedside table. He crossed the room, coming toward her, and her heart beat considerably faster. She tried to swallow, but her throat felt closed.

He passed the book to her. "If you get past the sixth chapter, don't tell me if he gets the girl."

Her fingers brushed his and need ignited deep inside her. "Doesn't he always get the girl?"

Sean was so close now the scent of his skin filled her senses. She wanted to reach out and run her hands over those broad shoulders. She wanted to trace every ridge and valley of the lean torso beneath that khaki shirt. She wanted to lose herself in the sensations and pretend her world wasn't a total mess.

He leaned his face toward hers. "I would really like to kiss you right now, but that's a bad idea."

She lifted her face, leaving no more than a couple of inches between their lips. "I was thinking the same thing."

He moistened his lips, and her breath caught.

"What do you want to do about it?"

Amber reached up slowly and fisted her fingers in his shirt. "I say we get it over with so we can move past it." She wet her lips. "My grandmother always said to go for whatever you wanted, otherwise you'd just go on wanting it."

"Smart lady."

His lips lowered to hers. The first contact had pure pleasure erupting inside her. His mouth was hot, his lips firm, but his kiss was slow and restrained. His fingers landed on her cheeks, tracing the lines of her face as his lips tasted and teased hers. She pulled at his shirt, drawing that amazing body nearer.

By the time he drew his lips from hers, her thighs were trembling and every part of her was on fire. He pressed his forehead to hers and whispered, "That was good."

"Uh-huh." She licked her lips, shivering at the taste of him.

"Should we do it again just to make sure we get it out of our systems?"

Amber closed her eyes and inhaled a slow, deep breath. She wanted to say yes so badly. "I think we should maybe wait until tomorrow and revisit the idea then." Otherwise she was going to drag him into that big, unmade bed.

"Agreed."

He drew away first and stuffed his hands into the pockets of his jeans as if he didn't trust himself.

Amber's entire being protested the loss of contact. "Well, good night."

He managed a stiff nod. "'Night."

Amber didn't breathe again until she was in the guest room with the door closed. She tossed the book onto the bed and dragged in a couple more deep breaths to calm her galloping pulse. When she felt in control again, she grabbed the tee and some clean underwear. She opened the door and peeked into the hall. Clear. She moved to the bathroom. He'd gone back to the living room and turned on the television. Once inside the bathroom, she closed the door and locked it. A glance in the mirror made her wince. She looked frightful. Her skin was even paler than usual. Dark circles had formed under her eyes.

With a groan, she turned on the water in the shower and undressed. How in the world had she allowed that to happen? What had she been thinking? Shaking her head, she stepped into the shower, and the hot water instantly banished all other thought.

For a while she stood there and allowed the water to work its magic on her tight muscles. It felt so good. She'd been so tense all day. Slowly, she reached for the soap and lathered it up. The clean, fresh scent of Sean filled the tiled space. She shivered despite the hot water.

A glutton for punishment, she closed her eyes and rubbed the soap over her skin. When she moved it over her breasts, her breath caught and she let the memory of his kiss consume her. By the time she'd lathered her skin, her body felt weak with want. In her mind his hands replaced hers, sliding the soap over her skin, his fingers tempting her nipples and trailing down her ribs. She trembled.

The soap slipped from her fingers and hit the floor. Amber jerked out of the fantasy. This was a perfect example of how badly the past few days had shaken her. She was fantasizing about a stranger. Sure they had spent the last forty-eight or so hours together, but they still didn't know each other.

Hurrying through the rest of her shower, she rinsed her body with cool water. Even after she'd toweled off, she was still burning up. She dragged on the tee and her underwear and reached for the door. Maybe she should give herself a few more minutes before chancing an encounter with Sean.

After taking a deep breath, she prowled for a hair dryer and set to the task. She massaged her scalp with one hand while directing the hot air with the other. Her fingers slowed as she studied her reflection. What did Sean Douglas see when he looked at her? She was attractive enough, she supposed. Braces had taken care of her teeth back in middle school. She hadn't suffered with acne like a lot of her friends, but she'd been teased endlessly about her freckles.

She didn't mind the freckles really. The makeup when she was on the air basically covered them up, but she didn't bother trying to hide them when she wasn't on the job. She hung her towel over the shower door while the dryer cooled off, and then she searched the cabinet under the sink for a spare toothbrush. She'd left hers in the guest room.

A knock at the door made her jump. She bumped her head on the counter.

"I noticed your toothbrush on the bedside table," Sean announced, his deep voice filtering through the door and wrapping around her. "You want it?"

Man alive did she want it, only it wasn't the toothbrush. Amber rubbed at her head. She cracked the door open the tiniest bit and reached out. "Thanks."

He placed the toothbrush in her waiting hand. "Welcome."

When he walked away she closed the door and leaned against it for a long moment. *Get a grip, Amber. Adrenaline is messing with your head.*

Five minutes later, teeth brushed, dryer put away and her clothes folded in her arms, she exited the bathroom and headed straight for the guest room. "See you in the morning," she called without a backward glance.

His deep voice followed her into the room. "Count on it."

Chapter Thirteen

Fourth Avenue North,
Thursday, October 20, 10:20 a.m.

The story was out.

For six years Amber had chased the story. She had gone to great lengths to uncover details and insights no one else could find.

Now *she* was the story.

She and Sean had been summoned to the B&C office right after breakfast. On some level she was glad for the escape. All night the memory of that kiss had haunted her. Meeting his gaze this morning had been difficult. Primarily because she'd wanted to resume right where they'd left off. *So, so not smart.*

On the way here, she'd focused on the case, hoping the summons meant there was good news, but judging by the look on Jess Burnett's face that was not the case. Buddy Corlew had called first thing this morning to let them know the phone records had been a bust. There were plenty of calls between Adler and his customers, but none between him and Thrasher except those to the floral shop.

Amber braced for more bad news.

Jess closed the folder on her desk and looked first at Amber, then at Sean. "Thrasher is still at large. His car was found abandoned near the Nineteenth Street bus station. It's possible he fled the city, but there's always the chance he could be in hiding close by."

It wasn't necessary to be an FBI profiler to understand why Thrasher would choose not to run. "He may want to finish what he and Adler started," Amber proposed.

Jess nodded. "Lieutenant Harper and I believe it would be best if you continued to keep a low profile for a few more days. We want to be sure you stay safe."

"Wow." Amber slumped in her chair. "This keeps growing more complicated." So many times she had interviewed victims and expressed her sympathy. Now she understood the look in their eyes after she offered the usual words of commiseration. A person couldn't possibly understand how *this* felt…unless he or she was the target. "So *you* believe I'm still in danger."

"I do. I've had time to review all the available information on Thrasher and Adler," Jess began. "Thrasher has spent his adult life dealing in flowers. He never married. No long-term relationships. His father died when he was ten and his mother passed away two years ago, so there's no family. No record of mental illness or counseling of any sort. No health issues on record. According to the interviews conducted by the lieutenant's team, his employees like him."

"Is that typical in a killer?" Sean asked.

The sound of his voice wrapped around Amber and made breathing difficult. She wasn't at all sure she could handle another night in the same house with him. She'd gone to sleep and awakened dreaming of making love with him. His voice, the way he moved, it all got under her skin somehow.

"Many killers are loners," Jess explained. "Most psychopaths are quite charming. Not all are murderers. In fact, I'm not convinced Thrasher is a killer. Adler may have been the dominant one, but I haven't found evidence suggesting as much. According to the interviews conducted by the BPD, Adler's parents are very religious. They raised their son in a strict environment. Those who knew him called him a loner, shy, quiet. Nothing was found in either man's home that tells us the rest of what we need to know." Jess clasped her hands atop the folder. "I'm not willing to take the risk there's another layer to one or both that I'm not seeing yet. Until we know more, we need to make sure you stay safe."

Sean glanced at Amber. "I guess that means you're stuck with me for a little while longer."

She produced a smile. "I guess so."

"If Thrasher and Adler were obsessed with you," Jess said, "he won't be able to stay away. He'll need to see you. To be close."

Her words sent goose bumps spilling over Amber's skin. "I understand. The station isn't expecting me back to work for a few days." She swallowed, wishing her mouth hadn't gone so dry. "I should stay home and not answer the door?"

A rap on the door drew Jess's attention there. Amber glanced over her shoulder to see the receptionist poke her head into the office.

"There are at least a dozen reporters lining the street out front. When Ms. Roberts is ready to leave I would suggest the alley exit."

Any hope of getting through this without mounting

attention in the media curled up and died in the pit of Amber's stomach.

"Thank you, Rebecca." Jess shifted her attention to Amber. "The more your face is in the news, the more Thrasher will be incited to make a move—if he's watching, as I suspect he is. If he's obsessed with you, he can't help himself."

"How difficult do you believe it'll be for the police to find him?" Amber pressed.

"His resources are limited, which helps, but there's no guarantee he'll be found."

She could be looking over her shoulder for the rest of her life. This time the inability to draw in a deep breath had nothing to do with the man next to her. Something Jess had said suddenly elbowed its way to the front of her worries. "You said you're not convinced Thrasher is a killer and that there's no absolute evidence Adler is. If they aren't killers, then who murdered those women?"

"Therein lies the rub," Jess admitted. "Consider Adler's murder. He was seated at the dining table having tea, presumably with his killer. If that killer was Thrasher, who is a far larger man than Adler, why get up from the table and go to the kitchen for a knife when you can easily overtake the victim?"

"You think there's a third killer involved." It wasn't a question. Amber could see the conviction in Jess's eyes.

"Lieutenant Harper has expanded the parameters of his investigation to include a potential third killer," Jess explained. "In my opinion, it's a necessary step."

Amber felt completely unnerved. Totally unsettled. "Wow."

"I would advise you to go someplace not a part of your routine," Jess offered. "Someplace the killer or killers won't know to look. Just for a few days. Let the BPD and us do what we need to do without having to worry about adding names to the victim list."

"What about the other woman who was being watched?" Amber worried Jess hadn't provided an update on the woman because it was more bad news. "Has she been found?"

"She has," Jess said. "Her name is Emma Norton. The employee the BPD spoke to had just returned from vacation and didn't realize Emma had taken her vacation this week. The lieutenant has spoken to her. She's visiting her father in Seattle. I received the call just before you arrived."

"I'm glad to hear it." Amber felt immensely relieved. It was bad enough two women were dead.

"Take a day or two someplace quiet while we sort this out," Jess repeated. "Sean will see that you stay safe."

He stood. "I'll make sure the alley is still clear."

Amber pushed to her feet. "I appreciate all you're doing, Jess. I can't imagine doing this alone."

With effort Jess stood and rested a hand on her rounded belly. "I'm glad we can help. You are our top priority."

Sean returned and ushered Amber to the rear entrance. Since the slots in front of the B&C office had been full when they arrived, he'd parked two blocks away. To avoid being spotted by her colleagues from the various stations around the city, they detoured another couple of blocks.

He opened her door, and Amber settled in the passenger seat. What if Thrasher wasn't found by Monday? How long was she supposed to keep her life on hold? She should call Barb and let her know what was going on. Was her sister in danger? Jess hadn't mentioned any concerns about Barb's safety. Calling her boss was unavoidable. He would insist she take as much time as she needed.

She didn't want to take more time. She wanted her life back. She wanted to avoid getting tangled up with her protector. She wanted to stay alive.

Amber looked around to get her bearings. She couldn't say how long Sean had been driving before she snapped out of her pity party. "Where are we going?"

"My parents have a place on the river. I thought we'd go there."

She hoped it was larger than his house. "What about clothes?" And other stuff, like a toothbrush and deodorant?

"We can drive past your house, but I'm guessing there are more reporters waiting there. We can stop for what we need once we're out of the city."

Amber resigned herself to her fate. It was either risk a confrontation with an obsessed killer or killers or spend time in a remote location alone with the man who had kissed her like she'd never before been kissed.

She stole a glance at him. She was in trouble either way.

River Road, 3:30 p.m.

JUST OVER A year ago Sean had escaped the hurt and anger by coming here. For six months after Lacy's death the press hounded him. The official investigation had cleared him of any criminal wrongdoing related to her death, but he hadn't been able to forgive himself. If he had paid closer attention...if he hadn't allowed things to become personal, she might still be alive.

Intellectually he understood that the choices she had made in her life were not his responsibility, but in his heart he carried the burden. He had trusted her...trusted the love they shared.

What an arrogant fool he'd been.

"So this is where your family spends Christmas?"

Sean shook off the painful memories and focused on the woman standing in the middle of the family room. "This is the place."

During the forty-five-minute drive from the city she'd initially remained silent. He imagined she grappled for some way to come to terms with the situation. As if she'd reached some understanding with herself, she had kept the conversation going from that point on, asking him question after question about the family cabin. His great-great-grandfather had built the room they were now standing in nearly a hundred years ago. Each generation had added additional square footage and renovated to include multiple bedrooms and bathrooms. His grandmother had been the one to insist on the huge eat-in kitchen.

"Take any bedroom you'd like." The sooner they were settled, the sooner he could walk the grounds to clear his head. In the past twenty-four hours the lady had managed to breach his defenses entirely. That kiss had blown him away. Even a month ago he wouldn't have believed he could feel that way again. He wanted to touch her and to kiss her...and a whole lot more.

She's an assignment, blockhead. Work. You can't go there.

"Which one do you usually take?"

Her question dragged him from the disturbing thoughts just in time to watch her turn all the way around again, taking in the enormity of the place. There were no frills, no chef's kitchen or jetted tubs, just homey spaces with decent plumbing and incredible views of nature.

"Top of the stairs, first door on the left." He hitched a thumb toward the door. "I'll batten down the hatches and bring in the supplies."

Since no one had stayed here since spring, there were a few things to be done before dark, like turning on the water and checking the generator in case there was a power outage. Then he had to bring in the food supplies and get the refrigerated goods stored. As long as he stayed busy, he would be good to go.

Maybe.

Sean did a quick walk-through of the house before heading outside. When he'd been a kid he'd dreamed of living here full-time. Of course puberty and girls had changed his mind. The occasional weekend here had felt like a world away from his school friends and whoever he'd been sweet on at the time. If only he had known how complicated life could be.

The sky was darker than usual. The rain would be here soon, along with a potential thunderstorm or two. All the more reason to check the generator. His father had taught him to ensure all the mechanics were in working order before getting comfortable. It wasn't like you could call for a service man who would show up in an hour or so.

With the water on and the generator checked, he took a walk around the house and confirmed all was as it should be. Down at the road a passing car drew his attention. He should probably call his parents and let them know he was here. Neighbors were few and far between out here, but they kept an eye on each other's property. His folks would no doubt get a call when the house lights were spotted tonight. Having his parents show up to investigate would not be a good thing. His mother had been complaining for years that she wanted grandchildren. Since his older siblings hadn't stepped up to the plate, his mother was now eyeing him to fill that void.

The image of little redheaded girls frolicking around the pond made his heart stumble. Shaking his head at the crazy fantasy, he carried the first load of grocery bags into the house. When he returned with the rest, Amber was putting away the refrigerated goods.

"You didn't tell me there was a basement with a wine cellar." She put the quart of milk in the fridge. "This is no run-of-the-mill cabin, sir."

"When my grandmother insisted on the kitchen expansion, my grandfather demanded the wine cellar with a smoking room."

A smile spread across her lips as she set the sandwich bread on the counter. Man, he loved the way she smiled. "Sounds like your grandfather knew how to drive a hard bargain."

"He did." Sean placed the bag of mixed greens in the fridge. "He died three years ago, barely three weeks after my grandmother."

"I'm so sorry."

He met her sympathetic gaze. "They were like that. Did everything together, and wherever one went, the other followed."

Sean had decided years ago his grandparents had the kind of love that couldn't be found anymore. People had stopped learning how to love that way. For the most part his parents' relationship wasn't far off the mark. He couldn't hope to ever share that kind of devotion with anyone.

"My grandparents were like that." Amber scooted onto a stool at the kitchen's center island. "My parents, too. I never really noticed until they retired and started traveling so much. It's like they've fallen in love with each other all over again. My sister says she and Gina have that deep bond. I'm not so sure people our age know how to love like that. Maybe we can't give so deeply."

"Is that what you're looking for?" He could have bitten off his tongue. Why the hell had he asked that damned question? Because he was this close—he mentally imagined his thumb and forefinger a fraction of an inch apart—to being a fool twice in one lifetime. At least he hadn't announced that he'd just been thinking the same thing. He'd already noticed far too many commonalities between them.

Her brow furrowed as she contemplated the question. He busied himself with stuffing the plastic grocery bags into the recycle bin.

"I absolutely want it, just not now. My career is top priority." She drew in a big breath. "Before I'm forty I'd like to be married and focused on making a family."

He allowed his gaze to rest on hers once more. The seriousness in her green eyes made his gut tighten. "Sounds like a plan."

He could see himself taking a similar path when he was older. Just another example of how alike they thought. Sean stopped himself. He was intensely attracted to Amber and they had a great deal in common, but that didn't mean they belonged together. *Get your head out of your—*

"Would you mind taking a walk with me?"

Sean blinked. "Sorry. What?"

"I've felt like a prisoner for two days. I need to get outside, breathe some fresh air and just walk off some of the stress. I hate to ask, but apparently I'm not supposed to go anywhere alone."

"Sure." He reached for the key. Usually he wouldn't bother locking up for a stroll around the property, but this was different. Until Thrasher and whoever else might be involved were found, Amber had to be protected.

The sky had darkened a little more but there was still plenty of daylight for a short walk. Over the years several paths had been formed along interesting views on the property. A long circle around the pond and then a meandering trail through the woods to the river. The air was crisp but not actually cold.

Maybe a walk had been a good idea.

"Do you come here every Christmas?"

The soft, lyrical sound of her voice meshed perfectly with the natural beauty around them. Funny how he noticed all those little things when he didn't want to. He should never have kissed her. That sweet taste would never be enough. "I do."

"I'll bet you cut your Christmas tree from these very woods."

Sean laughed. "We do actually. My grandfather insisted that two be planted for each one we cut. Every year on Christmas Eve, my parents drag two small evergreens up here to plant."

"Your grandfather was a smart man."

Sean wished he were a lot smarter and maybe he wouldn't be standing here dying to kiss her again. Then again, maybe what he really needed was courage.

Chapter Fourteen

The scent of marinara sauce filled the kitchen, and Amber's stomach grumbled. She placed the salad she'd prepared on the dining table. The long farmer's table seated ten. She could imagine the big family gatherings around the holidays. The large fireplace on the other side of the room would be roaring at Christmastime. The freshly cut tree would stand tall before the front window. She closed her eyes and imagined the smell of freshly baked cookies. Though her family holidays were usually celebrated in the city at her parents' Mountain Brook home, she'd gotten a taste of a true country Christmas as a child. Her grandparents on her mother's side had lived on a small farm in Blount County. She'd spent a few Christmases there.

She remembered the towering, freshly cut trees. Her grandparents always waited until Christmas Eve to place the final decoration on their tree. The star that topped its peak was saved for Amber's mother to set in place. Her grandmother insisted that her only child, Amber's mother, had placed that star atop the tree since she was old enough to hold it, and she wasn't letting go of that tradition as long as she was breathing.

By the time her grandmother reached thirty, she'd already been married with a daughter running around the home where she and her husband had started many wonderful traditions. Amber straightened the linen napkins next to the two plates. Her only traditions were spending holidays with her family—if work didn't get in the way. Those traditions were actually her parents', not hers. She didn't have any holiday traditions, or any other kind for that matter. She had work.

"Hot stuff headed your way," Sean announced as he moved around her to place the bowl of sauce and the mound of plated pasta on the table.

Amber bit her lips together to prevent mentioning that the food wasn't the only hot stuff in the room. Then and there she admitted defeat. The man got to her. He made her want to explore feelings she'd spent the past year telling herself she no longer cared about. After the breakup with her fiancé, she had decided she would wait a few years or ten before getting involved in another serious personal relationship. How had this man—in a mere seventy, give or take a few, hours—changed her mind so completely?

A hand waved in front of her face. "You still with me?"

Her gaze settled on his, and she melted a little more even as the sound of his deep voice made her shiver.

"Are you cold?" He rubbed his hands up and down her arms.

Her pulse skittered, and she mentally scrambled to find her voice. "No, no. I'm not cold at all." In fact, she was burning up.

"Sit." He pulled out a chair. "I'll run down to the cellar and get a bottle of wine."

Amber prepared her plate. A small serving of salad and pasta. The smell of the sauce had her mouth watering and her appetite resurrecting. Maybe eating was what she needed to take her mind off sex and Sean. Really, her inability to ignore her attraction to him surely had to do with twelve months of celibacy. Had she chosen to abstain from sex since the breakup? Not really. She simply hadn't taken the time to socialize.

The truth was she hadn't been on a date in six or seven months.

Sean returned with a bottle of wine and a bottle of water. He placed the bottle of water next to his glass and deftly opened the bottle of wine. He reached for her glass. "Say when."

Amber moistened her lips as he poured the red wine. "When," she remembered to say as the stemmed glass grew half full.

He set the bottle aside and claimed his chair. Rather than pour himself a glass of wine, he added water to his glass, and then reached for the pasta.

"You're not having wine?" She downed a hefty swallow to calm her nerves.

"Can't." He grinned as he smothered the angel-hair pasta with sauce.

The heat that had kindled inside her at just being in the same room with him extinguished. "Right. Of course. You're on duty." It was his job to be here with her.

She really, really was losing her grip. None of this was real. The silky texture of the full-bodied wine soured on her tongue. What was wrong with her? A man was dead, two innocent women—his victims—had been murdered. Being trapped on the radar of this former killing partnership had turned her life upside down. Had left her vulnerable to her own fundamental desires. The fear of death made her want to celebrate life. She downed another swallow of wine.

Since he'd already dug in, she forced herself to eat. Her appetite had vanished again, but she had the foresight to understand the wine would go straight to her head if she didn't eat. They had forgotten to pick up rolls. Saved her a few carbs.

"Is everything okay?"

She realized then that he'd already cleaned his plate and was going for seconds. "It's great." Another mouthful of wine covered the bitter taste of the lie.

He talked endlessly about his family and how much he'd missed the traditions when he'd lived in LA. To a large degree he felt the loving traditions of his family had helped him move past the tragedy. Amber hung on his every word—hard as she tried not to.

When he tossed his napkin aside, she realized he had stopped talking and was staring at her.

"Now I'm really worried."

She reached for her glass, but it was empty. She blinked and cleared her throat. "Worrying won't find the bad guy." She laughed. "We can do nothing but wait it out." The truth in her words made her shudder. There really was nothing she could do. For the first time in her adult life she felt helpless.

He reached out and entwined his fingers with hers. "This is hard—I know. We'll get to the bottom of what's going on soon. The BPD is moving quickly. Jess and Buddy are doing all they can." He squeezed her fingers. "I'm right here, and I'm not going anywhere until you're safe."

And then he would be gone.

Amber stood. "Thank you for a great meal. I'll be back to help clean up."

She hurried up the stairs to the room she'd chosen. She slammed the door shut and tried to calm her breathing. Squeezing her eyes shut, she cursed herself for jumping back into the pity pool. Her mood swings were about nothing more. She was a grown woman—an educated woman with a great career. There was no excuse for feeling sorry for herself. Yes, a bad man or men had put her life in danger, and, yes, her emotional neediness had prompted her to get all sentimental and filled with what-ifs, but this would be over eventually and she would be okay.

The least she could do was act like a grown-up about it instead of falling apart just because the man who had kissed her like she'd never been kissed before wasn't the knight in shining armor with whom she was destined to ride off into the sunset.

And then she laughed. When the laughter started, she couldn't stop it. Two women were dead, and she was upset because her bodyguard wasn't as enamored with her as she was with him.

A knock at the door had her wiping the tears from her eyes.

"You okay in there?"

Was she okay? *Absolutely not.* Would she be okay? *Probably.*

Squaring her shoulders and wiping her cheeks, she crossed to the door and opened it. "I'm perfectly fine."

He searched her face with those incredible blue eyes,

and she realized that he really was worried about her state of mind.

Amber laughed. Startled at her reaction, she pressed her fingers to her lips and muttered, "Sorry. I think I'm hysterical."

Concern lined his face. "Maybe I should get you another glass of wine."

Barely suppressing a second outburst of side-splitting laughter, she held up her hands stop-sign fashion. "No, no. Really, I'm fine. I just… I just…" She burst into tears. "Oh, God. I don't know what's wrong with me."

Could she do any more to embarrass herself? She simply could not get it together.

Sean pulled her into his strong arms and hugged her close. "Everything's going to be all right," he promised softly. "I'll keep you safe."

She drew away and shook her head. "I know the police will find Thrasher and whoever else is involved, and this will all be over eventually. That's not the reason I'm upset."

He squeezed her arm and smiled. "You're scared."

A burst of anger flared inside her, instantly drying the ridiculous tears. "I am not scared." She wasn't. She really wasn't. Not at the moment anyway. She had him… for protection.

He held up his hands in surrender. "Sorry. I'm only trying to help."

Calm down, Amber. It isn't his fault you're having trouble holding it together.

She smoothed a hand over her blouse and reclaimed her composure. "I apologize. I don't know why I fell apart there for a moment. I'm fine—I assure you. I should probably call it a night a little early."

Under no circumstances did she trust herself alone in the same room with him just now. She was on some sort of emotional roller coaster, and she had no idea where the tracks ran out. Ending up in bed with him was not where she wanted to crash-land tonight.

His face changed as if an epiphany had occurred to him. "Is this about that kiss last night?"

Her jaw dropped. The very idea that he would call it *that kiss* made her inexplicably angry. "What about the kiss? It happened in a moment of…a moment of neediness. It wasn't a big deal."

He frowned. "Ouch. I thought it was a huge deal." His gaze dropped to her lips. "I really hoped we might go for an encore." His gaze slid up to hers. "If you're as interested as it felt like you were."

A multitude of new sensations cascaded over her, shaking her newly regained composure. "I told you I don't do one-night stands." Even as she said the words she couldn't stop looking at his lips.

Before she could dodge the move, he had closed the short distance between them and forked his fingers into her hair. "Good, because I have no interest in a one-night stand with you." He pulled her mouth to his but hesitated before kissing her. "I want a whole lot more, starting with this."

He kissed her, his lips applying just the right amount of pressure. No matter that her mind was set to protest, her body melted against his. Her hands slid up his sculpted chest and curled around his neck. He cupped her bottom and lifted her into him, showing her the intensity of his desire.

"Say the word," he murmured against her lips, "and I'll stop."

"Don't stop." She kissed him hard, tangled her fingers in his hair and held his mouth firmly against hers.

He lifted her against him and carried her to the bed. They fell onto the plaid quilt together. He took his time undressing her and helping her nervous fingers undress him. It had been so long and she was so excited she couldn't seem to make her fingers work.

When they lay skin to skin, he slowed things down even more. He kissed her gently, tracing her face with his fingertips. She did the same, loving the ridges and planes of his handsome face. The high cheekbones and square jaw, the straight nose and strong brow. The silky feel of his blond hair and the amazing blue of his eyes.

He whispered sweet words to her as he kissed his way down her throat. *You're so beautiful. Your skin is so soft. Your hair drives me crazy.* He traced every inch of her with his lips and fingers, and she repeated each move with hers. By the time he moved on top of her, spreading her legs wide, she was gasping for air, her entire body pulsing with need.

They made love twice before moving to the shower and making love a third time. Afterward he dried her hair and teased her body to the point of insanity all over again. He brought her to climax again with those magic fingers and those equally skilled lips, and then he held her tight until she drifted off to sleep.

Friday, October 21, 6:30 a.m.

SEAN WOKE TO the sweet scent of Amber. He smiled and resisted the urge to wake her. He wanted to make love to her again, but he had to be sure she wanted to go there. Last night had been an emotional one for her. He didn't want her to look back and see one minute of their time together as a mistake.

He was serious when he'd told her he wanted more than just one night together. If he was lucky, she would want the same. The idea of a serious relationship had been the furthest thought from his mind. Since Lacy, he hadn't wanted to feel this way again. Amber Roberts had shattered his defenses and stolen his ability to resist without even trying. He was pretty sure she had been as surprised by the development as he was.

Her eyes opened, and she stared at him in surprise. Holding his breath, he hoped regret wouldn't be the next emotion he saw in those beautiful green eyes. A smile widened across her kiss-swollen lips, and happiness was what he saw in her gaze.

"Good morning," she whispered.

He grinned. "It's a damned good morning." He brushed her lips with his own. "I was thinking we'd make pancakes. You like pancakes?"

She nibbled at his lips with her teeth. "I haven't indulged in pancakes in forever, but I'm not really ready to get out of bed yet." One delicate hand slid along his hip until those cool fingers found his arousal. "It feels like you're ready for something besides breakfast."

He teased a rosy nipple with his tongue. "Always."

They made love slowly. Her soft whimpers made him want to go faster, made him want to plunge hard and deep into her over and over, but he refused to hurry. He wanted to show her how important she was to him. How much he adored every part of her. How much he wanted to know her innermost thoughts and secrets.

His body arched with the building need as she cried

out his name. He could hold back no longer. Still, he set an easy rhythm and pace, determined to make this last.

AFTER A SHOWER and a long morning walk, they were both ready for breakfast. She made the pancakes from a box of mix he found in the pantry. He brewed the coffee and rounded up the syrup.

"I don't know what your family does for the holidays," he ventured.

She licked her finger, making him smile. "Barb and Gina insist on hosting the family for Thanksgiving this year. We're eating lunch at one, so Barb and Gina can have the evening meal with the Colemans."

"That works out perfectly," he said, grabbing his courage with both hands. "Maybe you can come to dinner here with me and my family."

The smile started at one corner of her mouth and spread across her face, and the whole room lit up. "I could do that, if you're sure your family won't mind."

He downed a bite of pancake. "My family would be ecstatic. I warn you, though, they'll jump to conclusions. If you're not careful, my mother will start suggesting wedding venues."

Amber's tinkling laughter filled the air and made his heart glad. "I'm an expert at changing the subject."

He bit his tongue to prevent asking her if she had given up on the idea of weddings. He damned sure had— or he'd thought so. Funny, the notion of marriage didn't feel so difficult to imagine anymore. The realization should terrify him. Strangely it didn't.

Silence enveloped them for a minute or two. Sean recognized reality had intruded. They weren't kids punch-drunk after a night of incredible sex.

She set her fork aside. "What're we really doing, Sean?"

All of a sudden he didn't know how to answer that question. This—whatever it was—had happened so damned fast.

She nodded. "I can't answer the question, either." She exhaled a big breath. "I really like you. You make me feel things I haven't felt before, not even when I was wearing an engagement ring. I just don't know what it means."

"I'm in the same place." He shrugged. "I swore I'd never make this mistake again."

"Is that what *this* is? A mistake?"

The hurt in her eyes tightened his chest to the point where he couldn't draw in a decent breath. "I hope not." All that bravado he'd felt earlier abruptly deserted him. "I honestly don't know."

Obviously his answer wasn't the one she'd wanted to hear. "Wow. Okay." She stood and carried her plate to the sink.

Damn it. He grabbed his plate and joined her there. "I just meant—"

She backed away. "Let's not do this right now, okay?"

He piled his plate on top of hers and set his hands on his hips. "Is this your way of protecting your feelings? You just blow it off and walk away?" That was exactly what she was doing. Maybe instead of arguing he should take the easy way out and forget the whole damned thing.

"You're the one who called it a mistake."

Before he could respond, his cell in his pocket vibrated. He dug it out and glared at the screen. *The boss.* He dragged in a calming breath and answered. "Hey, boss. You have news?"

Sean listened to the update and tried to feel relief. Didn't happen. "Thanks. I'll let her know."

He ended the call and tucked his phone away. He had a bad feeling that what he was about to tell Amber would be the end of whatever *this* was. "The BPD found Thrasher. He's dead. He left a note apologizing for all he'd done."

Chapter Fifteen

"Peter Thrasher appears to have committed suicide. We can't officially call it a suicide until we have the autopsy report, but based on the ME's examination at the scene and the note he left, the preliminary call is suicide."

Lieutenant Chet Harper opened the folder in front of him and passed an eight-by-ten photo to Jess. Next to Sean, Amber tensed. He'd tried a dozen times on the way here to apologize for not being able to explain himself, but she refused to talk. She had been vulnerable, needy. He should have protected her without allowing personal feelings to get in the way. How could he make her see what he meant if she wouldn't hear him out?

He was supposed to be a professional. He was supposed to keep her safe. He'd fallen down on both counts and he'd taken advantage of her need to grab on to life with both hands. He had to find a way to explain to her that the mistake he'd meant hadn't been what she thought.

Jess passed the photo to Sean, yanking him back to the present. The preliminary report indicated Thrasher appeared to have taken an overdose of over-the-counter sleep aids. The empty bottle had been found in his pocket. Apparently when he'd abandoned his car, he'd hitched a ride to the greenhouses where he grew flowers. One of his employees, a worker who spoke little or no English, had given him a ride. The employee had no idea Thrasher was embroiled in a murder investigation. He claimed Thrasher acted like he always did. When they had arrived at the greenhouses, Thrasher had told everyone to take the rest of the week off with pay.

"Forensics found evidence from both victims, McCorkle and Pettie, on Thrasher's computer. He and Adler were sharing the videos via a cloud service."

Jess studied the forensic report before passing it to Sean. "Is there any possibility the evidence was planted?"

Sean had been about to ask the same question. As badly as he'd screwed up with Amber, he hadn't forgotten the case entirely.

"Are you suggesting that someone may have set up Thrasher?" Amber asked. "The potential third killer you mentioned before?"

"That's exactly what I'm suggesting," Jess confirmed. "Thrasher knew the BPD was looking for him and he goes to a greenhouse and puts himself to permanent sleep? Why not just disappear? Did he call anyone on his cell? This is not typical behavior for a serial killer, and I'm always suspicious of an alleged suicide note that ties everything up in a nice, neat little bow."

Chet Harper shook his head. "We haven't located his cell. We're hoping to have his cell phone records later today." Harper directed his attention to Amber. "The case will remain open until we've tied up the last of the loose ends, but we're confident Adler and Thrasher murdered McCorkle and Pettie. It's difficult to say who actually did the killing or if it was a joint effort. As for the potential third perpetrator, we'll either rule out the scenario or we'll find him." When he turned back to Jess, he flared his hands. "Any additional input you have is always extremely valuable to the team."

"I agree with your conclusions to a degree." Jess surveyed the photos and reports now spread across the table. "But we're missing something."

"One other thing." Harper reached into another folder and removed a report. He passed it to Amber. "The toxin that made you sick was azalea leaves. Someone chopped up the leaves and added them to your tea. Do you have a regular tea routine?"

Amber looked from the report to Harper. "I have a cup every evening when I get home from work."

"Adler and Thrasher would have known that routine," Harper said. "Since Thrasher worked with flowers and small shrubs, we checked the greenhouses. He was growing a variety of azaleas. The lab is attempting to determine if the leaves in your tea came from a plant in his greenhouse. The azalea leaves may have been added to your tea to disable you. One or both men were likely watching, prepared to act when the time was right for abducting you."

Sean gritted his teeth. The son of a bitch's carelessness with Amber's life made him want to beat the hell out of something...or someone.

"Did you find evidence that similar methods were used with McCorkle and Pettie?" Jess wanted to know.

"We've got the ME's office taking a second look," Harper confirmed. "Dr. Baron believes the screening tests wouldn't have picked up all potential plant toxins. She wants to run additional tests."

"I understand that the case is ongoing," Amber spoke up. "But are you saying Emma Norton and I are no longer in danger?"

Sean turned to Amber. She kept her gaze away from his. He'd made a mess of this morning and now she couldn't wait to get away from him. *Damn it.*

Harper and Jess exchanged a look. Harper said, "As far as the department is concerned, any threat these men posed no longer exists, but we are still investigating the possibility of a third person's involvement."

"I'm not completely comfortable with the facts in front of us," Jess said with obvious caution, "but to our knowledge the source of the threat is gone. If there is a third killer involved, he may believe he's tied up all the loose ends and will escape any consequences."

"But we can't be sure." The words were out of Sean's mouth before he'd taken the time to think through the statement.

All eyes were on him now. He might as well say the rest. "We can't say that Amber is no longer in danger until we rule out the third killer scenario."

A beat of silence echoed in the room.

"No doubt," Jess said, backing him up. "Amber." She turned her attention to the woman beside Sean. "The choice is yours. If you'd like to continue our security services a few days longer, we're more than happy to do so. Lieutenant Harper, I'm certain, will have more answers soon."

"I won't stop," Harper assured her, "until we know for certain. You have my word on that, Ms. Roberts."

Sean braced for Amber's decision.

"The cameras have been removed from my home," she said. "Adler and Thrasher are no longer a threat." She took a breath. "At this point, I feel secure on my own. I'll, of course, be watchful." She met the gaze of everyone at the table except Sean. "I appreciate all you and the BPD have done to bring a swift conclusion to this nightmare."

"Amber," Sean protested, "you should—"

"Get back to work." She stood. "I've had way more time off than I'm comfortable taking." She flashed a smile at Jess and Harper but still refused to even glance at Sean. "Thank you again."

"If you change your mind," Jess offered, "call. Day or night. We'll be there."

Amber gave her a nod and started for the door.

Sean pushed back from the conference table and followed her. He would owe his boss an explanation, but right now he couldn't let Amber leave this way.

"Amber, wait." He caught up with her at the elevator.

She jabbed the call button and reluctantly met his gaze. "We both have careers that need our attention, Sean. We don't need any distractions or personal entanglements. Spending more time together would complicate things. I'm not ready for complications. Clearly you aren't, either."

He touched her, wrapped his fingers around her forearm. Even that innocent contact made his pulse rush. "We should talk about us first."

For one instant he thought she was going to agree, but then her green eyes shuttered. "There is no us, Sean." She pulled free of his touch. "I have a very important event to attend tonight. Everybody who's anybody in Birmingham will be there—including your boss. I barely have time to pick up my dress from Martha's and get ready. Goodbye, Sean."

The elevator doors slid open, and she stepped inside. Sean watched her go. There was plenty he wanted to say, but none of it would come to him just now.

Eagle Ridge Drive, 2:00 p.m.

SEAN CLIMBED OUT of his car. Maybe he was way off base, but like his boss he wasn't convinced this case was as cut-and-dried as it seemed. It didn't feel right. He fully understood that part of what he felt was prompted by his feelings for Amber.

God almighty, he couldn't pretend those feelings didn't exist.

Problem was, he had his work cut out for him. Convincing Amber to give *them* a chance wasn't going to be easy. He had to find the right words to rebuild the trust he'd crushed with this morning's hurtful ones. Before he could worry about their relationship, he had to do whatever necessary to ensure she was safe.

He moved around to the back of Adler's house. What he was about to do was breaking and entering. At least the house was no longer a crime scene. His boss wouldn't be happy when she found out, but if he found a connection to a third killer, she would likely let his methods slide. He removed the lock pick from his pocket, glanced around and set to the task. He'd learned how to pick a lock from Buddy Corlew, but he wasn't supposed to tell Jess.

The door opened easily. Inside the place still smelled like blood. He wasn't exactly clear on what he expected to find. Mostly he intended to look until he was satisfied there was nothing to find. He pulled on a pair of latex gloves and started with the living room.

He scanned the framed photos, the books, unopened mail. As he moved through the house he checked drawers, shelves, cabinets and closets. Nothing.

Before closing the door to Adler's bedroom closet, he hesitated. Might as well check the guy's pockets and shoes. One by one, Sean went through his jackets, his shirts and his trousers. Nothing in the pockets.

"Damn it."

There was only one thing to do. Check out Thrasher's place.

Unfortunately, it was still a crime scene.

Killough Circle, 3:30 p.m.

SEAN WAS INSIDE Thrasher's house without a glitch. As he did at Adler's place, he moved from room to room, checking every available space.

He'd almost called it a bust, when he backed up to check a framed photo next to the television. A younger Thrasher with a couple of buddies. It wasn't the sort of thing the cops would consider relevant; still it was worth a look.

"Well, hell." Sean picked up the photo and scrutinized at it. There were three guys. Thrasher was in the middle, Adler on the left. Sean studied the dark-haired guy on the right. The kid, seventeen or eighteen, looked vaguely familiar. He flipped the frame over and removed the back. As he'd hoped, the names were written on the back of the photo. Thrasher, Adler and Guynes. Where had he heard that name? The three looked high school age. The clothes were definitely last decade's.

Sean went back to the spare bedroom and opened the closet door. School yearbooks were piled on the top shelf. He grabbed the stack and went through the autographed pages. The threesome had been friends for years. Maybe they'd lost touch, but then why keep the framed photo displayed? People, especially men, didn't do that unless the people in the photograph were more than a little important to their lives.

The senior yearbook gave him the answer he was looking for. Delbert Guynes had been injured in a football game his senior year. Making the winning touchdown, he'd suffered a spinal cord injury, which had left him paralyzed from the waist down. Sean skimmed the dedication page. Guynes was touted as a hero, as was his mother who always tailored the cheerleader uniforms.

Martha Guynes... Martha Sews.

She had spoken as if she hardly knew Adler. She certainly hadn't mentioned that her son and Adler were best friends all through high school.

Amber was picking up a dress there today.

Sean shook his head. The theory didn't make sense. Delbert Guynes was paralyzed and sentenced to using a wheelchair for the rest of his life. He was a big video game player. Did that mean he was also a computer buff? What did a guy whose life consisted of being stuck in a wheelchair and under his mother's thumb do for fun... or for pleasure? *The videos.* Maybe the cameras had been for Delbert.

Still, how could Delbert be involved with Adler and Thrasher's criminal activities without his mother knowing?

Memories from his and Amber's visit to the shop

the other day flashed one after the other through Sean's mind.

Were those shrubs lining the front of her shop azaleas?

Martha Sews, 4:30 p.m.

AMBER PEERED OVER her shoulder at the mirror. The back of the dress looked great. She smiled. "It's perfect, Martha." She turned back to the lady who had single-handedly kept Amber's wardrobe fitting right for years now. Being what the fashion world considered petite was a real pain. Not even the most expensive labels managed to make clothes that fit her body. "I don't know what I'd do without you."

Martha beamed. "I love taking care of you, Amber. You're my favorite customer."

Amber gave her another big smile before stepping back into the dressing room. "I'll change and pay so you can call it a day." It had to be five already. Thankfully that still left her enough time to get ready.

"Take your time. I'm locking up," Martha called. "Would you like some tea before you fight the rush hour traffic?"

Arching her back, Amber reached for the zipper. "Oh, that would be wonderful."

"Paradise Peach still your favorite?"

Amber almost stumbled stepping out of the dress. "Yes." She cleared her throat. "But whatever you have will be fine." Her stomach roiled. The ugly few hours she'd endured the other night had made her wonder if she would ever drink another cup of her favorite tea. Her response to Martha had been automatic. Amber's grandmother had taught her to love hot tea. Louisa Roberts would be immensely offended that someone would use tea as a weapon.

"I have tea cakes if you'd like one," Martha called. "You should treat yourself more often, Amber. You deserve it."

Amber paused again as she wiggled into the unwashed jeans she'd bought yesterday. She tugged the sweater on next. The memory of rushing through the discount store grabbing clothes with Sean made her heart hurt. How had he stolen a place in her heart in a mere four days? She hadn't meant to let that happen, but control had been taken from her so quickly her head was still spinning. Walking out of that meeting on her own today had been her way of taking back control. Adler and Thrasher were dead. She would be okay.

"You'll love the cakes," Martha said loud enough for Amber to hear. "They're my grandmother's recipe."

Evicting thoughts of Sean, Amber considered that she really wouldn't have time to eat before heading to the fund-raiser. A quick snack would be nice. "I would love a tea cake."

She stepped out of the dressing room, and Martha was waiting for her. Amber jumped.

"I'm sorry. I didn't mean to startle you, dear." She took the dress from Amber's hand. "Come along before your tea gets cold."

"You don't want me to pay you first?" Amber followed her to the kitchen.

"That won't be necessary." Martha draped the dress across the back of a chair. "Sit down and I'll serve."

Amber exhaled, feeling a burst of uncertainty. What was wrong with her? This was Martha. She'd known her for years. There was time before she had to get dressed. She needed to relax. If she were honest with herself, she would admit that it was Sean. Making love with him had touched her in a place no one had reached before. It was ridiculous. She barely knew the man and somehow it felt as if they'd always known each other. He felt like the perfect fit…her other half.

Ridiculous. Tomorrow Sean would wake up and realize the circumstances had triggered an out-of-control moment, and he'd never think of her again.

"Amber?"

She snapped to attention. "I'm sorry—what did you say?"

"I was asking about your friend Mr. Douglas."

"Oh." Amber accepted the cup of tea. "His assignment concluded."

"So you were working together." Martha gestured to a chair. She then placed a tea cake on a delicate china plate and set it in front of Amber.

"We were." *Close enough*, she supposed as she sipped the warm refreshment.

"He seemed like a nice young man." Martha settled into a chair across the table from Amber. "Quite handsome. I thought he was smitten with you—the way he looked at you, I mean."

"I…don't think so." Amber sipped her tea to avoid saying more.

"You certainly appeared quite taken with him."

Before Amber could protest, a howl reverberated through the house.

Martha jumped up from her seat. "Delbert?" She rushed from the room.

Amber sat there for a moment, wondering if she

should check to see if everything was all right. The silence that followed felt entirely wrong. She should see if Martha and her son were okay.

Amber stood and the room tilted.

Good grief. What was wrong with her?

She stared at the porcelain cup. *The tea.*

Where was her phone? Her purse?

Turning around, Amber grabbed at that table to maintain her balance.

"Now, now, take care there."

Amber tried to steady herself. Martha was suddenly at her side, guiding her forward. At least it felt as if they were moving.

"Martha…" Amber's tongue wouldn't work right. She felt horribly ill. Vomiting felt imminent.

"Don't you worry, dear. I'm going to take extra good care of you."

Amber leaned heavily on Martha. She couldn't hold herself up anymore. She tried to plead with her…but the words wouldn't come out.

"Here she is, Delbert."

Amber felt her body plop into a chair. The room was shifting again. In front of her a man in a wheelchair stared at her. Delbert. Martha's son. Behind him the computer screen that usually sported a video game was focused on a small room. Was that the dressing room she'd just been using to try on the dress? Amber groaned. She couldn't be sure. Her vision kept fading in and out. She just didn't know. She felt horribly sick.

"We thought we'd lost you," Martha was saying.

What was she talking about?

"You're the one he wanted," Martha cooed. "Of all the ones we offered, it was you he wanted."

Amber didn't understand. She tried to move. Couldn't.

"Rhiana turned out to be nothing but a whore." Martha heaved a big sign as she knelt in front of Amber and tied her feet together.

Amber told herself to pull away from her. To get up and run, but her legs wouldn't work.

"And Kimberly was a closet alcoholic. He just didn't like either of the two the boys and I picked out for him. It was you. It had always been you. He'd been watching you for years. He said you were perfect. You were the one. I even tried to discourage him. How could someone as famous as you be bothered, but then I understood what I had to do. I had to make you available."

Amber tried again to cry out. She tried to get up. Her body wouldn't work.

"And those stupid so-called friends of his almost ruined everything. You just can't depend on anyone anymore. They were only supposed to install the cameras on the candidates. But I knew when Kimberly went missing that they were up to something. The bastards were messing with those girls, and they killed them. But don't worry—I took care of those idiots. As soon as I found out what they were up to, I made them pay. All I had to do after that was find a way to get you here. I'm sorry about the tea the other night. That wasn't supposed to happen until I was ready. You'll be fine, though. I was careful about the dosage."

She tied Amber's wrists together. "Now. We're ready. I'm going to be taking you and Delbert to a special place where no one will ever bother us. You are to love him and take care of him from now on. He's ready for a life of his own, and he has chosen you to share it with him. I'll make sure you have whatever you need."

Another of those eerie howls echoed in the room.

"Hush now, Delbert. She's all yours." Martha got to her feet. "You can play with her all you want, every day from now on, and she'll take good care of you."

Amber closed her eyes in an effort to stop the spinning. She had to do something.

Martha screamed, and Amber's eyes snapped open. *Sean.*

Her heart leaped. He was here.

He and Martha struggled. Amber tried to keep her eyes open, but she couldn't.

The darkness consumed her…and then the silence.

UAB Hospital

AMBER OPENED HER EYES. She felt weak. Her brain seemed swaddled with cotton. She remembered throwing up in the ambulance. She remembered… *Sean.* He'd been right beside her through it all.

"There you are." His blue eyes twinkled as he smiled at her.

Her heart squeezed. She really liked his smile. She like his eyes and everything else about him. "Martha… oh, my God." Her mouth felt cotton dry. "She's done my alterations for years. How did you know?"

"Thrasher kept a framed photo of him and his best buds from high school—Kyle Adler and Delbert Guynes. I couldn't get the idea out of my head that there was a third player in all this. When I saw that photo, I knew I was right."

Amber reached for the water on the bedside table. "Let me do that." Sean poured water in the cup and added a bendable straw; then he held it to her lips. "This should help."

The water cooled her raw throat. She drew back and he set the cup aside. "I don't see how Martha thought she could get away with this." Amber shook her head. "They were helping her find a caregiver for Delbert. Why in the world would she do something so insane? She always seemed so normal." The whole idea was ludicrous.

"Jess called a little while ago and gave me an update." Sean's expression turned somber. "Martha is dying. It's cancer. The doctors have given her maybe six months to live. She doesn't want her son in some institution. When she found out Thrasher and Adler were using her shop to video women changing and then sharing that video with her son, she threatened to call the police."

"Wait." Amber's brain was still a little fuzzy from the poisoned tea. "Why did she threaten to call the police?"

"To make them cooperate with her. At some point after that she found out they were using the women for sex slaves. She killed Adler when she found out he was obsessed with you. She was after Thrasher next, so he killed himself. He knew his life was over anyway, so he ended it himself. Martha found him and left the note."

"The whole thing is just horrible." Amber fiddled with the edge of the stiff sheet. "What happens to Delbert now?"

Sean took her hands in his. "He'll be placed in a facility and receive the care he needs. It isn't what his mother wanted, but there's no other family. The important thing is that you're safe now and the Pettie and McCorkle families don't have to wonder if their daughters' killers will get away with murder."

"You were right." Amber squeezed his hand, tears burning in her eyes. "Still waters do run deep."

"Sometimes being right is not so much fun." He leaned forward and kissed her forehead.

"I was thinking," she ventured. "I feel like maybe it's time we learned how to have a real personal life. Together, I mean. Unless, of course, you really believe what happened was a mistake."

"You're behind the curve, Roberts." He grinned and shot her a wink. "I've already started. For the record, I never thought what happened between us was a mistake. I worried that the circumstances were the wrong time and place." He kissed her hands. "I don't care what brought me to you, all that matters is that I found you. I want to explore what we have more than I want to see the sun come up tomorrow."

That was the best news she'd heard all week. "I'm sure we can arrange for both to happen."

"Good." He kissed her lips this time.

Amber closed her eyes and savored the sound of his deep voice as he promised her the world. As soon as she was out of this hospital she intended to hold him to every single one of those promises.

Chapter Sixteen

3309 Dell Road, Mountain Brook, 9:00 p.m.

"She's growing too fast." Jess smoothed the hair back from her sweet baby girl's face.

Dan tucked the pink blanket around Bea. He turned to Jess, took her by the hands and drew her away from their daughter's crib. "She'll always be our little girl no matter how big she gets."

Jess leaned into his chest and closed her eyes as his arms went around her. "Is she going to be jealous of her little brother?" Jess peered up at him. "I don't think I could bear it if they hate each other when they become teenagers. Lil and I went through that stage, you know."

"You need some hot cocoa." Dan kissed her forehead and ushered her from Bea's room.

He looked back one last time before turning out the light. The princess night-light kept the room from being completely dark. Jess had always been afraid of the dark. She hoped her children weren't, but just in case she intended to make sure they felt safe.

"We have to finish decorating your son's room soon. He'll be here before we know it." She was feeling a little overwhelmed lately. The agency was off to a great start and even Sean had turned out to be a top-notch member of the team. Still, there was just so much to do, and she felt tired all the time.

Dan guided her to her favorite chair in their family room. Toys were scattered all over the floor. Jess groaned. She had sworn she would never be one of those people—the ones who spoil their children with far too many toys. And look at their home. Toys were lying about in every room.

"You sit tight, and I'll make the hot chocolate." He backed toward the door and stumbled when the stuffed animal he stepped on made a high-pitched sound. He swore under his breath and snatched up the pink bear to ensure it still worked. It did not.

"You killed it," Jess warned. "You better get rid of it before she notices."

Dan nodded. "Good idea."

He hurried away, damaged pink bear in hand.

Jess huffed out a big breath. This was her mother-in-law's fault. Katherine spoiled Bea endlessly. "Like you don't," she muttered.

With much effort and no shortage of groaning, Jess hefted herself out of the big plush chair and followed the path Dan had taken to the kitchen. He'd just put the milk in the microwave. She slid onto a stool at the island and watched as he readied the instant cocoa mix. It might be instant, but it tasted like the real thing. With a toddler in the house, they had both learned to appreciate plenty of *instant* fixes.

"What's on your mind?" Her handsome husband leaned on the island and studied her. "I can always tell when you're unsettled."

It was true. They had been in love since they were teenagers and could read each other like a book.

"This case reminded me of the one that brought me back home." The similarities were disturbing.

Dan nodded. "Me, too. I was terrified Andrea would end up dead, like the two women in this case."

Jess placed her hand on his arm and smiled. "But she didn't. She's in her senior year of college and doing great." Andrea was Dan's stepdaughter from a previous marriage. Though the marriage had been over for years, Dan still loved Andrea. Jess did, as well. She was a wonderful young woman.

"She didn't because you found her when no one else could." He touched Jess's cheek. "I am so thankful you came back to me."

"This is where I was always supposed to be."

The microwave dinged and he straightened away from the island. "First you had to go catch all those serial killers for the FBI."

She rubbed her belly as Dan prepared her cocoa. One of those bad guys had followed her back to Birmingham and no matter that two years had passed since she ended his reign of terror, he still haunted her sometimes.

The steaming cocoa appeared in front of her, marshmallows floating on top. "Drink up before it gets cold."

She arranged her lips into a smile. "Thank you. Where's yours?"

"I—" he reached into the fridge "—am having a beer."

She made a face. "Don't brag."

He twisted the top off the glass bottle. "The case brought up memories of Spears and Holmes." He traced his fingers over her forehead. "Whenever you're worried about a case you frown. And since the big case B&C was investigating is closed, it has to be about those two bastards."

He knew her too well. "Spears is dead. I don't worry about him. It's all his sick followers that keep me awake sometimes." Ted Holmes had tried his best to reenact Spears's obsession with her. He'd gotten far too close to her child. "I've had my moments since leaving the department," she confessed, "when I thought I'd made a mistake. That maybe I couldn't do as much to stop the evil out there."

Dan held his tongue and allowed her to continue in her own time.

"This case showed me I made the right decision." She held up her mug. "To the future."

Dan tapped her mug with his bottle of beer. "Hear, hear."

One more face of evil down. Jess sipped her hot cocoa and relished the victory.

* * * * *

"Are you out of your mind? Get back in the raft."

He leaned forward and stole a quick kiss. "You can slap me later. I've got a job to do." He rolled over the side and eased into the water without making much of a splash. His heart pounded as he stared at the tall grass near a mound of sticks and mud. He'd stay as far away from the alligator nest as he could, but he had to get the raft beneath the trees before the people in the helicopter spotted them.

Grabbing the tow line from the front of the raft, he held on tight and sidestroked, pulling the loaded craft with him. Everyone helped by paddling with their hands. They moved faster than they had before, but not fast enough to make the trees before the helicopter swung around and headed their way.

"Duck!" Quentin called out.

As the chopper neared, the sound of a machine-gun blast ripped through the air, but bullets didn't hit the water near the raft.

NAVY SEAL TO DIE FOR

BY
ELLE JAMES

All rights reserved including the right of reproduction in whole or in part in any form. This edition is published by arrangement with Harlequin Books S.A.

This is a work of fiction. Names, characters, places, locations and incidents are purely fictional and bear no relationship to any real life individuals, living or dead, or to any actual places, business establishments, locations, events or incidents. Any resemblance is entirely coincidental.

This book is sold subject to the condition that it shall not, by way of trade or otherwise, be lent, resold, hired out or otherwise circulated without the prior consent of the publisher in any form of binding or cover other than that in which it is published and without a similar condition including this condition being imposed on the subsequent purchaser.

® and ™ are trademarks owned and used by the trademark owner and/or its licensee. Trademarks marked with ® are registered with the United Kingdom Patent Office and/or the Office for Harmonisation in the Internal Market and in other countries.

First Published in Great Britain 2016
By Mills & Boon, an imprint of HarperCollins*Publishers*
1 London Bridge Street, London, SE1 9GF

© 2016 Mary Jernigan

ISBN: 978-0-263-91918-9

46-1016

Our policy is to use papers that are natural, renewable and recyclable products and made from wood grown in sustainable forests. The logging and manufacturing processes conform to the legal environmental regulations of the country of origin.

Printed and bound in Spain
by CPI, Barcelona

Elle James, a *New York Times* bestselling author, started writing when her sister challenged her to write a romance novel. She has managed a full-time job and raised three wonderful children, and she and her husband even tried ranching exotic birds (ostriches, emus and rheas). Ask her, and she'll tell you what it's like to go toe-to-toe with an angry three-hundred-and-fifty-pound bird! Elle loves to hear from fans at ellejames@earthlink.net or www.ellejames.com.

I dedicate this book to all of my readers. If not for you and your voracious reading habits, I would not have the career of my dreams. I consider myself lucky to have found what I want to be when I "grow up" and that I'm living that dream now. Thank you all from the bottom of my heart. Happy reading!

Chapter One

"Ahh, this is the way to travel." US Navy SEAL Quentin Lovett yawned and stretched, burrowing into the contoured seat of the Stealth Operations Specialists corporate jet. "I've never felt more rested. This beats commercial flights, hands down." He chuckled. "I don't even want to compare it to the back of a C-130."

"Don't get used to it, Loverboy." Dutton Calloway, Duff to his friends, sat with his eyes closed, his head tipped back across the aisle from Quentin.

"Maybe you should switch branches of service." Becca Smith blinked her eyes open and cocked her eyebrows at Quentin in the seat beside her.

"What? And give up the glamorous life of a navy SEAL?" Quentin lifted Becca's hand and brushed her knuckles with a light kiss. "Although, if I got to work with a pretty little thing like you, I might consider giving up the swamps and the honor of getting mud beneath my fingernails."

She frowned and pulled her hand from his. "Forget it, frogman. You're not getting into my pants. My mamma told me about guys like you."

He chuckled. "That you would be lucky to have a man as handsome and talented as I am?"

"No, that navy guys have a woman in every port and shove off when things get a little too permanent for them."

Duff, his six-foot-three-inch SEAL teammate, laughed. "She's got your number, Loverboy."

Quentin grinned. "We're just getting warmed up."

Becca gave Quentin a glance that should have chilled him to the bone, but he didn't give up easily.

"Before she knows it, she'll be madly in love with me." Quentin winked at Becca.

She rolled her eyes, leaned forward and asked Duff, "Is he really that full of himself, or is he pulling my leg?"

Duff cracked open an eyelid. "I suspect he's a bit of both."

Natalie Layne rested a hand on Duff's. "I'm so glad you're not a ladies' man."

Duff's other eyelid rose, exposing his green eyes. "Who said I wasn't?"

Quentin snorted. "Please. Leave the art of seduction to the pro."

Sawyer Houston laughed out loud behind Quentin. "Says the man striking out with the beautiful lady."

Becca raised her hand above the chair. "Thanks for the compliment."

"Not that I think she's more beautiful than you," Sawyer added for the benefit of Jenna Broyles, the woman riding in the plane beside him.

"I'm not opposed to my man looking, as long as he's not sampling," Jenna said.

Duff closed his fingers around Natalie's hand. "Sawyer has a point, Quentin. I've got a gorgeous babe. What have you got?"

Quentin loved the banter between him and his team-mates. He loved a challenge even more, and Becca Smith was a challenge. The way he saw it, he had until the plane landed in Mississippi to win her over and se-cure a date with the incredibly beautiful and extremely uptight lady, who intrigued him to the point of obses-sion.

She was wound up so tight, Quentin considered it his duty and responsibility to help her loosen up. He'd dedicated the flight from Cancun to Mississippi to win-ning over the pretty secret agent's interest. In the past few hours, he'd failed to get more than a "drop dead" glare out of her. His time was quickly running out. He had yet to succeed in his mission.

"Sawyer, I'm surprised your father agreed to go along with the faked death scenario," Becca com-mented.

"*You're* surprised?" Sawyer huffed out a breath. "I was floored. The man never had time for anything other than politics. I swear he didn't know my name half the time. My father had a cot set up in his office. He spent so many late nights working, it made more sense for him to sleep there."

"Must have been hard for you and your mother," Jenna commented.

"Nah. We were used to it. You don't miss what you never had."

Quentin could relate. His father had left him and his mother when Quentin was five. His mother, destitute and with a young mouth to feed, was forced to move in with her parents on their Iowa farm. His grandfather had been his male role model, for which he was for-ever grateful. He'd raised him to appreciate the fruits of a hard day's labor. Nothing in this world was worth anything if it was easy to attain.

Thus his interest in Becca. The woman who'd shown up in Cancun, Mexico, on what should have been Quentin's relaxing vacation, and helped them keep Sawyer alive when an assassin was hell-bent on ending his life.

"Speaking of assassins," Quentin said aloud.

"No one was speaking of assassins until you just brought it up," Benjamin "Montana" Raines said and yawned. "Could ya shut up for the next thirty minutes until we land? I haven't gotten my full three-hours' sleep in on the flight."

"You wouldn't have needed it, if you hadn't stayed up until four in the morning," Sawyer grumbled. "And then dragged yourself in, waking everyone up."

"Can I help that the last night of vacation they had to have Country Western Night at the resort?"

Quentin shook his head. "I didn't know one man could two-step for six hours straight."

"I've got stamina, unlike some of you boneheads." Montana pushed his cowboy hat down over his eyes. "Seriously, could you hold it down?"

"I've been thinking."

His buddies all groaned.

"No, really." Quentin frowned. "Just because we took care of the assassin-for-hire who'd been gunning for our buddy Sawyer, it doesn't mean that dirty dog is dead."

"What are you talking about?" Duff asked.

"Someone wanted Rand Houston, aka Sawyer's father, out of the way and was willing to use Sawyer as bait to get him to Cancun in order to get a clear shot at him. We got his hired gun, but the man who hired him is still on the loose."

"Your point?" Duff prompted.

"Who's going after him?" Quentin persisted.

"I don't know," Sawyer said. "But we have to report back to Stennis as soon as we get back. Which won't be much longer. We should see land soon."

Quentin leaned over Becca to stare out the window. Just as Sawyer said, land was within sight.

"Do you mind?" Becca said, her brows hiked. "If you're that interested in the scenery below, I'd be happy to swap seats with you."

Slowly leaning back in his seat, Quentin gave her one of his best smiles. His mother always said he could charm the chickens out of the trees with that smile. "Instead of agreeing to swap seats, why don't you agree to have dinner with me when we land?"

"I told you, I'm not interested." She turned her shoulders toward the window, effectively cutting him off.

"Okay, I get it. You don't want to go out with me for dinner. How about lunch?"

She drew in a slow, steadying breath and let it out. "No."

"Coffee?"

"No."

Undaunted, Quentin grinned. "You're making it really hard for me to get to know you."

"Not my problem. That one's all on you."

"Tell you what," Quentin said. "Before you reject me, give me one kiss. If the chemistry isn't there, I won't pursue you anymore."

"You'll leave me completely alone?" she asked.

Quentin nodded and held up his hand. "I promise."

"Fine. One kiss." She leaned toward him.

He faced her, puckering.

Becca reached out and turned his cheek. "On the cheek."

"How are you supposed to gauge the chemistry with a kiss on the cheek?" he protested.

"Not my problem." When she swooped in to land her kiss, Quentin turned at the last minute and caught her lips with his.

Her eyes widened, her breath hitched, but she didn't back away.

Quentin cupped the back of her neck and deepened the kiss, pressing her closer.

She gasped, her lips parting for a second. Long enough for Quentin to slip his tongue past her teeth for a taste of her. *Mmm.* Rum and coconuts from the drink she'd had earlier. So sweet and amazing, he almost groaned. When he lifted his head, he smiled down at her. "Was that so bad?" he asked.

Her drooping eyelids popped wide and she slapped him hard on the cheek she had intended on kissing.

Quentin could swear the plane shook with the force of the blow.

"What the hell?" Duff shouted, sitting up.

The plane shook and shuttered.

"Ladies and gentlemen, we've lost power to the engine and will be making an emergency landing," the captain said over the loud speaker. "Please check your seatbelts and hold on."

It took Quentin a full second to realize the slap he'd deservedly received had not impacted the plane. "What happened?" he asked, tightening his belt.

"Felt like we were hit," Sawyer said.

Quentin pressed a hand to his stinging cheek. Oh, he'd been hit all right. But the plane? "By what?"

"I don't know," Duff said. "But you better hunker down. It's gonna be a rough landing."

With the plane shaking like an old truck on a gravel road, Quentin doubted the landing would be an easy one.

A feminine hand slipped into his and he held on to it.

"Just for the record," Becca said. "You deserved that slap."

If he'd thought the dire situation would encourage her to apologize, he was sorely disappointed. "It was worth it. You taste so good. If I die in this crash, I will have died a happy man."

"Jerk," she whispered, but didn't let go of his hand as the plane pitched, dipped and plunged toward the ground at a terrifying speed. "For the record, if I make it out of this alive, I'm still going after the man who killed my father."

"I believe you," Quentin said. "If I can get more time off from my unit, I'll go with you."

"I don't need an amateur getting in my way."

"I'm not an amateur, I'm a SEAL."

"Yeah and you're used to kicking ass and shooting anything that moves. My kind of work takes finesse, something you are clearly lacking."

"Ouch," Quentin said.

"Loverboy, I believe you've been put in your place." Duff chuckled. "Give it up. She's not into you."

Quentin snorted. "This frogman won't give up without a fight."

"Yeah?" Montana said from the back. "Seems we're going down *with* a fight, now."

And he was right. It seemed as if the ground outside the window rushed up to meet them. Make that the *water* rushed up to meet them.

The pilot brought the plane in on a marsh, the only gap between tall cypress trees. The belly of the aircraft slid across the smooth surface like a hovercraft until it hit a berm of land, barely jutting a foot into the air.

The plane jolted hard on impact; the tail lifted and then crashed down with a big splash.

Throwing aside her seatbelt, the flight attendant ran for the emergency exit and struggled to open the exterior door.

Quentin released his seatbelt and hurried to help. Together they managed to open the door, the steps falling into the water.

"There are flotation devices beneath each seat," the attendant called out.

Quentin glanced out the door and shook his head. "I suggest we all get into the life boat or do our best to stay with the plane until help arrives. You do not want to get in that water."

"Why?" Duff staggered up the aisle to join him at the door.

"I believe we've landed in the middle of an alligator farm."

BECCA ROSE FROM her seat aboard the downed aircraft, shaken but refusing to show how much the crash-landing had scared her. She'd been shot at, held hostage and beaten by one of the meanest sons of a bitch known to the drug-dealing mafia, but never had she been in an airplane crash.

If Quentin hadn't been next to her, teasing her and holding her hand, she might have dissolved into a very embarrassing case of feminine hysterics.

On the ground…or in the water…they had survived. A few alligators were nothing compared to the instant death of a plane hitting the ground and completely disintegrating like she'd seen happen at the Baltimore International Airport one snowy evening a long time ago.

Her father had brought her to the airport to greet her mother after she'd been on a work trip to California. Becca had missed her mother, and looked forward to being held and cuddled in her arms. They'd watched as her mother's plane approached the airport on schedule. It appeared to be a perfect landing until a wing dipped and the entire plane performed something like a cartwheel on the runway.

Her father cursed and pulled the young Becca into his arms to hide her view of the burning wreckage. No one survived. Her beautiful mother would never come home, never hold her close or sing her to sleep at night.

Her heart hammered against her ribs and her belly soured at the memory. Where her mother had not escaped, Becca had cheated death in the SOS corporate jet. All her life, she'd flown in airplanes, pushing back the fear of crashing. Today she imagined what her mother might have felt when she realized the plane was going to crash. She could only hope it had happened so fast that none of the passengers had time to be afraid.

"Hey."

A gentle hand on her arm brought her out of her memories and back to the problem at hand.

"Are you okay?" Quentin asked.

"Yeah. I'm fine," she lied, barely able to stand on wobbly knees. Bile churned in her gut again, threatening to find a rapid path out if she didn't reach open air immediately.

She shoved Quentin to the side and staggered toward the doorway, where the flight attendant and Duff struggled with a life raft, blocking the exit.

"I need to get out," Becca said, her voice strained.

"You'll have to wait until we get this raft the right side up," the attendant said.

"You don't understand. I. Need. Out. Now." She shoved them aside, pushed the raft out of her way and jumped out of the plane into the water.

She hit at an angle and sank below the surface, sucking fetid swamp water up her nose. Panicking, and fighting to get her feet under her, Becca couldn't tell which way was up. She flapped and kicked, but couldn't get turned the right direction.

Something splashed next to her and an arm wrapped around her waist and yanked her out of the dark, dank water and into the bright sunshine.

Becca coughed and sputtered, gagging on the nasty water. All the while those strong arms held her, letting her get her feet beneath her on the silt bottom of the marsh.

The life raft plopped into the water beside them.

"Better?" Quentin's voice sounded in her ear, his breath warm on her cheek.

She nodded, still unable to form coherent sentences.

"Good, because a couple of alligators spotted us. They're on their way and we're getting out of the water now." He hauled her up and over the edge of the life raft, tossing her like a rag doll. Then he planted his hands on the sides and dragged himself up and in, along with enough water to threaten the small craft.

Her heart beating so fast she thought it might explode out of her chest, Becca peered over the side of the inflatable raft. The dark surface of the water appeared smooth, but there was tall grass all around. "I don't see any alligators," she said.

Quentin didn't answer. He'd turned back to the aircraft, smoke billowing up from the engine in the tail. "Everyone out!" he shouted. He reached up as Natalie Layne appeared in the doorway. "Lose the shoes."

She kicked off her high heels and leaned out into Quentin's arms. The raft rocked with the added weight. One by one, the SEAL team and Lance climbed into the raft, followed by the flight attendant, pilot and copilot.

Once everyone was on board the rubber raft, Quentin said, "Now let's get away from the fuselage before the aviation fuel ignites." The SEALs dug their arms into the water and paddled, doing the best they could to move the unwieldy craft through the marsh waters and away from the plane.

They hadn't gone more than the length of a football field when an explosion rocked the air.

Quentin shoved Becca into the bottom of the raft and threw himself over her body. Debris dropped into the water around them.

Quentin jerked and cursed. Then he sat up and looked back.

Without his weight on her, Becca sat up and followed his gaze. A mushrooming cloud of flame and smoke rose into the air.

Becca clutched the side of the raft, her body shaking. "Damn, that was close."

"Yeah." Quentin ripped his shirt open and dragged it off his shoulders, wincing as he did so.

"Hey, Loverboy," Montana said. "You took a hit."

Quentin nodded, his jaw tight.

"Let me see." Becca scooted around to get a look at his back.

A jagged piece of metal about two inches long stuck out of the man's shoulder. "Pull it out," he said through gritted teeth.

Becca bit her lip. She'd been trained to leave embedded objects for a surgeon to extract. But with no surgeon around, and no telling how long it would be until someone found them, she couldn't let him suffer. Picking up Quentin's discarded shirt, she wrapped it around the sharp edges of the metal and paused. "This might hurt a little."

"Just do it." Quentin's jaw tightened and he clenched his fists.

Before he finished his command, she gripped and pulled. The shard was only an inch deep, but once removed, the blood flowed.

"Here." Duff pulled his T-shirt over his head and handed it to Becca, along with a knife. She cut the shirt into long strips, wadded one into a pad and pressed it to the wound. "Hold this there," she said to Duff.

Duff held the pad in place while Becca tied the other strips of fabric together and then wound them around Quentin's shoulder. She created a big knot over the wound to add continued pressure to stop the blood flow.

All the while she worked on Quentin, she couldn't

help but notice the breadth of the SEAL's shoulders and how solid his muscles felt beneath her fingertips. If she didn't have a mission to complete, and if Quentin wasn't a navy SEAL, she might consider going out with him. Maybe. The truth was, she couldn't stop in her pursuit of finding her father's killer.

Once done, she sat back and assessed the damage. "Barring a swamp-water bacterial infection, you'll live." She turned toward the smoldering plane. "On the other hand, the SOS plane is a complete wash. What happened?"

"Something hit the plane," Duff said.

Quentin nodded. "And since it didn't impact the nose or the fuselage but knocked out the engine, we either sucked a pelican into the engine, or were hit by a heat-seeking missile."

"What?" Becca looked around the swamp. "We're in Louisiana, not the Middle East."

Sawyer pulled out his cell phone and held it up. "If I can get cell service, I'll contact our unit. We aren't too far from Stennis." He tapped the screen and waited.

Becca plucked at her damp blouse, realizing a little late that the wet white fabric did nothing to hide what was beneath. Thank goodness she had on a bra. She crossed her arms over her chest, feeling a little silly for the panic attack that made her leap out of the airplane into an alligator-infested bayou. "Where are we, anyway?"

Quentin pulled his cell phone out of his back pocket and shook it. "I'd tell you if I could get my GPS up. I think my phone is toast. These things don't do well submerged."

Becca twisted her lips. "Sorry."

He shrugged and tucked the phone back in his pocket. "What happened back there?"

She glanced away. "Nothing. Just a little claustrophobia."

Natalie snorted. "A little? You were getting out of that plane if you had to tear a hole in the fuselage to get there."

"I'm glad we all got out before it blew," Duff muttered staring down at the screen of his dry mobile phone. "We're in a marsh near the Pearl River. If Sawyer can contact the team, they can come get us."

Sawyer had his cell phone pressed to his ear. "This is Chief Petty Officer Houston, let me speak to the LT... I don't care if he's on lunch break. This is an emergency. Get him."

All faces turned to Sawyer.

Becca held her breath and strained to hear.

"LT, we have a problem. The plane we were flying in crashed in a marsh close to the base... Yes, sir. We all got out alive. Thanks to the pilot." Sawyer nodded toward the pilot, who'd landed the plane under the worst circumstances. "I've got the app to find my cell phone. You can track us with it." He gave the LT the login and password to track his phone. "How soon can someone be here? Twenty minutes? Make it less. We're sitting ducks in this life raft and we don't know whether the guy who shot us down is still out there."

Becca glanced around the marsh. So far the only other living creatures were those that belonged in the swamp. Theirs was the only boat afloat.

Quentin also stared around the bayou. "If someone shot us down, they might come back to finish off any survivors. And that smoke signal will make it all too easy to find us. Perhaps we should find some cover and concealment."

"Right." Montana nodded toward a stand of cypress trees a couple hundred yards away. "Let's make for the trees."

Without a paddle to propel the raft, they made slow progress toward the stand of trees. Everyone who could leaned over the side and paddled with their hands.

Already wet, Becca did her best tucked against Quentin, who sat behind her. All the while she watched the water for alligators, praying none of the crash survivors lost an arm to the gaping maw of one of the swamp reptiles.

Halfway to the trees, Becca paused and tipped her head, the thick humidity of southern Mississippi causing sweat to drip into her eyes. A sound reached her over the splashing of the water.

"Shh!" she said. "Listen."

All hands stilled.

There it was again. The thumping sound of rotors beating the air.

"Helicopter." Quentin twisted left and right.

Sawyer straightened, looking to the sky. "Where's it coming from?"

"Did you ask the LT to send a chopper?" Duff's voice was low and intense.

Sawyer shook his head. "The LT said he'd send out a boat."

"Damn." Quentin leaned over the side and paddled faster. "Let's get to those trees!"

Becca studied the horizon, turning for a three-hundred-sixty-degree view. "It could be a coast guard rescue helicopter."

"I'm not willing to bank on it." Quentin continued paddling, along with the other SEALs.

Becca bent over the side and contributed to the effort, glancing up, searching the horizon.

The dark silhouette of a helicopter detached from the horizon, rose into the air and headed straight for the burning hull of the SOS jet.

As the chopper neared the downed craft, it let loose a stream of bullets.

"Holy hell," Becca said, ducking automatically. She resumed paddling, praying the bright yellow life raft wasn't as easy to spot as the color intended. They only had moments to make the trees, still another fifty yards away.

Chapter Two

Quentin would give his left arm at that moment for a fully-equipped Special Operations Craft-Riverine, or SOC-R as they called it, and his favorite machine gun. Deadly accurate on his aim, he'd have that chopper down in seconds.

But they weren't in the navy boat. Instead they were in a raft designed to float, not move swiftly through the water. Hell, they could swim faster than they could maneuver the raft. But swimming wasn't an option. They were up to their necks in alligators and bad guys.

"Now would be a good time for the team to show up."

"Come on, LT," Montana prayed aloud.

"The only way they'd get here in time to help is if they were already on the Pearl, headed in this direction." Quentin sucked in a breath. "There's only one way to get us to the trees faster."

"You got a motor in your pocket?" Sawyer quipped.

"No." He slung his leg over the side of the raft.

"What are you doing?" Becca asked.

"Going for a little dip." He winked. "Can I get a kiss before I swim with a bunch of hungry alligators?"

She shook her head and reached for his arm. "Are you out of your mind? Get back in the raft."

He leaned forward and stole a quick kiss. "You can slap me later. I've got a job to do." He rolled over the side and eased into the water without making much of a splash. His heart pounded as he stared at the tall grass near a mound of sticks and mud. He'd stay as far away from the alligator nest as he could, but he had to get the raft beneath the trees before the people in the helicopter spotted them.

Grabbing the tow line from the front of the raft, he held on tight and side-stroked, pulling the loaded craft with him. Everyone helped by paddling with their hands. They moved faster than they had before, but not fast enough to make the trees before the helicopter swung around and headed their way.

"Duck!" Quentin called out.

As the chopper neared, the sound of a machine gun blast ripped through the air, but bullets didn't hit the water near the raft.

The chopper pulled up suddenly, altering its direction. More gunfire sliced through the marsh.

"God bless the lieutenant," Sawyer cried out.

Montana whooped. "It's the cavalry!"

Quentin swam to the side of the raft to see what they were yelling about and his heart swelled. A SOC-R watercraft skimmed across the water, headed for the hovering helicopter, the gunners firing live rounds.

"Don't stop paddling," Duff advised. "That helicopter is armed. If they take out the boat, they'll still come after us."

With renewed purpose everyone in the raft paddled and Quentin dragged them along, closing the distance to the trees and the relative concealment the overhanging branches would provide.

By the time he reached the shadows of the cypress trees, his muscles were screaming and he couldn't quite get enough air.

"Quentin, get in the raft. We can take it from here," Duff said.

"Just…a…little…farther." Too exhausted to say more, Quentin kicked and pulled.

"Get in the boat now!" Duff said. "Sawyer, Montana, get him!"

Sawyer grabbed the line Quentin held and dragged it back toward the boat, pulling Quentin up to the rubber sides.

"Get in, now!" Duff yelled. He grabbed Quentin's right arm, Sawyer caught the left and they hauled him over the side, dumping him into the bottom of the raft and then pulling his legs in behind him.

Quentin stared out at the helicopter and the navy boat duking it out a couple hundred yards away. "They could still come after us."

"Yeah, but there wouldn't be anything left of you to shoot at, if that giant gator got to you first." Duff nodded toward a small island.

Quentin sat up in time to see a twelve-foot-long alligator slip off the land into the water and head their direction. "Well, why didn't you say so? I'd have gotten in a lot faster."

"You don't think it will take a bite out of the raft, do you?" Natalie asked, scooching toward the center of the crowded craft.

"Never met an alligator that liked a mouthful of rubber. But if it's a female, and she's guarding a nest…" Quentin pointed to a large mound near the shore, "she might attack to protect her clutch of eggs."

"Not much in the way of choices." Montana shook his head. "Either we go out in the open for the helicopter to use us for target practice, or brave an angry mama gator."

Quentin wasn't as concerned about the alligator as he was about the helicopter circling around to attack the navy boat again. He wanted to be on that boat, manning his position as gunner.

The reassuring sound of the machine guns spitting out ammo was music to his ears. Several bullets hit their mark on the fuselage of the dark chopper. The aircraft jerked to the side and plummeted toward the ground for a few heart-stopping seconds and then leveled off. As if the pilot debated whether to continue the fight or cut his losses, the aircraft hovered over the marsh a couple hundred yards away from the SOC-R. Then it rose straight into the air and disappeared as quickly as it had appeared.

A cheer went up from the occupants of the raft. The navy boat turned and made its way toward the wreck survivors.

Quentin looked forward to getting out of the swamp and back to his apartment where he could strip down, shower and dress in clean dry clothing. In the heat and humidity, his wet jeans and shirt were beginning to chafe in all the worst places.

The navy watercraft pulled up alongside the life raft and stopped. "Rip" Cord Schafer, Trent Rucker and Jace Hunter leaned over the side to help the flight attendant, pilot and copilot into the boat.

Montana and Sawyer handed Jenna out of the raft and then heaved themselves onto the boat.

"What the hell kind of trouble did you stir up in

Mexico?" Rip held out a hand to Natalie and pulled her aboard.

"We'll brief you back at the base. Let's get out of here before that whirlybird returns." Duff hauled himself aboard and reached down to help Becca onto the craft.

Quentin steadied her and handed her off to his buddy. Then he pulled himself aboard, and lay on the deck, happy to let someone else take charge and get them back to base. He was wiped out from swimming and dragging a boatload of people.

He lay there with his eyes closed as Duff and the others manned the SOC-R.

"Are you all right?" a soft voice asked close to his ear.

"I'm fine. Just resting." He cracked one eyelid open and admired the pretty brunette leaning over him.

"Though I still think it was incredibly stupid and risky to pull a stunt like that...thanks," Becca said.

Quentin chuckled. "Does that mean I get a kiss or, better yet, a date?"

She shook her head, her lips twisting. "No to both. And that kiss you stole wasn't even a real kiss. So it doesn't count."

The boat captain revved the engine and set the SOC-R on a course for the base.

"Maybe you could show me what you consider a real kiss?" he said, increasing the volume, though it was hard to sound sexy over the roar of the boat's motor.

Becca's brows wrinkled, but the corners of her lips quirked upward for a brief second. "Don't you ever give up?"

"Nope." Quentin shook his head. "I'm a navy SEAL. It's not in our nature to give up."

With a roll of her eyes, Becca stuck out a hand. "Then maybe you should get up and get behind a weapon in case that helicopter returns to finish the job."

Quentin took her hand and let her pull him up to a sitting position. "I trust my brothers to handle the situation. They've got my six. Don't you?" He stared around at the men manning weapons and scanning the sky for additional threats. He trusted these men with his life, and they trusted him.

Duff nodded. "You know it. Now, stop trying to impress the lady with your brand of cheesy charm. She's not buying it."

Becca laughed out loud. "Thank you. Maybe he'll listen to you. He doesn't seem to take me seriously when I tell him I'm not interested."

"I'm a stubborn man." Quentin pushed to his feet and steadied himself against a machine gun mount. He helped Becca to a position next to Natalie and Jenna, seated on the deck near the rear of the boat. Then he stood behind a shielded weapons mount, watching the shoreline and the sky.

THE TRIP BACK to the Special Boat Team 22 base located at Stennis, Mississippi, took less than twenty minutes. Becca's clothes stuck to her skin. Along with the sweltering heat and humidity of late summer in Southern Mississippi, she was sweating and ready for a shower. They were met upon arrival by men in navy uniforms, standing on the dock.

As soon as the boat came to a complete stop, Becca,

Natalie and Jenna all stood. Quentin leaned close. "The tall one is the boss, Commander Paul Jacobs, and he looks mad. The man with the face of a bulldog beside him is Master Chief Joe Martin."

Commander Jacobs tilted his head toward the operations building. "Inside. Now. Before Homeland Security, CIA, FBI, FAA, state and local police and every other government entity descend upon us."

The men clambered off the boat, helped the women onto the dock and hurried them toward the building.

Once inside, the commander gave strict instructions to the SEAL manning the front desk. "Don't let anyone inside without notifying me first."

The man popped to attention. "Yes, sir."

The master chief led them to the end of a hallway and into the conference room lovingly referred to as the war room.

Becca slowed about halfway down the hall, and then stopped short, causing a pileup of people behind her. After all that had happened, she felt a gnawing need to get back to DC, the SOS headquarters and their impressive computers to look for another link to her father's killer. "I really need to check in with my boss and catch a flight back to DC as soon as possible."

Commander Jacobs shook his head. "No one's going anywhere until everyone's been debriefed."

Quentin hooked Becca's arm. "The sooner we go through the debrief, the sooner you can be on your way."

Becca allowed him to guide her into the war room, and then shook off his hand and lowered herself into one of the seats. Her leg bounced beneath the table. Every minute she was in Mississippi was another minute some bastard was loose, possibly planning on killing another member of the CIA or even her, since they'd targeted the plane bringing her and the SEALs back to the States. She glanced at Quentin, glad he and his friends had all made it off the aircraft before the fuel had ignited in a fiery ball of smoke and flame.

He stood near her, leaning against the wall, a smile playing on his lips, his gaze on his commander.

Commander Jacobs cleared his throat, drawing Becca's attention. "I have a mind to never again grant this navy-issue band of misfits leave," he began. "What the hell happened while you were in Mexico?"

"Sir, you might want to take a seat," Duff said. "This could take a while to explain."

The CO shoved a hand through his hair. "We don't have time to go into a lot of detail. Having a plane shot down on US soil is something we can't hide, nor do we want to. But that brings in a whole lot of scrutiny. Give me the digest version. And make it fast." He snapped his fingers.

Quentin stepped forward. "While in Mexico, we busted open a human trafficking ring, and then someone tried to kill Sawyer." He turned to Sawyer Houston, his teammate. "But that was an effort to get his father Rand Houston to fly to Cancun so that an assassin could kill the senator."

The commander shot a glance toward Sawyer. "I heard about the senator's death. I'm sorry."

Sawyer nodded acknowledgement. "Thank you, sir."

Duff cut in with, "As you see, Sawyer's fine and the rest of us survived with only minor injuries."

"Injuries?" A ruddy flush rose into Commander Jacobs's cheeks. "You were supposed to be on *vacation*, not running covert operations. Who gave you permission to get involved?"

Duff, Sawyer, Montana and Quentin all stood straighter.

Quentin answered, "Sir, we couldn't stand by and let women be sold into sex slavery."

Duff backhanded Sawyer in the belly. "And we couldn't let someone off Sawyer or his father."

"So, you assigned yourselves as the superheroes to save the world." The commander pounded his fist on the table. "Damn it! You're trained Navy SEALs. You follow orders. You don't take on the world without checking in with your commander."

"Sir, they really didn't ask to get involved," Natalie offered. "They did what they thought was best. If it hadn't been for your men, my sister and I would be in some harem in the Middle East or dead."

The CO turned toward Natalie, his eyes narrowing. "Who are you, and what do you have to do with all this?"

"I'm Natalie Layne. My sister was kidnapped while on vacation in Cancun. I went there to find her. Duff and his friends helped me locate the island she was being held on and free her and several others."

The commander faced Jenna. "And you?"

"I'm Jenna Broyles. I was on vacation in Cancun when I got the wrong suitcase. It contained a rifle and a file folder identifying Sawyer Houston as a target."

Sawyer rested a hand on the back of Jenna's chair. "Sir, if she hadn't warned me, I'd be a dead man by now. They wanted to get to my father by going through me."

Commander Jacobs paced the length of the table.

"For the record, Houston, I didn't hold your lineage against you because you've proven yourself over and over." The man stopped halfway across the room and faced all of them. "Still, none of you thought to clue me in on what the hell was going on?" He spun toward the pilot and copilot.

The pilot held up a hand. "Robert Van Cleave, pilot of the plane, this is Randy Needham, my copilot. I don't know what all happened in Cancun, but we experienced engine trouble after something hit the plane." He nodded to the man next to him. "We did the best we could to land the aircraft in an unpopulated location. We got everyone out before the fuel ignited and the plane exploded."

The commander nodded. "Thank you for getting them down in one piece and out of the plane alive." He turned to Becca. "And who are you and what do you have to do with what happened? Were you one of the kidnapped women being sold?"

"No, sir." Becca stood, too wound up to sit, and ready to get the heck out of the building and on her way to DC. "I'm Becca Smith, and I was in Cancun looking for the assassin who killed my father, a respected member of the CIA. I believe the assassin who targeted Sawyer was the same mercenary who killed my father. Unfortunately, he died before we could find out who hired him to do the job. Now, if you'll excuse me, I want to get back to DC and see if I can pick up the trail from a different direction."

Commander Jacobs held up his hand. "Hold your horses, young lady. Like I said before, nobody is going anywhere. You do realize you'll all be questioned in regard to the airplane you were flying in. And, by the way, you haven't gotten to letting me know how you managed to be returning to the States in a private jet."

Becca held up her hand. "I can explain that one. My boss offered to fly us back after all that happened in Cancun."

"Who the hell do you work for? The president?" the CO asked.

"No, sir," Becca said. "But my boss has connections in the government. I'm not at liberty to share his identity or the organization for which I work. I'd have to get permission from my boss."

Commander Jacobs crossed the room and stood toe-to-toe with her.

Becca lifted her chin and stared straight into his eyes, refusing to back down or be cowed by the man who towered over her.

"Well, I sure as hell don't have the answers to the questions the FAA will have about that aircraft. I suggest you get your boss on the line, ASAP."

"Do you have a phone I can borrow?" She fished hers out of her pocket. "Mine went for a swim with me."

Quentin chuckled, the sound sending warmth through Becca's chest.

"Chief Petty Officer Quentin, do you find something funny about this situation?" Commander Jacobs glared at him. "Because I sure as hell don't."

"No, sir." Quentin wiped the smirk off his face and stood at attention.

"Then show this woman to a telephone so that she can call home," Commander Jacobs snapped.

"On it." Quentin held out his hand.

Becca took his hand and let him lead her out of the

room. Once in the hallway, she asked, "Is he always that cranky?"

"Only when he doesn't know what's going on. We should have reported in sooner."

Quentin led her into an office with a telephone. "Dial 9 to get an outside line. I'll leave you to it." He stepped into the hallway and pulled the door closed behind him.

Alone at last, still damp with swamp water in her hair and clothes, Becca lifted the telephone and dialed 9 and Royce's cell phone number.

He answered on the first ring. "Yeah."

"It's Smith," she said.

"Smith, what's going on? The tracking device on the plane blinked out before you were due to land in Mississippi. Is everything all right?"

"No, sir. We think the plane was shot down." She explained what happened and their subsequent attack by the helicopter. "You might want to be here to explain the private plane and who it belongs to. The FAA and the Department of Homeland Security will be all over what happened."

"I'm on my way. I should be there early in the morning, if you can hold off the wolves until then."

"I'll do the best I can," Becca said. "When the FAA and DHS are done with us, I'd like to get back to DC and see if I can drum up another lead to follow. Whoever is behind my father's death could possibly be after me now."

"You're probably right. In which case, I need to assign an agent to protect you."

"I don't need anyone to protect me."

"Yes, you do," a voice said behind her.

Becca spun toward the door.

Quentin stood in the half-opened doorway. "Sorry to eavesdrop, but the CO is getting restless."

"Becca, is that one of the navy SEALs?" Royce asked.

"Yes, sir."

"Let me talk to him."

"Sir—" Becca hesitated.

"Hand him the phone, Smith," Royce commanded.

Becca held out the receiver. "My boss wants to talk to you."

Quentin entered the room, closed the door and raised the receiver to his ear. "Yes, sir."

Becca strained to hear what her boss was saying to Quentin.

"Chief Petty Officer Quentin Lovett, sir." He listened for a moment and then smiled. "I'd be happy to. No sir, I'm still on leave for a couple days, if my commander doesn't cancel it." He nodded. "I will, sir. No. Thank you." He handed the receiver to Becca.

She frowned, not liking that Royce hadn't told her what he wanted to talk to Quentin about. "Sir, I need to get back to the debriefing."

"Smith, Lovett has offered to be your bodyguard. I want you to stick to him like flypaper."

"But, sir."

"No buts. All other agents are assigned at this time."

"What about Natalie Layne? She could be my bodyguard."

"She's not officially on board. I have to bring her back on the payroll before I can assign her."

"Quentin isn't on your payroll," she pointed out.

"No, but he offered to spend his leave taking care of you. Let him."

"But—"

"I'm on my way. See you in the morning." A loud click indicated the end of the call. Becca stared at the receiver a moment before replacing it in the cradle.

"Looks like you and I will be together a little longer."

Becca spun to face him.

The man leaned his back against the door, his arms crossed over his chest.

Anger rushed up Becca's chest, filling her cheeks with heat. "Like hell we are." She marched up to him. "Move."

He stepped aside and opened the door. "Where are you going?"

"Anywhere but in the same room with you."

He raised his hands. "Hey, your boss asked *me* to look out for you, not the other way around."

She stared at him through narrowed eyes. "I don't care what he said. I have work to do."

"You heard the commander. No one goes anywhere until the FAA and DHS go through the motions."

"The sooner the better. And then I'm out of here."

"Not without me."

"We'll see about that." She marched past him and down the hallway toward the war room. The man was far too infuriating for Becca. He was irritating, persistent and annoying.

In the back of her mind she heard another voice extolling his virtues of bravery, determination and concerned for the welfare of others. She might not be alive if he hadn't jumped into the alligator-infested swamp after her, or if he hadn't gone in again to pull their life raft to the shadows of the trees.

Well, damn. Just when she thought she'd get away from him and his band of brothers, she'd been ordered to stay put by her boss. In the morning, when Royce arrived, she'd have to get him to call off the SEAL so that she could get on with her search to find her father's killer. She didn't have time to get involved with a sexy SEAL. His broad shoulders and tempting smile were beginning to wear on her. She had to get away before she did something dumb like kiss him.

Chapter Three

Three hours later, after they'd answered what questions they could for the FAA, DHS, county sheriff, state police and everyone else who could possibly be involved, they were finally allowed to leave the base.

Quentin needed a shower. He smelled like swamp water and, despite his discomfort, he was hungry. He could imagine Becca felt the same. Her anger seemed to have dissipated as the day wore into evening.

"Some of us are headed to the Shoot the Bull Bar for a beer. Are you coming?" Jace asked.

Quentin shook his head. "I need a shower and a gallon of coffee, not booze."

Becca rose from the conference table and stretched. Even in a swamp-water-dingy white blouse and wrinkled trousers, her dark hair in funky disarray, she was a beauty.

His groin tightened at the thought he would be spending the night in the same building as her, possibly the same room.

Rip entered the war room and handed Quentin a cup of coffee. "I'm headed to the bar, but I can drop you at your apartment on the way."

"You are a lifesaver." Quentin wrapped his hand

around the cup and inhaled the fragrant scent. "And yes, I'll take you up on that ride as soon as I convince Becca she's coming with us."

Rip grinned. "Did you score in Cancun?"

Quentin winced when Becca joined them at that exact moment. "No, he did not score, nor will he. If you don't mind, could you drop me at a hotel?"

"Sure," Rip responded.

"Then you'll have to drop me there, too." Quentin turned to Becca. "I'm not leaving you alone. Either you stay at my place where I have two bedrooms, or I stay with you in your room at a hotel."

"I'm not staying in the same room as you, Loverboy," she said.

"So you're telling me you want to stay in my apartment?"

"No. I didn't say that."

He leaned close to her. "Just so you know, when I give my word, I keep it."

"And like I told Royce, I don't need a bodyguard. We don't even know why they shot down the plane. It could have been someone after Sawyer, not me."

"Or it could have been you since you're on the trail of whoever hired the assassin who killed your father." Quentin crossed his arms over his chest. "Your choice. Togetherness in one hotel room, or sleeping in separate rooms in my apartment."

Becca's lips pressed into a thin line. She waited twenty of Quentin's heartbeats before she finally said, "Fine. Your place. But I'm not sleeping with you."

"You hear that, Duff?" Rip grinned. "A female who isn't falling for Loverboy's killer charm. This has to be a first." Rip turned to Quentin, shaking his head.

"What happened in Mexico? Are you losing your touch?"

Quentin ignored Rip's comment and raised his brows at Becca. "I didn't ask you to sleep with me. Besides, who said I wanted to sleep with *you*?"

Rip clapped a hand on Quentin's back. "If you two have things figured out, I'd like to leave while we can."

"We're ready." Becca sailed past Quentin and Rip and marched down the hall.

Quentin stood for a moment, admiring the view of her swaying hips.

Duff clamped a hand on Quentin's shoulder. "Forget it, she's not that into you."

"Oh, she is," Quentin said. "She just doesn't know it yet."

"That's right, feed the ego, Loverboy." Duff walked with him to the exit. "If you want to win her over, my advice to you is to get a shower. The only female you're going to attract smelling like you do is a female gator."

Outside, the parking lot was slowly clearing of the emergency and government vehicles. Rip hit the button to remotely unlock his truck. When the taillights blinked, Becca headed in that direction.

Before Quentin could open the door for her, Becca was inside, adjusting her seatbelt in the front passenger seat.

Quentin climbed into the backseat behind her.

Rip slipped behind the wheel. "So, Becca, is it?"

"Don't feel obligated to engage in small talk," she said. "It's been a long day."

"Gotcha," Rip said, a smile spreading across his face. He shot a glance at Quentin in the rearview mirror. "She's a real ball-buster, isn't she?"

Quentin ignored him. It *had* been a long day and he was tired of the smell and stickiness of his clothing against his skin. The sooner he got a shower, the more human he'd feel. Then he could continue his campaign to win over the pretty secret agent.

Rip pulled up in front of his apartment building. "Got a key, or did it go down with the plane?"

Quentin nodded. "I have a spare."

"Under the welcome mat?" Rip asked.

"Something like that," he replied.

"In this day and age, you're willing to risk someone finding your spare key?" Becca frowned. "Maybe the hotel is a better idea."

"We're here. Give my apartment a chance. If you don't like it, I'll drive you to the hotel myself." Quentin got out, opened Becca's door and held it while she climbed down. "Thanks, Rip."

"Don't do anything I wouldn't do," Rip said with a grin. Then his face sobered. "Hey, and if you need anything just yell. Hopefully, whoever took a shot at the team won't try picking you off one at time." Rip drove off, leaving Quentin with Becca. Alone.

Quentin had been thinking along the same lines. If someone was truly after Becca or the SEAL team, they'd gone to a whole lot of trouble to take them out with a fiery plane wreck and helicopter attack. After the failed attempt, wouldn't they come after them again in a subtler attack?

Perhaps staying alone in his apartment wasn't such a good idea after all. Granted, Montana lived in the same apartment building. Though Montana had opted to have a beer with the guys at the Shoot the Bull, he'd be back later. Since he was on the same floor of the apartment complex, he'd be within shouting distance should Quentin and Becca run into trouble.

With a sigh, Becca faced the building "Which one is yours?"

Quentin hooked her elbow. "I'll show you." He led her to his door and reached up to the porch light fixture and pulled the spare key from between the base plate and the wall. "See? Not under the mat."

"I feel so much better," Becca said, her voice dripping sarcasm.

"Great. We can get this evening off to a good start with the right attitude."

"The only thing that will improve my attitude is a long soak in a hot shower followed by a glass of wine."

He opened the door and reached inside to flip the light switch.

Becca entered and stared around at the small but comfortable room. "Are you sure you live here?"

"Yes, of course. Why?" He closed the door behind him and glanced around, trying to see the room through her eyes.

"It's...too..." she waved a hand at the room "...clean."

Quentin shrugged and stepped past her. "Not all men are slobs."

"Yeah, but this is almost sterile. I feel like I have to take off my shoes before I step inside." She toed the back of her shoe. "Actually, that's not a bad idea, considering where they've been." Barefoot, she walked through the living room and peered into one of the bedrooms.

"That's mine. You can sleep there or in the other room. Your choice. There's only one bathroom, shared between the two bedrooms." He unbuttoned his shirt as he walked into the small kitchen. "You can have the first shower, while I open a bottle of wine."

"Thanks. I'll take you up on both offers." She headed straight for the spare bedroom, entering the bathroom from there. Before she closed the door, she called out, "I'll try to save you some hot water." Without looking back, she closed the door.

A moment later, Quentin heard the snick of the door being closed on the other side of the Jack-and-Jill bathroom—the door leading into his bedroom. Then he heard the sound of the shower spray.

Quentin had the bottle out of the cabinet and two glasses on the counter when he realized Becca didn't have clothes to change into.

He entered his room and riffled through his dresser for a soft T-shirt for her to sleep in. He'd offer her pajama bottoms to go with it but he didn't own a pair. Instead, he grabbed a pair of clean running shorts with an adjustable drawstring. With the clothing in hand, he knocked on the bathroom door.

"I'm not done yet," Becca called out.

Quentin tried the bathroom doorknob in the guest bedroom, surprised to find it unlocked. He twisted the knob and pushed it open a crack.

Becca poked her head around the shower curtain. "What are you doing?"

"I brought clothes for you, unless you prefer to sleep in the buff."

She frowned at his offering and then nodded. "Thanks. You can leave them on the counter." The curtain whipped back in place.

Quentin set the shirt and shorts on the counter and

turned. Though he couldn't see through the shower curtain, he could clearly see the outline of Becca's naked body.

His heart skipped several beats and his blood raced south, tightening his groin. Yeah, she had all the right curves in all the right places.

A sopping wet rag flew over the top of the curtain rod and smacked him in the side of his head.

"Out!" Becca demanded.

"Going." Quentin left the bathroom and returned to the kitchen where he poured a large glass of wine and called in an order for pizza to be delivered. He had no intention of going back out and he didn't have much in the way of food in his refrigerator, having emptied it prior to the planned two-week vacation in Mexico, which had been cut short by all that had happened.

As he drank his wine, his gaze fixed on the bathroom door, his mind conjuring the silhouette of Becca standing behind the shower curtain. He had to have her. A thousand seduction scenarios ran through his head, many of which had been successful in the past with other women. But Becca was different.

The woman wanted nothing to do with him.

She'd be a challenge, but one worthy of the effort to win.

BECCA SCRUBBED THE swamp smell out of her hair and grabbed the soap, working up a good lather. As she smoothed it over her body, she was entirely too aware of the man on the other side of the door. As a physical specimen, he was perfect, and he wasn't a slob like most men she knew.

If she wasn't searching for her father's murderer,

she might be open to flirting with Quentin. Maybe even sleeping with him. At the thought of her father, her chest tightened and her hand stilled. He'd been her only family.

Becca prided herself on her independence, but she'd always had the safety net of her father. He'd said if she needed him, he'd be there for her. Well, he wasn't anymore.

Tears welled in her eyes and she dashed them away. Agents didn't cry.

She turned the heat down on the shower, and rinsed the soap from her hair and body, reminding herself why she was there and what she had to do.

Becca stepped out of the shower, toweled herself dry and finger-combed her hair into some semblance of order. Then she reached for the clothes Quentin had thoughtfully provided. The soft-white T-shirt smelled clean and freshly laundered, unlike the clothes she'd left piled on the floor, destined for the washer.

She pulled the T-shirt over her head and let it slide down her body, imagining how differently it would fit over Quentin's broad, muscular chest. On her, it draped loosely over her breasts and down to mid-thigh. She could wear it as a nightgown, all by itself. But Quentin had provided shorts, as well.

She pulled them up over her hips and cinched the drawstring around her waist to keep them from falling off. Completely covered, Becca still felt somewhat exposed. She didn't have panties or a clean bra beneath the shirt and shorts. The thought of stepping out of the bathroom into the living room where Quentin was made her nipples tighten under the soft cotton fabric.

Great. He'll think I'm turned on by him. She had to

admit she was attracted to the man, but he didn't need to know that. He'd probably press the advantage and sooner or later, she'd cave to his dogged determination to get her into his bed.

Becca pressed her hands over her breasts, hoping to warm them and make them quit puckering. But the more she touched them, the more she imagined Quentin's hands there and the tighter her nipples beaded.

Giving up, she plucked the shirt away from her chest and curved her shoulders inward, hoping to hide the telltale sign of her awareness of the man. Twisting the towel around her hair, turban-style, she straightened—clean, refreshed and ready to face the world and Quentin.

She gathered her soiled clothing in one arm, sucked in a breath and opened the door. Despite her determination to face Quentin head-on, she felt more vulnerable than she had in the alligator-infested swamp as she walked barefooted through the bedroom and out into the living room.

Quentin emerged from the small kitchen, carrying two glasses of wine, one of which was halfway gone. He'd shed his shirt, displaying a wide expanse of a tanned muscular chest. "Feel better?"

"Much." She took the goblet he proffered and focused her attention on the liquid in the glass, trying, but not succeeding in avoiding looking at Quentin's gorgeous body. The red wine warmed her insides enough she lifted her head. "You don't happen to have a washer and dryer in your apartment, do you?"

"I do. In the back of the kitchen. There's detergent and fabric softener in the cabinet over the washer. Help yourself."

"Thanks. If you throw your clothes out of the bathroom, I'll put them in with mine." Becca crossed to the kitchen and set her glass on the counter.

"I'll only be a minute in the shower," Quentin said on his way to the bathroom. He paused with his hand on the doorknob. "I called for pizza, I hope that's okay with you. Sorry, we don't have any other food delivery service in the backwaters of Mississippi."

She smiled. "I love pizza as long as it has pepperoni."

"Good, because that's what I got." He nodded toward the kitchen bar. "There's money on the counter. I don't have to tell you to look before you open the door. With all that's happened, you can't be too cautious."

She nodded. "Right. I'll pay you back when Royce gets here."

"My treat. It'll be our first date."

She frowned, but couldn't find it in her heart to be mad at him. He'd offered his apartment, his clothes and his protection, and he hadn't made another pass at her since she'd arrived.

Quentin disappeared into his bedroom, leaving the bedroom door open, but closing the door to the bathroom behind him.

Becca unwound the towel from her head and shook out her damp hair. Come to think of it, he hadn't even tried to coerce her into kissing him since Royce had asked him to be her bodyguard. Now that Quentin wasn't pressuring her, Becca had the odd sensation of missing his teasing and coy remarks.

The door opened and a pair of jeans landed on the floor.

Becca hurried forward to gather the clothes.

As Becca entered his bedroom, Quentin stuck half of his body through the opening, stopping short of exposing his private parts.

Becca's pulse quickened and she drew in a sharp breath, her gaze drifting down his torso to the slice of hip and thigh visible through the crack in the door.

Quentin winked. "Like what you see?"

Caught staring like a teenaged girl in the boys' locker room, Becca blushed. At a complete loss for words, she threw her towel at him, spun away and closed the bedroom door behind her with a snap.

A bark of laughter erupted behind her through the thick panels of both doors.

"Egotistical jerk," she shouted.

He laughed again.

Pressing her palms to her cheeks, Becca entered the kitchen in search of the washing machine. She found it behind a louvered door, threw her dirty clothing into the tub and started the water, trying to forget what she'd seen and heard. It was hard. The man didn't have an ounce of fat on his body and his thighs were just as muscular as his upper body. She could imagine what it would feel like to lie next to him, naked. Her softer body against his chiseled one.

Becca groaned. Thoughts like that would get her nowhere. No, they would get her into trouble, make her lose focus and forget why she was there in the first place.

She marched back across the living room, gathered Quentin's jeans and returned to the washer. Once she had the load going, she wandered around the kitchen, opening cabinet doors. Every dish, glass, cup and spice was placed neatly on the shelves. The man obviously believed in order and structure.

Becca did, too. Unfortunately, she hadn't had much of it since her father's death. Everything about her life was out of kilter. The lead she'd gotten from one of Royce's informants had led her to Cancun following the trail of a mercenary thought to be the one who'd shot her father in cold blood.

In Cancun, she'd stumbled upon the group of SEALs, one of whom was yet another target of the mercenary. Becca had helped them solve that case, but the killer she'd hoped to question had died in the subsequent firefight. With a trail gone cold, she'd been eager to return to the States and dig for more clues as to who had hired her father's murderer.

She hadn't planned on the plane she was in being shot down, nor did she have any contingency in her schedule to fend off a growing desire for the SEAL Royce had tagged with providing her protection.

Other than the neatness and orderly appearance of the apartment, there wasn't much else in the way of personal items that could give her anymore insight into Quentin Lovett.

While the SEAL was in the shower, Becca wandered into his bedroom. Here, the king-sized bed was neatly made, the pillows stacked by size against the headboard. Becca couldn't tell by looking at the mattress which side of the bed Quentin preferred to sleep on, or if he slept in the center. Becca preferred the left side. Not that which side Quentin slept on would pose an issue. Becca had no intention of sleeping with the man.

In his closet, all of his uniforms were pressed and hanging neatly, boots and shoes lined up on the floor.

His civilian clothing hung by type and color. For what appeared to be a man with OCD tendencies, he was somewhat of an enigma. How had he come to be a navy SEAL, dealing in the chaos and messiness of war?

The water switched off in the bathroom.

Becca hurried guiltily back to the kitchen near the washer. She didn't want Quentin to know she'd been snooping in his bedroom. He'd be drying off, rubbing the towel over all those lovely muscles across his chest, down his torso and across—

The doorbell rang, interrupting Becca's lusty thoughts. She jumped. For a moment she'd forgotten about the pizza delivery. Her stomach growled, a reminder that she hadn't eaten since the muffin she'd had in Cancun early that morning. She grabbed the bills Quentin had left on the counter and hurried toward the door.

A quick peek through the peephole reassured her the young man was indeed from the restaurant, complete with a uniform shirt bearing the name of a pizza establishment written in bold yellow lettering.

Becca slid the chain loose and twisted the deadbolt. When she turned the door handle, the door exploded inward, catching her across the side of her face, knocking her off balance. She squealed, stumbled backward and tipped over the arm of the sofa, landing on her back.

Two men dressed all in black from the tops of their heads to the tips of their toes rushed in, both carrying handguns.

With no time to think, Becca rolled off the couch onto the hardwood floor and shoved the couch as hard as she could toward the advancing men as they aimed their guns at her. Becca somersaulted across the floor and ducked behind a lounge chair.

The couch hit the men in the thighs as they fired their weapons, throwing off their aim. But it wouldn't take them long to regain their balance and fire again. The lounge chair wouldn't stop bullets, only slow them down. She had to get to a safer place.

Chapter Four

Quentin had just shoved his feet into his jeans when he heard Becca's scream. He rushed out of the bathroom into his bedroom, eased open his nightstand and pulled out the Sig Sauer P226 he kept loaded and on safe. Gunfire sounded, spurring him to move quickly across the floor, his bare feet making no noise.

He threw open the door to find two men in black advancing on the recliner behind which he suspected Becca had ducked.

"Fire another round and I'll kill you both," Quentin said, his voice low, his hand steady, aiming at the man nearest to the lounger.

The two men spun toward him, firing.

Expecting as much, Quentin dove and rolled as soon as he issued his warning, coming up behind the rear-ranged sofa.

"Hey, dirtbag!" Becca shouted from the other side of the room.

Quentin peered around the side of the sofa in time to see the recliner erupt from the floor, crash into the closest man and knock the gun from his hand.

The other man unloaded his magazine of rounds into the sofa.

Quentin didn't rely on the sofa for cover; he low-crawled around the side and aimed at the man's knee, careful not to fire toward the lounger. He hit dead on and the man dropped his gun and went down, screaming.

The one who'd had the gun knocked from his hand threw himself to the floor, grabbed for the other man's gun, rolled to his feet and raced for the sofa blocking his exit. Instead of going around it, he leaped to the back, tipping it over.

Quentin rolled out of range of the big piece of furniture and into his bedroom. Getting his feet beneath him, he poked his head around the doorframe.

The man in black had stopped in the doorway, his gun aimed at Quentin.

Quentin fired and ducked back inside his doorway.

A shot was fired, splintering the doorframe where his head had been a moment before. Another round went off, then footsteps sounded, leading away from the apartment.

Quentin left the bedroom and ran toward the lounge chair, his gaze swiveling from the chair, to the man on the floor, to the open doorway.

"Becca." With his gun trained on the man lying in the middle of his living room, he stepped around the upended recliner.

Becca lay face-down, flat against the ground, her arms over the back of her neck. She executed a full body-roll to the right and pulled her feet beneath her, ready to launch herself at him.

"Hey, sweetheart, it's me." He held up his free hand in surrender. "One's gone, the other appears to be dead."

She rose to her feet. "What are you waiting for? Go get him!"

"Hell no. I'm not leaving you. He could circle back and finish the job."

She went for the gun on the floor and held it in her hand like she knew what to do with it. "I can take care of myself. Either you go, or I will."

Since she appeared okay, he decided not to argue. "If he moves," he said, pointing at the man on the floor, "shoot him." Quentin bolted out the door and nearly fell over a young man lying next to a crushed insulated pizza delivery bag. "Got a man down out here. Call 911," he shouted and ran out into the parking lot.

Screeching tires alerted him to the escape car before it barreled toward him in the parking lot of his apartment building.

Quentin aimed at the driver's windshield and pulled the trigger, holding his ground until the last second. Then he dove out of the sedan's path. The car continued out of the parking lot onto the four-lane street. Barely missed by traffic from one direction, clipped by a passing vehicle from the other, the escape car came to an abrupt halt by smashing into a telephone pole.

Quentin ran out into the street, dodging traffic. By the time he got to the crashed car, he found the driver's door open and the seat empty. A shiny trail of blood led toward a grocery store where people hurried in and out, unaware of a potential murderer in their midst.

The farther away from the apartment Quentin ran, the more he worried about Becca. What if the man he'd shot wasn't really dead? What if he'd been playing dead and waiting to attack until Becca had her back turned?

Quentin continued on until he arrived at the entrance to the store, no longer finding a blood trail. Had the assailant ducked behind a car in the parking lot and circled back?

His pulse ratcheting upward, Quentin glanced inside the grocery store. Nobody seemed worried about a strange man bleeding amongst them. But Quentin worried he'd doubled back and was now almost to the apartment complex and Becca.

Keeping his gun out of sight of the shoppers, Quentin performed an about-face and ran back across the parking lot and waited precious seconds for a break in traffic so that he could run across the thoroughfare. He was sprinting by the time he reached the apartment building parking lot.

An SUV door opened and Montana got out, a frown creasing his brow. "Lovett, are you okay?"

He didn't slow, running past Montana, calling out over his shoulder, "We were attacked."

Montana fell in behind him, matching his pace to the closed door of Quentin's apartment.

Quentin pounded his palm on the door. "Becca! It's me, Quentin."

The door jerked open and Becca fell into his arms. Having her body next to his was the best feeling. She was alive and apparently unharmed, based on how hard she squeezed her arms around his middle. "When you didn't come back right away, I thought he'd gotten you."

"I'm sorry." He leaned back and brushed a strand of hair out of her face. "He crashed on the other side of the road."

"Is he dead?" she asked.

Quentin shook his head. "He escaped before I could get to him."

She leaned her forehead against his chest, reminding him that he hadn't fully dressed and he'd run across the street barefooted. "I'm just glad you're okay."

"You two want to tell me what happened here?" Montana asked. He stopped outside the door and squatted next to the young man just rolling over with a groan. "What's with the pizza delivery boy, and who's the stiff?"

Thirty minutes later, the team gathered in Montana's apartment. The police had cordoned off Quentin's apartment for an investigation of the attack. He'd filled in the men on what had happened.

"I guess it's pretty clear now that they are after Becca," Duff was saying.

Sawyer snorted. "Two attempts in the same day is a pretty big clue. And I wasn't anywhere near. They have to be after Becca." He touched his hand to his cheek, tilting his head to the side, studying Quentin. "Unless they were after Loverboy."

Montana narrowed his eyes. "You haven't slept with some rich dude's wife, have you?"

Sitting on a barstool, Quentin ran a hand through his hair. "Even I draw the line somewhere. I don't sleep with married women."

Becca paused in pacing the room. "Nice to know you have *some* standards."

He captured her gaze, holding it with a steady one of his own. "I won't poach on another man's wife or life. Never have. Never will."

"Needless to say, Becca is not safe staying in this apartment complex. They know where to find her now. If they're willing to fire a heat-seeking missile at an airplane, they might be bold enough to launch a mortar at this building," Duff said.

Becca's eyes widened. "Which means that by staying here, I put everyone else at risk."

"You don't have many choices," Quentin said.

"I can disappear. The fewer people who know where I am, the better." She started for the door to the apartment. "Thank, guys, but I need to get out of here."

His pulse quickening, Quentin stepped in front of her, blocking her exit. "You can't go."

"I have to leave. There are civilians in this building. We're lucky none of the bullets hit any of them."

"I agree, you can't stay here, but you can't go gallivanting around the country dressed like you are and without money or identification." Quentin took her hand. "Wait until Royce gets here in the morning."

"This building might be burned to the ground by then."

"Then we disappear to a hotel. Just you and me. We'll meet up with Royce at the unit in the morning."

"I don't want to put you at risk, as well. I can go by myself."

Quentin shook his head. "Whoever hired the assassins seems to have money to burn, recruiting enough people to form an army. So far they've used an expensive missile that is hard for the average person to get a hold of. They've sent multiple assassins to find and eliminate you, and we don't know how many others they will send in their place. You need someone to watch your six."

Duff pounded Quentin on the back. "And from what Loverboy says, your boss asked him to be that for you."

Quentin held his breath, thinking up additional words to counter any other arguments.

Becca glanced from Quentin to Duff and back. Then she sighed. "Fine. You'll be my six. But we do this my way."

Quentin popped a salute. "Yes, ma'am. I can follow orders when I need to."

Duff grinned. "He can. If the orders are going his way."

A frown pulled at Becca's brows. "Then you better start thinking my way. Our lives might depend on it."

"Thinking that way already," Quentin agreed, glad she was at least allowing him to tag along. When he'd come out of the bathroom to see two men holding guns on her, his heart had stopped momentarily. That she'd escaped alive was nothing short of a miracle. Quentin was determined to ensure her good luck held.

"We need to get out of here without being detected." Becca stared across at Sawyer, who wore an Atlanta Braves baseball cap. "I need your hat and shirt."

Sawyer handed over the hat and ripped the shirt over his head, holding it out. "I'll trade you," he said and winked.

Quentin took the shirt and hat. "Don't push your luck."

Sawyer grinned. "Just wanted to get a rise out of you. I'm not trying to steal your girl. I have one of my own."

"I'm not his girl," Becca insisted. She snatched the shirt and hat from Quentin and disappeared into the bathroom. After pulling Quentin's shirt off, Becca dragged Sawyer's on. Though she preferred Quentin's she'd have to leave it with Sawyer for her plan to work. She took a moment to stuff her hair into the ball cap, careful to get all of it hidden. When she emerged from the bathroom, she pointed to Duff. "Quentin will need your shirt." Facing Montana, she asked, "Do you have a pair of sweats and some shoes I can wear?"

"My sweats and shoes will swallow you."

"I don't have a choice. I need to walk out of here as Sawyer."

Montana entered his room. A few moments later, he returned with a pair of gray sweats that had seen better days, but had a drawstring she could pull tight to keep them from falling off. She pulled them on over her shorts and cinched the waist.

Montana handed her a pair of socks and tennis shoes. "The strings are long enough you can tie them around the shoe and your foot. Hopefully that will get you to the nearest vehicle."

"Thanks." She slipped into the shoes, her feet swallowed by the vastness of them. She tied the strings around the top of her foot and under the bottom of the shoe, praying they'd stay on long enough for her to get to a vehicle. When she had the string bound securely, she stood and practiced walking in the oversized shoes.

Quentin chuckled. "If someone doesn't shoot you first, you're going to trip over those boats and kill yourself *for* them."

"Can't be helped." She stared around at Quentin, Sawyer, Montana and Duff. "We need wheels. Sawyer's or Duff's since we're dressing as them."

Duff held up his keys. "You can take my SUV. I've been wanting to get a truck, anyway." He told them exactly where he'd parked.

Becca nodded, biting on her bottom lip, her nerves jumping inside her body. "Thanks." She faced Quentin. "Do you have any money?" she asked. "Enough cash for a hotel room?"

Quentin had swapped shirts with Duff and wore shoes he'd taken from his apartment before the authorities had arrived. "I grabbed my mad money before the police descended on us. If we're going to get out of here, we need to leave before we're questioned again, and before the parking lot clears of emergency personnel."

"I'm ready." She held up her empty hands. "I'm traveling light."

"We need to get you some clothes that fit as soon as we can stop long enough to hit a thrift shop."

"My clothes are not as important as getting out of here without being detected."

Montana tossed Quentin a ball cap. "You'll need this to shade your face."

Quentin jammed the hat on his head. "Let's go." He held out his hand to Becca.

She placed hers in his, her pulse pounding, adrenaline shooting through her veins. If someone wanted her dead, assassins could be waiting for her to leave, watching for her every move. Their deception could buy them enough time to get the hell out of the apartment building and into a hotel. When Royce arrived the next day, he'd bring her a new identity in the form of a driver's license, credit card and cash.

Quentin paused in front of Duff and touched his shoulder. "I'll get word to you on where you can find your vehicle."

"No worries. If I can't find it, I'll report it as stolen. The police will find it for me."

"Wait until we've been gone at least an hour before you leave Montana's place."

"Don't worry about us," Duff said. "We'll stay the night. We expect to see you two in the war room in the morning."

"If we don't see you, we'll understand that you think it's not safe," Sawyer added.

Becca had no intention of returning to the war room on Stennis.

Quentin was first out the door of Montana's apartment. He glanced around, then turned back. "Night. See you all in the morning. Oh, and Lovett, don't do anything I wouldn't do."

The men inside the apartment responded with forced laughter.

Becca stepped out, pulling the cap low on her forehead.

"And Duff, you better drive," Duff called out, doing his best to sound like Quentin. "Sawyer's had more than his limit."

"I got his six," Quentin said, pitching his voice low, like Duff's. He crossed the parking lot to Duff's SUV, leaving Becca to follow.

She squared her shoulders and tried to stand as tall as she could. Sawyer was a good foot taller than she was. By walking separately from Quentin, she hoped that from a distance, if anyone was watching, they wouldn't notice the height disparity. She sauntered for the SUV, pulling herself up into the passenger seat, sitting on a foot to appear as tall as Quentin, who sat in the driver's seat.

No sooner had Becca closed her door, Quentin had the SUV in gear, backing out of the parking lot, pulling between the remaining police cars. Once out on the road, he turned to the right and blended in with the traffic.

Becca glanced over her shoulder and checked in the side mirror, watching to see if they were being followed. After Quentin made several turns and no headlights stayed behind them, Becca relaxed. "I need to find a convenience store or truck stop selling disposable phones."

Quentin nodded without saying a word. He drove out to a highway intersection where a well-lit truck stop was located. He parked between two semi-tractor trailer rigs, turned off the engine and climbed out.

Becca got out and followed him into the store. She selected a disposable phone, flip-flops and a T-shirt with a big fish on the front and the words *Gone Fishin'* written beneath it.

Quentin found a straw cowboy hat and a fisherman's hat and added them to the pile on the counter along with beef jerky, trail mix and a couple of water bottles. "Anything else?"

She'd give anything to buy panties and a bra, but the truck stop catered to men, not women who'd been shot down, shot at and almost eaten alive by alligators.

Her body ached with exhaustion, and yet she couldn't let her guard down. Not yet. As soon as they were back in the SUV, she pulled the cell phone out of the packaging, turned it on and dialed Royce's number, let it ring once then hung up. She did it again, letting it ring only once before she ended the call, and then she waited.

Quentin glanced across the console at her.

She didn't say anything, figuring the less she spoke with him, the less likely she would miss him when she left him behind to head back to DC.

The phone in her hand buzzed, vibrating between her fingers. She pressed the talk button, recognizing the number as Royce's private line.

"Hey, it's me," she said.

"I take it things aren't getting better?" her boss said.

"Not by a long shot."

"Are you all right?"

"If you mean am I alive and kicking, then yes, I'm all right, but the recliner in Loverboy's apartment has seen the end of its days."

"Sorry to hear that." Royce chuckled. "Loverboy? Is that a nickname or does the man have mad skills?"

Becca snorted. "It's in his dreams. When will you be here?"

"Flying into Stillwell at eight in the morning. I have what you need."

"Good." She shoved a hand through her hair and stared across at Quentin. "I'm ready to move on."

Her bodyguard frowned.

"See you tomorrow," Royce said. "Stay safe."

"Don't you want to know where to find me?" she asked.

"I'll find you." Royce ended the call.

"That was short," Quentin commented.

"My boss doesn't waste words." She glanced out the window.

Quentin pulled into a really old motel that had seen better days forty years before.

Becca stared at the exterior with its half-lit neon

sign, peeling paint and sagging eaves. "Why are we stopping here?"

"This is where we're sleeping tonight." He parked at the end of the line of tiny rooms and shut off the engine. "It might not be pretty, but I doubt your followers will look for us here."

She wrinkled her nose. "I'll grant you that. But what about the local riff-raff? Not to mention the roaches and bedbugs bound to be in a place like this."

A long low Cadillac parked on the other side of the driveway. An older, rather rotund man climbed out of the driver's seat and rounded to the other side. He opened the door for a woman, less than half his age, wearing clothing that barely covered her breasts and butt.

Becca shot a glance toward Quentin. "I bet they rent rooms by the hour."

"And I'll lay odds they'll take cash and not ask questions. No credit cards and no need to show any ID."

He had a point. Becca didn't like it, but his observations were valid. Credit cards could be traced. Most of the nicer hotels required a credit card to secure lodging for the night.

"I'll get a room. Stay low until I get back." Before Becca could protest, Quentin had slipped out of the SUV and turned to face her. "Catch."

"Catch wh—" Becca held up her hands to keep from being hit in the face with the SUV keys.

"If anything happens, get the hell out of here."

"What about you?"

His lips tipped upward. "I can take care of myself."

Becca frowned. "So can I."

He tilted his head, his brows furrowing. "Do you argue about everything?"

Her lips quirked. "For the most part."

Quentin shook his head, pushed the lock button and strode back to the registration desk.

Becca debated making a run for it, leaving behind her assigned bodyguard. To use his own words, she could take care of herself. With her hand on the door handle, she paused. It was sort of nice to have someone watching her back. Normally, she worked alone. And it would only be for the night. She glanced at the sketchy couple making their way into one of the rooms. So, it was a dive. She needed sleep for the journey ahead.

By the time she'd talked herself into staying, Quentin was striding toward her. Becca's pulse raced and butterflies fluttered in her belly. From what she could see, he only carried one key, which meant one room... one bed.

Chapter Five

Quentin had paid for the room with cash, opting for a full night, not by the hour. He asked twice if the sheets were clean and the beds free of bugs. The clerk with the gauge earrings and multiple tattoos, smelling of marijuana and body odor, didn't make Quentin too confident in his answers. But he was assured the maids changed the sheets daily.

He didn't like leaving Becca alone for even the few minutes it took to pay the guy behind the counter and fill out a form, giving a fake name. Not only was he worried about her being attacked again, but he also figured she'd take off, preferring to go it alone.

At this point, Quentin couldn't let her walk away. After multiple attacks that had nearly gotten all of them killed, he couldn't let whoever was bent on taking out Becca finish the job. Yeah, he was getting used to her feisty attitude and damn, she could kiss.

As he reached the SUV, he climbed in.

She stared at the hand curled around the room key. "One room or two?"

"One."

"I prefer to have my own."

He shook his head and held out his hand. "Swap."

She placed the SUV key in his hand and he gave her the room key.

"Where are we going?"

He pulled out of the motel parking lot, turned onto the main street and took the first right. "I'm parking in the alley behind the motel. I don't want our friends to spot the SUV in passing."

She nodded, rolling the room key over in her hand. "Just because we're sleeping in the same room, doesn't mean we're sleeping together."

Quentin parked behind the motel and turned off the engine. He turned to face her, his brows raised. "Just because we're sleeping in the same room doesn't mean I want to make love to you. I made a promise to your boss to look out for you."

"With a nickname like Loverboy, I'd think you'd feel the need to uphold your reputation."

"Don't mistake the nickname with the man. I love women. So sue me. But I've never forced a woman to have sex with me." He pulled the key from the ignition, climbed out of the SUV and hurried around to the other side. Becca had opened the door. He reached for her waist and helped her down from the vehicle, holding her longer than was necessary. God, he loved the way she felt in his hands. "Every one of them was willing."

Becca's lips twisted. "All notches on your bedpost?"

"Hardly." He dropped his hands to his sides. "I make it clear that I'm promising nothing beyond the night."

"Oh, so you're allergic to commitment." She nodded. "I see."

Heat rose in Quentin's chest. She made him sound heartless, when he'd been kind and gentle with the women he'd bedded. None of them had gone away disillusioned. He jammed the key into the door lock and shoved the door open.

First order of business was to clear the room. He checked the closet, the bathroom and beneath the bed. No monsters lurked behind the shower curtain or in the shadow. The sheets appeared clean, if a bit worn. A dresser, nightstand and cushioned chair were the only other furnishings in the room.

Becca entered, carrying the bags of supplies they'd purchased at the truck stop. Once inside, she closed the door and set the bags on the dresser. "I'll sleep in the chair."

"Not necessary," Quentin said. "I'll be awake most of the night. You might as well get some shut-eye."

"I'm smaller than you. I can sleep sitting up."

"Look, I get it that you can take care of yourself. I know you're used to running ops on your own, but I promised—"

She raised her hand. "I know. You promised Royce you'd take care of me. Fine. I'll sleep the first four hours. You can have the next four hours. Royce should be in town by then and your commitment to me and Royce will be fulfilled."

"Deal." He didn't tell her that he had every intention of staying with her for the next four days, hoping to find the one responsible for the attempts on Becca's life. He wouldn't rest until he knew who had paid the mercenaries to shoot down the aircraft and come after her in his apartment. She might not want him tagging along, but damn it, they'd made it personal.

And he liked her bold attitude and dogged determination to discover the truth behind her father's murder. In a fight she was a ferocious opponent and a fierce ally. And the more he was with her, the harder it was becoming to keep his hands to himself. Her confidence and beauty made him want to kiss her again and again. More than that, it made him want to hold her in his arms…all night long…skin to skin.

Quentin busied himself unpacking the loot from the truck stop. "Want some beef jerky?"

"No, but I'll take a bottle of water." Becca pulled back the bedspread, inspected the sheets and then sat on the edge of the bed, testing the firmness of the mattress. "I think you gave me the bed because you know it will be hell to sleep on." She smiled. "You can change your mind, you know. I prefer the comfort of the chair for the night."

"Just go to sleep," he said, his tone a little harsher than he intended. Sitting on the bed, wearing Sawyer's shirt and the baggy sweat pants, she shouldn't look as desirable as she did. Quentin's ability to resist was rapidly deteriorating. He grabbed a bottle of water out of the bag and tossed it to her. "I need some air. I'll be outside within yelling distance should you need me." He started for the door.

Becca jumped to her feet and blocked his path. "Where are you going?"

"Just outside. I need the air." Balling his fists, Quentin fought the urge to grab her arms and pull her body against his.

"If I've made you mad, I'm sorry." She touched a hand to his chest, her gaze following her fingers. "I have a habit of alienating every guy I know by the stupid things I say. Please. Don't go. I promise to shut up."

"It's not what you say…"

Her palm flattened on his chest. "No? Then why are you about to run out that door like you're suffocating?"

"Because, if I stay..." his resistance crumbling, he reached for her arms and dragged her against him "...I'll do this."

Her eyes widened, and her tongue snaked out to wet her lips.

The motion and subsequent shine of moisture drew his attention to her mouth. With a groan he lowered his head. "And this," he whispered. He claimed her lips.

Her fingers curled into his shirt and her mouth opened on a gasp.

Quentin swept in and claimed her, caressing her tongue with his. He slid his hands down he arms, across the middle of her back, pressing her closer, molding her hips to his.

Becca raised her hands to his neck, threading her fingers into his hair. She pressed closer, rubbing her breasts across his chest, sliding a leg up the back of his calf.

Past reason, he cupped the backs of her thighs and lifted.

Becca wrapped her legs around his waist and Quentin carried her to the bed. He laid her down on the mattress and pressed a kiss to her mouth. "Stop me now."

She released her hold around his neck.

For a moment Quentin thought she was going to tell him to get lost. His gut tightened and he prepared to fight the lust raging through his system.

Then she reached for the hem of his shirt, dragged it up his torso and tossed it toward the chair. "You're not going anywhere until you finish what you started."

"I'm no quitter," he said, bending to press a kiss to the pulse beating wildly at the base of her throat.

Becca ran her hands over his shoulders and down his back, sliding into the waistband of his jeans.

Quentin fumbled with his belt and buttons, ripping them open. With Becca's help, he was out of his jeans and shoes in seconds. Then he worked on getting her naked. Off with the shirt and the baggy pants. She lay there, the light from the nightstand making her tanned skin glow.

He stood beside the bed for a moment, drinking her in with his gaze. "You're beautiful for a special agent."

"Uh. Thanks. You're not so bad yourself. For a SEAL." She took his hand and tugged. "Enough foreplay."

He dropped to the bed beside her and slid his hand over her arm and across her hip. "I like a woman who knows what she wants."

"You should know, having sampled so many." She kissed his lips, cupped his cheeks and kissed them again. "Show me what you learned."

He obliged, taking his time to fully appreciate the full lushness of her mouth, the taste of her tongue and the long, slim line of her neck. When he reached the mounds of her breasts, he rolled first one, then the other, nipple between his teeth, flicking the tips until they tightened into tasty beads.

She arched her back, pressing her nipple deeper into his mouth, a moan rising up her throat.

Her pure abandon made his groin tighten and his shaft harden to stone. He wanted to take her then, but he knew it might be the only time he would have with this woman. Vowing to savor every moment, he worked his way down her torso, dipping into her belly button and tonguing a path to the soft mound over her sex.

She threaded her hands into his hair, her fingers digging gently into his scalp. "Seriously," she said, her voice smooth gravel and sexy as hell. "Didn't any of those women tell you foreplay is overrated?"

He chuckled, blowing a warm stream of air over her heated center. "Are you sure about that?" Then he parted her folds and flicked that nubbin of desire with the tip of his tongue.

Becca drew up her knees, planted her heels into the mattress and raised her hips to his mouth. "Okay, you win. You were right. Holy hell, I'm going to come apart."

He tongued her again, sucking her flesh between his teeth and nibbling gently.

A moan started low in her chest and rose up her throat, filling the small room with the sound. "Oh, yes. You did learn something."

While he swept his tongue across that highly sensitive bundle of nerves, he touched a finger to her entrance. She was wet, ready for him and he was ready to take her. But she wasn't quite there. He focused all of his attention on that one little strip of flesh, flicking, licking and teasing her until she rose up from the mattress, her breath caught and her fingers flexed in his hair.

Her body trembled with the intensity of her release. When she dropped back to the mattress, she sucked in a long, steadying breath and said, "For the love of Mike, come up here already." She grabbed a handful of his hair and pulled.

"Hey, that hurts," he said, though he didn't care. He was on his way to where he wanted to go.

"I'll hurt more than your scalp if you make me wait a second longer."

"Yes, ma'am." He climbed up her body and settled between her legs, the tip of his shaft nudging her entrance. "Just so you know…"

"I know. You're not into commitment. I get it. Neither am I. So tomorrow, neither one of us will have regrets."

He kissed her and pushed a strand of her hair out of her eyes. "That's not what I was going to say."

"It wasn't?" She stared up at him, one of her legs wrapping around him, urging him to consummate their lovemaking.

"No. I was going to say, you know, I have protection in my wallet." He grinned. "The commitment thing is all on you." He winked, reached over the side of the bed for his jeans and unearthed his wallet from the back pocket.

He didn't let her know that her comment had struck a little closer to home than he'd thought it would. Yeah, he'd told every other woman he wasn't into commitment. But to have Becca beat him to it, well, it gave him a twinge of something like regret.

Pushing the feeling aside, he concentrated on the woman lying beneath him and the way his body reacted to hers. He found the packet buried in his wallet.

Becca grabbed it from his hand, tore it open and rolled it over his erection before he could protest. "Please, don't make me wait any longer," she begged.

"Wait? I thought you were enjoying the ride?"

"I'll enjoy it even better if you would focus on the

goal." She wrapped her hands around his buttocks and pulled him toward her.

Quentin slid into her tight channel, moving slowly, enjoying the way her muscles convulsed around him.

Becca wrapped her legs around his waist and dug her heels into him, forcing him deeper until he filled her completely. "There," she said and sighed.

He let her adjust to his girth, then he pulled out almost all the way and pressed in again. With her hands on his hips, he settled into a rhythm, pumping in and out, the speed increasing with every thrust until the bed shook and he lost himself in her.

Becca dropped her feet to the mattress and rose to meet him. Harder, faster, he moved within her, his insides clenching as he rose up to the peak and rocketed over the edge. He slammed into her one last time, buried himself deep inside her and rode the wave of desire all the way home.

As he eased back to earth, he lay down on her and rolled to the side, taking her with him to retain their connection.

Becca stared into his eyes and cupped his cheek. "Okay. I get it now."

"Get what?" he asked, kissing the tip of her nose and then her lips.

"Why they call you Loverboy."

"It's a play on my last name."

"The hell it is." She snuggled close, resting her hand on his chest. "It's one hundred percent your technique."

He laughed out loud, kissing her soundly on the mouth. "I'll take that as a compliment. Now, get some sleep. I'll pull first watch."

"I need it after that workout." She yawned and settled against him, her fingers light against his skin. "Wake me in a couple hours for second watch."

Oh, he'd wake her all right and he'd be counting the minutes until he did.

BECCA MUST HAVE fallen right to sleep. She didn't wake until sunshine peeked through the thick curtains, slicing across her eye. She reached out for the man in the bed beside her only to find the pillow empty and Quentin gone. She sat up straight and looked around the room, lit only by the light able to find its way around the curtain.

"Quentin?"

The bathroom door opened and Quentin stepped out, a towel wrapped around his middle, his hair damp. "Hey, sleepyhead. Decide to wake up, finally?"

"You were supposed to wake me for the second shift." She yawned and stretched, the sheet falling down to her waist.

Quentin's nostrils flared and the towel around his waist tented. He cleared his throat and closed his eyes briefly as if looking at her without touching her was straining his control. "I couldn't do it. You needed a break."

"You need to sleep, as well." She pushed her hair back from her face, watching his reaction as his gaze shifted down to her breasts. Becca almost laughed out loud at the hunger in his eyes.

Quentin shrugged those massive shoulders, making Becca's core tighten. When she'd first awakened, she'd thought making love to Quentin had been a lush dream. But the delicious soreness of her sex was proof it had all be too real. Despite her announcement that there would be no regrets, she was beginning to regret her announcement to that end.

One night wasn't nearly enough with Quentin. How the other women he'd loved and left must have grieved. He was that good, making Becca want more.

Quentin stood there, not making a move toward her, even though he was clearly aroused. What did she have to do to get him to come back to bed? Obviously, naked breasts weren't enough.

She threw back the sheet and swung her legs off the bed. "You could have at least woken me in time to share your shower," she said, making her voice soft and silky. Rather than throw herself at him and beg, she strode across the room, doing her best runway walk, every inch of her bare to him. As she neared him, she slowed and touched his chest. "I'd have scrubbed your back and anywhere else that itched." She lightly patted his cheek. "Too bad." Then she stepped around him and entered the bathroom, shutting the door behind her.

Her body tingled all over after only touching his naked chest. Becca turned on the water in the shower and stepped in, shocked at how cold the spray was as it hit her body. She prayed it would cool the heat and ease the throbbing between her legs.

She lathered the tiny bar of soap and spread the suds over her face, breasts and down to the juncture of her thighs. Yeah, he could have had her again that morning, if he'd wanted her enough to take her up on the offer. But he hadn't.

"To hell with him," she muttered out loud and ducked her face beneath the spray.

"Didn't your mother teach you it's not nice to curse?" A deep, sexy voice said as large hands circled around her belly from behind and pulled her against a hard erection.

She leaned into him. "I thought you weren't interested."

"Nothing could be further from the truth." He nudged her buttocks from behind. "And it was fairly obvious."

"Umm." She pushed the wet hair from her face and turned in his arms. "Is that what was hiding beneath your towel?"

He lifted her, wrapped her legs around his waist and pressed her against the cool tile of the shower wall. "I had to get protection before I joined you. Fortunately, I had more than one tucked into my wallet."

"They train that in BUD/S school?"

"Damn right. Never go into a situation unprepared." He nudged her with his fully cloaked erection. "Now, what was it you were saying when I stepped in the shower with you?"

Becca lost track of the conversation as Quentin slid inside her, filling her to full, stretching her tight. "I said something?" she whispered, unable to drag in a complete breath.

The cool tiles against her back barely chilled the heat building inside, and did nothing to slow the wild beating of her heart. This man had her turning inside out with the strength of her desire for him.

She rode him until she climaxed, Quentin following right behind her. Digging her fingers into his shoulders, she pressed her head back against the wall, her heart racing. She didn't come back to earth until the shower's spray turned cold.

Quentin lowered her to the floor of the tub and turned off the water.

The jangle of a phone ringing sounded from the next room.

Becca froze. "That could be Royce." She galvanized into action, stepped out of the tub, grabbed a towel and raced into the other room. The disposable phone continued to ring, the vibrations making it travel across the nightstand. It teetered on the edge as Becca reached for it.

As soon as she recognized Royce's number, she hit the talk button. "Yeah," she said, breathing hard after her mad dash.

"Becca? Are you okay?"

"I'm fine." She tucked the cell phone between her shoulder and ear and wrapped the towel around her body.

"I touch down in fifteen."

"Just don't run into any missiles on your way in," she quipped, but really meant it. She liked her boss and didn't want anything bad to happen to him.

"We're not flying into the airport. I'll shoot the co-ordinates to you," Royce said.

Her phone beeped, a text message coming through. She checked. "Got it."

"Be there. I'll brief you then."

Becca glanced across the room at Quentin buttoning his jeans, a towel slung across his shoulders, his hair still dripping. "That's our cue." She handed him the cell phone and grabbed her clothing.

He entered the coordinates on the map application and studied the screen. "I know where that is. It looks like a race horse farm from the road. I didn't know it was a landing strip."

"Royce has contacts all over." She jammed her feet into the baggy sweats and pulled them up over her hips. Then she dragged the T-shirt over her head, letting the towel drop to the floor. "Ready?"

He'd slipped on his shirt and pushed his feet into his shoes. Quentin straightened and headed for the door. "Wait for my signal."

"We don't have time."

"You need to take the few extra seconds to play it safe." He shook his head. "Otherwise, you'll have all the time in the world if you're dead." He narrowed his eyes and pointed at her. "Stay."

Becca bristled. "I'm not a dog that can be trained."

He tsked. "More's the pity."

Her lips pressing together, Becca crossed her arms over chest. "Fine. But get a move on. We have," she glanced at the clock on the nightstand, "twelve minutes to get there, and I'll be damned if I stand by and let someone take out Royce's plane with a rocket launcher." She followed Quentin to the door, but hung back.

Quentin poked his head out. A second later, he slipped through the opening.

Becca closed and locked the door behind him. She ran to the window and nudged the curtain wide enough to peer between its thick folds. For a second she couldn't see Quentin, then she noticed movement in the shadows. Quentin hunkered behind an old Ford Bronco with peeling paint and unmatched bald tires.

He glanced around the vehicle to the open parking lot at the center of the two motel buildings.

Becca prayed he wouldn't run into anyone eager to put a bullet in his chest.

Chapter Six

Quentin worked his way through the parking lot, scanning vehicles, windows and doorways for possible gunmen. When he was reasonably certain the coast was clear, he slipped to the alley in back of the buildings where he'd left the SUV parked. After a quick check over the vehicle for any hidden explosive devices, he climbed in and jammed the key into the ignition. So far so good.

Careful to check for any suspicious cars before he left the alley, he eased out and around the building and pulled up beside the room he and Becca had shared the night before. She yanked open the door and jumped into the passenger seat.

"I feel like this is overkill," she said, buckling her seatbelt.

Quentin pulled into the street and turned the direction the coordinates had indicated. "Better overkill than to be killed."

"True." Becca shook her head. "What I don't get is why my father's killers are now after me."

"Did he pass any secrets to you before they got to him?"

Becca shook her head. "Not that I know of. Hell,

I haven't been home since I started searching for his killer." Her eyes widened. "I wonder if he sent something to my apartment or to my post office box in Virginia. I didn't think of that."

"That might be the first place we head after we meet with Royce."

"We?" She cocked her brows. "You have a job with the navy. You're not a part of this case."

"I became a part of it when you joined us in Cancun. And I made a promise."

Becca rolled her eyes. "Seriously. I doubt Royce wanted you to be attached at the hip to me until this case is solved. Besides, you have a job here in Mississippi. And unless my knowledge of geography is off, Mississippi is a long way from Virginia."

"I'm on vacation."

"And you have three days until you have to report to duty." Again, she shook her head. "Three days only gets you to Virginia, you still have to get back. Never mind solving a case."

"My commander would let me have the additional time necessary."

Becca reached out a hand and touched his arm. "Thank you for offering, but I don't need your assistance. I'm a trained agent. I can handle this."

"Helps to have more than one set of eyes." He glanced at her. "Who'll cover your six when I'm not around?"

"Have you considered that I might work better alone?" She stared across the console at him. "That's what I do."

"Well, as long as I'm on vacation, I don't see any

harm in tagging along with you." He meant it, and he wasn't going to let her off that easy.

She faced the front windshield. "Look, just because we slept together doesn't mean either one of us owes the other anything."

Quentin's lips tugged upward. "Oh, I don't know…" He gave her one of his killer smiles. "I think you owe me a steak dinner. I'm told I'm pretty amazing in bed."

Becca laughed out loud. "I'll buy you that steak dinner, but not because I owe you one."

He nodded. "It's because I'm amazing."

She snorted. "Any of your conquests ever tell you that you're full of yourself?"

He tilted his head, pretending to think about his answer, then said, "No. Not one of them."

"Let me be the first."

"Ah, I love firsts. I'll be glad when we have our first official date."

"What was last night?"

"Amazing," he grinned. "But not a date."

"You don't ever give up." She pointed at the street he passed. "Based on your GPS, you should have turned right back there."

"I know." The smile slipped from his face. "I noticed a car following us at the last turn. I'd just as soon lose it than lead it to our rendezvous."

Becca swiveled in her seat. "Are you sure it's following us?"

"No. But better safe than sorry." He turned left at the next intersection and pressed down on the accelerator. "Let's test this theory."

He raced to the next street and turned left again. As he turned, he glanced over his shoulder. The car that had been tailing him was just turning onto the street he was leaving.

At the next street, Quentin turned right and whipped around a deserted auto repair garage and pulled into the alley behind the dilapidated building, parking behind a stack of old pallets and tires. He could just see around the pile to the end of the alley that led to the street he'd left a few seconds before. The car drove past, moving slowly. From what Quentin could see, there were two people in the front. One driving, the other seated in the passenger seat with the window rolled down.

"Seems awfully hot and humid to ride with the window down, in what appears to be a perfectly good vehicle," Becca commented.

"My thoughts exactly."

When the vehicle passed, Quentin pulled around the stack of tires and pallets and eased to the end of the alley.

"If you stop before the road, I can get out and check around the building." Becca unbuckled her seatbelt and leaned forward, her hand on the door handle.

Quentin stopped short of the end of the building. "Do it, but be careful."

Becca pushed the door open, leaped out and ran to the end of the alley. She peered around the corner, watched for a long moment and then ran back to the vehicle and dove into the open door. "They turned to the right two streets down. If we hurry, we can back-track and lose them."

Gunning the engine, Quentin shot out into the street and raced back the direction they'd come, glancing often in the rearview mirror.

Positioned in her seat to stare out the rear window,

Becca said, "I think we lost them." She turned to the road ahead and sat back in the seat. "How are they finding us? I don't even have my own phone, luggage or clothing. Hell, I don't even have any jewelry, and I'm not micro-chipped with a GPS tracking device."

"Unless they traced us through Royce's cell phone to the disposable."

"Royce doesn't give out his number to just anyone," Becca said.

"Doesn't matter if he's being watched, too," Quentin pointed out.

"If they found us by tracing us through Royce, they can find us again. Damn."

"It also means they might go after Royce, if we don't get there before they do."

"They could be working with others."

"Call Royce and warn him." Quentin stepped on the accelerator and turned away from the coordinates Royce had given them.

Becca dialed and waited for Royce to come on the line. "Hey, we might have a problem." She paused, listening. "Not good…an alternate location would be wise."

"Tell him aim for the Stennis airport, but bypass and land at the Slidell airport," Quentin advised. "We could get the jump on the others and meet him there."

Becca passed on the information and added, "We're ditching this phone, since we think it has been compromised. See you at the airport." She ended the call and lowered her window. "So much for staying off the grid." When she started to throw it out the window, Quentin stopped her with a hand on her arm.

"Wait."

A truck towing a horse trailer pulled to a halt at a four-way stop ahead.

Becca handed the phone to Quentin.

When the truck pulled past him, he lobbed the phone into the back of the empty trailer.

"That might help with our tail. Royce's tail will figure out their change of landing location, but it will take time for them to get there."

Quentin raced along the back roads toward Slidell, pushing the speed limits and praying the local police and sheriff's deputies didn't tag him. Being pulled over would drastically reduce all the time they might have gained by tossing their cell phone.

He didn't like being out in the open, subject to a mercenary targeting Becca. The sooner they met with Royce, the sooner they could drop off the grid altogether.

BECCA CHECKED THE side mirror often and turned in her seat, fully expecting to see another vehicle following them. Fortunately, the back roads were fairly clear. As they neared Slidell, traffic thickened. Quentin slowed their pace to match. Before long, he pulled off the highway onto an exit leading to the airport.

"Royce said they'd park the plane near the general aviation hangars. We could find them there," Becca said.

Quentin drove past the passenger terminal entrance and around the airport to the general aviation hangars used by local businesses. "Where? There are quite a few hangars."

As they passed one hangar, the tarmac was visible outside the next hangar. "There," Becca pointed excitedly. "That's Royce getting out of that small jet." She shot a glance over her shoulder. "So far no tail."

Quentin pulled into the parking lot. "Let's make this quick." He shoved open his door and hurried around to the other side of the SUV.

Becca was out before he could reach her door. She grabbed his hand. "Come on."

As they neared the door to the hangar, it opened and a man waved them inside. "I'm Joe Sanders, one of the owners of this hangar. Mr. Fontaine asked that you come inside quickly." He held the door for them and watched the road as they entered. Once inside, he closed the door and locked it. "This way."

They'd entered an office area with a front desk and a door with another lock. Sanders produced a set of keys, unlocked the door and led them through to the inside of the hangar, where several corporate jets were parked.

"Smith, glad to see you in one piece." Royce Fontaine, the head of the Stealth Operations Specialists, hurried toward her, his hand outstretched. When she put her hand in his, he pulled her into a bear hug.

"It's good to see you, Royce." And it was. He was now the only father figure in her life.

"You've had quite a time between what happened in Cancun and here in Mississippi." He glanced up at Quentin. "You must be Lovett." He didn't hold out a hand. "Let's save the introductions and debriefs for the trip." He turned, slipping Becca's hand through his arm.

"Trip?" Quentin asked.

"We're flying to New York. We'd better hurry, if we want to avoid another attack by our friends with the missile launchers."

"Do you think they'd be bold enough to attack in a more populated area?"

"You want to wait around and find out, or move on to the next clue in this increasingly complex can of worms you've opened?" Royce didn't wait for her answer. He continued toward the hangar door and out into the melting heat of the Mississippi sunshine.

The door to the plane was open and the steps were unfolded. Becca was first up. She turned to face Royce as he waited for Quentin to follow. "Royce, Quentin doesn't need to go with us. He's done more than his part to keep me safe."

Royce turned to Quentin. "You're back early from your vacation to Cancun, aren't you?"

Quentin nodded. "I have three more days on my leave and could ask my commander for more, as long as there aren't any missions slated."

Royce nodded. "If you want to bow out, now's the time."

"I'd like to put an end to the threats to Becca's life."

Fontaine jerked his head. "Climb aboard. When the time comes, I'll make sure you're back to report in. And if this mission extends beyond your leave, I'll make sure you're cleared for more."

"Let me guess, you have connections with the navy."

"Not specifically. But I have some friends in the Department of Defense."

"Really, Royce, I don't need a bodyguard," Becca protested as Quentin entered the aircraft and slipped past her.

"I have everyone else out on equally important assignments. I can't pull them back, or I risk revealing them." Royce turned to Quentin. "The man's a highly trained SEAL and he's willing. I say let him come if he wants. We could use more men like him on the team."

Becca frowned. "As long as you remember he belongs to the navy. They've invested a lot of time and money into his training. I'm sure they'd like him back in one piece."

"At the risk of sounding like an echo," Quentin leaned close to Becca and brushed a stray hair out of her face, "I can take care of myself. And you, if need be."

"Now that we have this settled, let's get the hell out of here." Royce nodded to the flight attendant, who closed the hatch and motioned for them to take their seats.

Becca sat in a plush contoured seat across a table from Royce. Quentin sat in the seat beside her, his thigh touching hers, sending tingles throughout her body. Damn the man.

If he continued to dog her every step, she could not be held responsible for her reaction to him. He was entirely too attractive for his own good. Having been outvoted, she sat back in her seat and pretended to ignore a man who was not all that easy to ignore, and focused her attention on Royce. "What do you have for us?"

The engines rumbled and the aircraft moved, taxiing toward a runway.

"I have your new identification documents, credit cards and cash to get you by. As soon as we're in the air, I'll show you what else you'll be issued."

The captain's voice came over the intercom announcing their departure from the airport.

Becca stared out the window, a chill slipping down her spine. As the buildings shrank, she slowly relaxed.

Quentin covered her hand with his. Only then did she realize hers was shaking. She gave him a weak smile. "I really hate flying."

"It's all right. After what we've been through, you're allowed." He winked and laced his fingers with hers, then turned to Royce. The plane had leveled off and was headed northeast toward their destination. "What did you do with your cell phone?"

Royce smiled. "I gave it to the owner of the hangar. He was on his way to lunch. I asked him to drop it in the restaurant's trash."

Quentin nodded. "We have to assume all of your communications are compromised."

"Understood. Our flight plan shows us leaving Slidell bound for Cincinnati, Ohio. We will be making a stop in Chattanooga to switch planes to continue our trip to New York."

"Why New York?" Becca leaned forward. "Did you find out any more information?"

Royce nodded. "The authorities found a body in the bayou not far from where your plane went down. Beside him, they found a Soviet-made hand-held, heat-seeking missile launcher. The man had been murdered. A bullet through the head. From the description, it was fired from a high-powered sniper rifle."

"So whoever hired the assassins aren't too attached to their help." Quentin shook his head. "They don't want to leave any loose lips behind to spill the beans."

"Exactly. However, we ran facial recognition software on the guy in the swamp. Fortunately, the alligators hadn't gotten to his face, yet. We found a match on the CIA's watch list. The man's name is Fuad Abuzaid. He was suspected of assisting with the Boston Marathon bombing, but they couldn't find enough evidence to put him away."

"Nice character. Why was Fuad in the swamps of Mississippi?" Becca asked.

Royce smiled. "That's why we're on our way to New York City. Our friend Fuad has been keeping company with a nasty piece of work out of the Bronx. His name's Samir Jabouri. The feds suspect him of supplying weapons to jihadists working on American soil. Again, they can never manage to catch him with the goods. The man's as slippery as they get."

"And we're going to find him?" Becca asked. "What do we hope to get out of a meeting with this Jabouri?"

"Answers," Royce said. "We want to know who provided him with the manpad?"

"How does one get a Russian-made man-portable air-defense system into the country undetected?" Quentin asked.

"I'd like to know that, myself," Royce responded.

Becca leaned forward. "Couldn't you trace his banking transactions?"

"Geek's on it, but hasn't been successful hacking into the man's accounts yet. If Jabouri is supplying the assassins, we might get him to rat out the man paying the bill. Or even better, if the man is local in New York City, we might follow Jabouri to his lair."

Knowing Tim "Geek" Trainer was working the data angle made Becca feel better, but computers and internet wouldn't have all the answers. "Do you have an address for Jabouri? We could make a call."

"I have it. We'll have to sneak up on him," Royce said. "From what the CIA intel report indicated, the man is usually surrounded by a full contingent of bodyguards. He runs a tobacco shop in the Bronx and lives not far from the shop."

"Tell me we have weapons," Becca demanded. "I don't like going into any situation unarmed. I'd prefer something with the force of a cannon, but is lightweight and can be hidden beneath my shirt."

"How about an H&K .40 caliber pistol?" Royce unbuckled his seatbelt, strode to a lushly upholstered wall panel and opened it to display an armory of weapons from .40–.55 caliber pistols to AR15s, ready for armed combat. And enough ammunition to start a small war.

Becca selected a .40 caliber H&K handgun, testing the weight in her palm. "I'll take this one."

"You know how to stock a plane. And here I thought corporate jets only carried wine and cheese." Quentin grinned as he selected a Sig Sauer P226. "Just like the one they issue me back home." He pulled open a drawer. "What's this? Plastic explosives? Remind me not to make Royce mad." He pocketed a few bricks of explosives and a couple of detonators.

"You might need one of these," Royce handed him a shoulder holster. "And check out these." He handed him a miniature night-vision monocular.

Quentin looked through the lens and weighed the device in his hand. "Nice." He shoved it into his pocket along with a small flashlight with the ability to change lens colors.

Becca selected a roll of duct tape, unwound it and rolled it into a tight wad the thickness of a cigar. "You never know when you might need some of this." She stuffed it into her pocket, along with several zip ties, and selected a .40 caliber pistol holster, slipped her arms into the straps and fitted it to her body. With a sigh, she ran her hand along an AR15. "Though I'd love to carry a rifle into the Bronx, I don't think I could hide it under my shirt." She glanced around the armory closet. "Speaking of shirts, I could really use some clothing. What I brought with me to Cancun was consumed in the plane wreck and subsequent fire. Until I get back to my place in Virginia, what you see is what I have." She held out her arms in the fishing shirt she'd purchased at the truck stop and sweatpants the SEALs had provided.

"I thought about that." Royce titled his head toward a locker-like closet to the left. "You got lucky. Tazer was in town. I had her throw a couple of outfits together for you."

Becca opened the door, happy to find a section of jeans, trousers, a dress, shoes and undergarments. "Tell her thank you from the bottom of my heart." She selected a pair of black jeans, a black long-sleeved sweater, panties and a sports bra. "If you'll excuse me, I'd like to change."

"Through that door." Royce pointed to the rear of the plane. "Take your time. We won't land in Chattanooga for another thirty minutes."

Clutching the clothing to her chest, Becca pushed through the door to find a very compact bedroom with a full-sized bed made up in expensive Egyptian cotton. She quickly changed into the clothing. The jeans were a little snug around her hips and too long, but she was able to zip and didn't care about dragging the hem around. Nicole Steele, affectionately called Tazer, was a good four inches taller than her.

Becca hadn't asked Royce where Tazer had acquired the clothing. Her bet was the woman had pulled it out of her own suitcase. Becca didn't mind. Tazer had excellent taste in clothes, one of the many traits she admired in the agent. That and her kick-ass attitude.

Becca was really glad Tazer had a man in her life after so many years flying solo. Unfortunately, now that Tazer was based out of the West Coast office in Oregon, Becca rarely saw the woman.

Dressed in a pair of jeans that bunched around her ankles, Becca couldn't be too unhappy. At least the dark tennis shoes fit her feet. She stepped out of the small bedroom and into the cabin where she found Royce and Quentin leaning over a computer screen built into the tabletop between the chairs.

"Ah, Becca, have a seat," Royce said. "We were just going over our plan to infiltrate Jabouri's apartment."

"Our plan?" She raised her brows. "Are you coming with us, Royce?"

He nodded. "I don't have anyone else to assign to you at this time. Besides, I wouldn't send any of my people into a situation I wouldn't be willing to go into myself."

"I admire the sentiment, but wouldn't it be easier for one person to sneak in and corner the man?"

Quentin shook his head. "According to Royce's input, the man could be surrounded by bodyguards. We'll need to hit him at night when the guards are least aware."

Becca slipped into the chair beside Royce, reluctant to sit with Quentin. Her body fired up and sizzled when she sat too close to the broad-shouldered SEAL. "Show me."

They huddled over the monitor for the next twenty-five minutes when the captain announced their arrival into the Chattanooga airport. As soon as the plane came to a halt inside a general aviation hangar, the trio left the plane, slipped from the hangar into the next one and climbed aboard the aircraft there.

Within minutes, the small jet left the ground, bound for Cincinnati. As soon as they were out of the air traffic control airspace, they switched direction and headed for Albany, New York.

With a plan firmly in place, Becca leaned back in her chair and closed her eyes. "You might want to get some sleep. This mission will require being up late, possibly into the morning hours." She raised an eyelid and stared across at Quentin.

"Will do," he replied, closing his eyes. "I just can't help wondering why someone would pay a lot of money to hire assassins to kill you."

Becca yawned. "Reason escapes me."

"I can have someone check your post office box back in Virginia," Royce offered.

"The key is on my spare key chain." She gave him instructions on how to find it and where to find the key to her apartment she kept buried in the dirt of a planter on her front porch in case of an emergency. Having her belongings burned in a crashed airplane would constitute an emergency.

"I'll get someone on it right now." Royce pulled a disposable cell phone from its packaging and placed a call to one of his agents assigned in the DC area. When he ended the call, he nodded. "Sam Russell will swing out to Virginia some time this evening. I'll let you know what he finds."

"Thanks." Becca closed her eyes and let the roar of the engines sooth her tangled nerves. She had a long way to go before she could call it a day. Having Quentin at her side made it easier to relax. Knowing he would be with her when they sought out Jabouri was both reassuring and a little scary. But for now, she didn't want to think about what lay ahead. If she wanted to be fully prepared, she needed the little bit of sleep to keep her energy level at prime level.

She must have fallen asleep. A hand on her arm woke her as the plane set down on the tarmac in Albany.

"Ready, Slugger?" Quentin's voice sounded in her ear, his warm breath stirring the hairs around her neck. *Mmm.* "I was dreaming we were back in that motel."

A deep chuckle warmed her insides. "Must have been a nightmare. That wasn't the nicest place I could have taken you."

She sat up and stretched. "Where's Royce?"

"In the cockpit, keeping an eye out for anything suspicious."

Becca blinked, fully awake now. "Any concerns?"

"None so far. But we need to get out of here and on the road. It's getting dark outside and we still have to get to the city."

"How are we going to do that?"

"Royce arranged for a rental car to be delivered here." As the aircraft came to a halt on the tarmac, Quentin stood in front of her and extended a hand.

She laid a palm in his, tingles of electricity running from point of contact up her arm and down into the lower regions of her belly. Becca let him pull her to her feet and into his arms.

"Are you ready?" he asked, brushing a strand of her hair back behind her ear.

"Yeah," she replied. For a kiss, for another caress, any scrap of attention he deigned to give her. Hell, she was getting far too used to having him around, touching her and seeing to her every need.

The door to the cockpit opened and Royce stepped out. "Oh, good, you're awake. The car is waiting. Becca, you have the identification documents you need, money and credit cards should you run into any problems."

She patted the pocket on her jeans where she'd stashed the cards and money. "Got them."

Royce turned to Quentin. "I can't ask you to go into a hostile situation. Now would be your last chance to back out."

Before Royce finished talking, Quentin was shaking his head. "I'm in."

"Then let's go." Royce led the way out of the plane into the hangar. A four-door, dark, nondescript sedan stood beside the plane. He slipped into the driver's seat.

Quentin held the front passenger seat door for Becca, but she opened the rear door instead. "You can keep Royce company. I think I'll finish my nap."

Royce drove out of the hangar and away from the airport, heading south to New York City.

Becca sat in the backseat listening to Quentin and Royce talking about football, baseball and the state of affairs in the Middle East. The lulling effect of their conversation made her sleepy. Leaning back, she drifted off, only to be jerked awake when the sedan swerved off the edge of the road and thumped over the rumble strips.

"What's happening?" she asked, blinking the sleep out of her eyes.

"We're being attacked. Stay down." Quentin pulled out his Sig Sauer P226 and leaned out the window of the SUV. A bullet hit the back windshield, shattering the glass.

"Stay down!" Quentin shouted as he twisted around and pointed his weapon out the ruined back window.

"The hell I am," Becca unbuckled her seatbelt and knelt in the cushions of the backseat. "If they want trouble, they've found it." She leveled her H&K .40 caliber pistol at the vehicle following theirs and fired. A headlight blinked out, the driver swerved, but the vehicle never slowed, quickly catching up.

Royce ran their vehicle off the side of the road, bumped down into the ditch and back up onto the access road paralleling the interstate highway they'd been traveling on.

The vehicle that had been following now ran alongside them. A man wearing a black ski mask leaned out the window with what appeared to be an AR 15 rifle.

Chapter Seven

"Look out!" Quentin shouted.

Becca ducked as a round shattered the window she'd been looking through only a moment before.

Quentin's insides bunched. "Brakes! Hit the brakes!"

Royce slammed his foot on the brakes as the man fired again.

The front of the sedan took the hit, but the engine kept running. Executing a one-hundred-eighty-degree turn in the middle of the one-way access road, Royce drove against the traffic, back the direction they'd just come.

The trailing vehicle's driver slammed on his brakes and rolled off the road into the ditch, only the slope was more pronounced, where he chose to exit. When the car hit the bottom, the nose buried in the dirt, bringing it to a complete halt so fast the tail of the car rose in the air and then crashed to the ground.

Becca laughed out loud. "That takes care of them. They won't be getting that car out without a tow truck."

Royce pulled off the access road at the first point he could and found a convenience store several blocks away. He parked in the darkest corner of the parking lot. "We need to find the nearest train station that will get us all the way into Penn Station."

"I'll ask." Becca shoved open her door and got out.

"I'm going with you." Quentin got out, cupped her elbow and escorted her to the door.

"I can handle questioning the clerk by myself," she insisted.

"Right, but you need to feed the beast. I could do with a candy bar and you're the only one with money." He winked and opened the door for her. "I don't have too big a problem mooching off a girl. For now."

Becca rolled her eyes, a smile tugging at the corners of her lips. "Fine. I'll buy you a candy bar. Happy?"

"I will be, as soon as we catch the bastard trying to kill you," he said in a low whisper only she could hear. Quentin pressed a hand to the small of her back and turned his frown upside down as they stepped inside.

While Becca inquired on the location of the nearest train station, Quentin selected snacks to hold them over until they could get a proper meal and brought the items to the counter.

Becca paid for the purchases and they left. Once in the car with Royce, she said, "The station is a couple miles from here. We can park the vehicle a block or two from it and hop on."

Following Becca's directions, Royce parked within a couple blocks of the station. The three got out and hurried to buy tickets for the next train to Penn Station. The train was leaving within a few short minutes and they had to run to the platform, leaping on seconds before the doors closed.

Once inside, Quentin selected seating close to a door and sat with his back to the wall so that he could watch everyone entering and exiting the car. Becca sat next to him and Royce across.

Because others were on the train within easy listening distance, they didn't talk, just watched and waited for their arrival in the heart of New York City. After a while, Becca leaned against Quentin.

The train arrived in the late evening. Passengers in a hurry to get on the train crowded them as they exited.

The station teemed with people heading home after a long day at the office, making it difficult to keep an eye out for any potential threats, while at the same time making it easy for the three of them to blend into the crowd.

Royce purchased tickets for the subway to the Bronx and they hopped on the next one leaving out.

Royce leaned close to the two of them. "It'll be several hours before we visit Jay."

Quentin understood Jay was code for Jabouri. "That should give us time to recon and come up with a plan."

"The main thing is to get in and out without getting killed," Becca reminded them. "This op isn't over until I find the one responsible for my father's death." Her determination blazed in her eyes.

Quentin found her hand and held it in his. "We'll get the information we need."

The train stopped at their destination. Royce pulled up Jabouri's last known address on the disposable phone and studied the street map. With a mile and a half of city streets between them and their destination, they had time to prepare for what they had to do next.

Their first stop was a store in the subway station selling baseball caps and jackets. The temperatures at night in New York City were quite a bit cooler than Mississippi. Becca selected a black cap to hide her hair.

Quentin found a long, black, baggy jacket to cover the designer black sweater Tazer had provided Becca. "We'll be entering some of the toughest gang-ridden neighborhoods of the city. The less like a fashion model you look, the better."

"Thanks for looking out for me." She smiled up at him. "So, you think I look like a fashion model?"

Quentin and Royce selected a couple of hats, jackets and dark, long-sleeved T-shirts. Once they'd purchased the items they found a bathroom in the station. Quentin left Becca with Royce so that he could change out of his short-sleeved shirt into the new one.

When he came out, he found Becca with her hair tucked up into the cap she'd bought, wearing the jacket that completely hid her curves and the expensive sweater. Royce entered the bathroom to make his change.

"Are you all right?" Quentin asked.

Becca stared across at him. "I'm fine. I've worked several operations in New York City. I know what to expect. Have you ever been in the city?"

Quentin shook his head. "Can't say that I have. I spent most of my life out west—Washington, Oregon, Montana, Colorado."

"How did you end up as a SEAL?"

He shrugged. "Someone told me I would never make it."

Becca touched his arm. "I'm betting it was someone close to you."

He nodded. "My father."

"So you had something to prove to him."

"More to myself." Quentin gazed out at the people passing through the station like a river of humanity. "I was on a one-way trip to nowhere until I joined the navy."

"How so?"

"Fresh out of high school, no direction, no desire to go to college and hanging out with the wrong crowd."

"So your dad challenged you to join the navy?"

"No, he kicked me out. Told me I'd never amount to anything."

"Well, you did, as a member of one of the most elite fighting teams in the US military."

He grinned. "Yeah. But I might not have done it if my father hadn't given me the needed kick in the pants."

Once they were set in their city camouflage, they left the station and ambled toward their destination. Though they looked like they had nowhere to be at any given time, they were carefully studying the streets, the people and the buildings along the way.

Tattooed men stood at street corners with their pants hanging halfway down their butts. Some had their ball caps turned backward, others smoked cigarettes.

Quentin could have been one of them had he not joined the navy when he did. Never had he been gladder that his father had more or less shamed him into taking that first step.

What he didn't like about walking on the streets was that the three of them were highly outnumbered by any one group. Thankfully, all three of them had training in self-defense. If things got bad, they could fight their way out. Preferably without use of one of the weapons they carried hidden beneath the layers of clothing.

"Hey." A big guy with droopy drawers, silver chains dangling low from one belt loop to another and wearing a Giants ball cap backwards stepped in front of Becca. "What you doin' hangin' with these losers?"

Quentin started forward, but Becca's hand held him back with a light touch, barely noticeable by the group of young men gathering around. This could be Quentin's worst nightmare about to happen and Becca could get hurt. Every protective instinct reared up and screamed to take the lead on this one.

Becca ran her gaze from the tip of the man's head to the toes of his ratty tennis shoes. Then she tipped her head with a jerk. "Better these losers than you."

Chuckles sounded from the teens and young men surrounding the big guy in the Giants hat. His eyes narrowed. Apparently he didn't like being laughed at in front of his peers.

Quentin's fists clenched and he braced his feet, ready to take on every last one of them if necessary.

"Do you mind?" Becca said, her voice low, tough, gravely and sexy as hell. "I gotta kid brother waiting for me at home. These two are just seeing that I get there."

Giants hat guy stared down his nose at her, his gaze slipping to Quentin and then Royce. Finally, he shrugged and stepped back. "I gotta kid brother, too." He glared at Quentin. "Make sure she gets there."

Quentin nodded without saying a word. The group of young men parted, allowing them through.

When they were a block away, Becca said through barely parted lips. "Thanks for not hitting him."

Quentin had yet to release his fists. He glanced to the left and right, getting a look at the guys they'd left behind in his peripheral vision, not so sure he wouldn't need to hit someone yet. "I would have."

"Me, too." Royce chuckled. "Nice line to deflect them."

"I figure even though they think they're tough, they have to have family." Becca kept walking, her head slightly down, her gaze seemingly on her feet. Quentin could tell she was looking all around her, but the hat made it hard for anyone else to know that.

Royce led them through a maze of turns, down one street then the next, leading them farther away from the main road into a labyrinth of tenements with laundry lines strung between the buildings. Windows were open to the evening breeze and some people stood on the metal fire escapes to get a breath of air or smoke a cigarette. The cries of children playing inside or a baby screaming for his mother reached them on the streets below.

But it was the smell of trash and human waste that filled Quentin's senses. The last place he'd been that had smelled this bad was New Orleans during Mardi Gras. Even the villages in Afghanistan didn't smell this bad. But then the buildings weren't stacked twenty to forty stories high, with garbage lining the gutters and filling the alleys.

"Jay's building is coming up on the left," Royce warned. "Time to split up. I got the front. I'll meet you two blocks past the building and two blocks to the left." He kept walking, while Quentin and Becca turned left at the intersection before they reached Jabouri's apartment building.

The people in this neighborhood appeared to be a mix of Middle Eastern descent. Women wore scarves over their hair and faces and dressed in long robes and were accompanied by men. Though they'd dressed for the rough neighborhoods, the three of them stood out.

Quentin had a tan from training outdoors and his time in Cancun, but his skin wasn't nearly as dark as that of most of the men in this community. He kept his head down as he passed others on the street, hurrying with Becca to the alley leading to the back of the apartment building.

Several huge trash bins lined the alley and rickety metal fire escape landings and ladders reached to the top of the twenty-story complex. Clotheslines stretched from the apartment building to the next one with everything from sheets to baby clothes, jeans and dresses hanging out to dry.

Without knowing the layout of the inside of the building, Quentin couldn't tell which apartment might be Jabouri's. They'd have to go in. He found that the worst combat situations were in urban terrain. Whether it was an Iraqi city or one in the US it could get hairy. He didn't have the equipment he usually had when conducting a military operation. No night-vision goggles or submachine guns equipped with sound suppression devices. But he did have the tiny night-vision monocular and a handgun. He'd have to make do.

Though he was certain Becca was a highly trained agent, they hadn't trained in this kind of operation together. It would be a crapshoot on how each would react to a tense situation.

He didn't like it. One thing was certain. If he didn't go with them into this operation, Becca would go in without him.

BECCA CHECKED EVERY WINDOW, noting which ones were open and which were closed with blackout curtains. Based on the address provided, Jabouri's apartment was probably located on the sixth floor. One set of windows on the farthest corner was closed with the curtains drawn. In fact, she couldn't see even a gleam of light escaping around the edges. Either all the lights were out, or they'd painted the windows black to keep anyone from seeing in or out.

At the end of the alley, Quentin and Becca emerged onto the street and nearly ran into a group of men hurrying toward the building they were studying.

Quentin stepped back, pulling Becca with him.

Several of the men gave them narrow-eyed stares. One in particular stopped, said a few words to another and then continued on. The one he'd spoken to fell to the back of the group, moving slower.

Quentin gripped Becca's arm and hurried across the street, turning left. He didn't slow until they reached the next road where he turned right.

As soon as he and Becca cleared the corner, she stopped. "Did he follow us?" Becca spun, preparing to peer around the corner.

Quentin laid a hand on her shoulder. "I think so. Now wouldn't be a good time to check and see. Let's take our time getting to the other corner. Maybe he'll step out and reveal himself."

He was right. If the man found Becca looking to see if he followed them, he'd be suspicious and alert his leader to the possibility of trouble.

Becca fell in step with Quentin, walking away from Jabouri's apartment building as if they were on their way somewhere and just passing through the neighborhood. As they turned to the left at the next street, she glanced back and noted the man leaning on the corner of the building.

A shiver slithered down the back of her neck. The man had to be one of Jabouri's men.

They kept moving, going one block past their designated meeting place. Through the gap in the buildings, Becca spotted Royce sitting like a homeless man at the corner. She could tell by the tilt of his ball cap it was him.

Once they were certain Jabouri's man wasn't still on their tail, they would circle back and join Royce. At times like these, she wished she had use of her cell phone to pass information to her boss. But the less communication by devices that could be easily tracked, the better.

Rather than turning right to take them to the block Royce was waiting on, Quentin made a left and backtracked a block, coming full circle to the one where they'd seen Jabouri's man. He was gone from the corner. Quentin and Becca retraced their footsteps down the path they'd taken to the next street and looked for the man. Again, he was nowhere to be seen.

"Did we lose him?" Becca whispered.

"That would be my guess," Quentin replied. "But it wouldn't hurt to take an even more circuitous route to meet up with your boss."

"Agreed." She turned right, away from the road Royce was waiting on. Quentin stayed abreast of her, his reassuringly big body blocking part of her view. At the next alley they ducked in and made their way around trash bins, pallets and rubbish. Becca held out her arm, stopping Quentin before they emerged from the alley onto the street where they would be meeting up with Royce.

She pressed a finger to her lips and eased her head around the corner of the building.

Royce hunkered against the corner of the next building. But he wasn't the only one on the street. The man who'd been following them was headed their direction. He slowed as he passed Royce, staring at him long and hard.

Royce held up a cup and moaned something.

The man shook his head and moved on, closing the distance between Royce and the alley where Becca and Quentin stood.

She ducked back and whispered, "Hide."

Quentin stepped into the shadow of a large trash bin overflowing with garbage and an old mattress. He pulled Becca in with him as Jabouri's man rounded the corner and entered the alley.

Becca held her breath, afraid to make even the slightest sound.

Something scurried across her foot. Becca jerked her foot backward, swallowing the natural urge to scream.

Jabouri's man stopped and stared at the bin.

Becca shrank back into Quentin's arms and remained motionless.

The rat that had crossed her foot ran out into the alley.

Jabouri's man leaped back and kicked at the creature, saying something in a language Becca didn't understand. Then he moved on, hurrying out of the alley, turning in the direction of Jabouri's apartment building.

Quentin and Becca stayed in the shadow of the trash

bin for a full minute before venturing out of the alley and back to where Royce sat huddled against the building like a homeless man begging for money.

"Was that your friend?" Royce asked, glancing left then right before pushing to his feet.

"We picked him up at the corner of Jabouri's apartment building."

Glancing down at the empty paper cup, Royce snorted. "He wasn't much into charity." He crumpled the cup in his hand. "What did you see?"

"Sixth floor corner apartment was the only one that seemed completely blacked out," Becca reported.

"No one hanging around the building before Jabouri arrived with half a dozen followers," Quentin added.

"Fire escape functional?" Royce asked.

"As far as I could tell. At least there is one from that apartment."

"Good. We might need it." He glanced past them. "We need to find a good observation point."

"The building across the alley from our target building is being renovated. Several of the windows were open with chutes for tossing down rubbish."

Royce nodded. "Let's see if we can gain access to it and watch from there until Jabouri's entourage leaves."

They walked back the way they'd come, stopping short at the building under renovation, facing the apartment building they would enter later that night. As Quentin indicated, this tenement was being renovated and many of the apartments were unoccupied. Royce was able to jimmy the lock on the entrance door while Becca and Quentin stayed at the end of the street in the shadow of the scaffolding being used to protect the people walking along the sidewalks from falling debris.

Quentin's hand rested low on Becca's back as they waited for their cue to join Royce. Becca didn't step away. She liked the feel of his big hand warm on her back.

Royce signaled. Reluctantly, Becca stepped away from that hand and Quentin's solid body. She hurried toward the entrance to the renovation project and ducked inside, Quentin on her heels.

Royce went up the stairs first, then Becca, followed by Quentin. They didn't stop until they reached the sixth floor. The going wasn't easy in the dark and they didn't dare use more than the pocket flashlight with the red lens Quentin had picked up on the airplane. On the sixth floor, Becca took the lead, turned left and hurried to the end of the hallway. The door at the end stood halfway open, the room filled with drop cloths, buckets of paint, rollers and brushes.

Light shone through the uncovered windows from the apartments across the alley, allowing them to make their way across the room without turning on a flashlight.

Quentin stood to the side of a window, pulled out the night-vision monocular and focused on the corner apartment window.

"See anything?" Becca asked.

Quentin stared longer and then handed the device to her. "I count six people from what I could tell." He glanced over at Royce.

The older man held his own monocular to his eye. "I got five or six."

Becca raised the small device to her eye and took a moment to train it on the right room in the apartment across the street. Green heat signatures appeared in the lens. She counted them, one by one. "I got six."

"That's two to one odds." Quentin shrugged. "I've been in worse scenarios, but I prefer to make a quieter entrance."

"We can't go in firing with both barrels," Royce said. "There are families in that building."

"Right." As Becca handed the monocular back to Quentin, their hands touched, sending electric shock waves up Becca's arm. *How did he do that?* "No collateral damage," she said, her voice a little gruff, her insides sparking with a desire she had no way to quench. Why was she so aroused by Quentin? Especially now. Maybe it had something to do with the adrenaline surging through her at the thought of the action ahead.

"No collateral damage," Quentin echoed. "In other words we wait until we get better odds or they go to sleep."

"We might be going in earlier than you think," Royce said. "Check it out."

Quentin raised his device to his eye. "Two, three, four of them are leaving." Again, he handed the monocular to Becca. "See them?"

She pressed it to her eye and focused on Jabouri's apartment in time to see four green figures walking toward what she assumed was the door.

She lowered the monocular and waited for the men to exit the front entrance to the building and circle around the way they'd come, passing the end of the alley. For almost a minute, she held her breath until a man appeared, then another and another. Four of the men she and Quentin had run into walked past the alley entrance. At least two remained inside. "I'm liking the odds much better now. Let's do this."

Chapter Eight

While they waited for several minutes for the foursome
to get far enough away from the apartment building,
Quentin took out his Sig Sauer P226, disassembled and
reassembled the pistol and checked the fully-loaded
magazine. It appeared to be in prime working condition. He didn't like that he'd never fired the weapon
and didn't know its quirks, if it had any. But it couldn't
be helped.

Three minutes after the four men disappeared down
the street, Royce placed a call to Geek's private number. "We're going in. Give us fifteen minutes, then call
the police and send them to this address. Tell them you
suspect terrorists live there and you heard gunfire."
When he ended the call, he shrugged. "It doesn't hurt
to have backup, even if the backup might mistake you
for the bad guys. We just have to be out in fifteen."

Quentin admired the way Royce thought. If he ever
left active duty, he'd like to work for a man like the
head of the Stealth Operations Specialists. "We will
be out of there in fifteen. Sooner, if we can get the information we need." Quentin led the way out of the
renovation building and across to Jabouri's.

Becca and Royce followed. The front door to the

building was locked. A knife applied to the right place on the doorframe got them in and they quickly climbed to the fifth floor.

"I'll go up the main staircase to the sixth," Quentin whispered. "You two take the stairwell. Let me get halfway down the hall before you exit the stairwell."

Royce and Becca nodded and took off for the stairwell at the end of the hallway. Quentin waited until they were through the door, then he continued up the stairs to the sixth floor and peered around the corner of the staircase to the hallway beyond.

Two men sat on the floor outside the end apartment door, their handguns lying beside them as they played a hand of cards. One yawned and spoke in a foreign language. Quentin couldn't make out the words, and didn't really care. A movement flashed in the small window of the stairwell doorway indicating the arrival of Becca and Royce.

On silent feet, Quentin entered the hallway and walked swiftly with his head down, his footsteps silent, one hand on the P226 in his pocket.

The men on the floor didn't look up until the squeak of the stairwell door. Both men grabbed for their guns.

Quentin jumped the closest one before the man could wrap his hand around his pistol grip. The other guy hesitated between facing the stairwell and turning back to his partner, giving Royce and Becca the time they needed to pounce on the other. Only one of the two men had time to yelp before their air was cut off by arms hooked firmly around their throats. The resulting scuffle was minimal and they were able to drag the two to the stairwell where Becca made quick work of duct-taping their mouths and zip-tying their wrists and ankles.

Quentin was back in the hallway before the others. He turned his ball cap around backwards, gripped the Sig Sauer in one hand and rapped on Jabouri's door with his knuckles.

"Who is it?" a man said from inside.

Royce and Becca joined him, standing to either side of the door.

"Pizza delivery," Quentin answered, leaning close to the peephole to let them see his face in a more distorted image.

"Go away. We didn't order pizza."

"The two guys I passed going down the stairs said you did," Quentin said with his best Bronx accent. "Look, I got a pizza with this address on it. Either you pay for it, or I have to pay for it out of my own pocket."

The man on the other side opened the door with the chain lock engaged. Quentin verified the face in front of him belonged to the guy who'd tailed them for several blocks before giving up.

The man started with, "I said I didn't—" He recognized Quentin and tried to slam the door.

Before the door shut all the way, Quentin reared back and kicked the door. The chain snapped free and the door swung inward, catching the man in the face. He staggered backward, reaching into his robes.

Quentin raced in, hitting him low in the belly, knocking him backward into a man stepping out of another room to see what was going on.

Both men went down in a heap on the floor of the apartment, and scrambled to reach for their guns.

Quentin pointed his P226 at the man nearest to him.

"Keep your hands where we can see them, or I'll blow a hole through you."

Becca and Royce joined him, all pointing their guns at the pair on the floor.

"What do you want?" the man in the back asked. "We don't have any money or drugs."

"Right," Becca said. "I imagine you keep your money in an offshore bank account."

The men didn't look at Becca, focusing on Royce and Quentin.

"I don't know what you are talking about," Jabouri said, addressing his remark to Quentin, not Becca. "We don't have any money."

Becca left the men and entered the next room.

Quentin didn't like that she disappeared. Especially when he didn't know if the other room was empty or had another terrorist waiting to come out shooting.

She reappeared a moment later. "The apartment is clear of other men, but there's a weapons stash in the flooring beneath the mattress in the bedroom. Enough guns and ammo to start a small war. All Russian. And another Russian-made manpad."

Royce stepped toward him. "We don't want your money. We want information."

"I don't know anything. I'm just a poor man in a big city."

"Look, Jabouri, we know you sell weapons and the services of mercenaries to the highest bidders. We want to know who hired you to kill Becca and Marcus Smith and Rand Houston."

Jabouri shook his head. "I don't know this Jabouri you speak of. No one by that name lives here. I'm Wayne and this is John."

"And I'm Peter Pan." Royce pulled a hypodermic needle from his pocket and removed the tube surrounding it. "You know what this is?"

The man's eyes widened briefly and he shot a glance toward the door.

Royce continued. "It's truth serum. You'll tell us one way or another who is funding this effort."

Quentin grabbed the top guy's hand, yanked him off Jabouri and twisted his arm up between his shoulder blades.

Becca moved in with the zip ties. While they were securing the man, Jabouri rolled to his side and scrambled to his feet, making a grab for Becca.

She jerked the zip tie tight on the man's wrists, jabbed her elbow into Jabouri's, slammed a fist to his groin, spun and knifed her knee into his face as he bent double.

The man went down, clutching himself, still conscious but in a significant amount of pain. He reached for his gun.

Becca kicked the gun out of reach and stepped on his wrist, pinning it to the ground. "I suggest you cooperate," she said, her voice low and dangerous.

"He will." Royce jabbed the needle into the man's arm.

Quentin slapped tape over his captive's mouth and shoved him into a closet, returning to assist with Jabouri. He glanced at his watch. "We have five minutes before Geek does his thing."

Royce nodded, waiting precious seconds for the drug to take effect.

Quentin helped Royce sit the man in a chair and

Becca bound his hands behind him with another handy zip tie.

"Jabouri, where were you born?" Royce asked.

The man's head lolled, blood dripping from his nose. "Syria."

"Do you support the Taliban?"

He straightened. *"Allahu Akbar."*

"Do you support ISIS?"

"Allahu Akbar."

"Who paid you to kill Rand Houston?"

"I don't know."

"Yes, you do," Royce said. "Who paid you to kill Marcus Smith, the CIA Agent?"

"Ivan."

"Ivan who?" Royce demanded.

"I don't know. He has no other name."

Quentin grabbed the collar of Jabouri's robe and snarled at the bastard. "Where can we find Ivan?"

"I don't know. I don't know!" Jabouri's eyes rolled back. For a moment Quentin thought the man had passed out.

Then in a soft voice Jabouri said, "He finds me. Coming tonight."

Becca's eyes widened and she ran for the door.

Before she reached it, the door exploded inward.

Two men rushed in, each carrying a pistol.

Jabouri's eyes widened. "Ivan!"

The first man through the door yelled in Russian and fired at Jabouri, hitting him square in the chest. The force of the pointblank shot toppled the man and chair backward and he crashed to the floor.

Becca kicked the wrist of the second man, knocking the gun from his hand.

Quentin grabbed the other man's arm, jerked it down as he pulled the trigger. The gun went off, the bullet missing the three of them.

Royce and Becca subdued one guy, while Quentin fought the other. When both men lay moaning on the floor, Quentin grabbed their guns with a cloth, ejected the magazines and the chambered rounds, and shoved them in his pockets.

Lots of footsteps sounded in the hallway and men shouted. Quentin slammed the door shut and shot the deadbolt home. It might slow them down, but not much.

Becca threw open the window to the back alley and swung her leg over the sill. "Time to go, boys." She eased out onto the fire escape and started down.

Royce knelt by Ivan, checking for a pulse. "We need to question him."

"No time," Quentin said. "Sounds like an army coming down the hall. We're outnumbered and the cops will be here soon."

Royce patted the man's pockets, removed a wallet and ran for the window. Quentin held a gun on the men in the apartment until Royce was halfway down. As he hiked his leg over the sill, Ivan clambered to his feet, staggered to the door and pulled it open. He shouted something in Russian and pointed back at Quentin.

"Yup. It's time for me to go." He slipped over the edge and dropped to the metal mesh of the fire escape and started down as fast as he could go. Several times, he vaulted over the railing and landed on the platform a level below the one he was on. Voices sounded from the open window above.

"Hurry!" Becca called out.

Gunfire echoed off the walls of the tenements.

Becca hovered behind a big metal garbage bin and returned fire, providing cover while Royce and Quentin made their way to the bottom.

Quentin had almost caught up with Royce when the older man dropped the remaining ten feet to the ground and took off toward the corner of the trash bin.

Before he made it a shot was fired.

Royce lurched forward and dropped to his belly on the ground, rolled and staggered to his feet, making it to the safety of the metal trash bin.

Quentin grabbed the railing on the last level, swung over the side, dropped and rolled on the ground. He sprang to his feet and ran in a zigzagging pattern. Gunfire sounded and he felt something sting his shoulder. He didn't stop until he dove behind the cover of the trash bin.

Becca fired several times at the window and then turned to Quentin. "Cover us while we make a run for the street."

"Got it. Go!" He fired at the window, keeping the men inside from taking aim at Becca and Royce as they dashed for the corner of the building. Once they made it, Becca returned the favor.

Once all three of them were around the corner, they ran for the next street and ducked down an alley. The sound of sirens wailing nearby was welcome, but no reason for them to stop running until they were far enough away that none of Ivan or Jabouri's people would find them.

Five blocks from the tenement, Royce staggered and fell to the ground.

Becca and Quentin draped Royce's arms over their shoulders and lifted him, guiding him to a darkened alley. When they eased him to the ground, rolling him to his uninjured side, that wet, warm oozing liquid Quentin had had far too much experience with dripped down his arm from the wound on the back of Royce's shoulder. A metallic scent filled the air.

Quentin shed his jacket and shoulder holster and then pulled his T-shirt over his head, ripping it into long, wide strips. He wadded one strip into a pad and pressed it into the wound. "Press that pad onto the wound and keep the pressure on to stop the bleeding."

Becca held the pad, applying pressure while Quentin wrapped the strip of his T-shirt around Royce's shoulder and knotted it over Becca's hand and the pad. Becca eased her hand out of the way of the knot.

Quentin pressed his hand to Royce's back. "Are you hanging in there?"

"I'm fine," Royce said, his voice less than convincing.

"Yeah, right." Quentin faced Becca. "He's lost a lot of blood. We have to get him to a hospital."

"No." Royce's voice was weak. He tried to sit up, but he couldn't, falling back to the hard pavement. He winced and grabbed for his arm. "Just leave me here and take this." He dug in one of his pockets and pulled out an electronic device. "I tagged Ivan. Follow him with this." He handed it to Quentin.

"Not until we get you to a hospital." Becca dug the phone out of Royce's other pocket and dialed 911. "Find out where we are," she ordered Quentin.

While he jumped up to investigate, she was on the phone with a dispatcher.

Quentin ducked out of the alley long enough to find street signs, and was back by the time Becca was ready to give their location. He relayed the information and Becca told the dispatcher. She remained on the line while they passed the information to the nearest first responders and then ended the call.

"I order you to go," Royce said. "The EMTs will find me. You don't need to stick around to answer questions."

She shook her head. "At the risk of being fired, sir... shut up and conserve your strength."

Royce chuckled and grimaced. "Insubordinate witch."

"I can be even witchier if you don't do as I say." Becca stood and paced to the corner, her gun ready. "Now be quiet. We don't need Ivan and his men finding us."

Royce looked up at Quentin. "Bossy, isn't she?"

"When she's right." Quentin continued to apply pressure to the wound, afraid if the medics didn't get there soon, Ivan would find them and they wouldn't need an ambulance. A hearse would be more in order. His gaze drifted to Becca. He worried that she might be seen, peering around the corner of the building. "Becca, trade places with me."

"No. I'm fine," she whispered over her shoulder. "You're doing a better job as a nurse than I would. Trust me. Just keep him alive, will ya?"

Within minutes, sirens sounded nearby.

Before Quentin could tell her differently, Becca left the relative safety of the alley and hurried to the intersection of the two roads Quentin had given her to flag the ambulance.

Quentin held his breath, straining his ears for the sound of gunfire.

"Go after her," Royce said. "She'll be in the open. If Ivan's men are drawn to the sirens, they'll see her."

Quentin shook his head. "You can't hold the pressure on the wound where it's located and Becca would shoot me if I let you die."

Royce snorted. "She was one of my best agents until she went rogue on me."

"Rogue?"

"When her father was killed, she didn't wait for me to assign another agent to help find the one responsible. She dropped off the grid and went out on her own."

"Yeah, we found her in Cancun." Quentin's gaze never left the alley entrance, his pulse quickening with each passing second as he waited for Becca to reappear. "We thought she might be the one after Sawyer until she helped save our butts in a firefight."

"I'm glad she had you and your team there to help her out."

"Hell, she helped *us*."

"She's a very determined young lady. It tore her apart when she learned of her father's death."

"I'll bet it did."

"Her mother died in a plane crash as the plane landed. Becca was there, waiting for her mother to get off that flight. She witnessed all of it. She was only six. Her father was the only family she had left. They were very close."

Quentin's chest tightened. No wonder she'd freaked out when their plane crashed into the alligator swamp.

Royce's gaze followed Quentin's. "Don't let her stubborn determination get her into too much trouble."

"I don't know that I have much say in the matter. But I plan on sticking close to her as long as I can."

"Good. As soon as the medics take me, go after Ivan. He might lead us to his contact. I can't imagine he's the one funding the mercenary killings."

"Will do." Quentin stiffened as a shadowy figure appeared, hurrying their way. It only took him a second to recognize Becca by the way she walked. She struck out like she had somewhere to go, and she wasn't wasting time getting there. Yeah, he'd have a hell of a time keeping up with her. But he didn't have much choice. He couldn't let her go it alone. He was beginning to care.

Chapter Nine

Becca stood in the shadow of the building waiting for the fire truck to stop at the street corner. When a paramedic dropped down from the passenger seat, she stepped out. Then she only stepped out long enough to say, "Over here. You'll need a stretcher." She waved and stepped back into the shadow of the building. The medics removed the equipment from the truck, asking questions as they pulled out a stretcher and what looked like a toolbox. She answered succinctly, anxious to get them to Royce.

So far, she didn't see Ivan or his men, but that didn't mean they weren't lurking somewhere, waiting for their opportunity to strike. With the police five blocks away, handling the aftermath of the firefight, maybe Ivan had cut his losses and gotten the hell away from the Bronx. Whatever was the case, Becca couldn't hold off getting medical attention for Royce.

A police car rolled up beside the fire truck and an ambulance pulled in, as well. Becca felt more confident that Ivan wouldn't try anything now. When the firefighters and EMTs were ready, she led the way to the alley.

The emergency personnel took over. Quentin and

Becca stood back, out of the way, and somewhat in the shadows.

When the paramedics had stabilized and prepared to move Royce, he raised a hand. "Wait."

The EMTs paused.

"Becca. Quentin." Royce waved them over. "I just remembered. Take my wallet. I don't want it to get lost." He winked and handed Becca the wallet he'd pulled off Ivan. "And don't forget to visit me after you take care of business."

"We'll be back," Becca promised. "I'll let your family know what happened." She'd call Geek with the name of the hospital. Hopefully, one of the SOS agents was in NYC and could be called upon to provide Royce with protection while he was there.

Royce was loaded into the ambulance and taken to the nearest hospital.

"We'd better go." Quentin glanced up from staring at the tracking device. "Ivan's on the move."

Although tired to the bone, Becca refused to let the opportunity pass because she was physically taxed. If Quentin could do it, so could she. "Let's go."

They chose a location on the street map and called for a taxi to pick them up in five minutes. That gave them just enough time to get to the location. And hopefully enough time to catch up to Ivan. Maybe he'd be moving on his own, not with his army of thugs.

Moving through some of the sketchier neighborhoods of the Bronx, Becca didn't have time to think about what they would do if they caught up to Ivan. She was more worried about getting out of the Bronx before they were mugged, shot or sold into sexual slavery.

When they emerged onto a busy main thoroughfare,

she let go a sigh of relief. A taxi pulled up to the designated location and they fell into the backseat.

Quentin pulled out the tracker. "Damn. He's moving fast, but it's not making sense."

"What do you mean?" Becca leaned against Quentin. He had blood on his jacket and beneath the jacket he wasn't wearing a shirt, but the hardness of his muscles spoke of his strength and ability to endure a lot of physical hardship. Becca melted into him, partly because her own strength was flagging, and partly because she wanted to see what he was seeing on the device.

Like Quentin had said, the little green dot on the screen was moving, but not tracking against the street map overlay.

"He's on the subway," Becca said.

"That makes sense."

"Where to, mister?" the cabbie asked.

"South," Quentin and Becca said as one.

The cabbie shook his head and made a U-turn in the middle of the street to a lot of honking and a few curses from drivers and pedestrians. Once he was heading south, the cabbie glanced into the rearview mirror. "I need an address."

"We don't have one yet. Just head south until we tell you otherwise."

"Look, I don't know what you're pullin' but I ain't got time to play games with you. Either give me an address or get out." He pulled to the curb and shoved the shift into park.

Becca pulled a hundred-dollar bill out of the stash Royce had given her and leaned over the cabbie's shoulder. "Take this for now and I'll give you another when we get out. Will that make up for the inconvenience of no address?"

The man stared at the bill, a frown denting his brow. "This ain't one of those counterfeit bills, is it?"

Becca locked gazes with the man in the mirror. "It's the real deal. Now, are we going south, or do we need to find another cabbie who wants to make a couple hundred dollars' tip?" She cocked her brows and waited for the cabbie's response.

"South it is." The man shifted into drive and pulled away from the curb, nearly hitting the car already in that lane.

Horns blared and curses flew through the night.

But they were on their way south on the streets while the green blip that was Ivan was headed south on the subway. The green dot only appeared at stops when a signal could get through. The taxi stopped at lights, but they slowly caught up with the subway.

"You two getting out at the train station?" the cabbie asked, turning onto the street at Penn Station.

"No," Becca said.

"Yes," Quentin contradicted. "Look, the green dot is moving, but not far from where he started. My bet is he got off the subway. If we hurry we can catch up with him."

Becca clenched the promised hundred-dollar bill in her fist. "Are you sure?"

"No, but what if he gets on a train? The taxi driver isn't going to follow a train out of here."

"If we pay him enough…?"

"We can't risk losing him."

"Fine." She leaned over the seat and handed the man

the second hundred-dollar bill. "Thanks for bringing us this far."

"No. Thank *you*. I can wait around for ten minutes if you think you might need me again."

"We appreciate the offer, but that won't be necessary." Quentin climbed out, rounded the vehicle to the passenger side and held the door open for Becca, glancing down at the tracking device several times. He held out his hand. "We'd better hurry."

Becca took the proffered hand and they ran for the entrance. Once inside, Becca craned her neck as she hurried alongside Quentin, following the green light.

"We should be getting close."

They ran into a gate. With no ticket they couldn't get past the barricades.

Becca stared at the display and then at a map on the wall. "Quentin, honey, this train is going to DC and it leaves in exactly three minutes."

She grabbed his hand, ran for the ticket kiosk and frantically fed bills into the machine, crumbling them so badly the machine only spit them out. "Damn it. This would be so much easier if I could just use a credit card."

"Let me." Quentin took the bills from her, straightened the wrinkles and patiently fed them one at a time into the machine.

Becca paced beside him, staring at the clock on the wall. "We only have two minutes to get tickets, get through the line and on that train," she said through her teeth. "But no pressure." She gritted her teeth, paced a few steps and returned. Holy hell, what was taking the machine so blasted long?

Finally, Quentin straightened and held up two tickets to DC. "Your train awaits, milady."

Becca grabbed his elbow and ran, dragging him along with her. A line had formed at the gate, slowing their entrance onto the platform.

They made it to the train in time to leap aboard two seconds before the doors closed.

Becca checked the car they were in and didn't see Ivan or any of his entourage. "Where is he?"

Quentin checked the tracker as the train lurched forward, moving slowly through the train station. Ivan's green light was moving, too. With them. "He's on this train."

Despite how tired she was, Becca jumped to her feet. "Let's go find him."

Quentin laid a hand on her arm. "Sit."

"But—"

"Sit."

"What about Ivan?" she asked, still standing.

"He's on this train. We can't interrogate him without drawing a crowd and possibly getting kicked off the train."

"We can't just sit back and do nothing." Becca paced a few steps down the aisle and back. "Ivan's the contact. He knows who paid to have my father killed."

Quentin nodded. "True, but he's headed to DC. We have to consider what that might mean."

Becca's eyes narrowed. "He's going to meet the man who hired him. We got too close. Ivan might be running scared." She glanced across at Quentin. He was right. "Then we can't let him know we're following him. But we'll need to stay on him. The bug Royce planted on him is probably somewhere in his clothing. If he changes, we stand to lose him."

"All the more reason to stick close to him."

Becca stared at the backs of the seats on the car they'd boarded. "Shouldn't we find him?"

"No, babe. He'd recognize us and we'd have a gunfight on board a train full of people. It's too dangerous."

Becca chewed on her bottom lip. "You're right." She settled in the seat beside him and stared down the aisle. "What if he changes clothing on the train?"

"Why would he?" Quentin asked. "He doesn't know we're on the train and he doesn't know he's been tagged. And considering he took the subway to get to Penn Station, I would venture to guess he didn't stop by his apartment and pack a suitcase or change of clothing for the trip."

Becca sat back against the seat. "I suppose you're right. Considering this is the only lead we have, I hate the thought of Ivan getting away." The door at the end of the train car opened and a man stepped through. Becca's pulse leaped. She reached out and gripped Quentin's leg. "Speak of the devil. He's headed this way. We need to hide. Right now." She shrank against Quentin's side, trying to get out of sight of the man heading directly toward them.

"Kiss me," Quentin urged.

"What?" She shot a glance at him. She'd wanted to kiss him all day long and wondered if he'd ever try to kiss her again. "Now?"

"Yes, now. Hurry." He swept the cap off her head, ruffled her hair, finger-combing it to let it fall around her shoulders in long, wavy curls. Then he gripped her arms and pulled her against him, pressing his lips to hers. Using her hair as a curtain to hide both of their faces, Quentin prolonged the kiss until Ivan passed them and walked through to the next car.

When the threat was gone, Quentin still did not let go of Becca. Instead, he pulled her across his lap and deepened the kiss.

Becca wrapped her arms around his neck. If Ivan came back that way, she never knew. All she knew was that if she died that moment, she'd die a happy woman. Quentin's kiss was that good.

The train lurched, throwing them out of the hold they had on each other. Becca lifted her head and stared around the interior of the train car. For the length of that soul-defining kiss, she'd forgotten about Ivan and the threat of starting a gunfight on a train full of people. Heat surged through her and settled low in her belly, a profound ache radiating inside her chest. She wanted to kiss Quentin and keep kissing him. More than that, she wanted to make love to him, and wake up beside him every day.

But she realized how impossible that would be. They were two very different people who worked in highly dangerous jobs, based out of different parts of the country. Nothing about a relationship with Quentin would work. She had to remind herself that he was a ladies' man—a navy guy with a female conquest in every port. Somehow the mantra didn't hold as much water, nor did it change her heart from feeling the way it did.

Becca's throat constricted. She swallowed hard to clear it and pushed free of Quentin's embrace, turning toward the aisle. Through a wash of moisture filling her eyes, she could see it was empty. "We're clear."

The kiss was nothing more than a charade to fool

their prey. She had to remember that and stop mooning over a man who wouldn't be in her life after this operation was completed.

No matter how much she reminded herself, the tightness in her chest refused to release.

QUENTIN SAT SILENTLY MONITORING the GPS tracking device, while his thoughts whirled around the woman sitting beside him. He longed to take her hand and tell her everything would be okay. They'd find her father's killer and make sure justice was served. But what then?

He'd go his way. She'd go hers.

Would he ever see Becca again?

He tried to recall the face of any one of the women who'd been in his life. None surfaced. None came to mind except Becca—the SOS agent with incredible combat skills and a warrior's heart. She was passionate about what she did, about the people she loved and equally passionate in bed. And that kiss...

What had started as concealment against discovery by Ivan had morphed into something much more. By the time Becca broke it off, Quentin felt as if a part of him leaned away with her.

What was happening to him? He'd never wanted a woman as badly as he wanted Becca. And not just for the sex, which was amazing, but for her—the intelligent, courageous woman she was, intent on finding the person responsible for her father's death.

Quentin could sense in her the deep anguish of losing the only family she had left, and his heart ached for her.

The train slid into a stop along the way to DC.

Becca turned to stare down at the tracker. "If he gets off, we have to get off."

"Right." Quentin focused on the small screen, his pulse kicking up a notch. They had to be ready to hop off the train if Ivan disembarked at the last minute.

People got on and some got off the train. The doors closed and they left the station, continuing on course to DC.

Quentin let go of the breath he'd been holding and relaxed against the seat.

Beside him Becca's stiff body slumped. "We need to get some rest. The trip takes about five hours. I can take the first shift." She held out her hand for the tracker.

Quentin, used to catching power naps whenever he could, handed over the device. "Wake me in two hours." He closed his eyes and forced all thoughts of Ivan on the train with them, Jabouri lying dead in his apartment, Royce laid up in the hospital and most of all Becca's warm body in the seat beside him to the back of his mind. His body needed rest. He fell to sleep.

The jungle around him was dark, the canopy so thick not a single star shone through as he and his team huddled beneath leaves and brush, awaiting the moment they would infiltrate the terrorist compound, dispatch the leader and detonate explosives around the weapons and ammunition cache stockpiled for an attack on the United States.

They'd done their homework, studied the intel and practiced the maneuver back at Stennis. They were ready.

"Initiate Operation Viper." The command came over his headset, setting the event in motion. SEALs

left their concealed positions and moved forward, sur-rounding the encampment. One by one they took out the sentries guarding the perimeter. Not a shot was fired. The guards didn't know they were in trouble until the blades swept across their throats.

Once inside the perimeter, the team split up. Montana set up a sniper position at one end of the camp. Duff and Quentin found the shed containing the stockpile of weapons and ammunition. They made quick work of setting the explosives and timers on the detonators.

Five minutes.

The team had a very short amount of time to dispatch the leader and get out of the camp before the charges detonated, setting off the fireworks. If they weren't halfway down the river by then, they might be caught up in the hundreds of rounds of ammunition going off, or be taken out by the stockpiled mortars or grenades that would be set off by the explosion and ensuing fire.

Quentin and Duff were to set the charges and work their way back to the river and man the boat that would take them down river. There they would wait for the rest of the team.

Duff and Quentin were at the edge of the camp when the first shot was fired. Shouts sounded and more rounds went off.

"Madre de Dios, I'm hit," Juan Garza's voice said into Quentin's headset.

"I have him," Trent Rucker said. "Headed for the boat."

"Target acquired," Montana said. "Get out. Now!"

Quentin and Duff dropped where they were, pre-pared to cover the team's exit from the camp.

"Loverboy and Duff will cover. Everyone else move out," Duff said.

One by one shadows emerged from the camp, crouched low, running.

Trent Rucker appeared with Juan slung over his shoulder in a fireman's carry. Montana was right behind them, another body wrapped around his shoulders.

The terrorists fired into the night, unable to see what they were aiming at. The brilliant blaze inside their camp made the surrounding jungle even darker. A vehicle engine roared to life and a truck spun, the headlights blinking on, pointed in the direction the SEALs ran.

"Damn." Quentin stared down his rifle's sights aiming carefully. He took a breath, held it and pulled the trigger. One headlight blinked out.

Duff took out the other. It gave them a few precious moments to get out of there before another vehicle was aimed their direction or someone found a spotlight.

Quentin shot a glance at the glowing dial on his watch. "One minute to lift off."

"Time to go, Loverboy," Duff said.

As the last word left Duff's mouth, the mother of all explosions shook the earth.

Quentin closed his eyes, ducked low and covered his ears.

A hand touched his shoulder. "Time to go, Loverboy." Duff's voice sounded different this time—lighter, more feminine and completely sexy.

Quentin blinked and stared up into deep brown eyes. "Duff?"

The eyes sparkled. "Sorry. Not Duff. We have to get off the train. We're in DC and Ivan disembarked a minute ago."

Jerking to his feet, Quentin woke instantly. He gripped Becca's arm and hurried with her off the train, his gaze scouring the crowd of people, on their way to work in the city.

"You were supposed to wake me in two hours." He glanced down at his watch. It had been over four.

"You were sleeping so soundly, I didn't have the heart to wake you." She glanced down at the tracker. "He should be really close."

Quentin glanced around, spotted a man about the same height and build as Ivan shoving bills into a ticket kiosk for the DC metro. "He's buying a ticket to the metro."

Ivan completed his transaction and turned toward them.

Quentin spun and grabbed Becca in a bear hug.

"What are you doing?" she said, struggling to free herself.

"He's looking our way." He bent his head, to hide his face. "Now kiss me, or risk being shot."

Becca complied, kissing him hard on the mouth. "Is he still looking this way?" she asked against his lips.

"No. He's headed for a turnstile. Come on, we have to buy tickets and get on with him." Quentin dropped his arms, grabbed her hand and ran for the kiosk.

Between the two of them, they fed bills into the machine and bought two tickets. Then they waited their turn at the turnstile, barely making it onto the metro train before the doors closed tight.

Fortunately, Ivan wasn't in the same car as they were. The GPS device indicated he was nearby.

His pulse pounding, Quentin circled an arm around Becca's waist. "Anyone ever tell you that you're kind of exciting to be around?"

She laughed, the dark smudges beneath her eyes a clear sign she was exhausted. "No. Most of my dates aren't subjected to what you've gone through in the past couple of days."

"You know how to show a guy a good time." He winked. "We have to get to a point where you can get some sleep or you'll run out of gas."

"I can manage," she said and yawned.

"Right. Total exhaustion starts manifesting itself like having had too many drinks."

The train jerked and sped forward. With the sudden surge of motion, Becca fell into Quentin. "You may have a point there, Loverboy."

Quentin's arm tightened around her. "Give me the tracker and relax against me."

Becca handed over the device and closed her eyes. Holding on to the pole for balance, she leaned heavily into Quentin. "I think I could fall to sleep standing up."

"I've tried it. I don't recommend it." His arm tightened. "But you can go halfway there and still remain upright."

"As long as you're holding me, I think I'll be okay."

God, he hoped so. Wherever this adventure led, he hoped she'd be okay, and that he could protect her from Ivan or anyone else targeting her for elimination.

Chapter Ten

"He's getting off."

Becca jerked awake at the sound of Quentin's voice, warm against her ear. She straightened and stepped toward the door.

Quentin held her elbow, steadying her to keep her from tripping or falling into the gap between the train and the platform.

Still fuzzy-headed from drifting off while standing in the curve of Quentin's arms, Becca shook herself and blinked several times. Her gaze panned the sea of faces concentrating on navigating the metro stop.

For a brief moment, she thought she spotted Ivan. "Was that—"

"Yes, that was him." Quentin grabbed her hand and hurried after the man. "We might lose him here, but we have the GPS. Until he changes clothes or discovers the chip, we can find him."

"Good, because he's getting into a taxi." Becca turned her back and pulled Quentin's face down to hers for a quick kiss while the taxi pulled away from the curb and passed them standing on the sidewalk.

As soon as the vehicle was gone, Becca stepped back. "Come on, let's get a taxi and follow."

"For the record, I'd rather finish that kiss." He nodded. "I know. Time for that later."

"Ha." Becca's insides warmed at the heat in Quentin's eyes. "Like we have time for playing around when a killer like Ivan is running loose in DC." She wanted to finish the kiss, too, but was afraid of letting Ivan get too far ahead. The man could find the tag at any time and they'd lose him. Then they would be back to square one.

Becca stepped into the queue for taxis. The line wasn't long. Two minutes later they were in a cab, following the GPS tracker. The cabbie didn't have a problem driving around without a set destination, as long as he was getting paid. Ivan's colored blip stopped before they caught up to him. He'd stopped at an inexpensive chain hotel.

Quentin and Becca had the driver drop them at a coffee shop across the street.

"Now what?" Quentin asked.

"We wait and see what he does next?" Becca responded. She pulled out the disposable phone Royce had given her and dialed Geek.

"Yeah."

"Geek, it's me, Becca."

"Good. I'm glad you called. Where are you?"

"In DC."

"I've got Sam Russell on standby to help out. When can you get to the office?"

"We've staked out Ivan." She told him the name and location of the hotel and coffee shop. "We can't leave until he makes his next move."

Quentin took the phone from her and said, "Any

possibility this Sam guy can take over and let us get a couple hours of sleep?"

"Absolutely," Geek said loud enough Becca could hear.

Quentin handed the phone back to Becca.

"I'll send Sam right over. Royce had me run a few checks. I have some information that might be interesting to you."

"Royce?" Becca shook her head. "Please tell me he's still in the hospital."

Geek laughed. "He called from his hospital room around three this morning, grumbling something about bloodsuckers. He thinks he'll be on a plane back to headquarters tonight."

"I hope he's all right."

"The docs said he'd be fine. The bullet missed all the bones and didn't do too much damage to the muscles. He'll have his arm in a sling for a couple weeks. Other than that, he's chomping at the bit to get back on this case."

Becca chuckled. "Sounds like Royce."

"Yeah," Geek said. "You can't keep the man down. Now let me get that call to Sam. Sounds like you two had a long night of surveillance."

"We did. I could use a shower and a change of clothes."

"After your debrief, you can head to your apartment."

"Speaking of my apartment, did Sam make it by? Did I get any packages?" She didn't add the thought that hurt the most—had she received any packages from her father?

"He did go by, but didn't find any packages in your

box or at the apartment building office. But don't take my word. Talk to him when he gets there."

Becca's hopes sank and the exhaustion that tugged at her eyelids dragged her down even more. "Thanks. See you in a few." She ended the call and lifted the cup of coffee Quentin had ordered for her.

"No package?" Quentin asked.

She shook her head and set the coffee on the table. "I really hoped my father would have left a message, a clue or something to help me figure out why someone would want to harm him. I feel like I'm clawing my way through a rather large spider web and not making any progress whatsoever."

"And I have the feeling that the spider is waiting to pounce," Quentin finished for her. He leaned across the table and covered her hand with his.

"Yeah. And I'll have no defense against whoever started this mess."

"You'll have me." Quentin squeezed her fingers gently.

Becca stared at their joined hands and sighed. "Not if this case drags on past your authorized leave."

"Royce said he could pull strings and get permission for me to stay on until the job's done." He lifted her fingers to his lips and pressed a light kiss to the backs of her knuckles. "Don't worry about me. You need to take care of yourself."

She liked how warm his hands were and how good it felt to have Quentin take care of her. "Someone has to keep an eye on Ivan."

"He's probably in that hotel sleeping the day away. Like we should be."

"And if he's not?"

"Sam is going to be here. If Royce trusts him to take over the surveillance effort, you should."

"I'd trust Sam with my life," Becca admitted. "He's one of the good guys. Along with Royce and the rest of the SOS team."

"That's the way I feel about SBT 22," Quentin said. "We're a tight-knit group. Closer than family, in most cases."

Becca's throat tightened around a knot forming there. The talk of family reminded her of what she no longer had. Her family. Her father.

"Hey." Quentin scooted his chair around the table to slip an arm around her waist. "I'm sorry about your father, and I understand why you're so dead set on finding the one responsible."

"Thanks." She leaned her cheek against his shoulder. "I haven't slowed down long enough to let it sink in too much. I'm afraid if I do, I won't be good for anything." She glanced up as the door to the coffee shop opened and a couple walked in. She'd recognize them anywhere. Sam and Kat Russell. Two of the most dedicated and effective SOS agents. And her friends.

Kat hurried forward and enveloped her in a hug. "I'm sorry about what happened to your dad," she said. "I tried to reach you when I heard, but you'd already gone to Cancun."

"Thanks." Becca hugged her back and then was enveloped in a hug from Sam, Kat's husband.

"You've been a very busy woman," he said, practically crushing her bones in a bear-like clench. "And what's this I hear about getting Royce shot?" He winked. "I'm sure the old man is giving his nurses hell in the hospital."

"He's a fighter. We just hope he's not fighting the doctors and nurses." Becca smiled at her friends. "Thanks for taking up the vigil. I'm desperate to get a shower and clothes that fit." She filled them in on the man they were watching, handed over the tracking device and waited to see if they had any questions.

"Sam and I have this covered," Kat said. "We'll let you know if Ivan leaves the hotel."

"Thanks." Becca yawned. "Now if I could only get a cab."

"Geek has one better than that." Kat grinned. "He sent the company car to take you to the office. It's waiting in the parking lot."

"You're kidding, right?" Becca could feel that day improving by the minute.

"I never kid about chauffeur-driven transportation." Kat cupped Becca's elbow and ushered her to the door of the coffee shop. "Go. Have your briefing with Geek and get to your apartment for some sleep."

"I will, thanks to you two."

"Any time," Sam replied for both of them.

Becca hooked her arm through Quentin's and led him out the door to the waiting limousine. The chauffeur opened the door for her and stood back.

Becca slid into the backseat and immediately melted into the plush leather. "This is heaven." She leaned her head back and closed her eyes. "You might as well close your eyes. It'll take a good thirty to forty-five minutes to get to the SOS office building."

"Hard not to in this ride," Quentin said.

Becca closed her gritty eyes and drifted to sleep immediately, waking all too soon when the driver stopped in front of the building that housed the headquarters of the Stealth Operations Specialists. She moaned. "Do we have to get out? Can't Geek come to us?"

"Come on, sweetheart." Quentin got out and reached in for her hand. "We'll ask him to make it short."

"It better be." She placed her hand in his and let him pull her out of the vehicle. Her foot caught on the curb, and Becca stumbled into Quentin's arms.

He scooped her up and carried her into the building.

"I'm capable of walking," she said, trying for a stern look which she found hard to do when he was being gallant, and it felt so good to let him.

"I know you are. But it's not often I catch you with your defenses down. I have to take advantage of it while I can." His lips lifted in that killer smile Becca was sure charmed the panties off every lady in every port.

Including her. She had to send him back to Mississippi soon, or she'd fall deeply, madly and stupidly in love with this big, strong navy SEAL. That possibility had "mistake" written all over it.

Geek met them at the door and held it open as they entered. "Are you all right, Becca?" he asked, concern etched into his young face.

"I'm fine, but this Neanderthal thinks I need to be babied. Please tell him that I'm a kick-ass agent capable of stopping bad guys dead in their tracks with nothing more than a killer look."

Geek laughed out loud, and then sobered when Becca glared at him. "Er...what she said."

Quentin finally set her on her feet. "As you wish."

Hell, she wished he'd kiss her and take her to bed. But setting her on her feet was a good start. Becca flung back her shoulders, pushing aside the intense fatigue plaguing her and faced Geek. "What information do you have for us?"

"This." Geek sat behind a computer screen and ran his hands over a keyboard. A screen popped up with a familiar face on it.

"That's Oscar Melton," Becca said. "He and my father were close friends in the CIA. He's like an uncle to me. His office is—was—next door to my father's."

Geek hit several keys and another screen came up with numbers scrolling down the side. "This is Melton's bank account." He pointed to the screen. "See the large sums of money added to his account and then paid out?"

Becca frowned. "Yes. So?"

"Those dollars match the ones hitting Ivan's secret account."

"No way." Becca shook her head. "My father trusted Oscar. They were really close."

"I'm not finished. Stay with me a little longer," Geek said. He pointed to the screen. "Note that the dates of these transactions show over a week ago."

"Yeah, about the time my father was murdered," she said her voice trailing off with the force of emotion welling up inside.

"Right, but when I dig deeper, I noticed the actual dates of these transfers are yesterday. The timestamps don't match the dates."

"What does that mean?" Becca asked.

"It means someone entered those dates to reflect what they wanted to reflect."

Becca's skin grew cold. "Someone is framing Oscar Melton."

"That's my guess." Geek leaned back in his chair

and stared at both Becca and Quentin. "One more thing. I found Ivan's room in the hotel, based on when he checked in. I've been listening in on his phone calls."

"And?" Becca prompted.

"Ivan made a call."

"To whom?" Becca asked.

"I have to assume to a disposable phone. I couldn't find it listed anywhere."

"What did he say?" Becca stepped toward Geek.

"It was all in Russian. I recorded it and played it back into translation software." He hit a button on his keyboard and played the recording. The electronic voice of translation software stated a time, date and address.

"That's tonight," Becca said. "That address is somewhere downtown."

"It's the address of a grand hotel hosting a fundraising gala with a lot of important political guests, including Oscar Melton, congressmen, the secretary of state and the vice president."

Becca's eyes widened. "Guests will be by invitation only. The building will be covered with security."

"Yes, it will. But there are always ways to get in. Especially if you have someone on the inside." He grinned and handed her two hotel staff ID badges. "Once you get in, you can go undercover as waitstaff, or change into formal attire and mingle with the guests."

"Geek, you're amazing," Becca said. "I could kiss you."

Geek's pale, freckled cheeks reddened. "Well, now. You don't have to go that far. But if you really want to,

I'm not opposed to it." He winked and returned his attention to the screen, without collecting on that kiss.

Becca leaned over and pecked him on the cheek. "Thank you. I don't know what any of us would do without you hacking into databases."

He shrugged. "That's nothing compared to you agents out in the field. You're lucky *you* weren't shot last night. It's bad enough Royce took a hit. I keep telling myself it could have been worse." He shook his head. "I can't imagine this agency without the old man in charge."

Becca sobered. Royce was the glue that held the group together. He was the mastermind they all turned to for direction. "He has to stop taking the risks he does."

Geek snorted. "Royce would never ask any of us to do something he wouldn't do himself."

"As he proved again last night," Becca muttered. "Okay. Let us know if anything comes up. Otherwise, we're headed for my apartment for sleep and then to do some shopping for our event tonight."

"I'll work on obtaining the work uniforms for the delivery personnel. In the meantime, the company car will take you to your apartment."

"Perfect." Becca felt as though some of the pieces were falling into place. She and Quentin left the building and climbed into the back of the chauffeur-driven company limousine.

"I have a few questions for Oscar when we see him tonight."

"I'll bet you do." Quentin pulled her into the crook of his arm. "Could I ask one favor of you while we're together on this operation?"

She glanced up at him. "What's that?"

"That you don't kiss other men until I'm gone." He raised his hand. "I'm just saying. I wanted to punch that nice kid, and that just wasn't right."

Becca's eyes widened. "You wanted to punch Geek for that little peck on the cheek?"

He nodded. "You bring out the animal in me."

"Mmm. I hope that's the case when we get to my apartment." She slid her hand inside his jacket to his bare chest beneath. "My shower is small, but just big enough for two."

He leaned down, his lips a breath away from hers. "I'm counting on it." Then he sealed her mouth with his, kissing her until her toes curled.

God, she was going to miss this man when he was gone. But until then, she hoped to make a few more memories to hold on to when she lay in her lonely bed.

QUENTIN KEPT BECCA nestled into the crook of his arm all the way to her apartment building. Then he held her hand until she found the key tucked behind the light fixture and opened the door, letting them in.

Once inside, she unzipped his jacket and pushed it over his shoulders. For a moment the garment stuck to his right arm. Then it ripped free and fell to the ground.

"What the hell?" Becca circled around behind him. "Damn it, Quentin, you were hit in that gunfight last night. Why didn't I see this?"

"It's just a flesh wound. I'd forgotten all about it." He shrugged. "It'll wash up in the shower."

Becca frowned, grabbed his hand and led him through her bedroom into the bathroom. "You should have said something. I can't believe I didn't see it before. That dark jacket must have hidden the blood stain." She pulled towels and a washcloth out of the cabinet. "Get out of those clothes and into the shower."

He reached for her shoulders and held her still. "Anyone ever tell you that you're sexy when you order a man out of his clothes?"

A smile quirked the corners of her lips and color rose in her cheeks. "I don't want you getting an infection in the wound."

"Is that all?"

She looked to the side, the color in her cheeks deepening. "Well, that and I like seeing you naked. You're not bad-looking…for a SEAL."

"Thanks. I think." He unbuckled his shoulder holster and dropped it and the P226 on the counter. "But it's only fair if I get to see you naked, too."

"Oh, you will." She unzipped her jacket and let it fall to the floor. "Count on it."

Within seconds, they were both standing naked beneath the shower's spray, a foil-packaged condom resting on an empty soap dish. Quentin had plans for that little item. Soon.

He kissed her forehead, her eyelids, her cheekbones, exploring every inch of her face. "You should be sleeping."

"I'm wide awake, and my heart is pounding." She raised his hand to her breast. "Do you feel it?"

Oh, he could feel it, and a whole lot more. He massaged the rounded swell and tweaked her nipple, rolling it between his thumb and index finger. The tip tightened into a bead.

Her back arched, pressing her breast into his palm. She grabbed a bar of soap and lathered it, then spread the suds over his body, from his neck down his back to his buttocks.

Sweet heaven, her hands were magic against his skin. "Where have you been all my life?" he whispered against her neck.

She laughed. "That sounds like a line, if ever I heard one." Becca lathered again and moved her hands between them, rubbing them over the contours of his chest and downward to the jutting evidence of his desire. She circled it with both hands and tugged him gently toward her.

"Not a line, sweetheart. The truth. I feel like you're the only woman I've ever *really* been with. Mind, body and soul."

"Pretty words for such a big, dangerous man." She slid her calf up the back of his and rubbed her sex against his thigh. "*Show* me what you're feeling." Capturing his face between her hands, she kissed him long and hard, thrusting her tongue between his teeth to caress the length of his tongue.

Lust, desire and something deeper surged inside him. He bent, lifted her up by the backs of her thighs and pressed her against the cool, tiles of the shower walls. "You're beautiful…" He kissed her lips. "Intelligent…" Pressing another kiss to the length of her throat, he said, "And sexy as hell."

Becca laughed and reached for the foil packet, tore it open and leaned away from Quentin, rolling the protection over his engorged staff. "A little less talk, and a little more action."

"As you wish." He lifted her up over him and slid into her, slowly, gently, all the way. He inhaled deeply and held her there, committing the moment to memory.

This was where he wanted to be, had always wanted to be. If they didn't see each other again after this night, he'd have what they shared now seared into his mind for the rest of his life.

Her legs tightened and she lifted herself up his length and lowered herself down. Her hands braced on his shoulders, fingers dug into his skin, and her head tilted back, eyes closed, the expression on her face one of intense concentration.

He matched her movements and more, thrusting again and again, the speed picking up with the rising wave of his desire. Soon he pounded into her, every nerve inside him tightening, sending electric jolts all the way to his fingers and toes. Then he catapulted over the edge, flinging himself into the stratosphere.

Becca cried out his name, her body shaking, her channel clenching in spasms around him.

One last thrust and he buried himself deep inside her, pressing his body flush against hers, holding her tight in his arms, never wanting to let go. Ever again.

When they both sank back to earth, Quentin set Becca on her feet. With deliberate and gentle hands, he washed her body, head to toe, shampooed her hair and rinsed her clean. Then he lifted her out of the shower onto the bath mat. With equal care, he dried her body, all the curves and crevices.

She returned the gesture, stopping long enough to care for his wound, applying antibiotic ointment and a bandage.

Then Quentin scooped her into his arms and carried her to the queen-sized bed in the middle of the bedroom, laid her between the sheets and slipped in behind her, spooning her body with his.

She reached back to cup his bottom. "Don't you want to go for round two?"

"Not now. You and I both need sleep."

"Big, dangerous and wise." She pulled his arm around her, resting it beneath her breasts, and promptly fell to sleep.

Quentin lay for a long time, inhaling the scent that was Becca, smoothing his hand over the curve of her hip and the soft swells of her breasts. He hoped and prayed this wasn't the last time he'd hold her in his arms. The very real threat of something bad happening that night made him want to keep her alone in her apartment, making love and ignoring everything else going on outside.

But he knew he couldn't. Becca's determination to set the world right wouldn't allow her to stay cocooned at home. And Quentin couldn't let her go it alone.

Chapter Eleven

Becca adjusted the collar of the waitress dress Geek had managed to acquire for their covert entry into the gala that night. She glanced across the back of the delivery van at Quentin.

Clean shaven, his hair cut high and tight, in the dark red uniform the waiters wore at the hotel, he was incredibly handsome.

Her heart beat faster, not because of the danger of sneaking into an invitation-only gala with the associated high level of security. No, her pulse quickened every time she looked into Quentin's eyes and he looked back. For that brief moment, they seemed to connect at the most amazing level.

The delivery truck swung in a half circle, forcing Becca to hang on until it backed into place against the loading ramp at the back of the hotel.

They had their entrance badges and their formal clothing packed inside the bottom of one of the boxes filled with pastries ordered from one of the most exclusive bakeries in DC, in honor of the vice president's attendance at the gala.

Quentin held out his hand. "Ready?"

She nodded, squeezed his hand briefly and waited for Sam, the driver, to open the back doors.

Sam and Kat had watched Ivan's hotel all day. A couple hours before the gala was to begin, Ivan had made his move. He exited the hotel and jumped into a cab headed downtown.

Kat and Sam had followed him all the way to the gala hotel. At that point, they'd met up with Geek. Normally a desk-jockey, he'd taken on the role of a field agent and commandeered a delivery van from the bakery earlier that evening, loaded with the special dessert. The hotel would be frantic looking for that last delivery of the VP's favorite confection.

Geek handed over the keys, badges and two sets of uniforms for Sam, a bakery uniform and a waiter uniform. For Kat, he had one waitress uniform. The two hurriedly dressed, then Sam had closed Kat, Quentin and Becca in the rear of the van and headed for the hotel.

As the back door opened, Sam leaned in. "Coast is clear. Move out smartly."

The three dressed in waitstaff uniforms grabbed a stack of dessert boxes.

Becca's stack had one box filled with her formal dress and shoes. She headed for the entrance door. Juggling her boxes in one hand, she swiped her badge with the other. The light next to the door lock blinked green. She released the breath she'd been holding and opened the door. Inside, dock personnel glanced up. A man with a clipboard hurried over. "Are these the desserts that should have been here hours ago?"

"Yes, sir. I ran into the delivery van outside and

thought I'd help bring them in. He said something about engine trouble on the freeway."

"Let my guys unload." The man with the clipboard reached out.

Becca pulled away from his reach. "No worries. There are a lot more boxes where these came from. I suggest you get some more help to get them inside and pre-positioned. I'll run on in and let them know the desserts finally made it."

The man hesitated a second and then hurried to open the overhead door. Three other workers converged on the van.

Becca, Quentin and Kat helped carry boxes into the hotel and slipped past the dock personnel while they hurriedly unpacked the van. Sam would drive the van away and park it nearby, returning in his waiter uniform when he had it hidden.

Once inside, the three hurried down a long hallway. Kat went ahead since she was already wearing her disguise. She'd work the tables and serve champagne to the guests, watching for Ivan. He had to be there somewhere.

Quentin opened doors along the hallway until he found a broom closet big enough the two of them could fit in. Pulling Becca inside, he closed and locked the door.

Becca ripped open the box with her evening gown, pulled out the tray of sweets and set them aside, then shook out the length of black fabric. There were no sequins or beads sewn into the dress. It was gorgeous on its own.

"Would you mind?" She turned her back to Quentin. "Unzip me, please."

"My pleasure." He ran the zipper down her back, his knuckles brushing against her skin. When he had it down all the way, he pressed a kiss to the back of her neck, just below her ponytail. "Mmm, you smell sweet."

Becca shivered, that ache low in her belly flaring with Quentin's touch. If only they weren't on a mission… "That's the desserts from the bakery you're smelling."

"Uh-uh." He nibbled her skin. "No. It's you, babe." He helped her push the sleeves of the waitress dress over her arms and down to her hips. His hands circled her waist and ran up to cup her naked breasts. She'd opted to go braless beneath the uniform as the evening gown was cut so low in the front and the back there would be no way to hide one. Now she was glad she'd left it behind.

Becca leaned into Quentin. "If only we had time, I'd—" She sucked in a breath and straightened. "Never mind. We have a job to do. The sooner we find Ivan the better."

Quentin wasn't so quick to give up. He pulled her back against him. "You'd what?"

Turning in his arms, Becca said, "This." She leaned up on her toes and pressed her lips to his. Her hands worked the buttons loose on his uniform and smoothed it back over his shoulders, letting it drop to the floor. Thrusting her tongue into his mouth, she tasted of his, nipping and sucking at him, while her fingers worked the button loose on his trousers. When she had his pants down, she stepped away, breathless. "And more." Wiping the back of her hand over her mouth, she dragged in steadying breaths. "We have to get going."

She raised the dress she'd chosen above her head and let it glide downward over her body. The V in the front came to just above her bellybutton, the back dipped low on her back, nearly to the swell of her bottom. It was the sexiest and most risqué dress she'd ever owned. Royce had sent her and a prepaid credit card to one of the most exclusive shops in DC with orders to get a dress that would draw attention to her.

Quentin had his trousers off, the tuxedo pants on, and his shirt halfway buttoned, when Becca straightened from slipping her feet into rhinestone-sparkled stilettoes.

He whistled softly. "Wow. And I thought you were gorgeous naked."

Heat rose up her neck into her cheeks. "Thank you." From the bakery box, she pulled out the glittering cubic zirconia necklace she'd purchased from a costume jewelry shop and handed it to Quentin. He smoothed her ponytail aside and hooked the necklace in place and then turned her around to kiss her forehead. "You really are incredible."

"Why do you say that?" She pulled the elastic band from her ponytail and then reached up to finish buttoning the shirt. He handed her the bowtie and she looped it around his neck.

"You can fight like a ninja, shoot like a world-class marksman, swim in the swamps with alligators, and still look like a million bucks in a go-to-hell dress and a pair of stilettoes."

She tied his bowtie and helped him into his tuxedo jacket. "I could say the same about you." She grinned. "Less the dress and stilettoes."

Quentin held out his arm. "Ready?"

She nodded and slipped her hand through his elbow. She was going to a gala with the most handsome man on the planet, dressed in the most expensive dress she'd ever owned. Why was she shaking on the inside? A nagging feeling of impending doom settled over her, something that had never occurred on any of her previous assignments as an SOS operative. She pushed that feeling aside, unlocked the closet door, pulled it open a crack and peered into the hallway.

A man in dock personnel uniform walked past her at that moment, pushing a cart filled with dessert boxes. Becca caught her breath and held it, waiting until the man disappeared around the corner. She opened the door wider and looked back in the direction from which he'd come. The hallway was empty.

She stepped out with Quentin. "Our story, should someone question why we're back here is that you were escorting me to the ladies' room and we got lost."

"Got it."

Fortunately, they were able to slip past the entrance to the kitchen, arriving at an empty service elevator. Quentin pulled her into it, punched the button for the next floor and waited for the door to close.

Becca didn't breathe until the two doors connected. "One hurdle crossed. Let's hope getting into the ballroom is equally easy."

"Let's hope the hotel security cameras aren't following us as we speak." Quentin glanced up at the camera in the corner of the elevator.

"That's Geek's job. The communication van he had stationed across the street from the hotel is his command center. He has the ability to tap into the security system and display what he wants the security personnel to see."

"Remind me to talk to Royce about my retirement plans."

"You're too young to retire from the military," Becca protested.

"Maybe so, but I like to keep my options open. Being a SEAL is a young man's sport. The older you get the slower you become. And it's soon time to let the new wave of recruits take it from here."

She stared at him, her brows furrowed. "Are you thinking of leaving the navy?"

"Someday." The elevator door opened on the level where the ballroom was located.

The two of them quickly stepped out and made their way through the labyrinth of service hallways to the one Geek had identified on the blueprint as the sound equipment closet. It had a door leading into the service area and one on the other side leading to the back of the stage where the band played.

Music drifted through the walls, the steady beat of the drums thrumming through the floors into the thin souls of Becca's shoes.

Hopefully, the electronics specialist would have completed all of his work and the room would be empty. They hadn't come this far into the hotel to be discovered and escorted out.

As Quentin twisted the knob, Becca held her breath.

QUENTIN FOUND THAT work as a covert agent was much different than that of a SEAL storming the streets and alleys of an Afghan village searching for the enemy. There, he would be fully equipped with a semi-automatic rifle, night-vision goggles and explosives should he need to blow up something. He'd be backed by his team of highly-trained combat veterans.

In the nation's capital, things were a lot different. He'd thought life stateside was a lot less complicated and safer than being in the desert surrounded by people who wanted to kill him.

So much for bursting his little bubble of trust. Becca had survived multiple attacks by someone paid to kill her. And that someone might be an official in her own government. Maybe even someone at this gala, dressed in expensive clothing, with a heart as black as the tuxedo Quentin had rented for the occasion.

Hopefully, that person wouldn't be taking potshots at Becca tonight. Not in a room full of people. An attack among the politicians and statesmen who would be present tonight would cause a riot.

With so many thoughts going through his head, Quentin had to go into combat mode and push them to the back of his mind in order to focus on what had to be done.

He turned the doorknob on the equipment room, surprised to find it unlocked. When he pulled it open, he found a man inside cursing and yanking on cables and electrical cords.

The man didn't look up from what he was doing. "Did you find the spare cables where I told you they were?" When Quentin didn't answer the man popped his head up. "Oh. You're not Ruben."

"No." Quentin smiled and held up a hand palm upward. "Sorry, but we went through the wrong door and got lost. Could you tell me how to get back into the ballroom?"

"You're not supposed to be back here."

"We figured that," Becca stepped forward, her leg standing out from the slit in her skirt.

The man's gaze went straight to the leg and his face burned a bright red. "Uh, ma'am, nobody's supposed to be back here."

"You said that, and we'd like to comply, but we can't find the door we came through. Is there another way inside?" She glanced at the door at the opposite end of the room. "Does that door lead into the ballroom? Couldn't we just go through there?"

"I'm sorry, ma'am, but I'm not authorized to let anyone through that door. You'll have to go out the service entrance and come back through the front of the hotel."

"In these heels?" She twisted her leg, displaying even more of her thigh than before. "I'll never get to dance if I have to walk all over creation to get back into the ballroom."

"Darlin'," Quentin murmured. "I told you that wasn't the shortcut to the ladies' restroom."

"'I told you so' isn't saving my feet for that dance you promised."

"Look, lady, as long as you're not packing a weapon I don't see any reason why you can't go through that doorway."

"I don't think I could fit anything but me inside this dress." Becca ran her hands down her body and hips. "See, smooth as skin."

Quentin had felt naked going in unarmed, but given the level of security, if he was caught with a weapon on him, they would throw him in jail first, ask questions later. He couldn't afford to set off any alarms. Now he was glad he hadn't insisted on even a small pistol hidden beneath his tux jacket. Opening his jacket, he let the guy see he wasn't carrying. He pulled out his pockets on his trousers, and even tugged his pant legs up to show he didn't have anything strapped to his ankles.

"Okay, okay. Go. But you never saw me or spoke to me."

"Scout's honor," Quentin said, raising two fingers in a salute.

Becca stepped over the cables and cords littering the floor, unlocked the door on the other side and pushed it open enough to slip through. The music volume was almost enough to make Quentin want to cover his ears.

Becca looked and then stepped out, bumping into a potted ficus tree positioned strategically to hide the door.

Quentin, right behind her, waited until she navigated around the plant and moved to the corner of the raised dais where the band was playing old classics from the Big-Band era.

Through the musicians and instruments Quentin could see the dance floor beyond, lightly populated with women in expensive gowns and men in tuxedos similar to the one he wore. He took Becca's hand. "May I have this dance?"

She nodded and slipped into his arms.

Being a ladies' man came in handy. Among the women he'd dated had been one who'd taught ballroom dance lessons. The band happened to be playing a waltz. Skillfully guiding his partner out onto the dance floor, Quentin was surprised to find that Becca could hold her own.

Blending in with the other dancers on the floor was

easier than he'd anticipated, especially with Becca. "Where did you learn to dance so well?"

She glanced up at him, the chandeliers sparkling in her eyes. Then she looked away, her lips dipping downward. "My father."

His heart squeezed in his chest at the shadow crossing her face at the mention of her father. "I'm sorry I brought it up."

"No. Don't be. I'm still trying to come to grips with his death." She smiled briefly. "When my mother died, my big, bad CIA father was determined to be everything to me. He saw to it that I went to dance lessons, even going to ballroom dance lessons with me. Living in the DC area, a lot of young women in the private school I attended were trained at a young age."

"Debutantes?"

"Yeah. I was okay at dancing, but they made it beautiful. I preferred going to the rifle range with my father, or playing basketball in the driveway."

"You play basketball?" Quentin grinned. She never ceased to amaze him.

"I might be too short to play professionally, but I can shoot some serious hoop." She blinked back a tear. "My father never 'let' me win. I had to earn it."

"Smart man. Not only are you beautiful, you're tough."

"He wasn't really happy when I told him I wanted to join the FBI."

"Why not the CIA and follow in the old man's footsteps?"

"He was working his way up in the ranks. I didn't want to be a conflict of interest for him. Besides, I wanted to make it on my own. Then I met Royce and found a different calling." She glanced around. "I've been watching the waitstaff. So far I haven't seen Ivan."

"What about Melton?"

"No. I haven't seen him, either."

Quentin waltzed her to the edge of the dance floor. "Let's mingle."

"Perhaps we should split up and meet at the dessert bar in the far corner." She nodded toward a corner of the room where the hotel staff was busy restocking the desserts, plates and cutlery.

Quentin didn't want to leave Becca's side, but knew they could cover more ground going different directions. "See you in a few." He raised her hand to his lips and kissed her fingers. "Thank you for the dance."

She dipped her head. "My pleasure." Becca turned away and weaved through the throng, making a wide sweep to the right.

Quentin headed to the left, stopping to say hello or shake hands with people along the way as though he belonged there. If they only knew he didn't, and that he was more at home in camouflage, knee-deep in swamp water than rubbing elbows with the rich and politically powerful.

"Darling." A hand descended on his arm, claw-like fingernails digging into his tuxedo. "Be a dear and fetch me a bourbon and coke from the bar. The night is young and I'm parched." The woman didn't release him to do her bidding; instead, her eyes narrowed as she raked him from head to toe. "Did the AC quit working, or did I bump into the hottest young man in the room?" She fanned herself. "Pardon my manners. I don't believe we've been properly introduced. I'm Victoria. Victoria Francis."

Quentin took the woman's extended hand, gave it a brief shake and let go. Her last name rang a bell in his memory, but he couldn't place it right away. "Nice to meet you, ma'am."

"Oh, please. Ma'am makes me sound so, so…" She reached out as a waiter passed with a tray of champagne and snagged two flutes, nearly toppling the rest of the glasses full of the sparkling liquid. "Old." She handed a glass to Quentin. "And who might you be?" She leaned close. "I don't believe I've seen you around."

"Quentin Lovett, ma'am."

She laughed out loud. "Lovett. That's perfectly marvelous." Victoria raised her glass. "Here's to living the dream."

Out of politeness, Quentin raised his glass to hers.

She tapped hers against his so hard he thought for certain it would break. By some miracle it remained intact and he touched it to his lips and pretended to take a drink. Although he didn't. He hated champagne, preferring a good beer with the guys.

His gaze shifted to where Becca stood talking with an older gentleman Quentin recognized from the pictures Geek had shown them earlier. Becca had found Oscar Melton. He'd give anything to be a fly on the wall, listening in on their conversation.

"Who's the bombshell?" Victoria asked, her gaze following Quentin's to Becca. "I used to look like that. But then that's what happens when you get older. Beauty fades and so does love."

Quentin tore his gaze from Becca, afraid he'd missed something the woman said. "Ma'am."

"Let's toast to love," she said and raised her glass

so fast, the remaining liquid sloshed over the edge. "I mean that's what life is all about, isn't it? *L-O-V-E*."

A man arrived next to the woman and seized the glass out of her hand before she could drink to her toast. A waiter passed by with an empty tray and the man dropped the glass on the tray. "Ah, Victoria, are you monopolizing this young man's attention?"

"No, darling, I was flirting with him." She straightened, shaking off the man's hand. "Killjoy," she muttered. Then she raised a hand toward him. "Let me introduce you to the man who stole my heart and made all my dreams come true." She emitted a derisive snort. "Mr. John Francis. And this is Quincy Lover."

Quentin didn't bother to correct her. The woman had obviously had too much to drink. From the way her husband was corralling her, it wasn't her first time with public intoxication.

"Pardon my wife. She's high-strung." John Francis nodded absently toward Quentin and then escorted his wife to the exit.

Quentin figured *high-strung* was code for *a deeply unhappy alcoholic*. He continued around the room, studying guests and waitstaff, searching for Ivan and anyone else who appeared nefarious. Although what that looked like, he hadn't a clue. Once he spotted Kat circulating through with a tray of hors d'oeuvres. At the far side of the room Sam Russell's head stuck out over many of the others. He worked the floor, carrying a tray of champagne glasses with a little less confidence than the other waiters.

Quentin searched again for Becca. His pulse kicked up a notch when he couldn't find her. He waded through the crowd toward the last spot he'd seen her. When he reached it he spun in a circle. No matter how hard he looked, he couldn't find her.

Although he and Becca had been on the hunt for the past twenty-four hours, he hadn't forgotten that she'd been the target of multiple attempts on her life.

Kat stepped up to him. "Care for an hors d'oeuvres, sir?" Then in a low whisper, she added, "What's wrong?"

"Becca. I can't find her."

Chapter Twelve

Becca had been making her way through the crowd, glancing across at Quentin every chance she got, when a man touched her elbow, bringing her to a halt.

"Becca Smith? Is that you?"

She turned to face a man with a shock of white hair and a neatly trimmed beard. "Mr. Melton. It's so good to see you."

He took her hands in his and pulled her into a hug. "I didn't get the chance to talk with you at the memorial service for your father. I'm so sorry for your loss." He shook his head. "For our loss. Your father was a good man, always doing the right thing."

"Sometimes the right thing makes people mad."

Oscar stared into her eyes. "Your father didn't let that stop him, or slow him down."

"Mr. Melton—"

"Oh, please, Becca. We're old friends. Call me Oscar."

"Oscar." She leaned close, her voice dropping to a whisper. "What was my father working on that was so dangerous someone felt the need to kill him? And what did it have to do with Rand Houston?"

Oscar's gaze darted to either side. "Becca…" He

looked around again. "Come with me." He grabbed her hand and led her to the side of the room, ducking behind a large decorative palm in a huge urn. "There are things you don't know. Things I can't tell you."

"Why? Are you the one trying to keep it secret? Are you the one hiring hit men to kill anyone who knows about it?"

"No, Becca. I would never have hurt your father."

"What about Senator Houston?"

"I don't know what you're talking about. I understand he was on vacation in Cancun and died of a heart attack."

Becca shook her head. "You know he didn't die of a heart attack. A mercenary was hired to kill him. You, of all people, should know the truth."

Oscar Melton stared into her eyes for a long moment and then bowed his head. "What do you know so far?"

"A paid assassin killed my father. I followed him to Cancun to find out who paid him. He tried to kill Senator Houston's son and managed to kill Senator Houston. I fly back to the States and the plane I'm in is shot down out of the sky. You tell me who's doing this." She shook with fury, her eyes filling with tears. "You and my father were friends. What happened?"

"I can't tell you."

"Can you tell me about the large sums of money moving in and out of your bank account?" Her lips pulled back into a tight line. "Can you tell me someone isn't paying you to keep others quiet?"

"What money?" Oscar pulled his cell phone from his pocket and hit the screen several times. "I don't know what you're talking about."

Becca leaned over his arm and stared down at the

bank application he'd brought up on his phone. The man stared at the screen, his face blanching. "I don't know where that money came from."

"No? Well, it went to a man named Ivan, a Russian immigrant who brokered the deal with the mercenary who killed my father."

Oscar ran a hand through his hair, standing it on end. "I have to go."

Becca grabbed his coat sleeve. "Not until you tell me what's going on."

"I can't. I have to go." He pushed past Becca and waded into the crowd.

Becca followed, determined to get the answers she'd come for.

Oscar was halfway across the floor before she spotted him again. He was talking with a man Becca knew as John Francis, the second in command at the CIA. She'd seen his face in the news several times and his portrait hung in the halls of the CIA building. The two men had their heads together, talking fast, their bodies tense, their brows pulled into deep frowns.

John stepped away, grabbed a woman Becca had seen earlier talking to Quentin and ushered her toward the door.

Oscar stood in the middle of the floor for a moment as though he wasn't sure what to do next. Then he turned and headed for the exit. A waiter blocked his path, carrying a tray filled with glasses of champagne.

It took a full second for recognition to dawn on Becca. "Ivan." She started forward, her mouth opened to warn Oscar. Before she could shout or scream, the Russian seemed to stumble, falling against Oscar, and the tray he'd been carrying slipped from his hand, the champagne flutes filled with liquid crashing to the floor and scattering shards of glass in all directions.

Women screamed and leaped out of the way of the mess.

Ivan pretended to duck down to collect the tray, but pushed through the crowd empty-handed. No one noticed but Becca.

"Stop that man!" She screamed over the shouts and cacophony of noise from the guests and the band still blasting '40s music through the room.

All attention was on the mess on the floor. No one noticed the man running for the exit. Becca started after him. But as she passed close to Oscar, she noticed he stood still in the middle of the melee, his eyes wide, his hand pressed to his belly, where blood trickled through his fingers.

"Becca," a familiar voice called out.

"Quentin?" She glanced across several people at the man who made her blood sing. "It was Ivan. He ran that way!" She pointed toward the man in the waiter's uniform, shoving people out of his way as he ran for a doorway leading to the exit.

"Will you be all right?" Quentin called out.

Becca nodded. "Hurry! Don't let him get away."

Quentin ran after Ivan. Sam joined Quentin as they neared the exit. Between the two of them, Becca hoped they'd catch the Russian terrorist. In the meantime, she had to get help for Oscar.

"Someone call 911," she said loud enough to be heard over the shouts and screams.

Becca caught Oscar's arm as he swayed. "Oscar. What happened?"

"I don't know." He lifted his hand and stared at the

blood. "I think I've been stabbed." Then he crumpled against Becca.

A woman screamed and fainted. Others cried out, turned and ran for the exit. Chaos reigned.

The man was too heavy for Becca to hold upright. She went down with him, falling into the broken glass and spilled champagne.

QUENTIN BURST THROUGH the doors of the hotel. The security guards standing outside lunged for him, tackling him to the ground.

"I'm not the bad guy. A waiter ran out this way." Quentin struggled, jabbing an elbow into one guard's gut. He swung his fist, hitting the other in the nose. Two more guards grabbed him, pulling his arms up behind him.

Sam shot through the door behind Quentin, dodged the guards and ran out into the street, chasing after Ivan, who'd already made it to the corner.

Not wanting to hurt the guards, Quentin didn't fight as hard as he could have. But, damn it, Ivan was getting away. In one final surge, he rammed into a guard, taking him to the ground. The men let go of him, he rolled to his feet and came up running.

"Stop, or we'll shoot!" the man called out.

"I'm a navy SEAL. If you shoot, you'll be damaging government property," he called out over his shoulder, refusing to stop. They had to catch Ivan. The man was too dangerous to be let go.

As Quentin reached the corner, he heard the sound of gunfire. He ducked, thinking one of the security guards had followed through on his threat to shoot.

But he felt no pain and kept going, rounding the corner at a full sprint.

Sam Russell knelt, pressed against the side of the building. "Get back!" he yelled. "Someone is firing from one of the rooms above."

Quentin flattened himself against the side of the building and took in the situation. A body lay in the middle of the sidewalk.

"Is that Ivan?" Quentin asked.

"Yeah."

Footsteps pounded on the sidewalk behind him and the four guards who had been at the front of the hotel came sliding to a halt, guns drawn.

One shouted, "Drop, or I'll shoot!"

"We're unarmed!" Quentin called out. "But someone inside the hotel is shooting."

The guards didn't budge from their position. All four had their weapons drawn. Sirens sounded nearby, getting louder.

"Get down on the ground!" the lead guard yelled.

Quentin didn't have time to fool with the man, but he didn't want to get shot. "Let us come back your way before we get down." He started to slide along the wall. Sam followed suit.

They'd only gone four feet each when the guard got nervous. "I said get down on the ground."

Quentin dropped to his belly, lying as close to the hotel wall as he could get. Shots were fired from above, the sound echoing off the brick walls of the buildings around them.

The guards fired at Quentin and Sam, bullets ricocheting off the sidewalks.

"We're unarmed!" Quentin shouted, his arms over

his head, praying the guards would stop firing. "The shots were fired from up in the hotel!"

"Cease fire!" the lead guard cried.

The sirens blared, but no more shots were fired in the street where Quentin lay. "Sam?"

"I'm okay," he said.

"Okay, you two, ease this way slowly. Keep your hands where I can see them." A flashlight beam pierced the shadows at the base of the building.

Great. Now the shooter will be able to get a bead on us. Quentin got up on his hands and knees and crawled to the edge of the building where he stood, raising his hands above his head. "You're stopping the wrong people. Someone up in the hotel fired on us. Whoever it was hit the guy lying in the middle of the sidewalk. He might still be alive."

The guard pulled a hand-held radio from a clip on his shoulder and spoke into it, "Check for a gunman on the upper floors. Secure the guests, but don't let anyone leave the building."

"Look, my date is inside the ballroom. I need to see if she's okay."

"What were you doing out here to begin with?"

"That man lying in the street stabbed CIA employee Oscar Melton. We were trying to stop him."

The guard nodded. "Right." He waved a hand at two men who worked their way down the sidewalk, hugging the wall until they were abreast of the body on the ground. One of them crossed to the man and pressed his fingers to the base of his throat. He glanced up. "This guy is dead."

The guard beside Quentin tightened his grip on the

pistol in his hand. "Sir, please turn around and lean against the wall."

Quentin did as he was told. The guard held his weapon on Quentin and Sam while another man patted them down, checking for weapons. When they were satisfied Quentin and Sam weren't carrying, they pulled Sam and Quentin's arms behind their backs and slapped zip ties on their wrists. Once they were secure, they herded them back toward the entrance of the hotel.

Ivan was dead. He hadn't been coming to the party to meet with the man who hired him. He'd come to kill Oscar Melton. One more person with a connection to Becca's father.

Quentin wanted back inside the hotel. The sooner the better. With a gunman on the loose and the entrances and exits blocked by guards and policemen, it might only be a matter of time before more people were killed. Quentin worried the gunman might be waiting for his chance to finish the job others had yet to complete. The job of killing Becca.

Chapter Thirteen

When Becca went down with Oscar landing on top of her, something sharp jabbed through her dress into her buttocks and her hand landed on broken pieces of glass. Becca cried out, shoving Oscar off her. She leaned to the side to alleviate the pain.

Cursing beneath her breath, she pulled a jagged shard from her hand and reached behind her to yank the one out of her bottom.

She balled her fist to stem the flow of blood from her hand. Nothing could be done about the cut on her backside until she took care of Oscar. "Someone get me a clean napkin or tablecloth," she called out.

A woman ran for one of the tables placed around the dance floor, grabbed a handful of cloth napkins and hurried back. "Will these do?"

"Yes. Fold two of them into four-inch square pads."

Her hands shaking, the woman did as Becca said. "Now what?"

Becca held out her good hand. The woman handed over the pads and Becca pressed them into the wound in Oscar's abdomen. Then she held out her other hand. "Now tie one around this hand and knot it over the cut."

The woman followed Becca's orders.

The CIA agent was pale but breathing for the moment. He'd lost a lot of blood before Becca could apply pressure to his wound. "Oscar, stay with me."

He moved, dragging his hand from beneath him. Blood oozing from the cuts, he dug into his pocket.

Thinking he might have something he needed like nitro pills or an inhaler, she asked, "What do you need? Let me help." Before she could reach into his pocket, he pulled out his wallet and handed it to her. "Becca, there are things you need to know." He closed his eyes and dragged in a rattling breath.

"You can tell me when we get you stabilized," she said, her heart lodging in her throat. The man's face was getting paler by the minute.

"No. Now." He handed her the wallet and whispered, "Find my CIA ID card."

She dug in his wallet and located his CIA access card. "Now what?"

He grabbed her arm and pulled her close.

Becca leaned over him, her ear close to his mouth.

"My access code is 982357."

She turned to look in his eyes. "Why are you telling me this?"

"Repeat it," he urged. "982357."

Speaking softly so only he could hear, she repeated, "982357."

His grip on her arm tightened. "Take the card, get into my office. There is a secret panel in my desk. Reach inside the first drawer and feel for a button against the underside of the desktop."

"Right side of your desk or left?"

He grimaced, his hand going to the wound in his belly. "Right. Button releases hidden drawer. Find the disk inside. No bigger than a quarter. Take it to Fontaine. He'll know what to do with it." He released his hold on her and slumped against the floor. "Hurry."

"But I can't just walk into the CIA building."

"It's night. New guard on the front desk. Tell him you're my secretary. You look a little like her."

Becca had to lean close to hear the last words, her heart beating so fast and hard it pounded against her ears. "Oscar?"

"Mmm," he said on a breath of air.

"Don't die, will ya? Losing my father was hard enough. I don't want to lose a friend, too."

Oscar's eyes blinked open. "I'll try." Then he passed out.

"Step back," a voice called out. Paramedics moved in and took over. Becca tucked the access card into the hidden pocket in the waistline of her dress and staggered to her feet.

A medic looked at her hand, cleaned and bandaged her wound. Then she turned around and let him lift her dress high enough to clean and bandage the wound on her buttocks while all of the guests looked on. She almost laughed, but she was too worried about Oscar to care if anyone saw her bare bottom.

When they cleared her, she stepped out of the way and watched as they moved Oscar to a stretcher, started him on an IV and carried him outside to a waiting ambulance.

"Becca!" Quentin's voice sounded over the wail of the ambulance's siren as it left carrying Becca's father's friend to the hospital. She looked around, spotting Quentin surrounded by police officers, with Sam next to him and Kat arguing with the leader of the men in blue.

She hurried over. "What's going on?"

"They think we killed Ivan," Quentin responded.

"He's dead?" She glanced from Quentin to Sam and back. "Are you two okay?"

"We're fine, but someone was shooting at us from inside the hotel."

Becca looked around at the guests. How would they find a shooter in this crowd? She turned to the police officer. "Who's in charge?"

"Command center is set up in the lobby." The officer jerked his head toward the lobby. "If you have questions, take them there."

"I'll be right back," Becca said to Quentin and Sam. She marched into the lobby and found the concierge. "I need to use a telephone."

The man told her to get in line. Guests who'd left their cell phones in their vehicles were anxious to call home and let folks know they were okay. Becca tapped her toe, anxious to get to the head of the line.

When the woman in front of her got on the phone and started sobbing hysterically, Becca had had enough. She pulled the phone from the woman's hand and spoke into the receiver. "She's fine and she'll call you back in a minute." Becca hung up on the man and dialed Geek's private cell phone line. The woman she'd taken the phone from sobbed louder.

"Lady, could you take it somewhere else? You're not doing anyone any good with all that noise."

Her eyes wide, the woman sniffed and turned to the concierge, who handed her a tissue.

Navy SEAL to Die For

Geek answered on the first ring. "What happened there? The scanners have been on fire."

Becca explained what had happened and ended with, "Get us cleared to leave the hotel."

"I'll call Royce," Geek said.

"I don't care if you call the president himself. I need out of here. Now." The card Oscar had given her was burning a hole in her pocket. The sooner she got inside the CIA building and extracted the data from Oscar's computer, the better.

Thirty minutes later, all four of them were allowed to leave. Whom Royce had called to manage that was a mystery to Becca, but she could always count on him to pull some pretty major strings. The man had connections. The Stealth Operations Specialists wouldn't be nearly as effective without them.

Good as gold, Geek had the company car waiting for them when they exited the hotel.

As they slid into the backseat, a dark sedan edged through the barricades and came to a stop in front of the hotel. A man in a black jacket and black pants got out and opened the back door of the vehicle. A German shepherd hopped out and followed his handler into the hotel. Before they passed through the doors, the handler held a cloth to the dog's nose. The animal sniffed and his tail wagged. He was ready to go to work.

Becca was glad to see the FBI had brought in a dog to search people for gunpowder residue. If the gunman was one of the waitstaff or guests, they'd find him. At least she hoped they would. Getting into the hotel hadn't been that difficult. Getting out might be equally easy for the assassin who'd killed Ivan.

"Back to SOS headquarters?" the driver asked.

"No," Becca said.

All eyes turned to her. She fished the card Oscar had given her out of her pocket. "We're not done for the night."

She closed the screen between the driver and the back of the limousine, and then explained what Oscar had said and what he'd wanted her to do.

"CIA headquarters?" Sam shook his head. "That can't be easy."

Becca held out her hand. "I need a cell phone."

Kat pulled one out of the V of her uniform collar and handed it to Becca. "Who are you calling?"

"Geek."

Sam chuckled. "If anyone can get you in, he can."

"I'm counting on it. I have Oscar's access card and code. If I can get past the front desk, I think I'll be all right."

"What about the security cameras?" Quentin asked.

Sam and Kat answered at once, "Geek."

"He can scramble them like he did at the hotel to get us in," Becca said. "Only this time, I'm going in alone."

Quentin shook his head. "No."

She raised her brows. "No?" Though her hand and butt hurt from the gashes, the biting pain didn't faze her as much as Quentin's adamant response. She was a bit shocked, but feeling pretty darned warm inside. After all that had happened, she'd never felt more alive. A lot had to do with Quentin. Knowing he was there during the whole gala event had made her feel somehow safer. Someone had her back.

The look on Quentin's face was one of worry, determination and protectiveness. She hadn't seen such a look before except on her father's face. That look made her feel cared for and protected, something she hadn't felt since her father's death.

"No," Quentin repeated. "If Oscar wants you to get to his computer, he must suspect someone inside the CIA is involved in the hits."

Becca nodded. "All the more reason to get the data that has someone worried enough to kill. This has to stop. And I'm the only one who has the card and access code to get in."

"You could give it to me and let me take it from here," Sam offered.

Becca shook her head. "I'm every bit as capable of handling this as you are, Sam. You know it. Just because I'm female doesn't mean I'm weaker."

Sam held up his hands in surrender. "You're absolutely right. Kat reminds me every day. I didn't mean to infer that. I have a lot of respect for your work."

She nodded. "Bottom line is that I have more of a reason than anyone to see this through. It was my father who was killed by the hired assassin. And my father's friend who was targeted by Ivan. And if I'm caught, I don't want any of you to take the fall." She turned to Quentin. "Especially you."

His brows dipped. "I'm not afraid of going in."

"Yeah, but you don't want to have a black mark on your military record for breaking and entering into the CIA building. You could get kicked out of the navy, or worse. You could go to jail."

His hand closed over hers. "I don't like the idea of you going in there alone."

She laced her fingers with his and spoke softly, "It's night. What are the chances anyone involved in this will be there?"

"Any chance is too dangerous," Quentin argued. "This guy is determined to keep his secrets and he's not afraid to kill everyone who stands in his way. He's already tried to get you several times."

WHILE BECCA PLACED the call to Geek, Quentin worked through all the scenarios he could think of that would get him into the CIA building with Becca. Short of walking in, punching out the guard at the front desk and bulldozing his way up to Oscar's office, he was stumped. The best he could come up with was to create a distraction to divert the guard's attention while Becca slipped past and entered the elevator.

Becca spoke quietly and rapidly to Geek. Between the two of them, they laid out the plan for her entry into the building. Geek was already on the way, driving the communications van with the necessary equipment he'd need to hack into the security system.

By the time they made it across town, Geek had caught up with them. They parked a couple blocks away from the CIA headquarters building.

All four of them crowded into Geek's van.

Quentin jumped in first. "Tell me you have something in this van that will make a loud and messy explosion."

Geek frowned. "I have a couple bricks of Semtex and detonators. Why?"

"Diversion," Quentin said. "All I need is a trashcan and a little bit of Semtex. I'll set small charges around the side and back of the building."

"Good idea." Sam held out his hand. "Show us what to do and we'll each take a side of the building. That way we can have choices over which one to set off and when."

"I'm not planning on hurting anyone or destroying property, other than a couple of trashcans. But if the guard gets sticky about letting Becca pass, we can set them off. It might give her the break in his attention to get her through."

While Quentin showed Sam and Kat how much of the plastic explosive to use and how to set the detonator, Geek fitted Becca with an ultrathin headset that fit in her ear, hidden by her long dark hair.

"Hopefully we won't need to cause a distraction. I'm counting on walking in, running the card through the turnstile and walking straight to the elevator," Becca said confidently.

"Yeah, and since when has this operation gone that smoothly?" Quentin pulled her into his arms. "Don't take any more chances than you have to. I'd like to see you come back out the way you go in. On both feet."

"And not in handcuffs or a straitjacket," Kat added with a wink.

"Or a body bag," Sam added.

"Geek, do you have a bottle of water? I'd like to get some of the blood off my dress and arm. I don't want to look like I just came from a warzone."

Geek handed her a bottle of water and a clean rag. Kat went to work on the back of Becca's dress where it was torn from the glass. "I can get the blood, but there's not much I can do about the rip."

"That's okay," Becca said. "I'll do my best to keep my back to anyone I come in contact with." She stood outside the van and started to pour water over her hand.

"Let me." Quentin took the bottle from her, poured

some on her hand and on a rag and dabbed at the dried blood until he'd cleaned it off completely. The bandage was on the inside of her hand. If she didn't raise that one, it wouldn't show. "Are you sure you're up to this?" he asked as he capped the bottle.

"I'm fine. A few cuts and bruises, but nothing I can't handle."

"Are you sure there's no way I can get into the building with you?"

She shook her head. "No." Then she leaned up and kissed him on the lips. "But thanks for asking."

He raised his hands to capture her around the waist. "I'm worried."

"Don't be. It's just another day at the office for me. A lot like you going on a special operation."

He nodded. "That's what I'm worried about. It's not safe."

She smiled up at him. "I never said my job was safe. But it's the one I have and love. It's part of who I am."

"Like me." He bent to press his lips to hers. "Just let me say *be careful* and let it go at that." Quentin nibbled at her earlobe and whispered, "I'm telling you I care."

"When you put it that way…" She reached up and cupped his face in her uninjured palm and turned him to face her. "I can live with it."

"As long as you live."

They kissed, long, hard and deep. She opened to him and he thrust his tongue past her teeth, sliding along the length of hers in a slow, sensuous display of affection. He ran his hands down her back to cup her buttocks. When she flinched, he remembered the cut. "Sorry."

"Me, too. I like how big and warm your hands are

on me." Becca threaded her fingers into the hair at the nape of his neck and deepened the kiss once more.

"Ahem. When you two are done sucking face, we might get on with this mission." Sam leaned out of the van. "Quentin, Kat and I have three trashcans to commandeer and position before Becca makes her grand entrance."

Quentin didn't want to let go of Becca. "See you in a few. Once we get the fireworks in place, we'll be listening for you in the van. Send up a verbal flare if you need help."

"And you'll do what?" Becca shook her head. "Don't be a hero and try to come into the building. I can take care of myself."

"I can't help it." Quentin kissed the tip of her nose. "I want to take care of you."

"Then plan what we can do to take care of each other when I get out of the building with the disk." She kissed him again and stepped into the van. "Let's do this."

Quentin's chest tightened with his frustration. He wanted to be at Becca's side through this operation. SEALs worked in teams for the most part. Becca needed someone on the inside who had her six. Too many things could go wrong.

And all he would be able to do was listen and maybe blow up a trashcan. Some help that would be.

Chapter Fourteen

The company car slid up against the curb and Becca got out. Her buttocks hurt every time she moved. She'd be glad when she could go back to her apartment and sleep until the pain went away. The medic said she might need stitches. Hopefully, the wound wouldn't reopen and start to bleed again. Keeping a low profile would be even more difficult if she left a trail of blood all the way up to Oscar's office.

Straightening, she winced. The stilettoes weren't helping. If she had to run, she'd end up kicking them off and running barefooted. She prayed it wouldn't come to that.

Get in. Get the disk and get out without stirring up any trouble. She repeated this mantra all the way into the building.

Pretending she belonged, she nodded toward the guard at the front desk and headed straight for the elevator.

"Excuse me, ma'am," the guard said. "I'll need to check you in here."

"It's okay. I left my reading glasses in my office. I'll just be a minute."

"I'm sorry, ma'am." He stood and started around his

desk. "It's SOP—Standard Operation Procedure. I need to see your badge and enter it in my log."

"Tell you what. If you'd just get my glasses for me, I'll wait here." In a whisper meant only for Geek's ears, she said, "I could use a little help here."

A loud bang sounded outside. The guard jumped back to his monitors. "What the hell?" He lifted his radio mic and said, "What the hell's going on out there? Sounds like we're under attack."

While the guard manned the radio and the screens in front of him, Becca slipped past to the elevator. An alarm went off and no matter how many times she hit the button to open the doors, the elevator was shut to keep anyone from going up or down. Spinning dangerously on her heels, she spotted a stairwell and hurried for it. "I'm taking the stairs," she said softly, hoping the mic picked up her words.

"Becca? Becca, can you hear me?" Geek said into her ear.

She didn't respond, wanting to get through the door before the man on duty tried to stop her.

The guard looked around, but an incoming call on his radio demanded his attention.

Becca ducked into the stairwell and started the climb to the fourth floor. "Geek, I can hear you. Can you hear me?"

Taking a few steps up the staircase, she strained to hear Geek's voice, but all she got was static. With no time to figure out the electronics, Becca hiked up her dress and ran as fast as she could in heels, twinges of pain shooting through her buttocks with each step.

Maybe she would have been better off letting Sam handle this. Her wound would bleed before she reached the floor with Oscar's office. He'd been on the same floor with her father, their offices side by side.

The few times Becca visited, she'd always stopped to say hello to her father's old friend, who'd greeted her warmly with a bear hug and a smile.

Her heart hurt the higher she climbed, not because she was in bad shape. Her chest tightened with memories of her father, whom she missed more than she ever imagined. When she got to the bottom of who'd sent the mercenaries to kill her father and her, she'd take the time she needed to grieve. Until then, she didn't have time for emotion. She had a job to do.

When she reached the fourth floor landing, she pushed open the door and peered into an empty hallway. Her father's old office was halfway down the corridor, and Oscar's just past it. She wondered who had inherited Marcus Smith's office and if they'd moved right in upon her father's death.

Pushing that thought aside, she dropped the hem of her dress and strode out into the hallway as if she owned the place. The emergency lights still blinked and she prayed the security guards were more worried about the outside of the building than the inside.

With a confident stride, she closed the distance between the stairwell and the door to Oscar's office. She ran the card through the scanner and keyed in the numbers she'd committed to memory. For a little more than a second, the lock did nothing, then a green light flashed.

Becca twisted the knob and pushed the door inward. The outer office consisted of a desk for Oscar's secretary. Becca hurried around the desk to the next door that led into Oscar's inner office. Once inside, she closed the door behind her and ran to his desk.

With the clock ticking in her head, she figured she didn't have a lot of time, if any. If Geek hadn't been able to tap into the security cameras, and Becca had been caught on camera in the stairwell, the security team could be on their way up now.

Becca eased into Oscar's chair behind his desk, pulled out the top right drawer and ran her fingers along the underside of the desktop. At first she didn't feel anything but the smooth texture of the wood.

She ran her hand back the other way, checking closer to the outer edges. Her fingers slid over something smooth and rounded and her pulse ratcheted up a notch. Giving it a firm push, she heard something click and a shallow drawer that had previously looked more like the rest of the trim around the edges of the desk popped out. Inside was a flat, rectangular card-like disk, no bigger than the size of a quarter.

Becca snatched the device, tucked it into her hidden pocket and pushed to her feet.

"I'm glad you found it."

Becca yelped and staggered backward, the backs of her knees hitting against Oscar's chair, making her sit back down, hard. Pain knifed through her as she landed on her injured bottom. She stared across the room at John Francis, the CIA's second in command. Her father's and Oscar's boss.

"I thought you were at the gala," she said, buying time while her brain processed what he'd just said.

"I had business to take care of at the office. I see you did, too." He held out his hand. "I'll take that disk."

"I don't know what you're talking about."

His face hardened. "Come, Becca. Your father didn't raise a fool. Hand over the disk."

She stood and walked around Oscar's desk. "Or what?"

"I'll turn you over to the security team and they'll take it from you when they frisk you."

She shrugged. "Then they would have it and you wouldn't." Becca tilted her head. "Go ahead. Call the guards."

When John reached beneath his jacket, Becca took the opportunity to charge him. Nothing stood in her way but five feet of carpet. She bent low and ran at him like a lineman going for the quarterback.

Hitting him in the belly, she knocked him backward and he hit the door. But he recovered quickly, grabbed a handful of her hair, knocked the headset out of her ear and stuck a smooth, gunmetal-gray Glock against her temple. "Don't push me, woman. You've caused more than your share of trouble, sneaking into a restricted-access facility."

"I take it you're the one behind the murders of my father and Rand Houston, and the attempted murder of Oscar Melton."

"Not attempted. He passed on his way to the hospital. The emergency room doctor called it. But I didn't kill him. That Russian waiter did."

Her heart stopped beating in her chest for a couple of seconds as emotion threatened to derail the functioning of her brain. First her father, now Oscar? When would the killing end?

"Come on, Miss Smith, hand over the disk. It contains classified data."

"I don't have it," she insisted.

"You can give me the disk, or I can take it from you. Either way, I'll have it." He pulled tighter on her hair. "Now, which is it to be?"

"You'll have to take it." She slammed her stiletto heel into his instep.

He grunted and loosened his hold on her hair.

Becca lunged for the door and ran through before John could grab her again. She was banking on the assumption that the man wouldn't shoot her in the building. It was a risk, but one she'd take to get the hell out with the disk in her pocket.

As she ran through the outer office, she shoved the secretary's rolling chair out in front of the CIA deputy director. He stumbled and cursed, giving her just enough time to make the outer office door.

As she reached for the door, a gunshot echoed through the room, tearing a three-inch strip out of the doorframe next to her hand. "Enough!"

Becca froze. Afraid if she opened the door, she wouldn't have time to take even one step before John put a bullet in her back.

He stepped up behind her.

Bunching her muscles, Becca prepared to defend herself. As she cocked her elbow, John pressed something against her side. "We quit playing games now."

A blast of electricity ripped through her. Her body jerked and shook. Her legs buckled and she dropped to the floor like a ton of bricks, her head bouncing against the door.

The knock on the head, more than the shock, made her fade in and out of consciousness. Everything in her body tingled and her vocal cords refused to work. She lay as helpless as a newborn while John patted her body, searching for the disk. As much as he tried he couldn't find the hidden pocket tucked against the waistline of her gown. The disk was so small it was barely discernible from the seams.

"Where is it?" the deputy director demanded, his face red.

Footsteps sounded in the hallway. Doors opened and closed along the corridor.

John pocketed the stun gun and holstered his gun. "We're getting out of here."

Becca wanted to tell him he wasn't going anywhere, but her body wasn't her own and she couldn't move anything, including her mouth. Forming thoughts was equally difficult.

John Francis lifted her in his arms and flung open the door. "Help. This woman is injured. I need to get her to the ground floor immediately."

Becca tried to cry out, willing her mouth to move and her voice to sound through her throat, but she couldn't make the muscles of her throat work. John ran with her to the elevator. The guards used their badges to override the safety shutdown, and they rode down together, John making up a story about an intruder on the fourth floor.

"Don't let him get away. You have to go back and find him. He's dangerous."

One of the guards who came down with them held the elevator door open. "Are you and the woman going to be okay?"

"Yes. I'll wait outside for the ambulance. I think she's in a state of shock." John stepped out of the elevator carrying Becca. He glanced back. "Don't wait with me. That maniac might hurt someone else!"

Please, don't let him take me! Becca shouted, but nothing came out of her mouth. A single tear slipped down her cheek.

Another guard hurried toward John. "Sir, it isn't safe to be in the building. Someone set off explosives on the perimeter. What happened to her?"

John shook his head. "I was showing my wife where I worked, but she obviously had too much to drink at the gala. Could you have my car brought around? My keys are in my right front pocket." He turned so the guard could fish the keys out of his pocket.

"I'll have someone get it for you. Wait right here."

When the guard left, John juggled her, reached for the stun gun and zapped her again.

Becca lost consciousness. When she came to, they were still standing in the lobby of the CIA building and her body still refused to cooperate. If only she could throw herself on the ground, it might slow John enough that her voice would come back and she could tell the guards John was kidnapping her.

But she couldn't even rock her body, or open her lips. A few moments later, a guard ran in. "Sir, your vehicle is out front. Do you want me to carry her for you?"

"No, no. She's my wife, I can handle it. Tomorrow I'm signing her up for an intervention. She's gone too far." He marched through the doors and out to the waiting car where a man in a guard uniform held the door.

Help me! Becca screamed inside. *Quentin, Sam, Kat, Geek! Can't you see?*

Police cars with bright blue strobe lights pulled in at the same time as John settled her in the backseat. A bomb squad van pulled up. The scene was chaotic.

John climbed into the driver's seat and a moment later someone tapped on his windshield.

He lowered it.

"Sir, you need to move this car away from the building. You could be in danger."

"I was just about to do that. I'll be out of your way in a second."

As he raised the window, Becca lay in the backseat, able to move the tip of a toe. Sweet heaven, how was she going to get out of this mess?

As soon as Quentin had his charge set, he raced back to the communications van and crowded in behind Geek, staring at images on the security cameras. On one side were the images Geek staged for the guards to see. The hallways were empty, nothing moved. On the other side were the true images. The lobby where Becca had been confronted by the guard, the stairwell she would take up to the fourth floor and the fourth floor hallway.

Kat and Sam entered the van shortly after Quentin, breathing hard from running the two blocks to the vehicle.

As soon as Becca encountered problems with the front desk guard, Quentin detonated his charge. Becca made it to the stairwell and then all the electronics went to hell.

The security camera screens turned to scrambled static.

"Becca, can you hear me?" Geek said into the microphone.

She never responded.

"What happened?" Quentin demanded.

"I don't know. It's as if someone is scrambling the signal."

Quentin leaned over and tapped the side of the monitor. "Make it come back."

"Hitting it isn't going to help." Geek's fingers flew over a keyboard. "I can't. Get. It. Back. I don't know what's causing the blackout."

They couldn't see, hear or contact Becca inside the CIA headquarters building. She would be flying blind and there wasn't much they could do about it.

Geek switched on the police scanner.

Reports of a terrorist attack at the CIA building spread across the police network.

"Damn," Kat said. "We're all going to jail."

His heart pounding, Quentin paced the length of the van—two steps—and spun. "I don't care as long as Becca gets out alive."

"I have her on the tracking device!" Geek shouted.

Quentin leaned over Geek's shoulder. "Where?"

"She's still inside the building."

"Where in the building?"

"It doesn't tell me what floor and room she's in, just that she's inside."

Quentin watched the screen with the others, praying for some idea of what the hell was going on. When he couldn't stand still any longer, he headed for the door. "I have to get closer."

"You can't. The place will soon be inundated with cops and the bomb squad."

"I can't do nothing."

"She's moving!" Kat exclaimed. "Look, the green dot is moving through the building."

Kat's excitement drew Quentin back to the screen.

Quentin leaned closer, studying the position of the dot on the street. "She's outside."

"She's outside the front door of the building," Geek corrected.

"That place has to be crawling with cops by now." Kat shook her head.

Sam punched numbers into his cell phone. "I'm calling Royce. I hope he can pull strings and get her cut loose."

"I'm going," Quentin said.

Kat touched his arm. "You can't. They'll have dogs out there. They'll know you were the one to set off the bomb."

"Becca could be in trouble." Quentin shook off her hand. "I can't just stand here and do nothing."

"Don't get close enough they see you. And Quentin—"

Quentin paused at the door.

Geek tossed a hand-held tracking device at him. "Take this."

Kat held out her cell phone. "And this. Let us know what's going on."

Sam pushed her hand aside. "Keep yours. I'll take mine. I'm going with him."

Kat straightened. "If you two are going, I'm going, too."

"I need someone to drive this crate if something goes down and we have to move."

Sam gripped her hands. "Kat, you're a better driver than I am."

"That's not what you tell me when I'm driving cross-country." She shook her head. "Fine. I'll stay. But don't let anything happen to you guys or our Becca."

Quentin couldn't wait any longer. He was out the door and halfway down the street before Sam caught up to him. They dodged between buildings and came out a block and a half away from the CIA building where several police cars, a bomb squad truck and a line of fire trucks were pulling in.

Glancing down at the tracking device, Quentin took a moment to orient himself with the dot on the screen. A car raced past on the street, barely missing him, when he realized Becca's dot was moving. Fast.

"Damn!" He spun and took off running after the car. "She's in that car."

"Quentin, you can't catch them on foot," Sam called out from somewhere behind him.

The car turned left at the next block.

Quentin cut down an alley between two buildings and emerged in time to see the taillights of the vehicle blink red as it slowed to turn right onto another road.

He ran until his lungs burned and his legs cramped, but he couldn't stop. Becca meant more to him than he'd previously realized. The smart, sexy, kick-ass woman had crawled under his skin like no other. He'd get her back if it was the last thing he did.

Chapter Fifteen

Becca lay in the backseat, struggling to regain control of her limbs. Eventually she was able to wiggle a toe, then another. She flexed her fingers and moved her jaw. Forcing air past her vocal cords she hummed, then tried for words.

"Can't."

"The effects wearing off, are they?" John said.

"Can't." She managed to swallow, forcing moisture down her throat and thoughts to congeal. "Get. Away. With. This."

"What's that?" He laughed. "You have something I want. I have ways of getting the information out of you. It's part of the job description. You know, the part they don't advertise. Interrogation techniques."

Becca rolled her wrists and moved her arms and shoulders. Before too long, she'd have full control of her entire body.

"The problem with hiring people for a job, they aren't always as thorough as you would be if you'd done it yourself.

"Take you, for instance. I asked Ivan to take care of you, so what did he do? He sends a sloppy mercenary after you. What was he thinking? What better way to announce to the world that you're a fool than to shoot down an airplane on American soil?"

"You killed Ivan," Becca said.

"Damn right I did. After I had him take out Melton. One less person to worry about. I'll find the rest. Make no mistake. They won't get to me or anyone else in this deal."

"What deal?"

"Ah, now that's where that little disk comes in. I suspect the information on that little storage device is enough to sink several ships. And I don't plan on being on the Titanic when it goes down. It should also tell me who was involved in the investigation."

"What investigation?"

"The one your father died for. You'll have to ask him all about it when you see him on the other side." John swerved sharply, the motion throwing Becca onto the floorboard. By now she was able to move her hands but they were secured behind her back, and the rest of her body still felt jerky and hard to maneuver.

The vehicle slowed and came to a halt. John got out of the driver's seat and opened the back door, grabbed her beneath the shoulders and dragged her out.

"I really don't care where you've hidden the disk. If it's on your person, it will go down with you. If you left it somewhere 'safe' its location will be lost with you. I'm tired of all the drama you've caused me."

"Why are you doing this?"

"You don't think the CIA pays me enough to keep my wife in booze, do you? I've acquired properties in different countries, I'm retiring next month and I'll be damned if you sabotage my plans to disappear off the grid before that time." He lifted her into his arms and carried her down an embankment.

It was dark out, but the city lights made the sky glow enough she could make out trees. They were in a park. By the sound of water lapping at a shore, she guessed they were somewhere along the Potomac River.

Her heartbeat quickened. He was going to dump her in the river while her body was still too dysfunctional for her to get out. She focused on her feet, praying they would move more than just the twinge or two she'd managed thus far. If he threw her into the water, it was deep enough she'd drown.

"Don't do this, John."

"I have to."

"Killing isn't the answer."

"How do you know? You have no idea what the question is. Walk a mile in my shoes and you'd come to the same conclusion." He held her over the water. "Gonna tell me where that disk is?"

Becca knew if she gave him the disk, he'd go after others who were involved in whatever investigation he was so determined to stop. Someone else would be murdered. A father. A mother. Someone's brother or son. She took a deep breath, knowing her next words would be her last. "I don't know what you're talking about."

"Have it your way. At least I'll be done with you." He let go of her and she fell.

Becca dragged in a deep breath just before she hit the icy cold water, and sank beneath the surface.

Her world went dark. With her hands behind her back, she had no way of treading water. Her legs were almost useless, her feet the only things moving. And barely, at that.

This was it. She'd always thought she'd die of a gunshot wound or in a fatal car wreck. Never had she imagined death by drowning. Her lungs burned with the need to release the air she held and the frantic urge to suck in another breath. The water was so black she couldn't tell what was up or down. And the numbing cold…

She thought of her father when he'd taught her how to swim. Of her beautiful mother so full of life before she died in the plane crash. And then she thought of Quentin and everything that might have been had she lived to get to know him better. It wasn't fair. She wanted to get to know him. What was his favorite food? What sports did he like to play? Did he like dogs or cats? Would he have taken her out on a date had they been regular people with regular jobs?

She kicked her feet, wanting to live so badly she refused to give up. Her foot touched the silty, muddy bottom of the river and she tried to push off to get to the surface, but she couldn't get much traction when her legs refused to cooperate.

Damn. This couldn't be the end. She wasn't ready to die.

QUENTIN RAN UNTIL he couldn't run any more. A horn honked behind him and he staggered to the side of the road as a van pulled up beside him.

"Get in," Kat yelled from behind the steering wheel. "Becca's somewhere ahead along the side of the river. Hurry!"

The side door slid open and Quentin fell inside next to Sam and Geek.

"They stopped in one of the parks along the river."

Quentin dragged in deep lungfuls of breath, willing his heart to slow so that he could hear over the pounding in his ears. "Whoever has her is going to throw her into the river. Can you make this thing go any faster?" He pushed to his feet and leaned over the back of the driver's seat.

Kat took a turn so fast the right side of the vehicle lifted off the ground and crashed down as soon as she straightened.

Quentin was thrown into a panel of electronics, jolting his injured shoulder. When he righted himself, he could see the glare of light shining off the surface of water. The river was dead ahead.

"She should be ahead about fifty yards," Geek called out. "Shut off the lights. We'll go in on foot."

Kat slowed the van, hit the switch throwing them into darkness with only the lights of the city providing a dim glow overhead. She pulled into the entrance of the park and turned sideways, blocking the drive for anyone who might wish to exit.

All four of them leaped out of the vehicle and ran toward the water.

A solitary figure stood at the edge of the river. When he heard footsteps behind him, he turned and ran.

Quentin reached him first and tackled him, hitting him hard. The man slammed into the ground, face first. Quentin flung him onto his back and grabbed him by the collar of his tuxedo. "Where is she?"

He laughed in Quentin's face. "I don't know what you're talking about."

"Becca. Where is she?" He lifted the man by the throat and slammed his head against the dirt. "Tell me!"

"I might have seen a woman throw herself into the water. But that was a few minutes ago. I looked but I couldn't see her."

Quentin's heart dropped to the sour pit of his belly. He punched the man so hard it knocked him out. Then he leaped to his feet and ran for the river's edge.

"Becca?"

He studied the water, looking for any sign. The moon drifted out from behind some clouds and shone down on the smooth surface. A few feet downstream, something moved. Were those bubbles?

Quentin ripped off his jacket and shoes and dove into the water. The chill hit him hard, but he refused to let it slow him down. He swam to where he'd seen the bubbles, tucked his body and dove beneath the surface, his hands out front, feeling for her, praying he'd find her. He didn't feel anything. Rising to the top he took a deep breath and went down again, his heart aching, desperate to find her.

Then he felt something light and silky float through his fingertips. He pushed deeper and wrapped his hands around hair. Long strands, attached to a head and body. He tugged the hair, pulling her up through the murky depths. When he could get his hands on her body, he grabbed her beneath the arms and kicked hard for the surface.

As he emerged into the cool night air, a scream rent the air.

"Quentin! Look out!"

Headlights blinded him as a vehicle raced toward

the water, launched off the bank and plunged into the river mere inches away from where Quentin held Becca in his arms.

A huge splash washed over them like a wave and the water sucked at them as the vehicle sank beneath the surface.

Struggling to keep himself and Becca from going down with the car, Quentin fought to make it to the shore. His lungs burned and his arms and legs strained with the weight of the two of them dressed in formal clothing.

Then Sam and Kat reached out and hooked Becca's arms, dragging her up the bank to lay her on the grass.

With the last bit of his reserves, Quentin crawled up beside her.

Once Quentin and Becca were out of the water, Sam dove into the river after John Francis's car.

Quentin didn't have the strength to help. After running through the streets and then diving in to find Becca, he had hit his limit. If John Francis drowned, so be it. He'd dumped Becca in the river. The bastard deserved to die.

Kat cut through the zip tie around Becca's wrists and went to work reviving her, pushing the water from her lungs and performing CPR.

Quentin knelt beside her. For every thirty compressions, Quentin sealed his mouth over Becca's and breathed air into her lungs twice. They repeated the process four times.

Quentin's heart pounded, his chest hurt and for the first time in a long time, he sent a silent prayer to the heavens. *Please spare her life.*

Becca bucked beneath them, and she lifted her head

to cough. She continued coughing until she'd cleared the majority of the river water from her lungs. Then she sank against the grass, raising her hand to cup Quentin's face. "You found me."

He laid his hand over hers and smiled. "Geek had you tagged with a tracker." Quentin didn't tell her the tracker did no good for finding her in the water. Faith, fate or something bigger and more meaningful than anything he'd ever known had led him to her. He squeezed her hand and helped her sit up.

Kat ran to the river's edge and watched for Sam.

A siren's wail sounded in the distance, getting closer.

Sam surfaced again and swam to shore, breathing hard. "Francis's car is too deep. I can't stay down long enough to get to him, and the doors are locked."

Geek ran to the van and returned with an emergency window escape tool. "Use this."

Quentin followed Sam into the cold water and, tracking the air bubbles, they found the car. Sam used the device to break the window and scrape the glass aside. Quentin opened the door, swam in with the tool and sliced through the seatbelt, grabbed Francis by the shoulder and hauled him through the window.

His lungs burned and he was desperate for air, but he worked his way to the surface. Sam had gone up for air and came back to bring Francis the rest of the way up.

When he emerged into the night air, Quentin sucked in deep breaths and tread water for a few seconds. Between him and Sam, they swam Francis to shore.

Geek and Kat hauled the big man up over the bank and started CPR.

Quentin left them to it and returned to Becca's side.

A fire truck pulled into the park and stopped, red strobe lights cutting through the night sky. Emergency personnel leaped out, grabbed their gear and ran toward their group huddled near the edge of the Potomac.

The paramedics took over from Geek and Kat, performing compressions and pumping air into Francis's lungs.

Geek went back to the van and returned with a blanket. Quentin wrapped it around Becca's shivering body and held her close.

"Are we going to get in trouble for breaking and entering in the CIA building and detonating explosives?" she asked, flexing her bare feet, her shoes lost somewhere in the Potomac. "Even Royce might have a problem on that front."

"He's fixing it." Geek knelt beside her. "They're calling it an unscheduled terrorist training event. Oh, and he'll be here in an hour."

"He shouldn't be out of the hospital," Becca said.

Sam chuckled, a violent shiver shaking his body. "The hospital staff had no choice. Royce was leaving whether they discharged him or not."

"Sam, you need this blanket more than I do." Becca tried to pull off the blanket.

"No way. I wasn't nearly drowned like you." He held up his hand. "Keep it."

Quentin held her against him, pressing his cheek to the top of her head. She was still shaking.

When the ambulance arrived, he reluctantly released her into the care of the emergency medical technicians. They covered her in warm blankets, started an IV and carried her toward one of the waiting ambulances.

She didn't need him anymore. The hospital would

take care of her, and the man responsible for killing her father was no longer a threat.

Becca reached out her hand. "Quentin."

He hurried to her side, glad to hold her cold hand in his. "Yeah, baby."

"Ride with me to the hospital. Please." She pressed his hand to her face.

He glanced at the medical personnel.

"It's okay," said the EMT. "She's not in immediate danger. We can spare the room."

"We'll catch up with you at the hospital," Kat called out.

Quentin sat beside Becca on the way to the hospital, holding her hand, wishing he could hold it forever. But that would be impossible. He wondered how they could make a relationship between them work, with her on the east coast and him stationed in Mississippi. He could ask for a transfer to one of the SEAL teams based out of Little Creek, Virginia. Then he could see her when he wasn't deployed on a mission. Whatever happened, he didn't want this to be the end.

BECCA HELD ON TO Quentin's hand like a lifeline. Never had she been so scared of dying, nor had she been so close. What hit her hardest was the realization that even though she'd lost her father, she had so much to live for. Her father wouldn't have wanted her to grieve her life away. He would have wanted her to live, to find someone she could love as much as he'd loved her mother.

Becca stared up at Quentin. Was he the one? He was brave, funny and sexy—everything she could have hoped for in a man. Her father would have loved him like a son.

Tears welled as she thought of her dad. "It was John Francis all along," she said. "He was the one who hired the assassins."

"Why?"

She shook her head. "My father, Rand Houston and Oscar Melton were involved in some kind of investigation." She stopped talking as a thought struck her. "Damn." Becca reached into the hidden pocket of her gown. When her fingers curled around the small, flat disk, she let go of the breath that had been caught in her throat. "He wanted the disk Oscar sent me after. Although, I don't know what good it will be after being soaked in river water." Becca handed the disk to Quentin. "Get it to Geek, and see if he can salvage the information on it."

"I will." He tucked it into his shirt pocket. "In the meantime, what's next?"

Becca raised her good hand to push the damp hair from her face. "I think we're going to need more help on this case. There's something big going on for John to feel like he had to kill those who knew too much."

"Yeah, but now your name and face will be known by anyone trying to keep this whole thing secret."

Her lips thinned and her jaw tightened. "We can't let this go. We have to get to the bottom of it."

Quentin brushed the backs of his knuckles across her cheek. "Maybe we need some fresh faces in the picture. Faces that haven't been involved so far."

Becca nodded. "I'll see what Royce can spare."

"And I'll talk with my commander. Royce seems to have some strings he can pull. I trust my team to provide backup and support."

"You are absolutely right. We need someone undercover," Becca mused. "Someone who isn't known in this area."

The ambulance stopped at the hospital's ER entrance.

The medics unloaded Becca and wheeled her back to a room to be examined by a doctor. A nurse asked Quentin to wait in the lobby while they took care of the patient. They'd call him back when they had completed their exam.

Kat, Sam and Geek arrived a few minutes later. And behind them Royce entered, his arm in a sling. His shock of white hair stood on end. He wore jeans and had a jacket slung over his shoulders. "Bring me up to date."

The four of them took Royce to a quiet corner of the lobby and gave him the details of all that had transpired since Quentin and Becca had stepped off the train in DC.

Quentin passed the disk to Geek. The young computer guru ran out to the communications van and returned with a laptop a few minutes later. He slid the disk into a slot in the front of the computer and waited.

Quentin leaned over his shoulder. "Anything?"

Geek pressed a few buttons on the keyboard. "An error message that the disk is damaged and can't be read. We may have to let it dry more." He tried a few more keys and shook his head as he closed his laptop. "I'll take it back to headquarters and see what I can do later."

Royce scratched his chin where the beginning of a beard showed up like a salt-and-pepper shadow. "Based on what we've learned from today, we still have work to do."

They all nodded. In this together.

A nurse found them in the lobby. "Excuse me, is one of you Mr. Lovett?"

Quentin stepped out of the group. "I am."

"Miss Smith is asking for you."

"Could we all go back?" Royce asked. He pulled his wallet from his back pocket and flipped it open, displaying a badge. "I have a few questions for Miss Smith."

The nurse frowned. "We usually don't allow more than two people, but if it's for an official reason, I suppose you can all go. Just don't disturb the other patients."

"Yes, ma'am." Royce smiled. "Thank you."

Eager to see Becca, Quentin followed the nurse through the doors marked Authorized Personnel Only. The rest of the group was only a few steps behind him.

They found Becca on a gurney in one of the rooms, her head raised so that she was almost sitting up, though she leaned slightly to one side.

BEING THE FOCUS of attention from five people, and still babying a gash in her bottom, Becca could feel the heat rising in her cheeks.

"If I'd known you all were coming, I'd have baked a cake. But then I don't know how to cook, so that's not true." Becca clamped her lips shut for a second when she realized she was babbling, something she *never* did. Instead, she held up her hand. "I think I'm still fuzzy-headed from the stun gun. They cleaned the river water out of my wounds, and then stitched my hand and...other parts."

She jerked her head toward her derriere and looked

away from Quentin, suddenly and inexplicably shy around the man who'd seen her naked, and made love to her twice already. "Okay, too much information. But I'm supposed to change the bandages daily."

Quentin smiled down at her, lifted her uninjured hand and pressed a kiss to her fingertips. "I can help with that."

"God, I sound like an idiot." Becca weaved her fingers with his. "And you have a unit to report to."

"I'll work on that," he said. "I still have thirty days of vacation I can draw on."

Becca's eyes narrowed as she stared across the bed at Royce. "Are you sure you should be out of the hospital? You're still a little pale. I mean you were shot less than thirty-six hours ago."

"Says the woman who nearly drowned in the Potomac." He patted her arm. "I'll be fine. *We'll* be fine."

"Damn right, we will," Becca said, leaning back. She winced and turned on her side again. "As soon as certain wounds heal."

Royce laughed out loud. "Right."

Becca glanced past them hopefully. "Now, if the doctor would come back in and sign my release orders, I can blow this joint."

"I'll leave the company car for you," Royce said. "I'm scheduling a meeting of available SOS agents as soon as you've had time to rest."

"I'm rested." Becca tried to sit up again and fell back on her side. "As soon as I get out of this place," she muttered, with a little less confidence.

"I have to call in some favors first." Royce leaned over and kissed her cheek. "You did an excellent job finding John. Let someone else take the lead for a while."

She frowned. "I'm perfectly capable."

"But word will have gotten around that Marcus Smith's daughter is on the case. They'll be watching for you. I need to get people in on this one who haven't been in the area and aren't known."

Becca nodded, having already thought of this.

Quentin raised a hand. "Sir, I have some ideas about that."

A man in a lab coat stepped into the room and frowned.

Royce waved the others toward the door. "Let's step out and let the doctor out-process the patient. You can tell me about your ideas then. Becca, I'll see you in a couple of days." As Royce left he shook hands with Quentin. "Thank you for doing such a good job taking care of my agent, Lovett. I think we can take it from here, if you need to get back to your unit."

Royce's words hit Becca square in the chest like a prize fighter's fisted glove. No. She wasn't ready for Quentin to leave her.

Becca suffered through the doctor's explanation of what she needed to do in order to guard against infection. He left her with a prescription for antibiotics and orders to stay off her butt.

Becca fought the urge to giggle.

"And go easy on the intercourse. You don't want to rip a stitch." She gasped and glared at the man.

To his credit, he didn't crack a smile or smirk. He tore a sheet of paper off his prescription pad and handed it to her. "You're free to go, as long as someone drives you home."

"Got that covered," she assured him as she slid her feet over the edge of the bed.

A nurse pushed a wheelchair into the room.

"Is that necessary?" Becca asked.

The doctor finally smiled. "In your case, no." He waved the nurse away with the chair. "You're better off walking out than sitting in the chair."

Limping, Becca followed the doctor to the exit and emerged into the lobby of the ER. Quentin was the only person left of their group. Her heart beating a little lighter for seeing his smiling face, Becca walked toward him and fell into his arms.

"Hey, baby. Are you okay?" He smoothed hair back from her face.

She nodded, unable to force air past the knot in her throat.

"I told them I'd see you back to your apartment."

"Why?" she asked. "We found my father's killer. I'm no longer in danger—therefore you don't need to look out for me."

"Have you considered I might *want* to look after you?" He looped an arm around her middle and led her toward the door.

"We're two different people in somewhat similar occupations." She waved a hand to the side. "Nothing we start between us would ever work or last for long."

"So you're thinking along those lines, too?" He tightened his arm around her. "Because I was thinking I could use a challenge and a change of pace. I might ask for a transfer to one of the SEAL teams at Little Creek, Virginia."

"What if I told you I didn't want you around after this?"

He grinned and shook his head. "Not a chance."

Becca stopped in the middle of the sliding doors and cocked her brows. "You're a cocky son-of-a-gun. Why would you think I'd want you around pestering me?"

His grin widened. "Sweetheart, it's in the kiss."

She snorted. "I don't know what you're talking about."

"Let me demonstrate." He swooped in to claim her lips.

Becca stood stiff for a full second, then melted against him and kissed him back. This man had gotten under her skin from the moment he made a pass at her on the plane back to the States. Why the hell was she fighting what he was proving true?

He was absolutely, undeniably correct.

It was in the kiss.

Next morning, 7:00 am

JERKED AWAKE BY banging on her apartment door, Becca rolled onto her backside and cried out.

"Oh, baby, you have to remember the stitches." Quentin leaned over and kissed her cheek.

"Mmm." She twisted her head around to kiss his lips. "I wasn't thinking about that all last night."

"I told you it would be easier on top."

More banging on the door brought Quentin's head up. "I'll get that."

"Thanks." Becca snuggled into the sheet, one eye propped open as Quentin rose from the bed and slipped on a pair of jogging shorts.

Quentin left the bedroom and entered the living room.

"Becca? It's me, Marcy," a muffled female voice called through the door paneling. "I hate to wake you up, but I have to be at work in twenty minutes."

Quentin opened the door as a young woman raised her hand to knock again. She stopped with her hand frozen in mid-knock. "Oh."

"What can I do for you?" Quentin asked.

The woman called Marcy let her gaze rake him from head to toes before she swallowed and said, "Oh, baby, you could do a lot for me, if I didn't have to go to work right now." She held a package in her hand. "Is Becca here or did you just move into her apartment? Please say you're single, available and moving in?"

"Sorry to disappoint. Becca's here. I'm not moving in, yet. But either way, despite what some might think, I'm a one-woman-man and that one woman is Becca."

Marcy sighed. "In that case, could you give this package to her? The postman dropped it at my apartment by mistake a couple days ago. I'm just now getting around to delivering it."

Quentin took the package from the woman. "I'll make sure she gets it."

"Thanks. And if you find yourself single again, I'm next door."

After Marcy left, Quentin took the package into the bedroom and handed it to Becca.

"So you met my neighbor, Marcy." Becca laughed. "She's a mess, isn't she? She's never met a man she couldn't flirt with. Did you think she was pretty?"

Quentin shrugged. "I really don't remember."

"Right answer." Becca turned the package over. "That's funny. There's no return address on it." She tore it open. Inside was an envelope with her name written in crisp block letters.

Becca's face paled and she slowly opened the envelope, tears slipping from her eyes. She pulled out a single sheet of paper and a small, rectangular disk fell onto the bed beside her. It looked just like the one she'd taken from Oscar Melton's office.

Quentin scooped up the disk while Becca read the letter aloud, her voice catching.

Becca,

If you receive this letter and disk without talking to me about it first, something bad must have happened to me. Take this disk to your boss. He might be the only one you can trust with this information. With his resources, he should have more luck cracking the codes to get to the bottom of what's going on.

I couldn't send this letter without telling you how very proud I am of the woman you have become. Please don't let your job be everything to you. Take time to fall in love. Your mother and I loved each other so much, and you were the result. You're a beautiful, smart and generous woman who deserves to love and be loved.

I will always love my little girl and I'll always be looking out for you.
Love,
Dad

Becca stared up at Quentin with tears in her eyes. His heart broke for her and he gently gathered her in his arms. "He loved you so very much."

"He loved my mother, too. And all he wanted for me was to know that kind of love, as well."

Quentin leaned over and kissed her lips with a light touch. "I think we might have a shot at that if we give it half a chance."

She sucked in a shaky breath. "I'm game, if you are."

"I am." He kissed her, so happy he hadn't taken her initial no for the final answer. This woman was the one for him.

When they finally stopped kissing long enough to form coherent thoughts, Quentin glanced down at the disk in his palm.

"Guess we'll be visiting Royce sooner than we thought. This story isn't over, yet."

* * * * *

Every cowboy has a wild side—
all it takes is the right woman to unleash it...

Keep reading for a sneak peek of the ebook
BLAME IT ON THE COWBOY,
part of USA TODAY *bestselling author*
Delores Fossen's series
THE McCORD BROTHERS.

Available in October 2016!

LIARS AND CLOWNS. Logan had seen both tonight. The liar was a woman who he thought loved him. Helene. And the clown, well… Logan wasn't sure he could process that image just yet.

Maybe after lots of booze though.

He hadn't been drunk since his twenty-first birthday, nearly thirteen years ago. But he was about to remedy that now. He motioned for the bartender to set him up another pair of Glenlivet shots.

His phone buzzed again, indicating another call had just gone to voice mail. One of his siblings no doubt wanting to make sure he was all right. He wasn't. But talking to them about it wouldn't help, and Logan didn't want anyone he knew to see or hear him like this.

It was possible there'd be some slurring involved. Puking, too.

He'd never been sure what to call Helene. His long-time girlfriend? *Girlfriend* seemed too high school. So, he'd toyed with thinking of her as his future fiancée. Or in social situations—she was his business associate who often ran his marketing campaigns. But tonight Logan wasn't calling her any of those things. As far as he was concerned, he never wanted to think of her, her name or what to call her again.

Too bad that image of her was stuck in his head, but that was where he was hoping generous amounts of single-malt scotch would help.

Even though Riley, Claire, Lucky and Cassie wouldn't breathe a word about this, it would still get around town. Lucky wasn't sure how, but gossip seemed to defy the time-space continuum in Spring Hill. People would soon know, if they didn't already, and those same people wouldn't look at him the same again. It would hurt business.

Hell. It hurt *him*.

That was why he was here in this hotel bar in San Antonio. It was only thirty miles from Spring Hill, but tonight he hoped it'd be far enough away that no one he knew would see him get drunk. Then he could stagger to his room and then puke in peace. Not that he was looking forward to the puking part, but it would give him something else to think about other than *her*.

It was his first time in this hotel, though he stayed in San Antonio often on business. Logan hadn't wanted to risk running into anyone he knew, and he certainly wouldn't at this trendy "boutique" place. Not with a name like the Purple Cactus and its vegan restaurant.

If the staff found out he was a cattle broker, he might be booted out. Or forced to eat tofu. That was the reason Logan had used cash when he checked in. No sense risking someone recognizing his name from his credit card.

The clerk had seemed to doubt him when Logan had told him that his ID and credit cards had been stolen and that was why he couldn't produce anything with his name on it. Of course, when Logan had slipped the guy an extra hundred-dollar bill, it had caused that doubt to disappear.

"Drinking your troubles away?" a woman asked.

"Trying."

Though he wasn't drunk enough that he couldn't see what was waiting for him at the end of this. A hangover, a missed 8:00 a.m. meeting, his family worried about him—the puking—and it wouldn't fix anything other than to give him a couple hours of mind-numbing solace.

At the moment though, mind-numbing solace, even if it was temporary, seemed like a good trade-off.

"Me, too," she said. "Drinking my troubles away."

Judging from the sultry tone in her voice, Logan first thought she might be a prostitute, but then he got a look at her.

Nope. Not a pro.

Or if she was, she'd done nothing to market herself as such. No low-cut dress to show her cleavage. She had on a T-shirt with cartoon turtles on the front, a baggy white skirt and flip-flops. It looked as if she'd grabbed the first items of clothing she could find off a very cluttered floor of her very cluttered apartment.

Logan wasn't into clutter.

And he'd thought Helene wasn't, either. He'd been wrong about that, too. That antique desk of hers had been plenty cluttered with a clown's bare ass.

"Mind if I join you?" Miss Turtle-Shirt said. "I'm having sort of a private going-away party."

She waited until Logan mumbled "suit yourself," and she slid onto the purple bar stool next to him.

She smelled like limes.

Her hair was varying shades of pink and looked as if it'd been cut with a weed whacker. It was already messy, but apparently it wasn't messy enough for her because she dragged her hand through it, pushing it away from her face.

"Tequila, top-shelf. Four shots and a bowl of lime slices," she told the bartender.

Apparently, he wasn't the only person in San Antonio with plans to get drunk tonight. And it explained the lime scent. These clearly weren't her first shots of the night.

"Do me a favor though," she said to Logan after he downed his next drink. "Don't ask my name, or anything personal about me, and I'll do the same for you."

Logan had probably never agreed to anything so fast in all his life. For one thing, he really didn't want to spend time talking with this woman, and he especially didn't want to talk about what'd happened.

"If you feel the need to call me something, go with Julia," she added.

The name definitely wasn't a fit. He was expecting something more like Apple or Sunshine. Still, he didn't care what she called herself. Didn't care what her real name was, either, and he cared even less after his next shot of Glenlivet.

"So, you're a cowboy, huh?" she asked.

The mind-numbing hadn't kicked in yet, but the orneriness had. "That's personal."

She shrugged. "Not really. You're wearing a cowboy hat, cowboy boots and jeans. It was more of an observation than a question."

"The clothes could be fashion statements," he pointed out.

Julia shook her head, downed the first shot of tequila, sucked on a lime slice. Made a face and shuddered. "You're not the kind of man to make fashion statements."

If he hadn't had a little buzz going on, he might have been insulted by that. "Unlike you?"

She glanced down at her clothes as if seeing them for the first time. Or maybe she was just trying to focus because the tequila had already gone to her head. "This was the first thing I grabbed off my floor."

Bingo. If that was her first grab, there was no telling how bad things were beneath it.

Julia tossed back her second shot. "Have you ever found out something that changed your whole life?" she asked.

"Yeah." About four hours ago.

"Me, too. Without giving specifics, because that would be personal, did it make you feel as if fate were taking a leak on your head?"

"Five leaks," he grumbled. Logan finished off his next shot.

Julia made a sound of agreement. "I would compare yours with mine, and I'd win, but I don't want to go there. Instead, let's play a drinking game."

"Let's not," he argued. "And in a fate-pissing comparison, I don't think you'd win."

Julia made a sound of disagreement. Had another shot. Grimaced and shuddered again. "So, the game is a word association," she continued as if he'd agreed. "I say a word, you say the first thing that comes to mind. We take turns until we're too drunk to understand what the other one is saying."

Until she'd added that last part, Logan had been about to get up and move to a different spot. But hell, he was getting drunk anyway, and at least this way he'd have some company. Company he'd never see again. Company he might not even be able to speak to if the slurring went up a notch.

"Dream?" she threw out there.

"Family." That earned him a sound of approval from her, and she motioned for him to take his turn. "Surprise?"

"Crappy," Julia said without hesitation.

Now it was Logan who made a grunt of approval. Surprises could indeed be crap-related. The one he'd gotten tonight certainly had been.

Her: "Tattoos?"

Him: "None." Then, "You?"

Her: "Two." Then, "Bucket list?"

Him: "That's two words." The orneriness was still there despite the buzz.

Her: "Just bucket, then?"

Too late. Logan's fuzzy mind was already fixed on the bucket list. He had one all right. Or rather he'd had one. A life with Helene that included all the trimmings, and this stupid game was a reminder that the Glenlivet wasn't working nearly fast enough. So, he had another shot.

Julia had one, as well. "Sex?" she said.

Logan shook his head. "I don't want to play this game anymore."

When she didn't respond, Logan looked at her. Their eyes met. Eyes that were already slightly unfocused.

Julia took the paper sleeve with her room key from her pocket. Except there were two keys, and she slid one Logan's way.

"It's not the game," she explained. "I'm offering you

sex with me. No names. No strings attached. Just one night, and we'll never tell another soul about it."

She finished off her last tequila shot, shuddered and stood. "Are you game?"

No way, and Logan would have probably said that to her if she hadn't leaned in and kissed him.

Maybe it was the weird combination of her tequila and his scotch, or maybe it was because he was already drunker than he thought, but Logan felt himself moving right into that kiss.

LOGAN DREAMED, AND it wasn't about the great sex he'd just had. It was another dream that wasn't so pleasant. The night of his parents' car accident. Some dreams were a mishmash of reality and stuff that didn't make sense. But this dream always got it right.

Not a good thing.

It was like being trapped on a well-oiled hamster wheel, seeing the same thing come up over and over again and not being able to do a thing to stop it.

The dream rain felt and sounded so real. Just like that night. It was coming down so hard that the moment his truck wipers swished it away, the drops covered the windshield again. That was why it'd taken him so long to see the lights, and Logan was practically right on the scene of the wreck before he could fully brake. He went into a skid, costing him precious seconds. If he'd had those seconds, he could have called the ambulance sooner.

He could have saved them.

But he hadn't then. And he didn't now in the dream. Logan chased away the images, and with his head still groggy, he did what he always did after the nightmare. He rewrote it. He got to his parents and stopped them from dying.

Every time except when it really mattered, Logan saved them.

LOGAN WISHED HE could shoot out the sun. It was creating lines of light on each side of the curtains, and those lines were somehow managing to stab through his closed eyelids. That was probably because every nerve in his head and especially his eyelids were screaming at him, and anything—including the earth's rotation—added to his pain.

He wanted to ask himself: *What the hell have you done?*

But he knew. He'd had sex with a woman he didn't know. A woman who wore turtle T-shirts and had tattoos. He'd learned one of the tattoos, a rose, was on Julia's right breast. The other was on her lower stomach. Those were the things Logan could actually remember.

That, and the sex.

Not mind-numbing but rather more mind-blowing. Julia clearly didn't have any trouble being wild and spontaneous in bed. It was as if she'd just studied a sex manual and wanted to try every position. Thankfully, despite the scotch, Logan had been able to keep up—literally.

Not so much now though.

If the fire alarm had gone off and the flames had been burning his ass, he wasn't sure he would be able to move. Julia didn't have that problem though. He felt the mattress shift when she got up. Since it was possible she was about to rob him, Logan figured he should at least see if she was going after his wallet, wherever the heck it was. But if she robbed him, he deserved it. His life was on the fast track to hell, and he'd been the one to put it in the handbasket.

At least he hadn't been so drunk that he'd forgotten to use condoms. Condoms that Julia had provided, so obviously she'd been ready for this sort of thing.

Logan heard some more stirring around, and this time the movement was very close to him. Just in case Julia turned out to be a serial killer, he decided to risk opening one eye. And he nearly jolted at the big green eyeball staring back at him. Except it wasn't a human eye. It was on her turtle shirt.

If Julia felt the jolt or saw his one eye opening, she didn't say anything about it. She gave him a chaste kiss on the cheek, moved away, turning her back to him, and Logan watched as she stooped down and picked up his jacket. So, not a serial killer but rather just a thief after all. But she didn't take anything out.

She put something *in* the pocket.

Logan couldn't tell what it was exactly. Maybe her number. Which he would toss first chance he got. But if so, he couldn't figure out why she just hadn't left it on the bed.

Julia picked up her purse, hooking it over her shoulder, and without even glancing back at him, she walked out the door. Strange, since this was her room. Maybe she was headed out to get them some coffee. If so, that was his cue to dress and get the devil out of there before she came back.

Easier said than done.

His hair hurt.

He could feel every strand of it on his head. His eyelashes, too. Still, Logan forced himself from the bed, only to realize the soles of his feet hurt, as well. It was hard to identify something on him that didn't hurt, so he quit naming parts and put on his boxers and jeans. Then he had a look at what Julia had put in his pocket next to the box with the engagement ring.

A gold watch.

Not a modern one. It was old with a snap-up top that had a crest design on it. The initials BWS had been engraved in the center of the crest.

The inside looked just as expensive as the gold case except for the fact that the watch face crystal inside was shattered. Even though he knew little about antiques, Logan figured it was worth at least a couple hundred dollars.

So, why had Julia put it in his pocket?

Since he was a skeptic, his first thought was that she might be trying to set him up, to make it look as if he'd robbed her. But Logan couldn't imagine why anyone would do that unless she was planning to try to blackmail him with it.

He dropped the watch on the bed and finished dressing, all the while staring at it. He cleared out some of the cotton in his brain and grabbed the hotel phone to call the front desk. Someone answered on the first ring.

"I'm in room—" Logan had to check the phone "—two-sixteen, and I need to know…" He had to stop again and think. "I need to know if Julia is there in the lobby. She left something in the room."

"No, sir. I'm afraid you just missed her. But checkout isn't until noon, and she said her guest might be staying past then, so she paid for an extra day."

"Uh, could you tell me how to spell Julia's last name? I need to leave her a note in case she comes back."

"Oh, she said she wouldn't be coming back, that this was her goodbye party. And as for how to spell her name, well, it's Child, just like it sounds."

Julia Child?

Right. Obviously, the clerk wasn't old enough or enough of a foodie to recognize the name of the famous chef.

"I don't suppose she paid with a credit card?" Logan asked.

"No. She paid in cash and then left a prepaid credit card for the second night."

Of course. "What about an address?" Logan kept trying.

"I'm really not supposed to give that out—"

"She left something very expensive in the room, and I know she'll want it back."

The guy hemmed and hawed a little, but he finally rattled off, "221B Baker Street, London, England."

That was Sherlock Holmes's address.

Logan groaned, cursed. He didn't bother asking for a phone number because the one she left was probably for Hogwarts. He hung up and hurried to the window, hoping he could get a glimpse of her getting into a car. Not that he intended to follow her or anything, but if she was going to blackmail him, he wanted to know as much about her as possible.

No sign of her, but Logan got a flash of something else. A memory.

Damn.

They'd taken pictures.

Or at least Julia had with the camera on her phone. He remembered nude selfies of them from the waist up. At least he hoped it was from the waist up.

Yeah, that trip to hell in a handbasket was moving even faster right now.

Logan threw on the rest of his clothes, already trying to figure out how to do damage control. He was the CEO of a multimillion-dollar company. He was the face that people put with the family business, and before last night he'd never done a thing to tarnish the image of McCord Cattle Brokers.

He couldn't say that any longer.

He was in such a hurry to rush out the door that he nearly missed the note on the desk. Maybe it was the start of the blackmail. He snatched it up, steeling himself up for the worst. But if this was blackmail, then Julia sure had a funny sense of humor.

"Goodbye, hot cowboy," she'd written. "Thanks for the sweet send-off. Don't worry. What happens in San Antonio stays in San Antonio. I'll take this to the grave."

Don't miss the ebook
BLAME IT ON THE COWBOY
by Delores Fossen,
available October 2016.

Copyright © 2016 by Delores Fossen

MILLS & BOON®

INTRIGUE
Romantic Suspense

A SEDUCTIVE COMBINATION OF DANGER AND DESIRE

A sneak peek at next month's titles...

In stores from 20th October 2016:

- **Landon** – Delores Fossen *and*
  Navy SEAL Six Pack – Elle James
- **The Girl Who Cried Murder** – Paula Graves *and*
  In the Arms of the Enemy – Carol Ericson
- **Scene of the Crime: Means and Motive** –
  Carla Cassidy *and* **Christmas Kidnapping** –
  Cindi Myers

Romantic Suspense

- **Runaway Colton** – Karen Whiddon
- **Operation Soldier Next Door** – Justine Davis

Just can't wait?
Buy our books online a month before they hit the shops!
www.millsandboon.co.uk

Also available as eBooks.

Give a 12 month subscription to a friend today!

Call Customer Services
0844 844 1358*

or visit
millsandboon.co.uk/subscriptions

* This call will cost you 7 pence per minute plus your phone company's price per minute access charge.

MILLS & BOON®

Why shop at millsandboon.co.uk?

Each year, thousands of romance readers find their perfect read at millsandboon.co.uk. That's because we're passionate about bringing you the very best romantic fiction. Here are some of the advantages of shopping at www.millsandboon.co.uk:

* **Get new books first**—you'll be able to buy your favourite books one month before they hit the shops

* **Get exclusive discounts**—you'll also be able to buy our specially created monthly collections, with up to 50% off the RRP

* **Find your favourite authors**—latest news, interviews and new releases for all your favourite authors and series on our website, plus ideas for what to try next

* **Join in**—once you've bought your favourite books, don't forget to register with us to rate, review and join in the discussions

Visit **www.millsandboon.co.uk**
for all this and more today!